TheVampire
Girl Next Door

Richard Arbib

HIGHGATE
BOOKS™

Cover illustration, layout and design
by Jose Pardo.

Author photo by Bkos.

ISBN-13: 978-0615572635
ISBN: 0615572634
LCCN: 2011944243

For more information, visit:
www.thevampiregirlnextdoor.com

The Vampire Girl Next Door

To Bob and Eileen —
Hope you both enjoy
reading my novel.
— Richard Arbib
July 10, 2012

Richard Arbib

HIGHGATE BOOKS™

The Vampire Girl Next Door

Part One

Chapter One

Dave pointed at the window and said, "There's a girl staring at you."

"Really? Who?" I asked. He nodded at the large windowed front of Gold's Gym that faced the street. Although sometimes people passing by stopped and stared at the weightlifters and bodybuilders, tonight not a single person stood out in front on the sidewalk.

"Where?" I scanned the front of the gym.

"That's funny. There was this girl staring at you, Mark. She must have left just a second before you looked up."

I couldn't tell whether he was pulling my leg or if it was true. With my lousy social life recently, I hoped to meet a new and different woman. Though I had dramatically improved my body in the past three years, from a slim 145 pounds to a more muscular 175, the number and quality of women in my life had not risen proportionately. In fact, I was meeting fewer. I attributed this to my lack of time, caused partly by my four-day-a-week schedule in the gym, Wing Chun kung-fu lessons, taking two film classes at San Francisco State University, and partly from working thirty hours per week selling advertising for a weekly newspaper. My social problems had gotten even worse when my six-month rollercoaster relationship with my girlfriend, Mary, ended with a split

1

just a month earlier.

I decided to test Dave to see if he was joking or serious. I asked him what the mysterious girl at the window had looked like. He frowned. "She was pretty in a strange way, but..."

"But what?" I asked. "Why are you making a face if she was pretty?"

"I don't know, but there was something weird about the way she looked at you." His expression and tone of voice were quite ominous and foreboding. This was a complete reversal of Dave's normally joking demeanor. Half the time, he grinned after any remark, implying that what he just said was only a joke, so I sometimes never knew what he really meant. He might tell me something just to see my reaction, then a minute later tell me that he was only kidding. This trait really annoyed me since I was always more serious.

Yet I could tell he wasn't kidding this time; something he had seen still disturbed him.

"What was it about the way she looked that was so weird?" I asked.

"I don't know." Dave shrugged his shoulders. "Something about her eyes."

"God damn it!" yelled Ron. "It's five to ten. If you guys aren't out of here in five minutes, I'm locking you both in."

Fifteen minutes later, we were leaving. Dave told me he'd see me there "tomorrow night, same time." Ron told us both to come earlier so we could leave on time. This said, we parted company. Dave left for home, Ron for his hot date, and I for the bus.

It struck me then that I should have brought my car, as I needed two buses to get home, and I would have to walk through one of the worst sections of the Mission District to catch the first one. I tried to reassure myself that no muggers would try to take me on when they could just as easily pick someone older and weaker. True, at five feet, seven inches tall, I didn't appear too formidable, but I did look strong for my height. The muggers could choose other victims, provided they were looking for money, rather than someone challenging to beat up. With this cheery thought in mind, I sauntered down Valencia Street, trying to exude confidence. Evidently, my attempt at false confidence only appeared to others as arrogance in that particular neighborhood.

"Hey you! What you doing on our street?" a rough voice challenged. "Yeah, you. You heard me."

I turned around and saw three guys, around eighteen or nineteen years old, drinking beer and glaring at me. They appeared to be from the housing project in the same block as the gym. Though the project had a quaint name, Valencia Gardens, it was ruled by young thugs in gangs who sold crack and had little use for outsiders who stepped into their territory.

I had the distinct and uneasy feeling they would make me their scapegoat. Dealing with them in an intelligent manner would have been as useless as trying to explain Einstein's theory of relativity to a barking dog, so I simply ignored them and walked a little faster. I just hoped that they would ignore me.

They didn't. As I turned away from them, a beer bottle suddenly crashed on the sidewalk just inches from my feet. I quickened my pace, and tried to consider my options. I could run, but they would probably catch me since I couldn't run that quickly. I tried thinking of other alternatives as I heard their footsteps approaching rapidly from behind. Perhaps running wasn't a good solution, but I already ruled out talking, as they certainly weren't in the mood for friendly conversation.

The only alternative was to fight. I didn't relish the idea of fighting three guys, especially since they could have been carrying knives, or worse—guns. Now, I realized, all my Wing Chun kung-fu drills that I'd spent years learning, but had never used, would be needed on the street in the next minute.

These various thoughts only played through my mind for a few seconds, when I felt a hand grab my shoulder. I swung my full weight around, so that my left arm knocked his hand away and created a clear path for a right hook with my full 175 pounds behind it. It was a wonderful punch; it knocked him flat onto the pavement. I was so satisfied with the result, I wished to stand back and survey the damage, but his friends had other ideas for me.

They backed me into an alley. One of them stood closer to me than the other, so I shot off a front thrust kick to his knee, then hit him in the face with four or five centerline punches in less than a second. Suddenly, a fist smashed me in the nose. The punch came from the other thug I had forgotten about. Blood ran out of my nose and down to my lips. In a fury, I turned to my new attacker and slammed him against the wall of the building, then kicked him in the stomach as hard as possible. When he lurched forward, I kicked him in the face with my other foot, which knocked him back against the wall.

Behind me, someone screamed. The shriek lasted only a second, then stopped immediately—as if it had been cut short by a hand clapped over the victim's mouth. I had no chance to speculate about this, however, until I finished with my opponent. So, I punched him once more, and watched him drop unconscious to the cement.

Satisfied that he would trouble me no longer, I spun around to see what had caused the scream.

When I looked, I experienced a strange sensation. Somehow time seemed to have jumped forward several seconds—or a minute—I couldn't really be sure. It was as if I were watching a movie and several seconds had been spliced out and the movie jumped ahead slightly in time.

4

Just as some people experience a blackout for several hours, this sensation felt similar, but lasted only seconds. I stood in the same place, but something had happened in front of me without my seeing it.

The alley was empty. Looking back toward the street, I recognized the form of my first assailant on the sidewalk. He still lay face down on the pavement, right next to his friend. One of them had his head completely turned around, facing backwards, just like Linda Blair in *The Exorcist*. Someone had snapped his neck. The one who screamed behind me had apparently disappeared. This puzzled me since I blocked his exit, and I knew he hadn't gone by me.

And then I saw it. Near my feet lay a .45 automatic, unfired. Several drops of blood dotted the area around it, and leading toward the back of the alley, the drops grew larger and formed a crimson trail. I clenched my fists and cautiously stepped further into the alley. Just a few yards away stood several trashcans. I approached warily, and then stopped when I saw his feet sticking out behind a pile of garbage.

As I bent forward for a better look, a panic seized me. His whole throat was ripped open, and blood spattered his face and clothes. His lifeless eyes stared up at the sky, and his expression portrayed his final seconds of horror. I glanced back at his gun lying in the middle of the alley. Why didn't he use it? Who killed him? Why?

As these thoughts rushed into my mind, another idea entered as well—I had better get out of there as swiftly as possible. If the police discovered me there under these circumstances, I could be charged with murder, and the one who might have survived would probably testify that I killed his friends.

Slowly, quietly, I made my way out of the alley and onto the deserted sidewalk. I knew if I could just reach the bus stop without being seen I would be safe.

I made it about half a block when I saw the police car. They drove towards me, but on the other side of the street. It moved along the street slowly, and I hoped that it wouldn't stop. The few seconds it took for the police car to pass me by seemed excruciatingly long. I breathed deeply and felt thankful it kept going. My relief was short-lived.

Just as I reached the corner of Sixteenth Street, the police car screeched to a stop at the entrance of the alley. The police immediately pointed their spotlight at the two guys I had knocked out on the sidewalk. It would only be a matter of seconds before they discovered that two of the three men were dead and the other one could identify me.

I was now in a good position to run without being seen by the police, so I quickly sprinted down Sixteenth Street for one short block and ducked into the BART station on Sixteenth and Mission Street. A train pulled up just as I reached the bottom of the escalator. I rushed into it along with a small crowd of passengers, and in just a few seconds it whisked me away from any worries about the police.

Yet I couldn't help but be concerned that someone might have witnessed the incident in the alley. To be absolutely certain that no one followed me, I walked through several cars of the train before settling down in a seat. I shifted my gaze behind my shoulder, and noticed that several passengers seemed to be eying me suspiciously. I turned away from them and towards the window, which looked out onto a black tunnel, and thus functioned as a mirror. In its reflection, I saw what the other passengers had been staring at—it was my nose, which had blood all over it from the fight. I tried wiping off the blood, but it had already dried, so I licked my hand and then rubbed part of it away. By repeating this procedure several times, I removed the blood from my nose and upper lip, though in the process, I was forced to taste the blood. I found this to be disgusting and nauseating, since the blood only reminded me of the boy in the alley with his throat ripped open.

When the train reached the Financial District, I took the California Street bus, which brought me all the way out to my apartment in the Richmond District. I left the bus three blocks from my own apartment so I could see if anyone was following me. This would have been highly unlikely, though, considering the precautions I had taken on the train, and I didn't see how anyone could have followed me on the bus. While I may have been unduly cautious, I did not consider my actions to be overly paranoid under the bizarre circumstances. I couldn't explain the murders in the alley to the police. They would never have believed me. I can't say that I would have blamed them, either. After all, I had no reasonable explanation of what really happened back in the alley. It still remained a mystery to me how anyone could move fast enough to kill someone armed with a gun in his hand and also kill the other man and leave without allowing me to see or hear a thing. As for a possible motive, my mind drew a blank.

The fog of the Richmond District was thick, and little droplets of mist hung by the streetlights, giving the air a soft quality, as in an impressionistic painting. In the distance, I could hear the sound of foghorns warning ships of danger lurking in the darkness.

The Richmond District sprawled along the northwest corner of San Francisco, just north of Golden Gate Park, stretching along its entire length to the Pacific Ocean. The neighborhood was mostly residential, initially settled by Chinese and Russian immigrants, and now solidly middle class. While not as trendsetting or as famous as the Haight-Ashbury, the Richmond had some fine Edwardian homes, an active nightlife scene, and a wide assortment of restaurants along Clement Street, just a couple blocks from my apartment building.

Yet, in this very ordinary neighborhood, once stood an all-black house, its windows always shuttered, at 6114 California Street—the Church of Satan. Founded by Anton LaVey in 1966, it had many famous visitors, including sex symbol, Jayne Mansfield, later decapitated in a freakish car accident. LaVey kept a pet lion on his property, and one of the topless dancers in his "Witches Sabbath" show was none other than Susan Atkins. Three years later, in 1969, she and the other disciples of Charles Manson would shock the world with their murders.

Sometimes, you just never completely know the person next door.

And so, as I walked from the bus, just one block from my apartment, came another sound—the light, but distinct tap of footsteps behind me, which seemed to step in unison to my own. I stopped and listened, but heard only the wind, and the foghorn blaring out its warning.

I started walking again, and the footsteps started right along with me, as if a dancer were trying to keep in step with me. I could stand it no longer, and spun around to see who was following me.

It was a girl, a block behind me. The second I stopped and stared at her, she stopped too. I suddenly felt embarrassed by my unfounded fears, and turned around and resumed walking to my apartment. After all, she probably worried more about being out late at night than I; she was certainly more vulnerable. She had to fear, not only the types of lunatics I just survived, but also rapists. She had far more threats to her security than I had to mine, and she didn't have my weightlifting and martial arts skills to help her deal with these problems. Yes, she had far more reason to worry than I did, and it was best that if the punks on Valencia Street had to attack someone, that it was me—not her. What might have happened if she had been in my place?

When I reached my apartment and checked the mailbox, I noticed that the girl was now across the street and walking by rather slowly as she regarded me with great curiosity. In the dense fog under the streetlight, she reminded me of a figure in an impressionistic painting. I stopped and glanced back at her, but in the fog and the dim light, I could only see her as a silhouette. Even as I opened the door to my building, she didn't turn to walk away.

George, the manager of the building, was in the lobby, checking the well-worn carpeting. "I think we may be getting some new carpet in here," he said to me, as he looked up.

"That would be nice. But what we really need is soundproofing."

"Soundproofing?" he asked, as something else caught his attention. "For Christ's sake, what happened to your nose?"

I felt my nose and realized that it had started bleeding again, so I quickly made up a story about talking to a girl in a singles bar and getting punched by her boyfriend. George asked who got in the last punch, and I assured him that I had. He'd been a boxer himself in his twenties and always liked to hear about a good fight. Too bad I was unable to tell him what had really happened. He would have enjoyed hearing a punch-by-punch description.

"Now, what were you saying about soundproofing?" he asked again.

"Well, you know Harry, my next-door neighbor?"

George nodded. He knew.

"That bastard plays his stereo all night," I said. "He has friends over at two in the morning. They all make a racket while I try to sleep."

"You may not have to worry about him much longer," George answered. "He told me he might move in

9

with one of his girlfriends in a month or two."

This was certainly welcome news. I had reached the end of my patience with the jerk. I had tried friendly discussions, threats, and finally, calling the police. None of these worked. The police even warned me not to threaten Harry, since they pointed out that assault was a far more serious crime than merely disturbing the peace.

I trudged up the four flights of stairs to my floor, and as I made my way to the end of the hall, several of my neighbor's friends came out of his apartment. The smell of marijuana wafted out to the hall, and the departing guests seemed to be in good spirits, cheerfully yelling back and forth like monkeys in a zoo. I looked at my watch. It was 11 p.m. His friends had left earlier than usual. What a relief, I thought to myself. Now, maybe I could get a good night's sleep. It would be difficult enough after the events of the evening, but important nonetheless. I had to be up at eight and at work by ten.

By the time I crawled into bed, the noise from next-door stopped, and I thought I might be able to sleep *undisturbed*.

I was wrong.

I had a dream that night. The memory of it was so fuzzy, I couldn't recall everything, only that someone was trying to get me—the paranoia that nightmares are made of. I remember the sound of fingernails scratching glass. I was *certain* of that.

But there was more to it than that—another part—perhaps a second dream. It wasn't a nightmare at all, but rather quite pleasant. I dreamed of a woman in my bed with me. I somehow knew her as she had been in my dreams for many years. Her beautiful face and her long black hair I had seen over and over in my dreams. And as clearly as I could picture her, she apparently was only a figment of my imagination and not anyone I had actually met in real life.

The nightmare could only be heard, and the pleasant dream could only be felt. In the nightmare, an unearthly female voice, like a whisper, but magnified, repeated the words, "*Sleep. Sleep. Sleep.*" The voice soothed and terrified simultaneously because I felt powerless to resist its command. One feature I distinctly remembered was the velvety smoothness of the woman's skin. This sensation was so vivid, that when I awoke, the sheets of my bed felt as rough as burlap in comparison.

The clock said 3:33 a.m. I dragged myself out of bed and noticed a draft in the room. By the window, the drapes rustled slightly as if a breeze were blowing through. Of course, that would have been impossible, since the window would have to be open for wind to be moving the drapes. I always kept the window closed at night. Out of curiosity, I walked over and pulled the cord.

I couldn't believe my eyes.

The window was wide open and the lock on the inside had been snapped right off! I bent over and picked it up off the carpet, examining both the lock and the window. It looked like someone tried to open the window, and upon feeling the lock, just pushed until it broke. I wondered how I had slept through this and how it happened, but could think of nothing to explain it away.

And then I realized—maybe my dream wasn't a dream at all.

Chapter Two

Not surprisingly, in the morning I had a vague recollection of a nightmare. It's said that we all dream every night, but we just don't remember. The dreams escape from our subconscious at night, then slip back into hiding before we get a chance to see them clearly.

I felt exhausted, completely drained from the night before, and in the mirror noticed a bruise on the side of my neck, no doubt caused during the attack near my gym. But things could have been worse. At least I wasn't murdered like the guys in the alley.

At work, I couldn't concentrate, but kept thinking about the slaughters. There had to be some logical explanation, yet even though the events might have been logical, that didn't mean I was safe. A fly captured by a spider may know he is about to be devoured, but such knowledge may be of little comfort or practical use.

I called one customer after another, but I made only one sale, and the manager came over to my desk at the end of the day and asked me why.

"I've had a difficult night," I explained, but went no further.

"I don't care about your sex life," Max laughed. He held an unlit cigar in his mouth. "Ah, what the Hell. You'll do better tomorrow. Right?"

"You can be sure I'll give it my best." It wasn't exactly a commitment, but what he wanted to hear.

"That's all I wanted to hear." He slapped me on the back before turning to talk with another salesman.

Max was an easy guy to get along with. He just demanded lots of sales so that he could get his commission override on the salesmen's work. I never worried about losing my job since the majority of the pay consisted of commissions. No sales, no paycheck. Because of this, the sales staff felt little pressure to be on time or to dress a certain way. The job fit in quite well with my schedule and my four-day-per-week exercise routine at the gym. I liked the flexible hours and the opportunity to make commissions, yet at the same time, I realized that at 33, I was not on track for a high-paying career.

A copy of the *San Francisco Chronicle* lay on the desk next to mine. I scanned it for news of the murder the night before and it was featured on page two. The article explained that the police had found the three guys together, two of them dead, and that the other one had been questioned, but then released when the police had found no motive for the killing, no weapons that could have cut the victims' throat, and besides, the survivor had submitted to a lie detector test which cleared him. The "suspect," the article went on, "apparently attacked the three boys, incapacitating the first one, while murdering the other two. The motive for the murder is unknown at this point, but police are looking for a man who fits the suspect's description. He is said to be around 30, with brown curly hair and about average height." Well, at least they didn't describe me as short, I thought.

It didn't really sound like the police knew where to look, which greatly relieved me. Yet it surprised me that the article didn't mention Gold's Gym, since the murders happened right next to it. I couldn't imagine any way the police would believe the truth at this point, so the only thing I could do was to keep it a dark secret for the rest of my life. As disturbing as the whole incident was, it couldn't be shared with anyone. What really bothered me was the fact that I still didn't know who'd killed the two boys, how they were killed, or why. Since the police were looking for the wrong person (with almost no chance of success), it seemed unlikely they would ever find the real killer.

"Isn't that just awful?" Max pointed at the newspaper and grimaced. He wore contact lenses, and his eyes were always bloodshot. Someone else might have mistaken him for an alcoholic.

"Yes," I agreed. "It's terrible—all the murders in the city. It's not safe to walk the streets at night anymore." I hoped that I sounded sincere, rather than nervous, but as I talked on, I detected an increasing dryness in my mouth as I swallowed.

"Murder? Who's talking about murder? I'm talking about the game the Forty-Niners lost yesterday. I could give a shit whether all those punks kill each other or not. That's *good* news." He pointed his finger at me for emphasis. "This just means there's two less muggers in this city, and now it's a little safer for you and me. Both of those punks who were killed had records for armed robbery and selling crack. Who needs them? I need them to shoot me after work some night? Or sell drugs to my daughter at school? Huh?"

I nodded in agreement with him, which made him feel good and added the validity to his opinions, which he felt was essential. "You know, Mark," he began in his fatherly voice, "you're a good guy, but if you don't mind my saying so, a bit, well, let's just say a bit inexperienced in the ways of the world." I felt no reason to remind him of my age, or to explain that 33 was really not so young after all. He knew my age, but everyone told me that I looked younger. Bouncers still occasionally stopped me in bars and asked for identification and so sometimes people forgot. I could have told him that, but decided against it since it was close to quitting time for the day. Perhaps it would have been difficult to explain why at 33, I was still attending graduate school and not pursuing a career the way most people were.

I didn't know how to explain why I was trying to earn a master's degree in English with a minor in film when the degree would not guarantee a teaching job, or why I spent so much of my time lifting weights to develop

14

the kind of body that most people wouldn't appreciate anyway. I couldn't rationalize my actions to Max. I had enough trouble trying to justify my goals (or lack of them) to myself, when most other people seemed to be busy earning money or engaged in some practical pursuit.

I decided to skip the gym, something I rarely did. But I couldn't afford to run into anyone who might have recognized me from the night before. I had to call Dave and make up an excuse for not exercising. I hated to miss the gym workout.

What bothered me far more, though, was the discovery that my window had been forced open. While I couldn't make any connection between the attack in the alley and my broken window lock, other than they both had happened on the same night, the two events played over and over in my mind. I resolved to go home and catch up on my reading for school.

Around eight o'clock I reached my apartment building. George was in the lobby, laying new carpet. It was a light brown, and brightened up the interior immensely, looking far more fashionable than the worn green one he was taking up.

"You're working late, again," I said. "Have you heard anything else about my neighbor moving?"

George put his carpet knife down for a second, and groaned while he rose. I could hear his knees creak as they straightened.

"Sorry Mark. Haven't heard a thing. And too bad for you! I had a chance to rent an apartment today. A young girl, and pretty, too—but in a strange way, She came by less than an hour ago and she said she just had to have an apartment."

"Why don't you evict Harry and let her move in next to me?"

He shook his head. "I can't. He pays his rent on time. He hasn't broken any law. I know he's loud sometimes,

15

but you've tried calling the police and you know it doesn't do any good."

"Yes. I know." And how I knew. I would have moved out myself, but I couldn't afford another apartment. The rents had risen so steeply since I had moved in three years before, that I was stuck there. I only hoped that Harry would move in with his girlfriend and the two of them would go deaf from playing their stereo too loud. It especially annoyed me to learn that a pretty girl could have moved in next to me—but didn't because Harry lived there.

"What was she like?" I asked George.

"Who?"

"The girl you said came by looking for an apartment."

"Oh. Her. Well, she was kinda young. Yeah, maybe in her early twenties. Hard to say. Like I said, she looked pretty, but a little *strange*."

"In what way?"

"I don't know. Maybe she was a musician. She asked about having a piano and a harpsichord in the apartment."

My heart sank. All I needed was another music "enthusiast" to keep me up all night.

"Yeah," said George. "She could be a musician. From the way she talked, I could tell she was from England. She was kinda cute, though. But she looked sorta weird." He made a face as if he were describing a carnival freak.

I asked him what looked so weird about her.

"Her eyes. I never seen eyes like that before. But you'll probably see her yourself."

"Why is that?"

"She's going to keep checking with me every night this week to see if there's a vacancy, She thinks that if she does that with all the apartments on the block, she'll find a place within a week. I thought she was crazy. I told her it's not that easy trying to find an apartment in this city."

"That's for sure," I agreed. "If she's cute, it certainly would be nice if she did move in, though." Perhaps it would be the perfect cure for my ailing love life. I had no reason to believe that this girl would move in and that we would fall madly in love, but I've always been an imaginative optimist, or as my friend Dave has said many times, "a daydreamer who lives in a fantasy world." Of course, he always said it in a joking manner.

"Yeah, she was cute all right," George repeated, then shook his head and corrected himself. "No. Cute is the wrong word. She was..." he paused. "Exotic."

"To me the most important part of the body is the face—especially the eyes. That, and a nice smile."

"Then you'll be out of luck on both counts with this one. She has the strangest eyes I've ever seen and she didn't smile at all."

"Maybe you didn't tell her any funny jokes," I explained. "Next time she comes by, why don't you have her watch you throw a pie in Harry's face. I'll be happy to come down and help supervise."

"Don't worry," George assured me. "He'll be moving soon enough."

"Tomorrow wouldn't be soon enough." I started up the four flights to my apartment since the building had no elevator. By the time I reached the second floor, I could hear the music. At the third floor, I could make out the lyrics, and when I turned the key to my own apartment on the fourth floor, Harry's music swelled out of his closed door like a tidal wave. It was only 8:15 p.m. and I couldn't even call the police about the noise until ten o'clock. They would only drop by and ask him to turn it down.

The lock from my window still lay on my living room carpet, and it brought my mind away from the trivialities of loud music to the reality of the night before—the murders in the alley and my worries about my broken window lock. I couldn't do anything to change what had already occurred the night before, but I could certainly try to forget about it. I tried. First, I sat on my recliner chair so I could stretch out and relax. Then I picked up a copy of *American Film* and began reading an old article about Roman Polanski, how he had directed horror movies like *Rosemary's Baby*, and a comedy with his wife, Sharon Tate — *The Fearless Vampire Killers*.

With the comfort of my recliner combined with the stress I had felt during the past twenty-four hours, I found myself dozing off. Occasionally, I would awaken for a few moments, then my eyes would start to close again. I believe I was either asleep or dreaming, when I thought I heard the sound of fingernails scratching at my window! I sprang up and rushed over in apprehension. I swiftly pulled the curtain aside, but there was nothing, absolutely nothing at all out there. I felt like a fool for being so frightened by a noise that was probably just part of a dream, yet it had sounded so real.

Laughter echoed out in the hallway as Harry's friends, drunk and stoned, left him alone to enjoy his music. At least, I thought alone. I hoped I could finally get back to sleep. It was only 10:15, but I was eager to get to sleep earlier than usual, so I could forget everything.

After getting my paperwork together for the next day's work, I was about to retire for the night. Then, through the wall, I heard Harry scream and the sound of furniture being thrown and broken. I didn't know whether he was having some sort of temper tantrum and smashing up the place, or whether one of his friends was fighting with him, but I had to do something.

"Shut up in there!" I yelled through the wall. It did no good. Another lamp crashed against the wall. I could take no more. I walked out to the hall to confront him and his "guest" right at his door.

Evidently, everyone else on the floor had heard the fighting too, for the hall filled with people pounding on Harry's door, yelling, "What's going on in there?"

The noise stopped as suddenly as it had started.

Mrs. McCoy, the elderly lady who lived in the apartment across from Harry, shouted at his door, "Why don't you answer us?" No answer.

The others in the hallway looked at each other. None of us knew quite what to do. One of the tenants had already phoned the police. Another suggested breaking down Harry's door. This was met by unanimous approval, and they instantly volunteered me for the job. I guess they felt I looked like the type of person who could handle it. I gave it my best and kicked the door as hard as I could. Unlike the movies, my kick didn't break down the door, but did crack the wood.

Inside, I heard a rustling sound and then a thud as if something or someone had been dropped on the floor.

"Someone's moving around," said Mrs. McCoy as she craned her head closer to the door to hear a little better. "Is that you, Harry?"

I placed my eye against the tiny crack in the door to see if I could make out any details, but the room had been plunged into darkness. Only indistinct forms could be perceived. And then I realized the same thing happening to me that occurred the night before—as I peeked through the crack in the door at the shadows of the two figures, I somehow "lost" several seconds. The transition of time jumped, as if a brief instant of my memory had been erased, like a movie missing several frames of film. Suddenly a shadow leaped up from the floor and dove right through the window, shattering the glass in its path.

A moment later, we all heard a much louder crash out in the street below, of broken glass and a car alarm shrieking.

"What happened?" the neighbors yelled at me.

"Someone jumped out the window!" I answered. I stood up and kicked the door a final time, and it flew open to reveal one of the most macabre scenes I'd ever witnessed.

The room was barely illuminated by the light from the hallway, so as we all entered, I turned on the switch next to the door for the overhead light, which lit up the ghastly room with a horribly sudden starkness. Furniture and broken lamps were strewn all over the floor. As we all burst in to see what had happened to Harry, the police arrived, and the room erupted into chaos. Harry lay sprawled out on the couch, his throat ripped open just like the victim the night before in the alley. Bloody scratch marks covered his face, as if a wild animal had clawed him.

My attention immediately went to the large bay window, with only a fringe of jagged glass remaining around the edges. I rushed over and swiftly glanced down at the sidewalk, four stories below. Right underneath the shattered window, in the street below, stood a police car with its car alarm still shrieking and its roof and windshield totally crushed from the weight of someone falling on it from four stories up. But there was no body on the top of the collapsed roof! The sidewalk was empty, except for broken glass. No body of a killer, no blood—just the emptiness that fills the night air after death.

I turned away from the view of the street to focus my attention back on the room. Yet, it was not the crowd of my neighbors, nor the police rushing in, nor even the bloody corpse of Harry that I stared at. All those things blurred into the background as one small item in the room burned its impression into my mind.

It was the broken window lock that lay at my feet.

Chapter Three

When the police noticed me staring at the broken lock from Harry's window, one of the detectives questioned me about it. I explained that my own lock had been broken off the night before.

"Why didn't you call the police?" Inspector Swenson asked me. He appeared to be suspicious, and stroked his gray mustache as he stared at me in a distrustful manner.

"At the time, it didn't seem important. It was just a broken window lock, nothing more." I said this as calmly as I could and hoped that my nervousness didn't show through.

Apparently he believed me, but he still wanted to see my apartment for himself. He looked around my living room without disturbing or touching anything, but his eyes scanned it for clues of some sort.

"How well did you know your neighbor?" He had a notebook open with a pen ready to write down information.

"Not too well. We really didn't talk much. He wasn't exactly a verbal person. He was into music—loud music. I hardly knew him, actually. He was just the noisy neighbor."

"You disliked him, then?" The detective's voice contained a slight accusatory quality that I found annoying.

"Not enough to kill him. Is that what you're leading up to?" My reaction came out rougher than I had anticipated. It surprised me as much as him.

He waved my fears away with his hands. "No, no. Not at all. I *know* you didn't kill him. You were out in the hall with everyone else when he was screaming. I got that from the neighbors. You're not a suspect. You've got nothing to worry about. Except for one thing."

"What's that?"

"The killer." The answer seemed obvious to him. I guess it should have been to me, too.

"You say your window was pushed open the same way last night. It's very possible that the killer was trying to get *you*—not your neighbor." He nodded in agreement with himself.

I looked at him, and then at my window with its broken lock. What he said made sense, but I didn't want to admit it. "Then how come the murderer killed Harry if he really wanted me?"

Inspector Swenson shrugged his shoulders.

"And why," I continued, "would anyone want to kill me anyway? No one's got any reason to kill me." But at this point, I couldn't even convince myself that I was safe.

"If people needed a logical reason to go out and kill other people, I'd be out of a job. I've been on the homicide squad for twelve years, and I don't think I've heard a good excuse for a murder yet. Oh sure, the killers think their reasons are valid, but I've yet to hear a dying victim tell me he had it coming. Not one."

He smiled at his little joke, but he had made his point. There was no way to know who killed Harry, or the motive. There was no assurance that I wasn't next.

"I'll do anything I can to help," I said, "but I really have no idea who killed Harry or why he did it."

He nodded and looked over my window. I'm sure he noticed it stood much too far from Harry's window for anyone to do any climbing. There also was no ledge to stand on. The roof jutted out several feet beyond the wall of the building. It would have been nearly impossible to enter the windows from the roof. The fire escape seemed the only way to slip through a window. He took all of these factors into account, and as he was leaving, could offer no solutions.

"If you hear anyone at your window at night, don't hesitate to call us. That's what we're here for." Right before he walked out my door, he turned to me and added, "Oh, and one of the reasons we're never around when people need us is people wait too long to call us. I guess they're afraid of looking silly or something. We're usually called afterwards. By then, it's a little late to prevent the crime."

The next day, the police were crawling all over the roof, searching for clues to Harry's mysterious murder. From what George told me, they learned absolutely nothing to shed any light on Harry's death. Sitting in my apartment alone as I listened to the police above me on the roof, the words of Inspector Swenson came back to me. But as much as I may have needed protection from the police, I didn't want them to look too closely into my life and possibly accuse me of the murders in the alley. By 9:30 a.m., I left my apartment for work, but arrived fifteen minutes late.

According to the newspaper, the police had let the third boy go after his polygraph test—and since they still hadn't contacted me, I felt that they didn't suspect the murderer of his other two friends to be a member of the gym. So I decided to return to my workouts. Later, at the gym, I told Dave all about the murder at my apartment building. He didn't seem particularly disturbed about Harry, but then, to be totally honest, neither was I. Dave did seem worried about me, however.

"Maybe you should move." He started loading plates onto one of the barbells, then faced me. "It's your turn."

"To move? Or be murdered?"

"To do the bench press." He pointed at the barbell.

I did a warm-up set, and then Dave did his. He started loading more plates on one of the ends. I loaded the other end, and then slipped under the bar. I did ten reps, then Dave did his.

It continued this way for about five minutes. Neither of us said anything. We had been exercising like this together for three years and we knew our workout schedule so well, it was unnecessary to talk since we knew just how much weight to put on and how much help to give each other.

"Maybe I should move," I finally said.

"Yeah, why don't you move this bar up and down? It may be better than just standing there thinking about your neighbor. I don't know why you're so disturbed. You didn't like Harry anyway."

"It's not Harry I'm worried about. It's me. I could be next."

"You will be next if you blow my workout by stopping in the middle of this," said Dave. He pointed at his chest, "Look. I'm going to lose my pump and then I'll have to do another set."

Ordinarily, his light approach to a serious problem would have annoyed me, but now I found Dave's joking attitude rubbing off on me and I became more engrossed in the workout and less concerned with the problems of the past few days. It became clear I had nothing to worry about. A drug dealer probably murdered Harry. He and his friends were always getting high and making noise. He probably had an argument over money with one of his dealers and the guy killed him. It happened all the time.

The only problem was this theory didn't account for the murderer getting in and out of the apartment unseen. How could someone jump through a fourth-floor window and avoid being sliced into pieces and then splattered all over the sidewalk? To have survived such a fall seemed implausible, to have vanished in the few seconds it took me to reach the window—impossible. It didn't make sense. My broken window lock somehow fit into this pattern. I didn't know exactly how or why. What really scared me was the similarity between the murder of Harry and the murder of the guys in the alley. Of course, it could have been just a coincidence. I wanted to believe that it was a coincidence, but how could I? Everything was too similar, right down to the quick and inexplicable exit of the killer. Who was he and why did he kill people, who, in both cases, were only about ten feet away from me?

I tried to think of something that both Harry and the victims in the alley had in common. It said in the paper that the victims were drug dealers. Harry may have been selling drugs too. Since I was not a dealer, maybe that meant I was safe. Then again, both Harry and the muggers in the alley were young men. So was I. Maybe the killer just went after younger men. Maybe I was next. But I didn't believe age had anything to do with the murders. Then it hit me. Both Harry and the other guys knew me, (though admittedly, the muggers in the alley didn't know me for long) and they were enemies. Was there someone out there who actually liked me so much that he wanted to kill anyone in my way? That made no sense at all. If Dave had been with me when I had been attacked, he undoubtedly would have come to my defense, but even Dave, my best friend, wouldn't kill someone for me. Why would anyone else?

But perhaps the strangest part of the two murder scenes was how I had the same feeling of losing several seconds, both in the alley and when looking through Harry's cracked door. Like watching a movie that skips ahead a few frames, I had lost sight of the critical moment when the killer struck. I was a witness who could not remember what I saw. Or had I seen the killer at all? I didn't know.

The more I thought about it, the wilder my theories became. I couldn't solve it. I could only wait it out and hope that whoever the killer was, he was out of my life for good.

Our workout at the gym took longer than usual, as my mind constantly wandered away from the exercise and back to the murders. I would take no more chances with walking casually through the same neighborhood again. My eyes darted back and forth scanning the sidewalks to make sure no one could approach me. If I were to meet up with the other guy I had fought the other night, it could turn out differently this time. He wouldn't fight me again. He'd just shoot me.

On my way home, I took different buses than usual, just in case anyone from the area of the gym might see or follow me.

I stopped by George's room on the first floor to get the scoop on what had transpired during the day while I was gone.

"You just missed her again," said George, as he motioned for me to step into his messy apartment.

"Missed who?"

"That girl that wanted to rent an apartment. You just missed her by not more than fifteen minutes. She came by and wanted to know if there were any vacancies. I told her about the apartment next to yours being available."

"Is she moving in?" I asked. "Or did you tell her about the murder and scare her away?"

"I didn't have to tell her. She already read about it in the paper. She wanted to move right in."

"Then it didn't bother her that someone was just murdered there last night?"

George shook his head. "It didn't even faze her. She just wanted to know how soon she could move in. I told her in a few days—once the police were through checking out Harry's apartment."

It amazed me that the landlord would rent the place out so quickly, but George explained that the police dusted for fingerprints the night before and took some personal objects out of the apartment that they felt might give some clues. Harry's parents were from San Francisco, and some friends of theirs would be moving his other personal belongings out of the apartment and back to his parents' house. How quickly the dead are forgotten, I thought.

"This whole thing has been bad for all of us," said George. "It's time to start over and forget. I'll clean up the apartment soon so she can move right it in."

"Won't you have to replace the carpet? I thought Harry bled to death."

"Nope. There wasn't a drop of blood on the carpet. The police said he was actually murdered on the couch. That's where all the blood was. Whoever killed Harry was nice enough not to ruin the carpet."

"You're right," I agreed. "I saw Harry lying on the lying on his couch. His throat looked like it had been ripped open. But I guess it wasn't on the floor." The memory of it nauseated me.

"Whoever killed him must have been careful, cause there was no blood on the carpet. I'm telling you. I ought to know. I was in there with the police. His place was cleaner than mine."

He motioned with his hand, pointing out his living room. It wasn't really dirty in a filthy way, just totally disorganized.

Newspapers lay all over the floor, dirty clothes on his couch, and his television blared, with a boxing match on.

"What about this girl who's moving in? What's she like?"

"I already told you everything I know. Why don't you ask her for her life story when you meet her? She says she's moving her furniture in the next few days."

"I guess it will be nice to get a different neighbor— especially if she's pretty," I admitted. "But it's a shame it had to happen this way."

Chapter Four

Several days later, I woke up to the sound of furniture being moved. I drew open the curtains. In the street below was a large van, double-parked. Two men carried furniture and boxes into the building. Their loud tramping and groaning could be heard in the hall as they struggled with their load.

After breakfast, I opened my door and glanced around from curiosity, hoping to catch a glimpse of the new neighbor, whom I had heard just enough about to make her somewhat mysterious. Maybe there was nothing mysterious about her at all, but from the description George had given me, I was just dying to meet her. It struck me as wonderful that she should be moving into the building on a Saturday, when I didn't work and would have the entire day free to get acquainted with her.

In this I was sadly disappointed, for though I spent the whole day at home, I saw no sign of her. I stood out in the hall and watched the two men carry up a French Provincial sofa and vanity dresser. Whoever the girl was, she certainly had good taste. I wondered if she was possibly an interior decorator. Then, to my horror, they carried in a harpsichord, a case for an electronic keyboard, and a large keyboard amp. Although I knew the acoustic harpsichord would not be loud, the keyboard and its amp would be a different story and the sounds would go right through the walls. The irony of the situation struck me. For the past two days, I had felt disturbed by Harry's violent death. Out of the tragedy, came only one benefit—though purchased at a very high price—and that benefit was the peace and quiet that I assumed would be mine now that he was gone.

Looking at the musical equipment, I could see that I'd been wrong. Harry's death was now totally negative for me.

I looked at the harpsichord in disgust as the two men struggled with it in the doorway. They saw me looking at them and stopped, huffing and puffing in the doorway, trying to figure out how to get it in.

"If you find this so interesting," said one of them as he turned to me, "maybe you'd like to help instead of just standing there."

"There's nothing I'd rather do on a Saturday. The only problem is these muscles of mine have to recuperate from my heavy workout at the gym yesterday." I hit a double biceps pose, then laughed.

They looked at each other and shook their heads as if I were crazy. "We don't need your help anyway," said the other one.

"Turn the harpsichord on its side and it will go right through the door," I pointed out.

They turned it on its side and sure enough, it went right through the door, all to their utter amazement. They glared at me for my advice.

"Is my new neighbor a musician?" I asked, changing the subject.

"We just get paid to move furniture," snapped one of them. "We don't ask no questions. I could give a shit what your neighbor is."

With this last remark, we parted company. They went back to their moving and I went back to my apartment. They worked until about five o'clock, then left.

The sun began to set around six, and not long afterwards I heard the door to the apartment next to mine open and close. There was the sound of boxes being lifted and pushed around. She had finally arrived and I was anxious to see what she looked like.

It seemed almost in response to my wish to meet her that my doorbell rang. I rushed to open my door.

Instead of a beautiful young girl in front of me, there stood two elderly women. One of them leaned towards me with a smile plastered on her face that didn't look quite genuine to me. The other one positioned herself back a few feet, smiling, but her nervousness showed through more.

"Hello," said the one closer to me.

"Hi," I answered.

"It certainly has been a nice day, hasn't it?" she asked.

My face must have registered my confusion, since she quickly added, "The weather, I mean. It's been a lovely day." She smiled weakly.

"Yes, I guess so." I wondered what she wanted. The answer to that came quickly enough.

"You know," she went on, "we're hoping that there are better days ahead. Wouldn't you like to see better times?"

I thought of the past few days—the murders on the street and the apartment, my declining social life, the pressure at work and school. "Yes, I'm all for better times."

She smiled at the little bit of encouragement I showed her.

"Well, good," she said, opening up a Bible. "God says that there are better days ahead. I'd like to read you something."

The situation clearly was spinning out of control. Once they started reading, they would never stop. I had to do something quick, yet tactful and effective. I wanted to meet my new neighbor—not carry on a religious discussion. I had never been particularly religious. An idea materialized where I could get rid of them and meet my neighbor at the same time.

"I agree with you one hundred percent." I nodded my head to show that I was on her side. Then, cutting her off before she had a chance to read the entire New Testament to me, I added, "The thing is, I've already been saved, praise the Lord."

"Praise the Lord!" they both echoed in unison.

"My neighbor, though, hasn't yet seen the light." I shook my head sadly at this revelation. "If you were to talk to her and explain your story to her, I'm sure she'd be grateful." Then, taking one step out into the hall, I extended my left hand to the side and said, "Here, I'll even press the doorbell for you."

It rang, and the two ladies stood facing my neighbor's door as I peeped my head out of my own door to see her answer.

The door opened and a slender, but curvy girl with long black hair stepped forward just a few inches. She wore a short, skin-tight purple dress that revealed shapely legs like those of an ice-skater. I couldn't see her face, as she wasn't turned in my direction, but rather, towards the two women.

"Yes?" she asked. Her voice was soft and smooth.

"It certainly has been a nice day, hasn't it?" asked the old woman, with her partner nodding nervously in the background.

"I really wouldn't know," the girl answered. "I've been sleeping all day."

This answer struck me as odd, since she couldn't have slept in the apartment with all the noise and the furniture being moved in and out. I assumed she meant she had slept somewhere else during the day, or perhaps she was only joking with the old woman.

Yet nothing in her tone suggested she was. Her voice, though soft, was rather emotionless and conveyed a sense of fatigue.

"Well," the old woman continued, "what I meant was it's been great weather we've been having."

"I really don't know. I haven't been out and about."

The girl had a strong British accent, which I found charming.

"You know," said the old woman, "we're hoping for better days ahead —"

"I wouldn't hold my breath if I were you," the girl interrupted.

The woman's smile started to crack and her partner nervously fingered her Bible. "Wouldn't you like to see better times?"

"Better than what? The only time we have is the present. The past is gone and the future never comes."

The old woman saw her opening and pointed to a passage in the Bible. "It says here that God has a plan for your life."

"No." The girl shook her head, her black silky hair swaying back and forth. "It's not *God* who has a plan for my life."

"Who does?" the old woman asked.

In answer, the girl opened the top button of her dress and pointed at something around her neck. Though I couldn't see what it was, the nervous woman in the background stared at it in horror, and then whispered something in the other woman's ear. Upon hearing the whispered secret, she let out a screech and they both hobbled away and down the stairs as quickly as their feeble legs would carry them.

The girl's head moved only slightly, then her eyes slowly scanned the scene till they came into contact with mine. There was something unsettling about the gaze of her eyes. They moved independently of her head as if they had a mind of their own. The way her eyes moved so smoothly and then clicked into place jarred me. I now realized she had been aware of me from the moment she opened the door, though that seemed impossible since she hadn't looked in my direction and I had made no sound.

I don't know how long we just stood there, staring at

each other before we spoke, as we observed each other in silence, unblinking.

She was, quite simply, the most beautiful girl I had ever seen in my life. Her eyes were large and dark, and shaped in a most unusual manner—they flared upwards at the edges, so that the outside corners were higher than the inside. Her lashes were exquisitely long and thick, and black, just like the long hair of hers that framed her delicate face with soft bangs. That silky hair tumbled over the smooth bare skin of her narrow shoulders. Her figure tapered to her waist—a waist so tiny, it made her hips flare out provocatively. Her long legs gave her the same height as me, but accentuated her daintiness. She stood as still as a statue of a goddess, and I stood as still as an idiot who could think of nothing to say.

Something in her stare mesmerized me. I felt powerless to look away, just as I couldn't speak. A similar problem had always plagued me when confronted with a girl of exceptional beauty. I sometimes found myself unable to articulate as well as with a woman of average appearance, yet it had never been so serious as right then. I couldn't speak. Finally, after what felt like an eternity, there came an almost imperceptible movement of her lips into what might have become a smile—only her full, sensuous lips never parted. The smile originated in her eyes as much as in her lips, as if she didn't want to open her mouth into a big smile.

She took two steps toward me so that we were close enough to be within one arm's distance, and still without breaking that stare that had begun when she first turned her eyes at the door, she said, "I'm Sylvia Martin. You must be my next-door neighbor."

"I'm Mark Sheridan," I said, but I could say no more. Something strange was going on that I couldn't explain, and it went beyond mere shyness. Something physical, a sort of magnetic energy emanated from her body out to mine. This drew me to her even as my heart beat faster and faster.

I felt my entire body being drained and absorbed by her and we were blending into one person, with one mind. I didn't have to say anything at this point because I sensed that she could see right into me and that no matter how clumsily I would phrase any attempt at communication, she would understand what I meant, even if I were to say the wrong thing.

"Aren't you going to invite me in?" Her face looked at me questioningly, her large eyes like one of the sad children in a Margaret Keane painting.

"Yes. Come in. Come in. I'm sorry. Forgive my lack of manners. It's just that I…"

"Yes?" she questioned in her soft voice.

"It's just that I have *never* in my life seen a girl as beautiful as you. Never. And I just couldn't think of anything to say."

"You're doing just fine." She entered my apartment and looked at me, waiting while I closed the door.

She turned her gaze away from me and surveyed the apartment. I hoped it looked clean enough, and that there would be something in it to spark a conversation and keep it going. I had amazed myself with the frankness I had shown towards her from the very beginning and hoped that she would appreciate my candor, rather than perceive it as a possible sign of weakness or desperation.

"You must be from England," I said, noting her accent.

"Yes. London. Have you ever been there?"

"Yes. I went there as a tourist. I'd love to go back. Have you been here long?"

"Oh no. Just about a week."

"A week! You certainly are lucky to find an apartment in a week. Sometimes it takes months to find what you're looking for in San Francisco."

"I'm a lucky person," she nodded in agreement. "This flat already had a tenant when I called here a few days ago and then it became empty just when I needed it."

"Actually, it was more than just luck in this case." I stopped, wondering why I had said that. Even though she knew about the murder, perhaps it would have been as well to save such a subject for a later date.

"You mean what happened to your neighbor? But that is still a matter of luck. Bad luck for him—good luck for me." She shrugged her shoulders.

Her nonchalance astounded me under the circumstances. It was great to see that she wasn't disturbed by the murder, but her attitude didn't match her look of innocence.

"Then it doesn't bother you?" I inquired.

"Why should it? I didn't know him, so why should I care about him? And I'm not worried about myself. After all, lightning rarely strikes twice in the same spot."

I could have told her that it did—that three strangely related murders had taken place within twenty-four hours of each other, and that both murder scenes had happened within close distance of me.

There would have been no purpose in frightening her with such stories or in revealing what only I knew about these murders.

Apparently, my surprise to her statement must have shown, for her face immediately changed to a more solemn expression. She touched me gently on the shoulder with her delicate hand and said, "I'm sorry. I hope I haven't offended you in some way. Was he a friend of yours?"

"Harry? Oh no," I reassured her. "He and I hated each other, if you must know the truth. Of course, it's terrible when anyone dies the way he did, even if he's not a friend."

She asked me how he died and I told her the whole

story because of her obvious interest. Yet, the way she looked at me, I sensed that she somehow was more interested in how I felt about it than the actual facts, which I'm sure she had read in the newspaper anyway. She quickly got off the subject, though, and began looking around my apartment, as if trying to think of something to say.

I became aware of a certain vulnerability that had escaped my immediate impression of her. When our conversation about the murder ended abruptly and she looked around, for a moment she seemed as if she were lost and frightened. I realized then that she was every bit as nervous talking to me as I was trying to talk to her.

After casually inspecting my living room, she cast her gaze back towards me, and fixed those wonderfully large eyes of hers on mine, as she observed me with an intense fondness that I found peculiar. Such an unblinking stare from anyone else would have prompted me to look away, but she had such a beautiful face; it was a joy to be able to look upon it so freely. Yet, I found myself puzzled as to why she stared at me in such an unusual manner. She smiled strangely, as if in recognition.

"Somehow, I almost feel like we've met before," I told her. "But I know we haven't. If we had, I'm sure I wouldn't have forgotten your face."

"Nor I, yours." Her full lips drew back slightly as her smile widened, but they still covered most of her teeth.

Suddenly it hit me. "You're the girl of my dreams!"

She smiled wider this time. "What a nice thing to say."

"No, you don't understand," I explained. "I just realized you're the one I've been dreaming of—when I sleep at night."

"And in this dream of yours, were we in bed?" Her eyes twinkled.

"How did you know?" I wondered if she read my

mind.

"Tell me about your dream." She sat down in a chair, crossed her legs and pantomimed as if she was a psychiatrist writing about me in a notebook.

I blurted it all out—how I had dreamed for years about a beautiful girl in bed with me and how I was often aware that I was dreaming at the same time.

"I'm afraid your dreams just make you normal," she said.

"But it was *you* in the dream!"

"Why do you think it was me?"

"I recognize you."

"Freud would call this wish fulfillment," she pointed out. "Be careful what you wish for."

Then, noticing my large bookshelf, she examined it and asked if I was a student. I explained that I studied English and film at San Francisco State University.

"How wonderful!" She beamed with pleasure. "I just love going to the cinema!"

Seeing my cue, I responded, "In that case, why don't we go see a movie together tonight?" I hoped she would say yes.

"I'd love to," she answered, smiling.

"Great, let's stop and get something to eat first. What kind of food do you like?"

"I'm not hungry." She shook her head. "Oh no. I don't want anything to eat." She said this as if I had mentioned something she found extremely distasteful, but then she immediately brightened and added, "But you eat and I'll come watch if you like."

I was about to tell her that she certainly didn't need to be dieting since she had the fantastic figure of an ice-skater or a dancer, but then it struck me that it had nothing to do with her desire to be slim at all; she just seemed not to have much of an appetite.

We entered my kitchen, and I realized it would be

rude to eat dinner in front of her, so I just opened up a protein drink, took a sip and asked if she would like one, too.

"No, I'll just watch you." With that, she tipped my bottle up with her finger as I had it to my mouth, causing me to gag as it spilled slightly on my chin. She immediately grabbed a dishtowel and wiped my chin. "I'm so sorry," she said, "but I thought it wasn't too much to swallow. I think you need more practice."

Her wiping my chin with the dishtowel felt comfortable and familiar. I asked her if she knew anyone else in San Francisco.

"Only you," she replied.

Her answer amused me. After all, we had only talked for a few minutes. How could she say she knew me? I almost laughed at her remark as if she were joking, when I realized that if she knew absolutely no one in the entire city, and had just moved into an apartment where a murder had recently taken place, she might not find the whole situation so funny.

"I have no real friends here." Her voice was so matter-of-fact, as if she were quoting statistics out of a textbook.

"Then do you have any relatives here in this country?"

"No, neither here nor in England."

"Where do they all live, then?"

"They're all dead." Her voice dropped in tone and then cracked as she continued. "Everyone is dead. I have no family. I'm all alone." She broke off eye contact and looked away. Her eyes began to mist over.

I put my hand on her shoulder. "I'm sorry if I brought up painful memories."

She placed her hand on mine, and closed her eyes for a moment and leaned her head slightly against my hand so that it stayed resting on her shoulder. Then her eyes opened, and she looked into mine, and straightened her head back up. She moved both her hands, resting them on me between my shoulders and my neck. In response, I put both of my hands on her shoulders. She kept her hypnotic gaze upon me and said, "Yes, Mark. I do have some painful memories. And here in San Francisco, where I am all alone, I'm glad to have found a friend. You will be my friend, won't you?"

"I promise. I'll be anything you want me to be." Perhaps it was a strong statement. Perhaps I had committed myself a bit too far without realizing it. But in light of her frank and open display of her own feelings, I felt compelled to be as sincere with her as she was with me. So, there we stood in the kitchen, my hands on her shoulders, her hands resting on the sides of my neck, facing each other, having achieved a level of intimacy that some men and women never attain even after a long time together.

But as we held each other, a strange thought occurred to me.

Harry's death had led to Sylvia moving into the apartment next to mine. The death of her family moved her emotions strongly enough to push her into my arms at that precise instant. It was ironic that the birth of our romance grew from the death of others.

At that moment, I sincerely hoped that the future of our relationship would not depend on other people's tragedies.

Chapter Five

Sylvia gradually loosened her embrace from my neck and leaned back at arm's length from me. Though the tears on her face were visible, I was surprised not to see smeared eye make-up, but after a more careful look, I could see that she didn't wear any. This was remarkable, considering how dark and thick her eyelashes were, but evidently they were that way naturally. "I'm sorry for being so emotional. It's so unlike me," she said. "But somehow, I felt that I could be honest with you. I've been holding back my feelings so long, it was like a dam bursting."

"I'm sorry that it's taken thirty-three years for me to meet someone so nice as you."

"Are you really thirty-three?" she asked. She looked surprised.

"Yes, Why?"

"You looked younger to me."

"I still get stopped at bars sometimes," I said. "How old are you?"

"A woman shouldn't tell her age," she answered.

"But you're much too young to start lying about your age. That shouldn't happen till you're about thirty, and I'd guess that you're in your early twenties—twenty-five at the oldest."

She smiled, but this time her mouth opened fully, revealing perfect, dazzling white teeth. She pointed at my neck. "You must have a girlfriend. I see a love bite."

I looked at myself in the mirror and saw a slight bruise there. "I don't know how I got that. But it's not from a girlfriend. We broke up about a month ago."

"How interesting." Sylvia took me by the hand and pulled me down onto my couch so we sat next to each other. "Tell me all about it."

"You don't want to know."

"Oh, but I do." She leaned forward and looked into my eyes. "Were there any sexual problems?"

"No, no problems there. And I'm sure all the other men who were dating her during our exclusive relationship could attest to that."

"How awful." Sylvia put a gentle hand upon my shoulder. "Tell me more."

I wondered how many details to give, but since she persisted, I told her the relationship lasted about six months with numerous breakups because Mary traveled for work and wanted to have an exclusive relationship, but also liked to date other men while out of town on business.

"What a bitch!" Sylvia exclaimed. "I would never do something like that. I couldn't live with myself if I did." She stood up and held her arms stretched out. "I think you need a hug."

Who was I to argue with the most beautiful girl I had ever seen? I stood up, prepared to give a friendly hug, but it was even friendlier than I anticipated. She held me tighter than I held her and didn't let go. It was not one of those Platonic hugs where the woman bends forward at the waist so that only the shoulders and arms touch. No, this gorgeous girl stood straight up, not just close, but pressed against me from head to toe, like we were Siamese twins joined in the front. Our cheeks touched and I could feel her silky black hair against my face, and I could smell the fragrance of her shampoo. About halfway down my body, I began to feel aroused. I pulled my head back just enough so I could look her in the eyes and noticed I was looking up slightly.

"Hmm. It looks like you might be an inch taller than me," I noted.

"That's okay. I think you grew a few inches during our hug. Like the story of Pinocchio, only for adults."

"I'm sorry. It couldn't be helped." I let go of her and

broke off the hug. An awkward moment of silence followed as I tried to think of what to say next.

Instead, she changed the subject abruptly with, "Maybe we shouldn't go to the cinema tonight."

I was taken aback by her statement and hoped I hadn't said something to offend her. She must have read my reaction, for she immediately added, "What I mean is, I've only been in San Francisco less than a week and we don't even know each other. I'm not going to learn anything about this city or you by sitting in a film theater. Why don't we do something else?"

Her clarification relieved me. "What would you like to do?"

"I don't know. What do the tourists do?"

"There's Fisherman's Wharf, Chinatown, the clubs on Broadway, the cable cars, Golden Gate Park, Market Street, the Golden Gate Bridge."

"What would you recommend?" she wanted to know.

"It's too late for Golden Gate Park," I said. "After dark, the only thing to do there is get mugged. Market Street has a lot of stores, but they're all closed now. At night, the only thing to do there is go to the movies. Chinatown has some great restaurants and so does Fisherman's Wharf."

"But I'm not hungry," she reminded me.

"Broadway has mostly strip joints. Topless bars."

She shook her head at this description. "What about the Golden Gate Bridge? I'd like to see that."

"That's very close to here."'

"Could we go for a walk together on the bridge, then?"

As I looked at her beautiful face questioning me, she could have suggested both of us jumping off the bridge together and I probably would have accepted.

"It's pretty cold and windy on the bridge at night, " I warned her. "You better wear a warm jacket."

"How cold is it?" she wanted to know.

I told her that although the temperature was probably no chillier than the high forties, the strong wind on the bridge made it feel much colder.

She told me to wait and she'd be right back. She was true to her word. It couldn't have been any longer than five minutes later that she returned from her apartment, dressed in black velvet pants and a jacket that matched and a pair of black athletic shoes. Her outfit didn't appear particularly warm, but it looked fabulous on her. I told her so. Her face brightened with my remark. Compliments certainly weren't wasted on her.

When we got to my car, a yellow 1987 Lotus Esprit Turbo, she looked approvingly. "So you like cars from England?"

"And women from England, too, now." I opened the door for her.

I started to tell her it was the same model James Bond drove in the 1976 movie, *The Spy Who Loved Me*, but it was unnecessary; she already knew that.

"Does yours turn into a submarine, too?" she asked.

"No, I'm afraid not. And it doesn't come with a machine gun."

"Mine didn't have those features either. It was similar to this, except the steering wheel was on the right side."

I thought it an interesting coincidence that we should both have owned the same car, especially an uncommon one like a Lotus Esprit.

Half an hour later, we strolled along the narrow walkway of the Golden Gate Bridge. Traffic zoomed by in both directions. The bridge was particularly well traveled since it was Saturday night. A few other strollers walked on the bridge as well, but they were some distance from us. The wind blew briskly, but the air was so clear and fresh making it worth the cold. The skyline of San Francisco, with its lights stretching out over miles of

43

steeply rising hills, looked like black mountains covered with stars.

"It's beautiful!" said Sylvia. The wind lifted her long, thick hair, and both wind and hair flowed in unison, like the waves far below us. As light and ethereal as she looked, l half expected the next gust of wind to pick her up and carry her away from me.

She gazed down at the ocean, about two hundred feet below, then turned to me. "Shall we jump?"

"Don't even joke about it," I said. "About two people a month jump off this bridge."

"How sad," she agreed. "I would never kill myself. I'm an incurable optimist. I believe things can always get better."

"Things got better for me starting today," I agreed.

She looked down at the water below again. "How many people have jumped off this bridge?"

I tried to remember. "I think it was about eight hundred the last time I read. Something like that. I'm not exactly sure. But quite a few."

"Life is so short. Only a fool would commit suicide." Sylvia took an elastic band from a pocket and put her hair through it so it wouldn't blow across her face.

I turned away from her and pointed at the San Francisco skyline, and remarked about the great view.

"Do you like gymnastics?" she asked, her voice no longer next to me.

I spun around to see Sylvia standing on the ledge of the bridge.

"I asked if you like gymnastics," she repeated.

My heart raced. "My God! What are you doing? Don't jump! Please don't jump."

"Who said anything about jumping? I only asked if you like gymnastics. This is just like the balance beam. It's even a little wider than the four inches of an official size beam. This should be much easier."

"Are you crazy? It's two hundred feet down to the ocean if you fall."

"No worries. I can *swim*."

"Don't look down," I warned.

Sylvia closed her eyes. "Okay, I'm not looking down now. It will be more difficult to do this without actually seeing, but I'll do my best."

"Open your eyes!" I yelled.

"Well, make up your mind. And don't get upset. You're liable to make me nervous. You don't want to make me nervous do you?"

"You're making *me* nervous. Please get down. I'll do anything you want if you get down."

"Anything? At any time? Do you promise?"

"Yes," I agreed. "Anything at any time. I promise."

"All right, then. I'll get down. But first I have to show you this!"

With that, she leaped backwards in an arc with both arms. Her feet left the ledge as she did a back handspring—not once, but three times in a row, landing on her feet again and again. I had seen the movement in the Olympics on the balance beam, but never on a bridge. I heard the sounds of glass shattering as several cars slammed into each other on the bridge, obviously from drivers distracted from seeing a crazy woman on the ledge of the bridge who appeared about to jump. I didn't bother to look at the cars. My attention focused only on Sylvia. She landed back on the pavement of the sidewalk and I rushed up to her, grabbing her hand before she could change her mind and get back up on the ledge. We both turned toward the center of the bridge and saw several fender benders—drivers who had glanced over to see Sylvia and ran into the car in front of them. No one appeared hurt, but cars were dented. Some drivers yelled at us, while others seemed to believe I was a hero for talking a suicidal woman down from the bridge.

45

I started walking hand-in-hand with Sylvia away from the crowd as quickly as possible.

"Don't forget your promise," she said.

"What promise?" I asked.

"I knew it. You forgot already." Sylvia pointed at me accusingly. "You promised to do anything I wanted at any time if I got off the bridge. I got off the bridge, so now you have to fulfill your promise."

"All right," I said. "What is it you want me to do?"

"I'll ask you later when we know each other better. Right now, I'm feeling a little shy."

"Yes. I can see that," I answered, feeling both irritation at her crazy stunt, yet relief that she was safe.

We arrived back at the apartment building about half an hour later, and I pondered what to do next. I didn't know whether to suggest going out for a drink, or if she might be too tired. I wondered whether to invite her in again or if she would invite me to her place. She solved the dilemma by stopping right in front of my door and waiting for me to open it for her.

Once inside, she paced back and forth like an animal in a cage, repeating over and over, "What are we to do now?"

I asked her what she meant. She looked so restless, yet she didn't appear upset, only in a highly energetic state.

"I meant it's still so early yet. What are we to do now?" She looked concerned.

It seemed better to leave the answer up to her. If it had been totally up to me, the solution would have been simple—we would have made love all night. As alluring and sexy as she looked, it would have been the most honest answer. But I was not about to ruin my future chances with her by moving too quickly on the very first night. True, she had been somewhat forward herself, and certainly hadn't pulled back from me in any way. I was hitting green lights all the way so far, with no stop signs in sight. Even so, Sylvia was not just a beautiful woman and potential bed partner for the night. Not at all. From the very moment that our eyes locked onto each other in the hallway, I knew that there would be something special between us—that she would be different from any other woman. I wanted her badly that night, more than I had ever wanted any woman in my life. But I wanted more than just that night with her. I wanted her to be my girlfriend permanently. Though we had only spoken for a few hours, it was obvious to me that I had met someone who differed from other women I had gone out with.

Her eyes were different. They penetrated into mine with an intimacy that was hypnotic. Every time she looked at me, I felt that she could read my thoughts, and perhaps even control them.

"What would you like to do?" I asked. "I've already been to most of the places that I want to go to in this city. What do you like to do?"

"Oh, I don't know. Anything." She slumped into the sofa as if she had been poured into it. "I just can't go back to my apartment right now. It's so lonely."

"I can understand that," I agreed. "Especially after what happened in there to Harry."

"Oh no. It's not that." She dismissed the idea with a wave of her hand. "No one's out to kill me that way."

It was an odd remark. What in the world did she mean? Was someone out to kill her in some other way? If so, why would she be so casual about it? She was a constant mystery to me.

She saw my confusion over her remark and quickly added, "What really bothers me is staying up all night bored."

"You're welcome to stay here as long as you like. And whenever you like."

"You should be very careful in saying that to me," she

warned. Her tone of voice surprised me with its seriousness.

"Why is that?"

"I can be very difficult to be rid of." She said this just as seriously as her last statement.

"But I don't want to be rid of you," I said with a smile. "You're the nicest girl I've ever met."

She didn't return my smile. She stared at me with melancholy eyes. "I hope you can still say that *after* you know what I—" She paused for a moment, then changed to, "after you know me better."

I sat down on the sofa and put my arm around her. I wanted to pull her tightly to me and hug her. The moment I touched her, she leaned closer to me.

"I want to know you better. And I will. We only have a wall between us. We're next-door neighbors after all," I said.

"The wall between us isn't physical." Her remark hung in the air like a cloud.

I looked at the wall and then at her for clarification.

"I want us to know each other," she said. "It will be difficult for you to understand me at first. And it will become more difficult before it gets any easier. There will be certain things about my life which I cannot talk about right now, even though I would like to."

"I'm now more confused than before, but I do trust you. Of course, I want to hear everything about you, but if there is something that you can't tell me right now, I'll try to be patient. After all, we've got plenty of time."

She looked at my clock radio on the large oak bookshelf. "Yes, we've got plenty of time," she repeated, as much to herself as to me. Her reflective state lasted only a moment, then she added, "But why don't you tell me all about yourself?"

Who could refuse such a request? I could easily talk about myself. Besides, her interest in me seemed so genuine. I told her about my classes at San Francisco State University, and that my hobbies included photography. She listened intently as I rambled on about different movies that I liked. I don't think she blinked or turned her eyes or head away from me for a fraction of a second. Her attention span never wavered for an instant. In comparison to her, it was as if everyone else in my life had never heard a word I said. Every time I paused for even the briefest amount of time, she'd ask another question, as if she were afraid that too long a breathing space might result in our conversation toppling down, After telling her that I had only one more semester to go before finishing graduate school, I asked her if she was a student or planning to enroll in one of the colleges in the area.

She shook her pretty head, and her long, glistening, black hair swept back and forth across her face and shoulders. "Oh no. I read enough at home. I have thousands of books."

"Thousands?"

"Yes. Thousands. Mostly back in England. I brought some of them. I'll show them to you tomorrow, after I clean up my apartment and get everything in order. I still have a few boxes to unpack."

"I'll help you if you like," I volunteered.

"That's very nice of you. And I'm sure you'll be strong enough to help with my heavy lifting." With that, she squeezed my arm, as if I had flexed my bicep for her.

"Well, I'll be over at noon. How's that?"

"Oh no. That's much too early. Why, I don't even get up till after five or six."

"At night?"

"Yes," she replied. Her eyes were downcast, as if revealing a confession in the making. "I sleep all day."

"Just when you've had a late evening, or all the time?"

"All the time. I get up about five or six, then stay awake till about five in the morning, then go back to sleep. It's always the same." Her eyes pleaded with me. "Don't you see? That's why I'm so bored. Sometimes I think I'll just go mad!" To punctuate her point, Sylvia crossed her eyes, stuck out her tongue, and pulled her hair out to the sides. She held this pose for only an instant, then resumed her normal facial expression.

"How come you don't go out during the day?" I didn't want to pry, but it struck me as rather bizarre—to sleep all day and only venture forth at night like some nocturnal creature.

"I have an unusual medical condition." She glanced away for an instant. "The sunlight is very bad for me. It hurts my skin and eyes."

"You mean like an albino?"

"Yes, very similar to that."

"But you don't look like an albino at all. Your hair is dark. Your eyes are *very* dark. As a matter of fact, you have the darkest eyes I've ever seen. Albinos have no color in their hair or eyes."

"Look into my eyes and tell me what you see," she said enticingly, as she leaned closer to me.

Her eyes were not more than six inches from mine, and the light from my lamp on the side of the sofa shone on her face, I could now see her eyes more clearly than I had all evening, and what I saw startled me. Her eyes had no iris, just black pupils which were the same size as most people's pupil and iris together. It looked as if her pupils were twice normal size.

"Your eyes have no color. They're black." This surprised me.

She kept staring at me, and I suddenly became aware of a peculiar sensation—like falling into her eyes. They became more than eyes; they were a doorway, beyond which lay something unknown and forbidden. My entire body felt light and somewhat numb, and my vision began to blur. With great effort, I pulled my eyes away from hers, and immediately felt normal again.

"Did I say something wrong?" she asked in a sweetly innocent voice. Her eyes asked the question as much as her lips.

"No. Not at all. Perhaps I said something wrong."

She shook her head and stroked my face lightly with her smooth hand. "No. You just said that my eyes have no color, and it's true. They don't. My pupils are open all the time. That's why the bright light hurts my eyes." She said it so logically, as if she were a biology professor giving a lecture on the anatomy of the eye.

Her explanation sounded logical, but it didn't account for the hypnotic effect her eyes had when I looked at them for more than a few seconds. It didn't explain the actual physical phenomenon that had just occurred—the lightheadedness and blurring of vision. These were *real*. I did *not* imagine them.

But there would have been no point in bringing up this observation to her at that time. Perhaps I already appeared nosy enough to her, but then, she had certainly behaved the same way towards me. It only took a moment of reflection to recognize this, and to realize that since both of us were so interested in each other and had been so honest already that evening, either of us could say anything at all to each other, as long as it wasn't an outright insult.

So I nodded my head in agreement with her explanation and then added, "You have the most beautiful eyes I've ever seen. I'm sure many girls would give up the bright sun during the day if they could look half as beautiful as you at night."

She stared at me adoringly, then took her hand, which she had placed around my head, and pulled my face towards hers—and those full lips that tantalized and

51

invited me. I ran my fingers through her thick hair and along the velvety smooth skin of her face—skin smoother than any woman I had ever known. Just kissing her was more erotic than making love to someone else. It felt as if our bodies were melting into each other, and I was overcome with the same feeling that I had experienced when I first saw her in the hall—that sensation of being drawn to her like a magnet and absorbed by her at the same time. It was a strange sensation, simultaneously alluring and disturbing. Her tongue probed deeply into my mouth. I loved her sexual aggressiveness. It filled me with ecstasy—body, mind, and soul. I could feel her wanting me as much as I wanted her. Though her initial movement towards me and the beginning of the kiss suggested a simple appreciation of a sincere compliment, it quickly grew into an uncontrollable compulsion. Her gentle caress changed to a tight grip on the back of my neck, and I could feel her sharp fingernails start to pierce my skin.

Breathing heavily, she quickly pulled herself back from me and stared at her hands, checking her nails. For a brief instant, she reminded me of Lady Macbeth, seeing blood on her hands that had been washed away after murders long ago. Yet there was nothing on Sylvia's dainty hands, and I wondered what she was staring at and so concerned about.

"I've got to go now." Her voice was agitated and she appeared to be on the verge of an emotional tidal wave of some sort. She held her hand to her throat, and her breath came so quickly, I feared she would have some kind of seizure right there.

She gasped for breath, as if she were choking on something, and kept raising her hand to her mouth.

"Are you all right?" I touched her gently on the shoulder. Instantly, she jerked away as if I had burned her shoulder with my light touch. She held her hands out at me like a stop sign, then slowly backed away from me.

"No. Please don't touch me, Mark. I'm sorry. I'm not feeling well. I have to go now." She said this with regret. I could see by the sad look in her eyes that she did not wish to leave, yet I couldn't figure out why she had reacted so strangely.

"What's the matter? Is there something wrong with the way I kiss?"

"No, no." She shook her head and I could see that her eyes were already starting to mist. "It's me. I have a problem. Please don't be mad at me, but I must go now. I must go back to my apartment right away." Her eyes wore that sad expression I had seen earlier.

"But why do you have to leave like this? Can't you tell me what's wrong?"

"No, I can't tell you, and I don't want to lie to you— ever. So please let me go and I'll explain *everything* to you later."

I shrugged my shoulders and walked to the door and held it open. There would have been no point in arguing with her. She was certainly free to leave if she so chose, though I couldn't help but feel hurt. The way she kissed me so passionately—almost violently—and then to jump away from me so quickly and want to leave, shifted my emotional gears a little too fast for comfort. I didn't know what to think. She confused me completely.

Sylvia slinked by me towards the door. I noticed that the color in her face that existed earlier in the evening had left completely. The sad expression I saw earlier had returned.

"Will I see you tomorrow?" I asked her.

"Oh yes. Of course! You'll see me every night, unless you don't want to. It's all up to you." Her voice sounded sincere, and though her words didn't quite fit with her actions of the past few minutes, I hoped that tomorrow would be different.

"What time tomorrow?" I asked.

"I'll come over the very minute I wake up. I promise. And I'll stay until you get sick of me." She smiled with her remark.

"You may have to wait a long time for that. I doubt I'll ever get sick of you."

"I've got plenty of time to find out." Her smile ended abruptly as she suddenly clutched her stomach.

I went toward her to help, but she held her hand out to keep me away. "No. Please. I'll be all right. See you tomorrow."

She forced a smile, but I could see that something inside her pained her more than she wished to reveal or discuss. As she walked by me, she affectionately stroked my face good-bye with her hand as she departed. I watched her open the door to her apartment, gaze longingly back at me, and then close her door.

Her fingers felt like icicles, and it took almost a full minute before the chill of her handprint left my face.

Chapter Six

Sometime in the middle of the night, I awoke from a dream. Unlike many other dreams I've had, I remembered this with every detail lucidly intact.

I dreamed that I was sleeping in my bed with Sylvia's gentle hands caressing me. At first, I felt her velvety smooth touch. Her actual presence wasn't verified till I opened my eyes. When I did, she was lying on top of me, but under the sheets, and though it was difficult to see well in the darkened room, I could feel her naked body on top of mine. I tried to speak, to ask her what she was doing here while I was sleeping, but no words would come out of my mouth. She hugged me tighter and tighter until I thought I would suffocate, so I tried to push her body up, just slightly so I could breathe and see her face more clearly. The more I pushed, the harder she hugged me, till I couldn't even move my arms. She kissed my face over and over, then raised up her head just a few inches so that I could see her face clearly. For several seconds, we just stared at each other, until my vision began to blur. Then I became aware that I was in the middle of a dream and I remembered a feeling similar to the dream sequence in *Rosemary's Baby* and I thought, *This is no dream—this is really happening!* The dream ended at this point, before either of us had a chance to do anything. So I was cheated out of sex again, even in my dream.

I slept on till about 10 a.m., when my doorbell woke me. I stumbled out of bed, slipped on a pair of pants as I looked in the mirror to verify whether I looked as tired as I felt (I did), then opened the door.

Dave grinned and walked past me into the apartment. "Getting to sleep late, are you? Don't you know bodybuilders need their sleep?"

"Then why'd you come wake me up if I need my sleep?" I felt exhausted, almost faint, but couldn't figure

55

out why. I had gone to sleep no later than 1 a.m., which meant I had slept nine hours—two hours more than usual. Normally, seven hours were adequate for me, but at that moment, I felt as if I had been awake for three or four days. My body felt so weak, I walked back to my bedroom and sat down on the bed to relieve my dizziness.

"I came by because there was no answer on your phone."

"You know I always unplug it before I go to sleep."

"Why do you do that?"

"So that no one can call and wake me up in the morning," I said, in a mock accusatory tone.

"It doesn't seem to work too well, does it?"

"I'll have to get my doorbell fixed too, I guess. What's up?"

"Gail and I thought we'd see if you wanted to go with us to the movies tonight."

"What are you going to see?" I almost didn't care. I asked him more out of politeness. My exhaustion still bothered me and I couldn't understand what could be causing it.

"It's a double feature. *Romeo and Juliet* playing with *Night of the Living Dead*."

"You can't be serious," I said with a laugh.

"No, it's true. I got the message over the phone when I called. They got one of the movies by mistake." Dave laughed over this and then asked me again if I wanted to go to the movies with him and Gail.

"I don't know. Probably not. Last night I met this fantastic woman and we'll probably be going out tonight."

"It's about time you met a girl. Gail's always asking me why you don't have a girlfriend—or why you don't go back with Mary. She'll probably feel more comfortable if there are four of us instead of three."

"If I had known how Gail felt," I said sarcastically, "I would have gotten married just to be sure there would be four of us to go out on dates together."

Dave ignored my remark and asked me where I met this new girl.

"Right here. She's my new next-door neighbor."

"Wow! What luck! How did you meet her?"

I told him the amusing events with the evangelists and how Sylvia invited herself in.

In the middle of explaining it, Dave stopped me and said, "I wish I could have seen the two women running down the hall. It sounds pretty crazy. But I still don't understand why they ran away." He waited for me to explain.

"I don't really know," I admitted. "Sylvia pointed at something she wore around her neck that was under her dress. As soon as the old women saw it, they just took off. It was pretty weird."

"So what was she wearing around her neck?" Dave looked curious.

"I don't know. Whatever it was, she tucked it back under her dress."

Actually, when Sylvia had walked up to me in the hall, her beautiful eyes and face had so mesmerized me, that I had forgotten to check and see what so frightened the two old women. At the time, it seemed inconsequential next to Sylvia's hypnotic beauty. But now, as Dave mentioned it to me, I wondered, too. Why *did* the two old ladies run away? I resolved that I would ask Sylvia the next time I saw her.

Dave asked me what Sylvia was like and I told him where she was from, about her English accent, her friendly, open manner, and what a joy she was to have around. I didn't know quite how to describe her to him, since I really knew almost nothing about her. The main thing I was sure of was how great I felt being with her.

"What does she do?" asked Dave.

"I don't know," I confessed.

"You mean you spent several hours with a beautiful girl and you don't even know what she does for a living? You must be crazy. She probably won't go out with you again because she'll figure that you're not interested in her. You should read this book I got on how to pick up girls. It tells you just what to say to get them into bed right away. You have to pretend you're interested in them." Dave emphasized his last sentence with an air of confidence, as if he had written the book himself.

"I'm not just trying to go to bed with her," I explained. "Sure, I want to, and I think I will. She seems to like me as much as I like her. Maybe that's why I didn't get to find out that much about her."

"What do you mean?"

"All she wanted to talk about was me. As soon as I started to talk about her past, she switched the conversation to me again."

"She must like you."

"I hope so. I sure like her. She's the perfect girl I've always wanted. It's really great that she's my neighbor."

Dave sat down on the edge of my bed and nodded in agreement. He had been going with Gail for two years and I often wondered how they stayed together. Gail was a born-again Christian who resisted Dave's sexual advances for the first four months that they went together. Dave kept his patience by making it with every woman he possibly could behind Gail's back. At the end of four months, she rewarded his patience and "celibacy" with her body, and he rewarded her by reducing the number of affairs he had with other women. Of course, Gail knew nothing of this. If she had known the truth, she would have broken off her relationship with him. As things stood, conflicts arose anyway when she wanted him to go to church with her and he had no interest. Indeed, only after they became engaged, did she agree to live with him. I often wondered how they could stand each other, and Dave's romantic advice to me seemed like it came more from opinions than experience, so I took everything he said far less seriously than he did.

I walked over to the window and drew the curtains open. The blue sky and bright sun shone down on the street below, where I saw people riding bicycles and children roller-skating. At this sight, I felt disappointed that Sylvia would be sleeping all day. I wanted to take her roller-skating in Golden Gate Park on such a warm, sunny day. With great regret, I pulled my eyes away and turned to Dave, who sat on the edge of my bed. He grinned at me across the room.

"Mark, why didn't you tell me you already made it with this girl on your first date?" he asked. "Shit, here you are saying you *hope* she likes you and you've made it with her on the first date. What more proof do you need?"

"I don't know what you're talking about. All I did was kiss her. We never got into bed."

"Then whose is this?" He picked at my pillow and held out in front of me, a long black hair.

I picked up the hair that he held out to me and looked at it closely and at the bed and the pillow.

"This is impossible. Sylvia and I never got into my bed. I went to bed after she left. I don't know how it could have gotten there."

Dave laughed. "The good fairy must have put it under your pillow while you were asleep." He chuckled at his remark, then took the hair from my fingers and dropped it back onto my pillow. "You never know when she may come back for it,"

"That's strange. I had this dream last night." I then told him about it. He listened with amusement.

"Well, that explains everything," he said. "She had sex with you while you were sleeping. You must have turned her down last night and she just couldn't wait another night to get you into bed. So, in the middle of the night, she broke into your apartment, screwed you without waking you up, and then she left and locked the door behind her once she was in the hall." His tone was sarcastic.

Dave had a special talent for taking a minor detail and blowing it out of proportion to make a joke out of it.

"How would you know whether she locked my door?" I asked, as I played along with his game.

"That's easy. You were asleep when I rang your bell, and when you came to your door, you unlocked it and took off the chain, just like you always do."

It was the only logical thing he had said regarding the whole incident, but since nothing else he said made any sense, I tried to just forget about it all—the dream and the hair, and whatever other strange things might possibly come my way. We dropped the subject of dream interpretation since we were getting nowhere. I resolved to either figure it out later or forget about it.

Dave suggested that we go to the kung-fu school and practice together. It was on Leavenworth Street, right in the middle of the Tenderloin District, a sleazy area renowned for its junkies, prostitutes, drag queens, and other interesting characters. When we pulled up in front in Dave's car, there were about six or seven broken down men standing on the corner drinking wine out of paper bags. I had always wondered why they used paper bags. Was it to make the sober people of the world believe that they just had a Coke hidden in that paper bag? Were they trying to fool the police? Were they trying to fool themselves? It was a wonderful diversion for me to try to unravel the mysteries of San Francisco's street people. It was certainly more amusing and less disconcerting than trying to sort out the strange events that had come into play with my own life recently.

As soon as we entered the unlit hallway, and before

60

we could see the inside, we could hear the sound of people punching the heavy bags and the slap of the jump rope on the wooden floor. Several students were performing the first form, Sil Lim Tao, and in another corner of the room, others were practicing Chi Sau—the Wing Chun sparring exercise of sticky hands—rolling their arms back and forth in contact with each other, feeling for an opening, then striking without warning. Dave and I hit the sand bags. Some of the newer students watched us punch the bags, trying to see if we were as strong as we looked. I don't know whether we fulfilled their expectations or not. It occurred to me how our expectations of others are formed by our physical appearances, and I wondered just how much of my impression of Sylvia was based on her appearance and how much on what lay inside of her.

What actually lay inside that beautiful face and body still remained a mystery to me, and I kept asking myself why I was so crazy about her after only a few hours of knowing her. Perhaps it was because of her interest in me, or her air of mystery, or because I sensed in her an unusual combination of innocence and the forbidden. There existed in her, an essence behind the beautiful face and charming manner that I sensed differed from her outside appearance. I couldn't put my finger on it; it was just a feeling that there was more to her than met the eye.

The main instructor wasn't at the school that afternoon, so after hitting the bags for a while and about fifteen minutes of sparring, Dave and I left. We had lunch in a little greasy coffee shop just half a block away. I felt sure that he and I were the only two people in the whole place who weren't drunks or junkies. The little restaurant reminded me of a drawing of *Dante's Inferno*. I asked Dave if he really wanted to eat there, and he assured me that they had the best prices on steak and eggs, and that bodybuilders needed all the protein they could get. I acquiesced reluctantly, and hoped we wouldn't get anything else as part of the bargain, like fleas.

As I looked over the patrons, I realized that even though the last week had been terrible for me, with grisly murders occurring close to me (too close), my life still remained relatively unscathed. The terror and anxiety of the week had been partly offset by the introduction of Sylvia into my life. If I hadn't met her, perhaps the sum total of the week would have affected me more severely. However, since meeting her, everything else fell into the category of trivia, even the murders. I could think of nothing but her. The restaurant, the patrons, the other martial artists—none of these mattered to me. I felt like a prospector, who, after searching unsuccessfully for gold all of his life, discovers a nugget as big as a boulder, and then is afraid to let it out of his sight. Sylvia appeared too good to be true. I feared that at any moment, something terrible might happen to take her away from me. With three murders committed so close to me, I had a small, but growing fear that not only I, but also Sylvia, could be the next victim. I immediately pushed such macabre thoughts out of my consciousness. There could be no logical connection between the murders. They had to be a coincidence. After all, strange coincidences happened all the time. The only difference was now they were all happening around me.

Dave and I returned to my apartment about 5 p.m., just as the sun began to set. As I admired the view from my window, Dave asked to use the phone to call Gail. He talked to her for a few minutes, then told me that a girlfriend of Gail's would drop her off at my apartment in a few minutes. Dave wanted to know whether I wanted to date Gail's girlfriend tonight.

"No way." I shook my head. "Sylvia will be coming over any minute and I don't want to miss her. Besides, she and I will probably be going out tonight."

Dave cupped the phone mouthpiece with the palm of his hand.

"Instead of waiting for this neighbor of yours to come by, why don't you go ask her right now? That way, if she says, 'no,' you can still go out with Gail's friend."

"No. I can't do that, I might wake her up."

Dave glanced at his watch as he covered the phone with his palm. "Are you out of your mind? It's after five o' clock."

"She told me she's a late sleeper," I explained.

"Sure, probably sleeping with her daytime boyfriend."

I got into a boxing stance and pretended to throw a punch at his head, but stopped an inch short. It was a common gesture between the two of us, whenever we wished to show disapproval of something the other said. We always pulled our punches, though.

Dave held out the phone as protection. "Sorry if I said anything wrong. Look, you keep your date with Sleeping Beauty, and I'll tell Gail to find someone else for her friend."

Dave talked to Gail for only a few more seconds, but I didn't know what they discussed, for all I heard him say were one-word answers, like "okay," and "sure."

We practiced some kung fu for a few minutes, since we found that easier to practice than boxing when we had no boxing gloves with us. We always pulled our punches, but sometimes we slipped.

Today, it was Dave who slipped, and the side of his hand slapped against my neck.

"Why don't you use some control?" I asked. I checked my neck in the mirror. Sure enough, there was a bruise on the other side of my neck. I now had *two* bruises, one for each side.

Dave reluctantly apologized. "I saw those two marks this morning when I came over. You must have done it last night. Or maybe it was your new girlfriend from next door."

Then I remembered how Sylvia had dug her nails into my neck as she kissed me the night before. That almost explained it, except that she scratched the *back* of my neck. These marks were on the side and looked more like the bruise on the side of my neck I had gotten days earlier.

The doorbell rang, and Dave told me that would be Gail, coming by to pick him up for the movies. I told him it would be Sylvia. Unfortunately, Dave was right.

Gail entered my apartment and took off her coat, which I assumed meant she would stay awhile and talk. I hoped she wouldn't. It wasn't that I disliked Gail. She was pleasant enough. But I wanted to be alone with Sylvia. Though things had gone fairly well the night before, the evening had certainly come to a strange conclusion, with her scratching my neck and then leaving suddenly, as if staying would result in some terrible consequence. I wanted to be alone with Sylvia and make sure everything was all right, and that I hadn't said or done anything that had triggered her strange reaction to me. Because, in spite of the last minutes of the evening, the rest of the night had been perfect. I had never felt myself grow so attached to any other woman in just a single night. I needed time alone with Sylvia, time to find out all about her—her past, her hobbies, her interests, her likes and dislikes. I needed Dave and Gail to leave.

"Dave tells me you have a new girlfriend," Gail said. "Why don't we all go see a movie together?"

"Gee, thanks Gail, but I just met this woman last night and I'd like to get to know her better before going out on a double date."

"What he means," interrupted Dave, "is he thinks that if we're around, he can't get into this girl's pants." Dave grinned.

"Oh stop it. Will you?" Gail demanded of him. She hated it whenever Dave mentioned anything about sex in front of her and someone else. I could see it in the look she shot him after his remarks and the swiftness with which she changed subjects. "Mark, I just talked to Mary at church on Sunday. She's so nice, and I know she'd like to try to work things out with you." Since Gail had been responsible for introducing me to Mary in the first place, she knew all about our breakups and reconciliations. Gail started listing Mary's good qualities, such as her good looks and career, and she counted the fingers on her hand at the same time. I could see that she would soon run out of fingers before she ran out of things to tell me.

My mind drifted back to the previous night with Sylvia. "I would rather jump off the Golden Gate Bridge than try to work things out with Mary one more time."

"Don't worry," said Gail. "I'm sure you and Mary will get back together."

"First of all, I'm not worried. Secondly, she and I will never get back together."

"How can you be so sure?"

In answer to Gail's question, the doorbell rang.

"Saved by the bell!" I yelled, as I walked to the door.

I opened the door, but before I even had a chance to say hello, Sylvia kissed me lightly on the lips and walked in cheerfully. Only a second later, she stopped and froze in the middle of the room.

"Oh, I didn't know you had guests," she said apologetically. She stood as still as death, while Dave and Gail stared back at her. I couldn't figure out why she appeared to be so disturbed by the presence of Dave and Gail, but she obviously felt uncomfortable. Her eyes shifted nervously from Dave to Gail and then back to me.

Yet her reaction to them was slight compared to their reaction to her. In Dave's face, I saw an instant wave of recognition, as if he had seen Sylvia before. His face, which usually wore an expression of joviality, was as serious as I had ever seen. He actually appeared frightened of her, as if seeing her were some kind of shock. He looked at me in alarm, and appeared to be on the verge of blurting something out, but said nothing.

Gail stared at Sylvia too, but I could see that her eyes were not focused on Sylvia's face, as were Dave's. She was staring at a small silver medallion around Sylvia's neck.

I hadn't noticed it before, probably because Sylvia wore it inside her dress. I wondered whether this was what had scared off the two old ladies.

On the medallion was the figure of a goat's head inside a pentagram. The pentagram was inverted, with two of the five points facing up and one point down. Around it was a circle inscribed with foreign characters I couldn't read. It looked vaguely familiar, but I couldn't place its meaning.

After a short, but awkward silence, I introduced everyone and tried to break the ice, but this proved impossible. Gail kept staring at the little silver medallion around Sylvia's neck as if she found it disquieting for some reason known only to her. But I couldn't understand why.

Dave appeared so shocked at Sylvia's entrance to my apartment. He seemed to be concentrating on Sylvia's face, unlike Gail, whose attention focused only on the medallion.

Gail pointed at it, with an apprehensive expression on her face. "That symbol. I've seen it before, in a horror movie about witchcraft."

"Oh *this*." Sylvia held it between her fingers and looked at it as if she just discovered it around her neck. "It's the symbol of Baphomet." When Gail's expression revealed her mystification, Sylvia clarified by saying, "It symbolizes Satan."

66

"Satan!" gasped Gail. Her eyes widened in horror. "Oh my God! You're a Devil- worshipper!"

Sylvia shook her head. "There's no such thing as a Devil-worshipper. I'm a Satanist."

"*I'm* a Christian," Gail declared.

"Then our little group has diversity," said Sylvia. "Isn't *that* nice?"

"Why would you wear such a thing around your neck?"

"Because it's a symbol of my religion," answered Sylvia. "The same reason you wear your cross."

"My cross is a symbol of my closeness to God and Jesus Christ." Gail assumed a self-righteous tone. "It's the symbol of everlasting life, as given by the Savior." Gail smiled triumphantly as she spoke these words. Indeed, every time she discussed religion, her tone of voice would change, as if she were about to mount the pulpit for a sermon.

Sylvia shook her head. "Your cross is a symbol of death. Personally, I think it's crazy to have a miniature symbol of an execution device hanging from your neck to display your religion. What's next? A religion that has a replica of a guillotine or a hangman's noose?"

"It's a symbol of everlasting life!" declared Gail.

"If *I* were to start a religion about eternal life, I wouldn't use a cross. I'd use a positive symbol, maybe a butterfly or a rainbow," Sylvia pointed out.

"You'll never know eternal life as a Satanist," Gail said smugly.

"Maybe. Maybe not," answered Sylvia. "But whatever time I have here will be lived fully. I won't put off any pleasures for the afterlife. Priests do that with their vows of celibacy in this life and so do the suicide bombers who kill themselves and others thinking they'll get their seventy-two virgins in the afterlife. Not for me, thank you. I don't want seventy-two men who are virgins — I just want one man who knows how to satisfy me." Sylvia looked at me and put her hand on my shoulder, indicating that her sexual satisfaction would be my responsibility.

"I'll do my best," I answered.

"I'm counting on it." Sylvia gave me a mischievous smile.

Gail scowled at me. "Mark, don't you know that Satanists perform animal and human sacrifices?"

"Absolutely not!" yelled Sylvia. "Animal sacrifice is in the Old Testament and not practiced by Satanists. And we certainly don't sacrifice people. That's an old rumor started by the church hundreds of years ago. They charged people money for baptisms and then said that witches sacrificed unbaptized babies, just so they could get their baptism fees. It was all for money. The same reason priests couldn't marry — keep the money in the church — no heirs for priests to leave money to. The church tortured and executed tens of thousands of people for witchcraft and then often took their property. They had to grab all the power and all the money. Don't even get me started on this subject."

Sylvia stunned even me with her little speech. I had always felt that Gail had gone on too much about religion, but Dave and I usually just ignored what she said rather than challenging it so boldly. Though Sylvia shocked me, too, I couldn't help but be amused to see Gail meet with resistance for once, instead of just silent suffering, which most people had borne during her religious sermons.

Gail's anger rose within her like a boiling kettle, while Sylvia appeared quite content once she had said her piece.

I tried to quickly change the subject. "So, I hear there's a double feature playing tonight!"

"I think Dave and I should go now." Gail picked up her purse.

"Do come back again," replied Sylvia, beaming. "I just adore religious discussions."

Gail glared at Sylvia, then grabbed Dave's hand and pulled him out the door. I went to follow them to make sure that everyone involved held no ill feelings, even though that may have been expecting too much.

As they passed out my door, I told Sylvia I'd be back in a second, then rushed out and stopped them in the hall.

"Look," I said, "I just met Sylvia. I don't think you're being fair to her. What difference does it make what religion she is?"

"She's a Devil-worshipper, Mark! Don't you know about the things they do?" Gail pointed her finger at me. "Who knows what kinds of things she's done? Or what she'll do? And to you!"

"I wouldn't lose any sleep over it," I told her. "Sylvia and I like each other. She's not going to do anything bad to me."

"I wouldn't bet my life on that," added Dave. "You said you just met her yesterday?"

"Yeah, why?"

"You've never seen her before that?" he asked.

"No, of course not. She just moved in yesterday."

"Then tell me this," said Dave. "Why was she at the gym about a week ago, watching you through the window?"

"Not Sylvia. It must have been someone else."

"No way. I remember those eyes. The way she stared at you. Those *eyes*!" He shook his head. "If I were you, I'd want to know why she was outside the gym watching you that way and why she just happened to move in next to you."

Chapter Seven

My mind whirled as I made my way back to my apartment and Dave and Gail made their way out of the building. Somehow, I had to get to the bottom of this. I didn't like Dave's accusations, but then I had no explanation for what he said about Sylvia being at the gym. I hoped that Sylvia did.

She stood in the middle of my room, just where she had when Gail had stormed out. Her hands were folded in front of her and she hung her head down, as if in shame. Her black hair covered her face completely. When I closed the door behind me, she slowly lifted her delicate head, like a wax figure coming to life. Her dark eyes followed me around the room as she stood motionless.

"I'm afraid that your friends don't like me," she lamented.

"You're right. They don't. But I do."

With that remark from me, she flung her arms around me and hugged me tightly. Her embrace soothed me, but again I felt the sensation of sinking and being drawn into her and absorbed. The instant she touched me, my entire body's sensations changed. I could feel something like an electrical current that flowed between us, binding me to her. It was a deliciously erotic sensation, yet at the same time disturbing, because it felt as though I were relinquishing control over my body, and my mind as well.

"I hope you're not mad at me," she said in a melancholy voice.

"No, I'm not mad. But I am confused. Dave said that you were watching me at the gym last week, before you moved in. Were you?"

"Yes," she answered, but offered nothing more.

"Why didn't you say anything to me before? Not that it's important, but..."

"No, it is important. But I just don't know how to explain it to you. I did see you at the gym, but I thought that if I had told you, I—well, it might have looked like I was following you."

I laughed. "I should be so lucky to have someone as beautiful as you follow me." She brightened when I said this. "Why, the last time someone followed me," I began, and then stopped in mid-sentence, realizing that I almost told her of the three muggers that jumped me.

"Go on," she prodded. "You were saying something about what happened the last time someone followed you."

"Uh, right." She stumped me. What could I say? At this point, I couldn't very well tell her about the murders in the alley. I would carry that secret to the grave.

"So what happened?" she implored me. Her eyes pleaded with me to tell her the truth. She knew that I was holding something back from her and my withholding it was now even more important than the secret itself. It was the first time I had to keep something from her, and she knew it.

"I'm afraid I can't talk about it right now."

"Ah, a secret," she said with glee. "I love secrets! Will you tell me yours?" She looked into my eyes and smiled, waiting for me to pour my heart out. If only she had known what it was! Not some minor piece of gossip, but two murders that were still unsolved by the police, and which I could be held as a suspect, since I had no way to explain how they happened.

She shrugged her shoulders. "Okay. You don't have to tell me if you don't want to. But you already know two things about me that could have been secret—that I am a Satanist, and that I saw you before I moved here. It would be nice to have you share your secrets with me."

"I'm sorry. Maybe I can tell you about this later on. But it wouldn't be important to you anyway."

71

"You're right. It probably wouldn't. The important thing is our trust of each other. That will come, in time. But I have quite a few secrets of my own, you know. And before I tell you all of them, I want to know about this one."

"Why?"

"Because it's so important for you not to tell me. So when you do tell me, then I'll know how much you trust me."

What a corner I had verbally painted myself into! I had not only shown a certain amount of distrust, but had now given her reason to hold back parts of her own mysterious life. However, I could not resist asking her about her religion, especially since she hadn't tried to hide it.

"It's a religion," she explained, "but not the way your friends think of it. It's really an applied magical philosophy that helps us to do what we want without the conventional moral restrictions."

"But isn't it supposed to be evil?"

She laughed at my question, then answered it with a proverb, which she recited like a nursery rhyme.

"For every evil under the sun,
There is a remedy, or there is none;
If there be one, try and find it,
If there be none, never mind it."

"But what about things like human sacrifices? Isn't that part of worshipping Satan?" I asked. I was concerned with what Sylvia was involved with, because if it affected her, it would eventually affect me too, in some way.

She took me by my hand and led me onto my sofa. When I was seated, she sat down on my lap and placed an arm around me.

"First of all, we do no human sacrifices. Those rumors were all started by churches to keep their own members faithful. Those people who did sacrifices, killed needlessly, and out of ignorance. Satan does not ask for sacrifices. He doesn't want sacrifices. And he doesn't want people to get on their knees and worship him."

"Then what does he want?" I asked her. As she sat on my lap and stroked my hair with one hand and my face with her other, the light weight of her hips and legs on my groin aroused me, which I knew she could feel through my pants.

"Satan only wants to be your friend, just like I do. *Please* give me a chance, Mark. Trust me." She gazed into my eyes with her longing stare, her black eyes bottomless pits of mystery. The eyes—windows of the soul. I wondered what I would find behind those windows once they were opened to me.

I didn't know quite what to think of her involvement in Satanism and magic, but she told me only that she would soon explain everything more fully.

At this point, the conversation took a cautious detour from the subject of magic, and onto the subject of her past. I learned that she came from a small family, and that her childhood had been spent in the English countryside. Her family was well-to-do, owning a large amount of farmland that many other people worked on. They lived near a village, but it wasn't until after she left, that she became involved in the practice of black magic. At first, I thought that perhaps her family had also practiced black magic, but she told me that their magic differed. She explained that she didn't become involved in Satanism until after they all died. When I asked her how her family died, her face saddened and she looked as if she were about to cry, but she held back her tears, and then said, with a trace of an angry memory in her voice as she recounted it. "They were murdered."

"How horrible," I said. "How did it happen?"

"I'll tell you all about it someday." She sat silent for a

73

long while after saying this. I could see in her face that she was reliving the incident, and I felt guilty for bringing up the subject. But what could I do? Sylvia's past seemed so strange. I was sure that I could have started a conversation with her on almost any topic and it would have ended in something that she could no longer discuss. Sorting out her life was like running through a maze, with detours and dead ends that appear to lead nowhere, because as soon as I would ask a simple question like "When did this happen?" or "In what city did that happen?" she would fall silent again, and ask me to be patient with her for not revealing everything at once. It would not be long, she assured me, before she could make everything as clear as a cold winter night.

"Would you like to see my apartment?" she asked me, as she deftly changed the subject. "I've gotten everything in order now."

That was an understatement. I had thought that in only one night of sleeping at her new apartment, that Sylvia couldn't have organized everything so soon. With all the furniture the movers had carried in just the day before, and all the boxes, it amazed me how quickly she had fixed it up.

The carpet, brown and plush, was the same as before. Everything else in the room had changed. The previously bare walls now had framed posters of famous artworks. The frames had the titles, the names of the artists, and the dates. One, *Girl with a Hoop*, by Renoir, resembled what I imagined Sylvia might have looked like at eight or nine years old if she had been that age when Renoir painted the girl in 1885. Another painting was a total contrast to the portrait of the young girl. *The Spell*, by Francisco Goya, pictured a group of witches in black, one sticking pins into a doll, while another held a basket filled with several babies. Painted in 1797, it played into people's fears of witchcraft at the time. The two paintings certainly clashed with each other.

The entire apartment was furnished in French Provincial, and looking at the love seat, I felt sure it was an antique, not merely a copy. She had a writing desk that matched the love seat, and several other small pieces that apparently were part of a set. I complimented Sylvia on her good taste and she was pleased.

Every part of the room had something about it that would have made any apartment look unique; with Sylvia's antique furniture, every square inch of her living room titillated the eye.

In the edge of the room, sat a harpsichord, an English bentside spinet, asymmetrically shaped, like a curved triangle with keys running at an angle to the strings. The keyboard had black naturals and white sharps, the opposite of a piano. Sylvia sat down and began to play. Her delicate fingers glided along the keys effortlessly, and the most enchanting music filled the air. The piece was complex and faster than almost anything else I had ever heard. Sylvia looked at me, not at the keyboard as she played.

"What do you think?" she asked, as she continued.

"I've always liked the harpsichord. And you certainly know how to play."

"Thank you. That's because I've been playing so long," she explained with a smile.

I asked her whose music she was playing, and she said it was something she composed herself. Then she asked me if I liked Bach. When I assured her I did, she played for almost twenty minutes without ever looking at any sheet music, then told me it was *Partita Number 2 in C minor*, by Bach.

"I wish I could play like that," I told her.

"You can. I can teach you how to play this just as well as I do."

"That would take years!"

"Yes, I know." She stopped her playing and folded her hands in her lap as she turned toward me. "But I have plenty of time."

We looked at each other for several seconds in silence. I tried to imagine just what she meant. It sounded like a commitment of time that went beyond what one might promise to someone known only two days, but somehow, coming from Sylvia, it didn't appear as unusual as some of the other things she had already told me.

I decided to press her to clarify what she meant. "What if one of us moves before I learn to play?"

"Don't move," she replied.

"What if you move?"

"I won't," she came back. "Unless you want me to."

"Want you to move?" I asked, with a laugh. "Why in the world would I want you to move? I like you. I hope you stay here just as long as I do."

"And then what?" Her eyes as well as her voice questioned me.

I just realized she had switched the whole conversation around and that it now was my responsibility to explain myself more clearly.

"I don't know. I really hadn't given much thought to either of us moving. I never had any intention of leaving, and you just moved here. So there's really no point in either of us going anywhere right now. Right?"

By the expression on her face, I could tell that I hadn't answered her question. Evidently what she had meant when she asked "then what?" was she wanted to know what would happen to us, and between us. How could I come up with an answer to such a question after having known her for only two days, and a strange two days at that? True, I felt drawn to her like I had to no other woman, she was the most beautiful woman I had ever seen, and she obviously liked me. She also appeared to be unattached, considering that she had only been in

San Francisco a few days, and had told me she had no real friends. So why was I being so reluctant in telling her how much I liked her? I suppose it came from the silly notion many men have that a man shouldn't tell a woman that he's crazy about her. Disclosing this secret, it is assumed, will lead to the woman thinking that we are desperate, and it's further assumed that the faster one falls in love, the less genuine it must be. What illogical nonsense that is! Yet I had been influenced by it, too. So there I stood in front of Sylvia, with her eyes bearing down on me. I knew I had sidestepped her question, and she knew.

"I'm sorry, Mark. There I go again, being too pushy. I don't wish to force myself upon you. It's just that... Well, I've been by myself for so long, I don't know how to talk like normal people do. So, if I feel lonely, or I like you, I just come right out and say it." She stood up and backed away from the harpsichord and walked across the room.

Directly behind her the wall displayed several more framed posters, mostly soft, romantic impressionist paintings such as flowers by Monet or ballet dancers by Degas. Below that was a low bookshelf. Upon closer examination, I noticed that while many of the books were about art, literature, and music, some were about witchcraft, Satanism, demonology, vampires, and other aspects of the occult. At least a hundred books filled this bookshelf, and on the opposite wall, a smaller bookshelf must have held another hundred books. The striking difference between the two was that the smaller one had a Baphomet symbol above it in black and silver, about a foot across. Black velvet draped the top of the bookshelf, and on its surface lay two black candles, a silver chalice, and a dagger. This had many jewels in the handle, and appeared expensive. The blade gleamed under the light, but I noticed that one of the blade's edges didn't shine as brightly as the rest. It appeared to be slightly tarnished with rust, or at least that's what I preferred to think, but I had to admit, it looked more like dried blood.

Sylvia noticed my inspection of her altar. "Do you like the way I've decorated the apartment?" Her dark eyes searched mine.

I glanced nervously at the dagger and wondered what she used it for. "Well, your *furniture* is beautiful," I managed to remark.

"Thank you." She gave a curtsy.

"You certainly do a lot of reading." I picked up two of her books and read the titles aloud. "*The Vampire: His Kith and Kin* and *The Vampire in Europe*. Hmm, interesting. Both by the same guy—Montague Summers." I examined the books, then turned to Sylvia. "Is this stuff supposed to be real?"

She took the books and replaced them back on the bookshelf and pointed to the other volumes on vampires, witchcraft, and the like.

"Ninety percent of this is just superstitious nonsense," she informed me, as she tried to push away their credibility with a wave of her hand.

"What about the other ten percent?"

Her face had been turned toward the bookshelf, as if she were contemplating one of the titles. Slowly, her head rose, and the dark hair that covered her pale face parted, revealing a serious expression.

"The other ten percent is true," she answered, as she placed a hand gently on my shoulder.

"Which ten percent?"

"Curiosity killed the cat," she warned.

"Satisfaction brought him back," I retorted, remembering the old school rhyme.

"Yes, I suppose it did." Her voice sounded sad, and her large eyes became reflective again. I wondered where her mind went on these brief, but distant flights.

Her expression quickly changed, however, as she smiled again, and then said, "You know what I'd like to do? Go dancing. Do you dance?"

"I'm not that good, but I'm willing to try if you're willing to."

"Oh, don't worry," she reassured me. "If you don't know how to dance, I can teach you quickly enough." With that, she waltzed around the room, taking smooth steps as she glided almost on air by herself.

"Between the music and dance lessons, do you think either of us will have any time to work?" I asked.

"I don't know," she said, as she continued to dance around the room, "because I don't work."

"If I'm not being too nosy," I began, though I knew it was nosy to ask, "what do you do for money?"

She stopped her dancing. "You're not any nosier than I am," she said, as she shrugged her shoulders. "I already have some money saved up. I'm paying for my trip here to San Francisco with some money I won in Las Vegas, about a week ago."

"Your trip?" I asked. "You make it sound like a vacation."

"Well, in a way, it is. Except that there are no time limits. I can stay as long as I like."

I told her that I hoped that her "visit" here would not be of short duration, and she assured me, most emphatically, that it would not. This relieved me. I didn't want to become romantically involved with someone who I thought might be moving to another country soon, but I made no mention of this. It probably would have been unnecessary to bring it up, because I was certain that Sylvia felt the same way. Despite her peculiarities, I had a strong feeling that Sylvia and I were very much alike, but had simply not discovered those common points yet.

"Which games did you play in Las Vegas to win this money?" I asked.

"Just twenty-one. It's the only one where skill can play a part in winning."

"And I had thought it was all a matter of luck."

"Not when you're counting cards," she answered.

So that was it! She was a card-counter—one of those rare people with such an incredible memory, she could remember all the cards played, so that as the game progressed, she had a better idea of which cards the dealer had left. She could play her own hand accordingly, and with each hand dealt, the accuracy of her predictions rose. Casinos hated such people, and when they discovered one in their midst, the very least that would happen was the gambler would be thrown out. Other times the casinos were more harsh, and used physical force. Who knows how many card-counters lay beneath the hot desert sand just outside of Las Vegas? Shallow graves containing the unrecognizable remains of people were discovered periodically in the Nevada desert. The reasons why certain people wound up there were probably many and varied, but I always believed that money had a lot to do with it.

"You should be careful," I warned Sylvia, and told her about what happened to people the casinos disliked. "That could be dangerous."

"I should be very lucky if that were most risky thing I did. Anyway, after I teach you how to dance and play the harpsichord, I'll teach you how to count cards, too."

"Great," I answered, with a short laugh. "They'll bury us in the same grave in the desert. We'll be just like Romeo and Juliet."

"It's better than being buried alone," she said, as she slipped her slender arm around my waist and pulled me toward her.

Chapter Eight

As soon as we turned on the radio in my car, I discovered Sylvia could sing, as well as play the harpsichord. Other than having someone smoke in my car, the one thing that has always driven me crazy was to have a singing passenger. I always believed the best solution would be an ejection seat to dispose of unwanted passengers, just like James Bond had in his Aston Martin in *Goldfinger*.

Sylvia, however, was different. No matter what song played on the radio, she imitated every female vocalist with amazing precision. Her voice, soft and pleasing in speech, could change to any tone while singing. With the first song that she sang to, I told her that her singing voice sounded just like the girl on the radio. This, in itself would have been amazing. But to compound my astonishment, she demonstrated that she could imitate *any* female singer with equal clarity. As we drove on toward the bright lights downtown, I felt like there was a female rock singer sitting next to me in the car, and one song later, it would be another.

"You should be a singer professionally."

She shook her head. "Not really. I don't want to be famous. I like being free to come and go as I please without people following me down the street, or reporters trying to interview me to find out what kind of toothpaste I use. Do you want to be famous, Mark?"

"You bet I do," I said. The lights of downtown surrounded us as we reached the top of a large hill on the corner of California Street and Mason Street. We passed the Mark Hopkins Hotel and the Fairmont Hotel. "I'd like to be rich and famous, like the people who are staying at those two hotels," I said, as I pointed them out to her.

"But you don't have to be famous to stay there," Sylvia responded.

"True, but you do need money—more money than

they pay me for selling advertising."

"There are many ways to make the money you want. Far more money than you even need," she said. There was an odd tone of certainty in her voice that forced me to take my eyes off the steep hill we were descending and look at her eyes, which glittered wildly under the illumination of the full moon. She stared back at me out of the corners of her eyes, with her thick, sensuous lips hinting at a smile.

For a brief instant, the odd thought occurred to me that in two nights, Sylvia usually didn't fully open her mouth when she smiled.

She caught me glancing at her. In response, she edged herself closer to me. I put my arm around her, and she laid her head against my shoulder. It felt so comforting to have her next to me. I wished it could go on forever like that.

As we rolled down California Street with my brakes on, a cable car, on its way up the steep hill, slowly passed us on the opposite side of the street. Tourists jammed into every square foot, and the conductor rang the large bell as it passed us. Sylvia turned her head to watch it go by.

Her eyes took in all the sights. "I think I'm going to like San Francisco."

"I sure hope so," I answered. "It wouldn't do to have you leave. I like you too much."

To my surprise, she asked me why I liked her so much. I told her it was a combination of several things — her beauty, her honesty and frankness in telling me how she felt, her affection towards me.

"But I think there's more to it than that," I explained. "There was something I felt the very first second I saw you, before you even said a word to me. It was a feeling of predestination almost. I felt as if I had to like you. You didn't use any of your witchcraft to cast a spell on me, did you?"

"I wouldn't do that. Attraction must come freely. I wouldn't try to create it out of nothing. Besides, there was no reason to cast any spells like that."

"Why is that?" I asked. At Grant Street, I made a left turn into Chinatown and continued driving north slowly along the one-lane street so that I could show her Chinatown and North Beach.

"Everything will happen on its own." Sylvia didn't have to explain further. I knew what she meant, and she was right. If I liked her so much in only two days, how would I feel after a month or two?

We continued on Grant Street through the heart of Chinatown, past the restaurants, the throngs of tourists packed on the sidewalks, until we reached Broadway, where I turned right, taking a long scenic route so Sylvia could see more of downtown San Francisco. She looked out the window at the topless bars and nightclubs as we passed by. Barkers stood outside each one, enticing tourists with explicit descriptions of the shows inside. I had only been to one of these shows myself in the many years I had lived in San Francisco, and found it to be overrated and overpriced. I never returned for a second time.

Just two blocks later, we turned right on Montgomery Street, drove through the Financial District till we crossed Market Street, then parked a few blocks further down in the South of Market Area (SOMA), known for its trendy nightclubs.

"Here we are," I announced.

I opened the door for Sylvia, then arm in arm, we entered. Dance music blared from the huge speaker system. In comparison to most other dance clubs, this one would have appeared to be crowded, but by its own standards, it was just an average, or even calm night. On Friday and Saturday nights, it would take fifteen minutes for a couple to squeeze their way from one end of the club to the next. But tonight was Sunday, and evidently most of the people who went the night before were now home and getting their eight hours of sleep for work on Monday morning. I explained this to Sylvia, and promised a more exciting crowd to her on Friday and Saturday.

"That's all right." She took my hand. "We just came here to dance, not to meet other people. Besides, this gives us more room on the dance floor."

Strangely enough, space on the dance floor didn't pose a problem, for the instant we started dancing, the other couples moved out of our way. For the first few seconds, I wondered if they were merely polite, but then I noticed in them, a certain wariness that I couldn't account for. Sylvia danced like a professional, never missing a beat. With all I had learned about her in the past two days, this hardly surprised me. In fact, I would have been shocked if she had been anything less than fantastic. What *did* shock me was how well I could dance with her. I had always been a mediocre dancer, so I rarely went to dance clubs, and consequently never improved on my lack of ability. But now, I felt like John Travolta in *Saturday Night Fever*, and Sylvia and I became the center of attention.

I could perform any dance step perfectly, and somehow anticipated exactly what movement Sylvia would do. Just a fraction of a second before she would do it, I would initiate it, so it looked as if I were leading her. Only I knew the truth. I couldn't have led her because I didn't know those dance steps, or any others, for that matter. She led me, but somehow I knew in advance what movement she wanted.

We stopped at the end of the song and a number of people watching us from the side applauded. I took Sylvia's hand as we walked off the dance floor.

"How did you do it?" I asked her. "How did you

make me dance like that?"

"What do you mean?" she questioned. She appeared confused by my remark. "You danced just fine."

"Yes, I know I did. But that's just it. I can't dance like that. You must have done one of your magic tricks."

She laughed—and it was as pleasing to the ear as her sweet and soothing voice. "Magic tricks indeed! I have done no magic. We dance well together. That's all. If you must know the truth, I don't usually dance that well myself. At times, the sum can be greater than the parts."

"If you're saying that you can't dance either, then I don't see how we could have just danced like that. Two bad dancers don't make a good dancing pair." We held our heads inches from each other as we spoke so that we could hear our voices above the din of the music.

"Sometimes two plus two equals five," she explained. "And this is just the tip of the iceberg. Just wait. You'll be truly amazed at some of the things we can do together."

"If we can dance this well together when I don't even know how to dance, just think how we would be at making love together!"

"The thought has crossed my mind." She smiled and nodded.

"Now that," I declared, "is the best news I've had all year."

A trace of her smile lingered on her lips, as her dark eyes grew more reflective. She slowly coiled her arm around my neck and pulled me closer to her so that her smooth face brushed against mine. Then she spoke into my ear, at a loud whisper, "Just remember, Mark, that there are certain strings attached."

"Really? Whatever they are, I'm sure you're worth it."

She held her pretty face back a few inches, so that we could see each other, then gave me a serious look. "Are you so sure?" She spoke slowly and deliberately, taking great care to make sure every word came out clearly. "What would you give up to be able to keep me?"

I laughed at her choice of words, "*Keep* you? I wasn't thinking of buying you or owning you. I just like being with you and I'd like us to be closer."

"Closer? Like this?" she asked, as she took one step forward so that our bodies were touching. "Don't you want to keep me?"

"I'm not sure if I understand what you mean."

"Of course you do," Sylvia countered. "Look, if you needed to drive every day, and you found a car that you liked more than any other car, what would you do?"

"I probably wouldn't do anything. If I liked the car that much, I most likely couldn't afford it."

"Imagine that you could afford it. Would you buy it or rent it?" she asked.

"If I had the money, I'd buy it, of course."

"Why?"

"Because," I explained, "then I could keep it."

Sylvia pointed her finger at my nose in triumph. "You see! You'd *keep* it! Well, people are no different. You can keep a person, too. I'm just asking what you'd give up to keep me."

I told her I didn't know and asked her what I would have to give up. She thought about it for a few seconds and then answered, "Everything."

I just shrugged my shoulders. "Sure."

I didn't understand what she had meant, but I didn't ask for an explanation or another car analogy. She had the ability to be both amusing and cryptic when explaining things to me. I always felt that there existed in all of our conversations, an ulterior meaning behind everything she said.

"But although you must give up everything," she went on, "you'll get far more in return."

"Sounds fair to me," I answered. I was not about to

play this silly game any longer. I would just go along with what she said, and if she wanted to talk in riddles, I wouldn't try to answer them.

Her face grew suddenly sad. "You think I'm joking with you, don't you?"

"I don't know what to think. You're so honest and direct with your feelings, but sometimes I get the impression you're hiding something from me, and I'm sure that whatever it is, it's important."

She nodded her head, then suggested we leave the noisy dance club and find somewhere suitable to talk. I recommended the Top of the Mark, appropriately named, as it was a fancy restaurant and lounge at the top of the Mark Hopkins Hotel on Nob Hill.

It only took a few minutes to drive there, yet surprisingly, no time at all to find a parking space. Although at 19 stories high, it wasn't the tallest of San Francisco hotels, it stood at the top of a hill, and so had a panoramic view of the entire city. I had been inside before, of course, so I knew what to expect, and Sylvia appreciated the hotel's luxurious interior. Built in the 1920s, it exuded traditional amenities and attention to detail from an earlier time.

"Ooh," sighed Sylvia. "It would be nice to live here."

"*Live* here?" I questioned. "If we stayed here just one night, it could cost half my month's rent."

Sylvia shrugged her shoulders. Evidently money matters didn't concern her as much as they did me. I hoped I didn't sound cheap to her, but then I figured she would understand. Besides, if she had loads of money, what was she doing in my apartment building anyway? Not that it wasn't a nice building, but for someone with a lot of money, Pacific Heights would have been more appropriate than the Richmond District. True, the neighborhood that I lived in was clean, had a low crime rate, and interesting restaurants and shops, but it lacked the ritziness of Pacific Heights or the Marina. Judging from Sylvia's attitude towards money, and by her furniture and taste in music, I wondered just why she picked my street to search so hard for an apartment.

"Here we are at the top." She clutched my hand and pulled me out of the elevator and towards the cocktail lounge. The view inside, as I expected, took her breath away, She hardly noticed the cocktail waitress asking her what she wanted to drink.

"Oh, I don't drink," she said quickly, then went right back to her inspection of the view. The cocktail waitress, undaunted by Sylvia's air of disregard, stood her ground, waiting for one of us to order something.

"I'll have a Perrier," I told her. I rarely drank alcohol and wanted to keep my head clear.

Sylvia turned towards the waitress and gave her an icy stare for a second or two before ordering. The waitress squirmed nervously under Sylvia's scrutiny. "I'll take a Perrier too." Sylvia then turned back to me and said, "Isn't it funny? We both drink the same thing."

The cocktail waitress returned and set my drink down on the table, then clumsily bumped against the other glass, spilling the water onto the edge of Sylvia's dress. Sylvia leaped up, and for a moment, I thought she would grab the waitress and kill her on the spot. The hate in her eyes could have done the job easily, so intense was her anger. The waitress apologized of course, but even I had the feeling that perhaps Sylvia's anger was justified. The accident looked intentional. As the girl walked back to the bar to replace the spilled drink, Sylvia glared at her as the waitress looked back at us and laughed with one of the other waitresses.

And then, my thoughts somehow were spoken aloud. "That's strange. I thought she looked familiar and now I remember. She's a friend of Mary."

Sylvia eyes flashed in anger that I hadn't seen before.

She seemed in a trance. I called her name and she didn't hear. Just as the girl picked up a new bottle, I touched Sylvia on the arm. At the exact instant my hand touched Sylvia, on the other side of the bar a glass shattered right in the waitress's hand. She screamed as blood dripped from a large cut.

Sylvia looked at the girl's hand and then at where I had touched Sylvia's arm. Her lips drew back into a large and cruel smile.

Her teeth were a dazzling white, just like an actress in a toothpaste commercial, but some peculiar trick of the lighting made it appear that two of her teeth were longer and sharper than the rest, as if ready to attack, like a wolf or a snake.

The sight shocked me for a second, no less for the strange juxtaposition of the image of the waitress screaming as she stared at her bloody hand.

"Ah, me," Sylvia sighed, as she gazed into my eyes, oblivious to the commotion surrounding the screaming girl. "Why don't we go somewhere more quiet? That girl's screeching is too loud for me. I have sensitive hearing."

For a moment, she stopped up her ears and frowned, then clutched me by the hand and strode out the door, barely giving me time enough to leave some money on the table for the poor cocktail waitress.

Back at her apartment, Sylvia was in good spirits once again, playing classical music on her stereo as she waved her hands like a conductor. She saw me standing there watching her, so she stopped her conducting, placed an arm around me and began to waltz around the room. Again, though I had never waltzed before, we did just fine together now.

"It's been a strange evening," I said, as we danced around the room.

"It's only the beginning," she answered with a charming smile. "Things will get even stranger. Just wait and see."

I then mentioned to her that in two days, I had only seen her smile broadly a couple times, and I asked her why she kept her mouth almost closed when she smiled, since she looked so pretty.

"If you like, I can smile like this," she said, and she opened her mouth all the way, so that her beautiful white teeth gleamed back at me.

"How curious," I remarked to her. "Your teeth looked different at the cocktail lounge."

"Of course they did. So did yours. The lighting was different."

"They looked sharper than now."

Sylvia looked at me as if I were crazy. "My teeth were sharper back there than they are now? Oh my. What was in your drink? LSD?"

"No. Really," I said.

She kept her mouth open and licked her lips slowly and ran her tongue along her teeth. "All the better to bite you with, my dear," she joked, using the familiar line from "Little Red Riding Hood."

"Be my guest," I told her.

She stared at me for a moment, with a serious expression on her pretty face. Then her eyes slowly left mine and her gaze fixed on my neck. At the same time, her hand, which had been on the back of my head, slid down inside my shirt and stroked the back of my neck so softly that it almost tickled. Then Sylvia opened her large mouth even wider and placed her lips upon my neck. It was such a light touch as to be almost imperceptible. I could feel her breath on my skin and the wetness of her lips, and then her teeth resting there. The softness of her lips and the hardness of her teeth intermingled to form a strange sensation. She breathed heavily against the wet skin of my neck, then whispered, "Do my teeth feel sharp now?"

"No."

"Good," she responded, and immediately pushed me away, holding me at arm's length. "I'm glad you think I'm normal."

"I don't know if I would go that far. You are—an *unusual* woman."

Sylvia smiled and nodded. "You have no idea. You'll never meet anyone else like me. For better or for worse."

She leaned back to inspect the damage. "That's all I dare do," she said, "If I had bitten you any harder, you'd bleed. And that's one thing I don't want."

"You can bite me any time you like, as long as you kiss me afterwards."

"Now that's an offer I can't refuse." She wore her devilish smile.

I wondered what time it was, and tried to sneak a glance at my watch without Sylvia noticing. I had to be at work Monday morning at nine, and though I wanted my sleep, I wanted Sylvia far more. She caught my glance to my watch.

"It's almost two, in case you're wondering. You're welcome to stay here as long as you like, and talk to me, but I can't make love to you tonight, I'm afraid."

"Of course you have to know me longer. I completely understand," I said.

"I just don't want to do anything with you tonight that I might regret tomorrow. And if you spent the night with me, you would never make it to work tomorrow."

"You're probably right," I agreed. "No rush at all. I understand you need to feel strongly before getting that close physically."

Sylvia stared at me in disbelief. "You really *don't* understand at all! I'm not holding back because my feelings aren't strong enough. I'm holding back because they are too strong. You thought your life was turned upside down with Mary? That's nothing compared to what can happen with me. I really don't want to hurt you, but I can make a real mess of things. You just can't imagine."

"What could possibly go wrong between us?" I asked.

"I've been unlucky in love. You won't find any former boyfriends around to tell you how wonderful I am."

"I'm glad to hear there are no former boyfriends around," I said. "I hate former boyfriends."

"And I hate former girlfriends," Sylvia said. "So I'll never be friends with your Mary." She looked me in the eyes with an expression, half serious, half smiling.

"You've already made me forget what's-her-name," I said. "And nothing could ever scare me away from you."

"I hope you're right," she said, as she hugged me. "May I come see you tomorrow?"

"Of course! I'd like to see you every single day."

She smiled happily when I said this, then gave me a kiss. "What time do you get home?" she asked.

I said that I would work from 9 a.m. to 3 p.m., exercise at the gym with Dave until 5:30, and then would arrive back at the apartment by 6 p.m. She told me that she would come by then.

We kissed each other good night, then I went back to my apartment. A kaleidoscope of images from the past two days with Sylvia filled my head as I lay in bed and wondered what kind of surprise she had in store for me next.

Chapter Nine

Max scowled as I rushed into the office. He looked at his watch and then glared at me. "You're late!" he announced.

I looked up at the clock. It was almost 11 a.m. "You're right. I am late. Sorry, but I overslept. I stayed up kind of late last night."

"Oh you did, did you?" he asked with a sarcastic tone. "Well, I hope you had a good time. After all, putting out a newspaper is only a hobby for us. The important thing is that your social life is not being disturbed." He grinned with an artificial smile.

"I'll try to be on time tomorrow," I promised.

"Oh, don't put yourself out for us, After all, this is just a job. If it's not convenient to come in on time, don't come in at all. We'll get by somehow." With that, he walked off into his own office.

The rest of the day passed without much improvement. I found it difficult to sell advertising, because I could think only of Sylvia. I could see her beautiful face, feel her smooth skin, hear her pleasing voice, As I tried talking over the phone, I kept forgetting whom I was speaking to, and several times, called customers by the wrong name. When I complimented one of our customers heartily on the quality of his company's products, he became irate. After I realized that I had mistakenly called him by his competitor's name, I understood just how distracted from my work I had become.

Fortunately, I was able to take my mind off my work when I met Dave at the gym at 3:30. However, the conversation and my thoughts both revolved around Sylvia.

"So, how was your date with the Devil-worshipper?" he asked with a grin. "Getting any pussy?"

"The same amount that you got from Gail by your twentieth date with her," I countered. I knew that he and Gail had gotten a slow start on their sex life due to her religious beliefs.

Dave and I walked to the locker room to change.

"Hey, I'm sorry about Gail starting up with her religious bullshit again," he said. "But as you know, she has some pretty strong feelings about the subject."

"Yes, I know," I said with a laugh. "So does Sylvia. I hope this doesn't mean that the four of us can't go out together."

Dave shook his head as he stuffed his gym bag into the locker and closed it. "Oh, don't worry about that. Gail will either try to convert Sylvia, or she'll just forget about it."

"I think Gail would do better not to try and convert Sylvia. I don't think she's the type who becomes a born-again Christian."

"Neither am I," Dave confessed. "But Gail and I still get along fine. Don't worry. She and Sylvia will get used to each other. What's she like, though? If you'll excuse me for saying so, she seemed pretty weird to me."

I explained to Dave as best I could what Sylvia was like, but I found it difficult, since there were several things, such as the incident with the waitress, Sylvia's odd reactions when we kissed passionately, and the wide range of her emotions, which I felt would be better left unsaid. I also decided to omit any mention of the incident with the waitress at the Top of the Mark.

"She's a great dancer. Not only that, she can sing, too." I described to him how Sylvia had a wonderful gift, to be able to imitate any singer on the radio.

"She sounds very musical," said Dave.

"She is! In her apartment, she has a harpsichord, and she's very good on it."

"Really?" Dave asked. "Since Gail studies classical

music, too, maybe we could come over and hear Sylvia play sometime. It might be a good way to smooth out their differences."

I agreed, but wondered how Gail and Dave would react when they discovered the Satanic altar in Sylvia's living room. I felt awkward talking to Dave this way, concealing as much from him about Sylvia as I explained about her. This type of secrecy had never existed between us before. We'd been best friends for nearly ten years, and shared every confidence with each other. It bothered me that I now had to keep the most important part of my life partly a secret to him, yet I felt suspicious enough myself about Sylvia's odd characteristics. I didn't want anyone else passing judgment on her until my own mind was made up.

After our workout at the gym, I went straight home and waited for Sylvia to come over. As I sat in my reading chair relaxing, I wished that Sylvia's hours were different, so we could go out together during the day. I couldn't walk into work late again, yet if I wanted to spend long periods of time with her, I would either have to stay up until dawn, or she would have to go out during the day sometimes, at least on weekends. It didn't seem like much to ask of her. Surely she had exaggerated her sensitivity to the sun.

There was a knock at my door. Sylvia stood there in the hall, as I expected. But instead of entering my apartment, she took me by the hand and led me to hers. "I've got something I want to show you," she explained.

Classical music played from her stereo as we walked into her apartment. She waved her hands in time with the music like a conductor leading a symphony, as we walked through the living room and into her bedroom. "Do you like art?" she asked.

I told her that I wasn't an expert on the subject, but that since I studied film at college, and had taken courses on cinematography, I knew something about composition. She nodded her head, and still holding me by the hand, led me to her bed, then nudged me gently to sit down. I waited silently as she rummaged through her closet.

She pulled out several picture frames, covered with wrapping paper, which she quickly peeled off, and then set one of them on the bed. The oil painting was of a beautiful countryside, with lush, green trees amid fields covered with flowers on a bright sunny day. The picture looked so realistic, it could have been mistaken for a photograph, had it not been for the cracks that ran through the painting in numerous places. "That's where I grew up," was all she said.

Laying the painting aside, she placed another on the bed. This one contrasted sharply with the first. Instead of a beautiful daytime scene with flowers, it consisted of an old deserted graveyard, with crosses and tombstones, decaying with age, which leaned over, as if about to surrender to the earth. The sky was a deep, dark blue, as it is in those hours of twilight, after the sun has gone down, but before the stars have come out. A few trees stood here and there, but all of them had lost their leaves and appeared to be dead. The one quality and mood that exuded from the painting was one of impending darkness.

"Both of these were well painted," I remarked, "though the mood of the two is as different as day and night."

"Don't you see a similarity?" Sylvia pointed at the paintings.

I looked at the first one again and then the other. "Yes, you're right. They both were painted in the same realistic style, almost like a photograph." I observed the incredible detail in the wood of the trees and the blades of grass. "Yes, it looks like they might have been painted by the same artist."

"They were. I painted both of them."

"I should have known," I said with a laugh. It seemed there was nothing Sylvia couldn't do,

"I hope I don't seem like a show-off, but it's so nice to be able to reveal what I do to someone else, No one has ever seen these before. You're the first."

"They should be in a gallery, where lots of people could see them. You could be a famous artist."

"I don't *want* to be famous. I just do this for my own pleasure. But now I must show you the special painting I've done."

With that, she carefully unwrapped another of the paintings and set it on the bed. It, like the other two, had the same photographic quality. Unlike the others, it was a portrait of Sylvia and me together!

"A marvelous likeness, don't you think?" asked Sylvia. I sat there stunned. The image of the two of us looking back at me was certainly a compliment. The amount of time and effort Sylvia must have spent impressed me.

"It's very nice," I said. "I don't know if my eyes look quite so intense, but the detail is incredible. It seems to have a life of its own. How in the world did you finish it so quickly?"

"That's an artist's secret. If you're interested, I can teach you how to paint." She picked up the first two paintings and carefully placed them back in the box, then pushed the box back into her closet. She left the portrait on the bed.

"I want to give this to you," she said.

"Are you sure?"

"I don't need it anymore. I can look at you if I want, so I don't need a painting," she explained.

I thanked her and told her I would like to return the favor by making a portrait of her with my camera equipment. I had been thinking of doing that anyway, since she was so beautiful, and now I had the perfect excuse to make a photo of her and keep one for myself.

"Oh, but I *hate* to be photographed! No, please, no pictures of me!" She shook her head vigorously to punctuate her point.

"But I'd love to photograph you. You're the most beautiful woman I've ever seen in my life, and I'm a good photographer. Besides, I'd like to have a picture of you, in case you should ever move."

"But I already told you I'm not going anywhere," she insisted.

"Even so, I'd like to be able to look at you whenever I like."

"That's easy enough. Just knock and I'll let you in. Then you can look at me whenever you like. What could be simpler than that?"

"What if I want to look at your picture while I'm at work?" I asked. "Like today, all I could think of was you. It would be nice to have a picture of you on my desk."

Sylvia shuddered as if I had mentioned something awful. "Then everyone in your office would see it. I don't want my face in an office, especially not a newspaper office."

"What's wrong with newspapers?"

"They're always looking for news. They might make up a terrible story about me, and then use that picture to show everyone what I look like." She shook her head again. "Oh no. No pictures of me."

I dropped the subject at this point. Though I felt this to be a silly fear on her part, I didn't wish to appear insensitive to her feelings. Whatever her reasons for not wanting me to take her picture, I would respect them. After all, if she really would see me every day as she promised, perhaps I didn't need her picture after all.

The conversation switched back to her painting of me. Her incredible artistic talent shouldn't go unappreciated, I told her. "You know who should see this?" I asked. "Robert Stoker."

"Who's he?"

"He's one of our neighbors. Lives right downstairs. He's a very well-known artist." I then explained how Robert's artistic style resembled hers in that his drawings and paintings were so lifelike, they appeared to be photographs. Even prints of his works sold in local galleries for several thousand dollars.

Sylvia told me she was flattered by my comparison of her work to that of a famous artist, and that if I liked, she would paint another, of any subject I wished.

"You know what the subject is," I said, as I pointed at her.

It surprised me how quickly she agreed to paint a self-portrait, considering her refusal to pose for a photograph. Why she would let me have a large painting of her, but not a photograph, baffled me, but I wanted the painting of her, and told her I was anxious to see how it would turn out,

"How long will it take you to paint it?" I asked.

She hesitated a moment before answering. "I don't know. It's difficult to say exactly. Not too long, I'll have it finished before you know it."

"Great. Let's go show this to Robert right now. I know he'll want to see it. You'll enjoy meeting him too,"

She hesitated, then shook her head. "No. You go. I'll wait here. When you get back, then we'll do something together."

"What do you want to do?"

"I'm not sure yet," she answered, "But I'll think of something."

Robert was working on one of his drawings when I knocked at his door. He invited me in and I held Sylvia's painting so the light would hit it just right.

"What do you think?" I asked.

"It's great," he answered. "Who did this?" As he

asked, he leaned closer to the painting to examine the detail.

"Sylvia did. She's the girl who just moved next door to me. Isn't it something? I thought you'd be able to appreciate it."

Robert held the frame in his hands and scrutinized it more closely. "You mean that the artist of this lives here in the building?"

"Sure, She just moved here three days ago. That's probably why you haven't met her."

"What's her full name?"

"Sylvia Martin."

"That's strange." He rubbed his bearded chin and looked at the painting. "I've never heard of her."

I answered that it would be impossible for him to know every artist alive, but he insisted that someone who could paint that well would be so famous, that her work would be instantly recognized by anyone familiar with modern artists. Robert also worked as an art professor, so he was familiar with the work of many other artists.

"She doesn't exhibit her work," I explained.

"Well, she certainly should. When did you meet her?"

"Like I said, she moved here on Saturday afternoon."

"Yes, but when did you pose for her?"

"I never posed for her. I guess she just painted it from memory."

"You mean you knew her before she moved here?" he asked, with a puzzled expression.

"No, she moved here Saturday. We went out that night—and the next night, too. She gave it to me today. So she must have painted it on Sunday." As I said this, I realized it made absolutely no sense. Since Sylvia had slept all day Sunday, and woke up late, she had spent almost every waking moment with me since she had moved in on Saturday.

"Mark, a painting like this isn't finished in a day, a week, or even a month. If she works fast, and it doesn't look like she does, but if she does work fast, maybe three or four months. And that's with a model or a photograph to work from." To verify his statement, he brought the painting to his face and sniffed. "Another thing. If it were a day or two old, you would be able to smell the oil. This painting is dry. It may be months old, so if you add that time to the minimum of three months to paint it, it means she must have started it at least six months ago."

"But we didn't know each other then," I protested.

He handed the painting back to me and shrugged his shoulders, then brought me to one of his most famous works, *Journey Into Hell*, an incredibly detailed drawing that resembled a photograph of a nightmare. Men and women were running from pointy-tailed demons into a lake of bubbling fire, where they slowly sank in anguish. The demons ironically had features similar to the men and women, but looked more primitive, and some had savage smiles that seemed to delight in the carnage as their pitchforks were pointed at the escaping people below.

Robert pointed at his drawing. "That took me a *year* to complete." He laughed as he looked back at Sylvia's painting. "And she did *this* in one day? Impossible. I'll bet she spent as much time on hers as I did on mine."

I didn't know what to say. Everything Robert told me made sense, yet I knew that Sylvia had some logical explanation for this.

Whether I would get the explanation or not was another thing.

"It's a fantastic painting though, Mark. She must really care for you, to have spent that much time on it, especially with no intention of selling it. It appears so realistic, as if it has a life of its own. She only made one mistake that I can detect."

"A mistake? What do you mean?"

"You've got brown eyes, right?"

"Yeah. Why?"

"Take a close look at the eyes in the painting," he said.

Under the bright lights of Robert's studio, I examined the painting closely and felt a slowly growing panic rising up my neck. The eyes were completely black, with no iris, only wide-open pupils.

Just like Sylvia's eyes.

Chapter Ten

As I walked back to Sylvia's apartment, I wondered just how long before she moved in had she seen me. She had admitted to having watched me a week earlier at the gym, but at the time I took it as a possible coincidence that she happened to move into the same building. Now I wasn't quite sure whether it was a coincidence or not. Yet, as hard as I tried, I couldn't figure out why she had to lie about any of her motives with me. Her beauty and charm enchanted me from the very moment I met her anyway, so anything beyond that was only overkill.

"Did your friend, the artist, like it?" she asked, as I stepped back into her apartment.

"Yes. He thinks you're very talented and should exhibit your work."

"Mark, what's wrong? Is something bothering you? Please tell me."

She stared at me with her large melancholy eyes as if she were about to cry, and I realized that she knew what Robert had said about the portrait. "When did you paint this?" I asked. "And why did you make my eyes like this? My God, you've given me eyes just like yours!"

Several tears rolled down Sylvia's cheeks. "I thought you *liked* my eyes."

"I do like your eyes. What's bothering me is the secrecy behind so many of the things you tell me. My friend said it would take much longer than a couple days to paint this." I told her this as gently as I could, to avoid hurting her feelings. After all, she had spent an incredible amount of time on the painting, and I felt sure she cared for me, so even though some of her actions made me suspicious, I knew she had some reasonable explanation for them.

She placed her arms around my neck and hugged me tightly. Her face, wet with tears, pressed against mine.

"Of course it takes a long time. Anything of value takes time. I painted you from my dreams a long time ago. Do you remember that when you said you saw me in your dreams, I told you that I had seen you in my dreams? Well, now you have proof that what I said was true. Otherwise, how could I have painted your picture?"

"I don't know. Your painting is great and I really appreciate it. But I don't think we should keep secrets from each other."

"I don't like keeping secrets from you either. I want to tell you everything about me, but..." Her voice trailed off sadly.

"But what?" I set the painting against the wall. She held me by the hand, then led me to the couch so we could both sit down. I put my arm around her and she moved closer.

"If I tell you all about me right now, you won't understand."

"Try me. I'm very understanding."

"But I don't want to lose you. I could tell you the truth right this minute, but then—Oh no. I just can't do it." She shook her head. Her eyes gazed sadly at mine.

"I'm sure you know I like you very much," I began. "To be honest, I've never liked anyone so much. Never. And I've only known you a few days, but it's strange. I feel like I've always known you, like you're a part of me, and at the same time I feel like I don't know you at all. That you're really different than you appear."

"I'm glad you like me." She didn't sound glad, though. Her voice registered disappointment. "If you can ever say that you *love* me, then perhaps I can tell you all about me. Anything you want to know."

"But usually people get to know each other and then they fall in love. Of course, I probably will fall in love with you anyway."

"When you are sure, let me know," she said.

Sylvia's serious manner amazed me. After all, we had scarcely known each other three days. True, I felt myself strangely drawn to her, but I kept telling myself that to be so transfixed with someone I knew practically nothing about was crazy.

Yet, to be completely honest with myself, I felt more attracted to Sylvia than to any other woman I'd met, despite my belief that true love took a long time to grow and mature. Apparently it didn't take so long at all.

Somewhat nervously, I rubbed my hands against the soft velvet of the love seat. Sylvia took one of my hands and placed it back around her neck. I pulled her towards me and kissed her. She leaned the weight of her slender body against me and we held each other. As she caressed me, her eyes probed mine. Up so close, they looked not only exotic, but also bizarre, with her large black pupils penetrating my soul.

"I'm sorry if I'm being too serious Mark, but I like to say what's on my mind. And the truth is — I'm already in love with you."

Her words shot straight through my chest into my heart. "You're in love with me? Why? You've only known me a few days. I don't have any money, just an average job. And when I get my master's degree, I won't have any guarantee of getting anything better. A degree in English and film doesn't secure a job in teaching or in the movie industry. I don't have a lot of money now, and —"

"Must you always talk about money?" she asked, with some annoyance in her voice and expression. "I don't need your money. I have my own. I don't care about your future in the movie business or teaching. I have my own plans. You don't need your degree. It's just a piece of paper, nothing more. Stick with me and you won't have to worry about school, your job, or anything else. You don't need to worry about work again. I don't."

"What I can't understand is why a woman, as beautiful as you, with as much money as you've said, moves into a very average apartment like this, and in three days, falls in love with a very average guy like me. Don't you realize you can have anyone you want?"

"We're soul mates. We can change each other's lives. You're the one man capable of loving me."

"Many men could fall in love with you."

"No. Many men would like to have sex with me. Falling in love and *staying* in love—that's different. I think even if you knew everything about me, you'd still love me."

"What don't I know?"

"There's a lot you don't know. I don't want you to love me now for whom you think I am. I want you to love me in *spite* of who I am."

"You could have anyone you want."

"Perhaps," she replied nonchalantly, with a shrug of her shoulders. "But I want you."

I laughed. "It's okay with me. But to be honest, I think I'm getting the best part of the deal. I'll tell you the truth—"

"Please do," she interrupted.

"When I first saw you—I mean the very first second in the hall—I knew that you were different from any other woman."

"Really?" she asked, feigning surprise. "In what way?"

"For one thing, the way you look. You are unique. Absolutely no other woman in the world looks like you. Your eyes, your mouth, your hair, and your skin. You look completely different from any other woman. But it goes beyond your looks. You make me feel good whenever I'm around you. You're so different from anyone else I've been with."

Sylvia smiled at this. "I am completely different."

Then her face became more serious, and I could detect a hint of sadness. "But you don't know just how different." Her eyes avoided mine as she said this.

I held her head with my hand and motioned for her to look at me again. When she did, her eyes had that melancholy look again. "Is there something you want to tell me?" I asked.

Instead of answering, she just hugged me so the side of her face brushed against mine. We sat thus, entangled in one another's arms for a long time, when at last she said, "Oh, I could just stay like this forever."

Just as I told her I agreed with her, the doorbell rang. She almost jumped out of the chair, then looked at the door with a puzzled expression on her face.

"I hope it's not an ex-boyfriend coming for a visit," I said.

"You don't have to worry about *that*," she said emphatically. "I don't have any ex-boyfriends. I don't even know anyone."

She took me by the hand and led me to the door. "You come with me for protection. If they get out of line, break their nose." She giggled.

We opened the door to see Dave and Gail standing in the hall. "Whose nose should I break first?" I asked Sylvia.

She rolled her eyes toward the ceiling and grinned.

"We thought we might find you here," Dave said to me.

"Why don't you both come in?" Sylvia gestured invitingly with a sweeping motion of her arm.

The first thing they noticed was the harpsichord. Gail gave it a backhanded compliment, saying, "What a nice looking spinet you have. At the Conservatory of Music, they have a real harpsichord."

"A *real* harpsichord?" Sylvia looked indignant. "A spinet is a real harpsichord. My parents gave me one like this for my thirteenth birthday. This is a replica of the harpsichord that was most popular in early eighteenth-century England. This is what most families owned, not the full-size harpsichord."

"Perhaps," said Gail. "But it would be even nicer to have a full-sized one."

"I own one that's Flemish, one that's German, a French one, an Italian harpsichord, and this English bentside spinet." Sylvia rested her hand upon the instrument case.

Gail pointed at Sylvia's Yamaha keyboard. "Well, your electronic keyboard looks good. At least it's got eighty-eight keys."

"My piano in London has ninety-seven."

Gail's face suddenly registered a shock of recognition. "The only piano I know of that has ninety-seven keys is—"

"A Bosendorfer. That's right. I have a Bosendorfer concert grand piano and five harpsichords."

"All that would cost hundreds of thousands of dollars," countered Gail.

Sylvia nodded. "It was a good investment. I play them every day."

"You must be very talented with all that practice," Gail said.

I could see the wheels turning in her head as she was lining up her next line of attack.

"I can play anything you like," answered Sylvia.

"Anything?" Gail's voice hinted of trickery. She reached inside a shopping bag she had been carrying and produced a brand new music book. "Try this. *Fandango*, by Antonio Soler." Gail offered the book to her, but Sylvia shook her head. "I thought as much," said Gail. "Only God can give someone the talent to play this."

"Oh no, it's not that." Sylvia shook her head. "It's just that I don't need your music book."

Gail's eyes widened. "You can't mean you can play this from memory. That would be quite a feat. It's four hundred and sixty bars long!"

"Four hundred and sixty-one," Sylvia smiled as she stepped up to the harpsichord. She smoothed out her dress as she sat on the bench. With her long, glistening, black hair trailing down her back, and the bright yellow dress flowing over the front and sides of the bench, she looked more like a doll than a person. So perfectly graceful, like a work of art, she sat motionless for only a moment, then her dainty hands flowed along the keyboard. The contrast of the stillness and silence with her abrupt movement and the music that issued forth jolted the rest of us. Sylvia's playing absorbed me partly because of my strong feelings for her, but Dave and Gail were equally enchanted by her musical ability. *Fandango* was a musical rollercoaster, faster than anything I had ever heard. In some of the passages, Sylvia's fingers struck so many keys so quickly, that all I could see was a blur of hands. Sylvia's performance stunned Gail. I couldn't have been happier, especially after the snide look Gail had cast at Sylvia when she first asked Sylvia if she knew how to play the harpsichord.

"How did you learn to play like that?" Gail stared in astonishment.

"Many years of practice."

Gail shook her head as if bewildered. "I know harpsichordists in their fifties who've been playing since childhood—but none of them can play like you."

"Don't you wish you were me?" Sylvia asked Gail.

"Definitely not! You're going to Hell when you die."

"Maybe so," Sylvia agreed, "but that's a *very* long time from now, and besides, I think Mark is coming with me, so I won't have to be lonely."

"It's nothing to joke about," Gail scolded.

"It's okay," I said. "In Mark Twain's book, *Letters*

from the Earth, he wrote that people don't have sex in Heaven; they just sing hymns. So maybe Sylvia and and I will have a better time in Hell. Certainly the music will be better. Sylvia has a real gift for music."

"I do have a certain gift," replied Sylvia, with a mischievous gleam in her eyes. "A very *special* gift."

"Now, *I'd* like a gift like that," I told her.

Sylvia flashed her large eyes at me and held me in her gaze with a strange intensity. "*Would* you now?"

Since Sylvia only stared at me with a peculiar smile on her lips, an awkward silence arose, which Dave broke with dramatic flair.

"By the way," he announced, "Gail and I are getting married next weekend!"

"But I already know that," I said.

"Of course you know," admitted Dave. "But Sylvia doesn't know."

This certainly caught Sylvia by surprise. She looked at me and kept staring at me, as if analyzing my reaction for future reference.

Dave explained to Sylvia how he and Gail had planned on holding the ceremony at Grace Cathedral a couple months away, but that a wedding for this coming Saturday had recently been canceled. Now that it was available, they had grabbed the opportunity to hold their wedding in one of San Francisco's largest and most beautiful churches.

"On such short notice," Dave continued, "we couldn't send out formal invitations, so we're just calling everyone. So consider yourself invited." He looked at both of us for a second and then at Sylvia. "Of course, Sylvia is invited, too," he added.

Sylvia smiled at the invitation, but said nothing. Gail did not smile. I felt sure she would rather not have invited Sylvia, but since we now spent all of our time together and she certainly appeared to be my girlfriend, it would have been in poor taste to ignore her.

"As a matter of fact," Dave went on, "as long as we've got the use of the chapel, why not make it a double wedding? The four of us could all get married at the same time. We could share the cost of the wedding, and you and Sylvia could split the rent on just one apartment. It's really the most practical thing to do."

He smiled at his little joke, but Gail didn't. Though she knew he was only kidding, obviously even the thought of sharing a wedding ceremony with a Satanist she detested, disturbed her. She shot Dave an angry stare. Had we been seated at a table, I'm sure she would have kicked him in the shin.

"Just a minute here," Gail said. "For months, my friend Mary was planning to attend the wedding with Mark. What am I supposed to tell her?"

Sylvia faced me. "Is this Mary the same ex-girlfriend you said was cheating on you?"

"The very same one," I told Sylvia. Then turning to Gail, I said, "What you should tell Mary is that she can take any of her other boyfriends to the wedding and that it's absolutely no problem at all for me."

"You know perfectly well that Mary doesn't have another boyfriend," replied Gail. "She just has friends in all the places she visits."

Sylvia looked at me. "Sounds like a sailor who has a girl in every port."

"Exactly," I agreed, nodding my head.

"You and Mary looked very good together," said Gail.

"Better than us together?" asked Sylvia.

"Mary's very good looking," Gail pointed out, "and she has a perky personality."

"Really?" Sylvia asked. "I hate women who are perky. I think it's better to have perky breasts than a perky personality. Don't you agree, Mark?"

"Absolutely," I said, as I deliberately avoided looking at Sylvia's breasts at the same time.

"They're probably not even real anyway," said Gail.

"What? Not real?" Sylvia fumed. "We'll just see about that!" Sylvia turned to face me directly, grabbed both of my wrists and placed my palms directly on her breasts. "Go ahead and feel them. Tell Gail if they're real or not."

Even though I couldn't see myself in the mirror, I think my eyes must have popped open as much as Dave's and Gail's, but I tried to maintain my composure, and managed to say, "Well, if you absolutely insist."

Sylvia held my hands to her, revealing a bust as firm as any woman I had ever touched in my life. "What can I say? They're perfect to me. And they're definitely real."

"Do you need a second opinion?" Dave asked.

Gail, Sylvia, and I simultaneously glared at him.

"Only kidding," he protested.

"And I don't know why you thought they were fake," Sylvia told Gail. "They're not that big. They're thirty-four C, which makes me thirty-six, twenty-three, thirty-eight. A twenty-three-inch waist makes everything else look bigger."

"Yes, it's certainly making your ego bigger," answered Gail.

"Well, I think you're perfect," I told Sylvia. "And you're better than Mary in every way. You're prettier, have a better figure, you're more cultured, and more fun to be around. More importantly, I can trust you."

"Unlike Mary, I would never cheat on you," Sylvia assured me, as she put her arm around my shoulder and pulled me closer.

I turned to Dave and addressed what he had said just a minute before. "If Sylvia and I knew each other a lot longer, we'd probably take you up on your suggestion of a double wedding even though you were just joking."

Sylvia appeared delighted by everything I said and also at Dave's double wedding suggestion.

She flashed me a big smile and raised her eyebrows questioningly, as if mentally answering Dave's suggestion with, "Why not?"

I avoided Sylvia's questioning smile by looking away for a second, but my eyes were drawn back to hers. When I returned my glance to her, I found her still staring at me in the same manner. Then, in response to my silence, she turned to Dave and addressed me indirectly.

"I'm afraid Mark wouldn't like that," she explained to Dave, as she threw her hands up in mock exasperation. "Besides, the wedding ceremony I must follow would differ from yours. I daresay you might *all* find it somewhat—" and here she paused as she looked at me while she finished her answer to Dave. "Suffice it to say that my own ceremony would be done in private, with no large crowds."

Since I knew nothing of Satanic weddings, I really didn't understand what Sylvia meant, but she gave me the impression that her religion didn't allow church weddings. That much was obvious, but apparently there was more to it than that, I wondered what would take place at a ceremony that she thought we would all find so objectionable. Fortunately, Dave didn't seem to catch any hidden meaning in Sylvia's words; he just responded to her comment on large crowds.

"Actually, our wedding isn't really going to be all that large. Grace Cathedral may be big, but we're not holding it in the main part of the church. It's going to be held in the Chapel of Grace, which holds about a hundred people. We should be having seventy or eighty guests. It depends on who accepts our invitations."

"Well, Mark and I certainly accept your invitation," Sylvia said cheerfully, much to my relief. "It's been so long since I've been to a wedding." She gave a perplexed look at all of us. "Oh, I don't know what I shall wear."

"I'll tell you one thing you better not wear. Don't wear your Satanic medallion where it can be seen," demanded Gail. "And if I were you, I wouldn't wear high heels, either. You're obviously taller than Mark."

"Maybe an inch," Sylvia admitted.

"More like two inches," Gail countered.

"I rarely wear heels anyway. I like low athletic shoes so I can run at a moment's notice."

"Why would you have to do that?" I asked.

"I have enemies. There are some people who don't like me."

"Imagine *that*," remarked Gail.

"Don't worry," I assured Sylvia. "No enemies here."

"Yes, I can see that I'm among friends here," Sylvia agreed.

Gail still wouldn't give up. "If you wear heels, you'll tower over Mark and you'll both look ridiculous."

Sylvia would not be outdone. "So what you're saying is that instead of being happy finding my soul mate that I should pick someone who matches my *shoes*? Now I think *that's* ridiculous!"

"I'll be happy to help you pick out what to wear," volunteered Gail. "I have to do some shopping this week and we could go out together."

This sudden reversal of Gail's disposition could have taken me by surprise, had I not understood the reason behind her offer. What she really wanted was to ensure that Sylvia didn't show up at Gail's wedding in something that would have been embarrassing. Undoubtedly, she pictured Sylvia at the wedding dressed all in black, with an oversized Satanic medallion around her neck and a large button declaring, "God is Dead." By taking Sylvia out to look for clothes, Gail could avoid this, and make sure that Sylvia wore something more in keeping with the spirit of the wedding.

If Sylvia also realized Gail's ulterior motives, she showed no hint of it. Rather, she responded to Gail in a most friendly manner, and stated emphatically how much she loved to shop for new clothes.

"The only problem is that the wedding is Saturday," said Gail, "so there won't be a single afternoon when we can go."

"Why don't you go tonight?" I asked. "The Stonestown Galleria Mall is open till nine. You've got plenty of time."

Gail turned to Sylvia. "We can all go together in Dave's Cadillac — unless you want to squeeze into Mark's old sports car."

"Old sports car!" I protested. "It's a Lotus Esprit. The same car James Bond drove in *The Spy Who Loved Me*. It's a classic."

"Yes, it's a wonderful car," agreed Sylvia. "I owned one too."

"What do you drive now?" asked Gail, searching for a different angle of attack.

"An Aston Martin."

"Is it also twenty-five years old?" questioned Gail.

"If you absolutely must know, it's a brand new DBS."

Gail turned to me. "Is there anything you want to ask Sylvia?"

"You bet." I turned to Sylvia. "If I visit you in London, can I drive your Aston Martin DBS?"

"Of course you can. I'll even put on some music by John Barry so you can imagine you're James Bond."

"If I'm not being too nosy," interrupted Gail, "how much does one of those cost?"

"You are being too nosy," I said, though I wondered, too.

"About two-hundred and sixty-thousand dollars," Dave answered. "I read the *Robb Report* article. That's the car James Bond drove in *Casino Royale*."

Sylvia nodded, and then deftly changed the subject. "Why don't we take two cars? I want to ride in Mark's Lotus Esprit. It brings back pleasant memories."

"It's okay with me," said Gail as she turned to Sylvia. "Do you mind shopping at night, instead of during the day?"

"Oh, I don't mind at all," Sylvia replied sweetly. "Why, I rather prefer going out at night." She looked at me and smiled as she said this.

She may not have smiled had she known what Gail and Dave had told me once before—that Gail had always wanted her wedding to be held on a warm sunny afternoon. So, even if Sylvia were to avoid a daytime shopping excursion, she wouldn't be able to do so with the wedding on Saturday. She would have to put aside her dislike for daytime activities, at least for one afternoon, if she planned on attending their wedding.

I felt it only fair to tell Sylvia about the proposed schedule for the ceremony, just as soon as I could get her alone. If she did have some compelling reason for not attending an afternoon wedding, I wanted her to explain it to me, but not with Gail and Dave present.

With Sylvia's peculiar habits and personality, I had a feeling that possibly her reasons for her nocturnal existence went beyond a mere sensitivity to the sun.

116

Chapter Eleven

We sped to the Stonestown Galleria Mall in my yellow Lotus Esprit Turbo. Sylvia smiled, obviously pleased that we drove there alone without Dave and Gail in the car. I always believed sports cars to have a strong romantic advantage to other cars—not just because many women liked them, but also because their two seats excluded outsiders. Sylvia knew I liked John Barry's movie soundtracks, so she brought a CD with his most famous compositions, which she played on my stereo.

With a stick shift, holding hands was impossible, but Sylvia rested her left hand on my leg. I reflected on this, remembering that of all the time she and I had spent together, there had rarely been an instant when there had been no physical contact at all. Indeed, at almost every single moment, we either held hands, or walked arm in arm, or she was leaning against me as we sat down. Her affectionate manner won me over completely, and both times we had parted in the past two evenings, I felt as if she were a part of me being taken away, like a Siamese twin being split in half, and unable to survive alone.

The four of us met at Macy's, and then went to Nordstrom, where Sylvia not only picked out a delicately laced yellow dress, but also shoes, a purse, and a hat to go with it. She put on the entire outfit in the store, and looked so lovely, that for a moment I imagined that the wedding was for us. I stood there admiring her feminine and dainty form, when she turned to me and smiled.

"Do you like it?" she asked. After I told her how great she looked, she asked me what I planned to wear.

"I don't know. I really hadn't thought about it. I suppose I'll have to rent a tuxedo."

Sylvia shook her head and grimaced at my statement. "You can't rent a tuxedo. They'll never be able to alter it to fit properly. You'll have to buy one and have them alter it for you."

What she said was true. Since I had gotten into bodybuilding, I had a very difficult time finding clothes that fit right. Either the chest and shoulders would fit me too tightly, or the waistline of the shirt and jacket would be incredibly baggy, like a tent. The tuxedo rental tailors would only do a small amount of alterations, and it wouldn't look right. Only if I were to purchase one, would they be able to make all the necessary alterations.

I nodded in agreement with Sylvia. "You're right. It would look better if I bought one." My credit card would take care of it for the moment and I would pay it off gradually over the next few months. I couldn't let her know how much of an unnecessary expense it seemed to me—especially since she was spending so much on her own clothes. Her dress, shoes, hat, and purse came to over $3,000, but she shrugged it off as inconsequential as she pulled out her credit card.

As we left the store, I joked with her that she should be careful about carrying around such expensive clothes from shopping in San Francisco, and that I would hate to see her get mugged for her clothes, but that I'd do my best to protect her. She only giggled at this and replied that she was sure that between the two of us, we could handle any muggers we might come across in San Francisco. Of course, I didn't dare tell her about my own experience with the muggers in the alley next to my gym. I did not want to alarm her unnecessarily.

The four of us passed by numerous shops, when Sylvia suddenly spied a pet shop, and asked if we could go in and look at the animals. Dave and Gail went to a music store while Sylvia and I browsed in the pet store.

We walked in, and Sylvia immediately engrossed herself with the lizards and snakes. Unfortunately, they did very little but sit under the hot light, as if too busy to do anything but get a tan. Sylvia reached into one of the cases and pulled out a boa constrictor, some three feet long, and let it coil itself around her arm.

"Aren't they nice?" she asked. "They love to wrap themselves around you. It's their way of saying they like you."

"How friendly of them," I remarked, "but don't they do the same thing when they are about to kill something?"

"Yes, they do," Sylvia admitted.

"Then how do you tell whether they like you, or just want to kill you?"

"If they kill you, then that means they didn't really like you," she explained, as if talking to a biology class. "If they don't kill you, then they must like you."

"They must be a lot of trouble to feed, though," I said, since I knew that snakes needed live food.

"Oh no! Why, they're no trouble at all! Just watch." With that, Sylvia turned around quickly and scanned the other cages till she discovered one filled with mice. She watched the salesclerk out of the corners of her eyes, then swiftly reached in and pulled out one of the mice by its tail. It tried to bite her, but Sylvia ignored it, and opened up the cage to the large snake and threw the mouse in. The boa struck immediately, by taking a bite of the little mouse's head, then coiling itself around the poor victim and squeezing it to death instantly. It then swallowed the mouse whole, making a large lump in what could have been called his neck. "Now what could be simpler than that?" asked Sylvia, jubilantly. "No muss, no fuss. They only eat once a week."

"That's great," I said without enthusiasm, "but what about the mouse?"

"Ah," she said with a wicked smile, "that is why it is so much better to be a snake than a mouse."

"Perhaps," I agreed, "but I feel kind of sorry for the mouse. Such a useless existence—to live for a short time—only to die at the jaws of a creature so much more powerful."

"But that is life, Mark. Don't you see that? One must die, so another may live. For all of us feed off each other in *some* way." Here, Sylvia's voice became sad, and her eyes, though staring straight at me, appeared to see something else, perhaps something that distressed her. She was off in deep thought again, but only for an instant, then she suddenly snapped herself out of it and regained her composure.

We rejoined Dave and Gail briefly, and then they decided to leave since they knew we had purchased our clothes. Sylvia and I stayed on at the mall to find a wedding gift. In one of the other stores, Sylvia giggled and said, "How about this for Gail?" as she held up an ear and nose hair trimmer for inspection.

"She would never speak to us again," I answered.

"Really?" Sylvia's eyes widened as she smiled. "In that case, I should definitely buy it."

"Absolutely not. Dave is my best friend. And anyway, Gail doesn't need it."

"I was thinking ahead for when she gets older," Sylvia explained.

We looked around and then some figures in Steuben glass caught Sylvia's attention. Two swans in an embrace, with a description that said after a long courtship, swans mate for life. "How romantic. This is perfect as a gift from the two of us."

I gasped at the price. "It's over one-thousand, five-hundred dollars!"

"Yes." Sylvia nodded. "Years from now, they'll always remember this present after all the towels and sheets and toasters fade from their memory."

"I really can't afford to buy that for them."

"You don't have to," Sylvia answered. "Just sign the gift card with me."

"But I can't make you pay for it."

"Mark, you've never made me do anything I didn't want to do." With that, she pulled out her wallet.

"Well, after this present, Gail can never complain about you again," I said.

"I wouldn't bet money on that if I were you!" Sylvia poked me affectionately with her finger.

A little while later, entering our apartment building, an awkward silence ensued as we made our way upstairs. We hadn't planned the rest of the evening, so I didn't know whether she would want to go to her apartment alone or spend some more time with me.

As we reached my apartment, she circled my waist with her arm and kept walking so that we stopped in front of her apartment. She led me to her love seat and motioned for me to sit down, as she turned on her large stereo. I recognized the music as the second album by The Doors, one of my favorite bands even though Jim Morrison, the lead singer, actually died before I was born. I always liked the classic rock bands of the 1960s and 1970s, and classic cars like my Lotus Esprit. Sometimes I wondered if I had been born at the wrong time. The title of the album was *Strange Days*, and "When the Music's Over" was playing, the longest song ever performed by The Doors. Sylvia and I sat on the love seat together, listening to the song, and I happened to glance over to her Satanic altar against the wall. As I examined the detail in the silver Baphomet, the face of Satan stared back, and Jim Morrison's lyrics implied he was going to Hell instead of Heaven after death. I wondered if my attachment to Sylvia would lead to the same fate for me.

"Isn't that a nice song?" asked Sylvia.

Her voice pulled my eyes away from her altar and back to her again. "Yes," I agreed. "It's one of my favorites. I've always liked The Doors. I still do, though I suppose they may be considered out of date by now."

"Not really. Jim Morrison may have died years ago, but Bach died almost two and a half centuries ago, and I still play his music on my harpsichord. Time is relative. The longer you live, the more time changes." She looked at me reflectively, as if about to collect her thoughts for further discussion on the subject. She put another CD in the stereo and handed me the album cover. The title was *The British Beat: Best of the '60s*. "I'm different from you because I'm English. We look at time differently. America is a little over two hundred years old. Great Britain is about two thousand years old. If a song is forty or fifty years old, that's not too old for me. I have a different perspective on time."

After noting the words in The Doors' song, and hearing what Sylvia had to say about death and time, I had to find out what she felt about death from her position as a Satanist. "Do you believe in Heaven and Hell?" I inquired.

She shook her head and smiled. "No, of course not. At least not in the way most people envision it."

"Then you're not worried that being a Satanist now could lead to some sort of punishment after you die?"

She almost burst out laughing. "Such worries are the furthest thoughts from my mind, I can assure you of that."

"I only ask you out of curiosity," I explained. "I've never been religious myself, but I am curious about your beliefs."

"Mildly curious, or interested in becoming like me?" she asked, her eyes hypnotically beckoning.

"Perhaps a little of both. I've always had some interest in the occult, but little faith."

"Faith will not be necessary for you because soon you'll have all the proof you need."

I asked her for an explanation, but she only repeated that soon everything would be clear to me, and that she would explain who she was and who I was.

"I already know who I am," I told her, "and I hope I know who you are."

"We are not just Mark and Sylvia. We are something more than that. We are more than these bodies that we inhabit."

"That's true," I agreed. "We're mental as well as physical."

"But even more than that," she went on, "we are more than that. If you were to take away our minds and our bodies, there would still be something else left—something even more powerful. Something far older, which lived before our bodies, and continues to live on."

"Yes, that's what many people believe about reincarnation—that everyone keeps living in some other form after death."

"No, this is different. I'm not talking about another form. And I'm not talking about everyone. I'm talking about you and me, Mark. Just the two of us. *Only* us. I cannot explain it all now, but suffice it to say that you and I are unique. We are quite different from the average person."

"Maybe so, but it seems that everyone probably believes that they're different in some special way. For myself, I think I'm really not that unique. On the other hand, you *are* different than any other woman I've met. For one thing, I've never gone with a Satanist before."

She pulled me toward her and kissed me tenderly, then I felt her hands sliding over my head and neck. When she pulled her hands away, I could feel something around my neck. I reached for it with my hand and looked down. Sylvia had placed her Satanic medallion around my neck, and it dangled there from a silver chain, halfway between my heart and my throat. The medallion was about the same diameter as a quarter, and appeared handmade. I looked at Sylvia questioningly, about to ask her why she put it on me.

"Now you're different, too." Sylvia flashed her mischievous smile. She fingered the medallion, then stroked my chest with her hand. "It looks quite good on you, I think." She nodded her head in agreement with her appraisal.

"But it's not mine," I said, as I began to remove it.

Sylvia quickly placed her hands on mine and stopped me in the middle of my movement. "Oh no! Please, Mark You mustn't take it off. It's my gift to you."

"But I'm not a Satanist. It would be hypocritical for me to wear it."

"It's a symbol of my love for you," Sylvia answered, her eyes pleading with me. "Please don't take it off, Mark." She hugged me and rocked back and forth. Her smooth face rubbed against mine, and her touch mesmerized me. "Wear it always, as a symbol of our commitment," she whispered softly in my ear.

Though I hadn't yet told Sylvia I loved her, apparently it was unnecessary. She already knew. Her gift acknowledged our feelings, though I still hadn't said it aloud.

"What will you wear?" I asked.

"Do you mean for Satanic rituals, or do you mean what will I wear to symbolize your love for me?" Sylvia stared into my eyes.

"Both." Then I realized in an instant that I had just indirectly told her that I loved her.

"You can decide what you want to give me," she answered, "and as far as my rituals are concerned, now that you have my medallion, I guess you'll just have to be part of my ritual. So we'll simply do it together. That will be quite wonderful, it will. Oh yes! I want to do everything together with you."

"I'm not so sure about that. I really don't know anything about these rituals you're talking about. Maybe you'd be better off doing them without me."

"Oh, I couldn't do that!" she said, alarmed at my suggestion.

"Why not?" I asked.

Her sensuous lips drew back into a large smile, revealing her teeth. "Because," she answered, as she pointed her finger at me, "you are the object of the ritual."

Chapter Twelve

Sylvia's medallion remained around my neck for the rest of the night. Although it didn't give me much cause for insomnia, I couldn't help but think of her parting remarks for the evening, and as I lay in bed alone, I wondered just what kind of ritual she had in mind.

Even at work, I kept my promise to her, and left the medallion on, but underneath my shirt and out of view. It was a fairly ordinary workday, except that I made almost triple the usual number of sales.

Max, gratified by my results, which would bring him a nice commission override, came over to my desk to congratulate me.

"A great day, Mark. Keep up the good work. You should be selling like this every day. Then you'd be the top salesman. Just so you can repeat this tomorrow, what do you think is responsible for these results?" He held out the sales sheets.

I pointed to the medallion, taking it out of my shirt. "It must be this. My girlfriend gave it to me last night."

"Then be sure and wear it tomorrow. And hang on to your new girlfriend. Maybe she brings you good luck. Christ knows, with what you made last week you'll need all the luck you can get."

With that parting remark and a chuckle, he disappeared into his office.

The atmosphere at the gym was a welcome change from work, and since Dave and I had started our workout at five o'clock, I exercised as quickly as I could, so that I would be finished early. I wanted to get back to the apartment and Sylvia as soon as possible. Fortunately, for some reason or another, I felt stronger than usual, and had no problem rushing through the same routine with almost no rest.

Dave must have had the wedding on his mind, for we

had been exercising for a full fifteen minutes before he noticed the medallion around my neck. When he did, a look of shock crossed his face.

"Good God, Mark! Don't tell me you're a Devil-worshipper too, now!" He shook his head in disgust. "For Christ's sake, whatever you do, don't wear that God damn thing at the wedding. I'll never hear the end of it from Gail if you do."

"Sylvia gave it to me last night. I promised her I would wear it all the time," I explained, as I positioned myself into a Nautilus shoulder machine.

"Why did you make a promise like that?" Dave wiped the sweat off his face with a towel.

"Because she asked me to," I told him rather sternly, then continued lifting the weight on the machine as he continued to talk.

"If she asked you to kill yourself for her, would you do that, too?" he challenged.

I finished my set before answering, "I don't know. She hasn't asked me yet. But to tell you the truth, I think I'm falling in love with her."

"Are you nuts? You've known her for maybe a week! How could you be in love with her?"

"Surely you've heard of love at first sight?" I asked. "Well, that's what this is. It really didn't take a week. I felt something strong the first time I saw her."

"So did I," interrupted Dave, "and it wasn't love. To tell you the truth, she gave me the creeps from the first time I saw her, watching you at the window. And you thought I was bullshitting you. But I wasn't. She looked at you like —"

"Like what?" I asked, annoyed at the turn of the conversation.

"Like she was a wild animal, about to kill you." His serious tone of voice irritated me.

"You're completely misreading Sylvia. And no matter

127

what you say, I'm still in love with her."

"A minute ago, you said you just *thought* you were falling in love with her."

I motioned for Dave to take his turn at the shoulder machine.

"Time flies," I remarked. "I guess I've been trying to tell myself that I'm not supposed to fall in love with someone so fast, but at this point, I really don't care what I'm *supposed* to do. I just know how I feel. And who made these rules about love anyway?" Without waiting for Dave to respond, I took advantage of the fact that he was the one exercising and unable to talk for a few seconds. "I've gone out with plenty of other women in my life and never felt like this about anyone else. It's not the amount of time. Sylvia's different."

"Speak of the Devil." Dave pointed at the front window.

Sure enough, there was Sylvia staring at me from the window of the gym, smiling and waving at me. She wore a form-fitting white knit dress that ended just above her knees. It fit her like a second skin, showing off her great combination of curves with her tiny waist. To top it off, she wore a white silk ribbon tied at the top of her shiny black hair. Just her appearance at the gym brightened my whole day.

I walked toward the door to meet her, and could hear Dave complaining in the background about me walking off in the middle of his set when he needed a spot from me. Ignoring him seemed like the best policy, so I greeted Sylvia at the door.

She kissed me passionately at the entrance, and with such ardor, that several of the guys looked over at us to see what was going on. Perhaps they watched us because Sylvia kissed me so intensely, or maybe it was the way she looked in that dress. It did make her appear somewhat out of place, but then she didn't seem to care about the other gym members' opinions anymore than she considered what Dave and Gail thought.

"I thought I might come here and surprise you," she said cheerfully.

"It is a surprise, and a pleasant one. But I thought you always slept till dark."

"It's dark enough now," she replied, with a turn of her pretty head. "The sun has already gone down. And I rather prefer spending time with you to sleeping all day."

I thanked her for the compliment, then asked her to come in and talk while Dave and I finished our workout.

"If you're sure I won't be a bother," she said as we reached the dumbbell rack where Dave stood waiting impatiently.

"No bother at all," I replied, as Dave turned his head away in exasperation at having our workout interrupted. Indeed, Sylvia's presence pervaded the entire gym, and I became aware that a number of people were looking at us, as if we had interrupted all of them, and they wouldn't be able to get their minds back on their exercises until she left. While some of the men ogled Sylvia the way they often did when a pretty woman happened to drop in and watch, other members scrutinized her with a certain amount of hostility that I felt oddly inappropriate. Perhaps her light and cheery manner annoyed them, since some were trying to act ridiculously macho, with grim expressions, and they believed that any intrusion on their training mood would weaken them or maybe they did not want any distractions—no matter how sexy and appealing. Whatever their reasons, they regarded Sylvia even more suspiciously than Dave did, and I felt sympathy for her, since I alone understood her and liked her.

As we stood there, Sylvia reached out, touching the medallion she had given me, she let her slender fingers move down my chest. Poking me in the stomach with her fingers, she smiled and said, "My, what a hard stomach you have. And my Baphomet certainly looks nice on you. I'm ever so glad to see you wearing it."

While Dave and I continued with our workout, Sylvia followed us around, talking cheerfully about the wedding coming up on Saturday, how well-equipped the gym was, and any topics of conversation that popped into her mind. Dave ignored her; I listened, and ignored Dave. Sylvia talked happily as she gestured and waved her hands for emphasis, quite oblivious of the other members of the gym. It wasn't until we were right next to a couple doing the bench press that the problems began. The man stood several inches taller than me, while his girlfriend was a few inches shorter than Sylvia, but far more muscular. As Sylvia gestured while talking with me, her hands almost bumped the barbell that the man was in the middle of pressing. It was loaded to weigh 275 pounds, and just as I was about to ask Sylvia to stand a little closer to me, the man's girlfriend spoke.

"Will you get out of our way?" she yelled at Sylvia. Her deep voice reflected anger and also indicated to me that she used steroids.

"It's not very civil of you to talk that way," scolded Sylvia. "Haven't you any manners?" she inquired, just as the woman's boyfriend prepared to lift again.

He released his grip on the barbell and sat up on the bench, ready for a confrontation. "Will you shut her up and get her out of here before I get pissed off?"

Now I was mad at the rude gym members. Instead of answering the man or his girlfriend, I turned to Sylvia. "Don't mind them. They're suffering from roid rage. That's what happens when they take too many steroids. It causes psychological problems."

The man stood up, revealing the difference in our sizes. Somehow, his shaved head made his muscles look bigger. But I knew what I was doing. If he was going to start a confrontation in the gym, I wanted everyone see him swing first so I would have the legal right to retaliate fully.

"What did you say?" he challenged, making two big fists.

"You heard me," I said with a smile that everyone else in the gym could see so I didn't look like the aggressor. "You may be able to lift more weight, but I can hit a lot harder than you can and I'm much faster."

Dave interrupted me and addressed the man. "He's not kidding. We've been practicing kung-fu together for years. Don't even think about fighting him."

"Right," Sylvia chimed in. "No fighting. Better to have a weightlifting contest."

The man suddenly smiled. "A lifting contest between me and him?" he asked as he pointed at me.

Oh shit, I thought. *Now what have you gotten me into?* Although I could have beaten him in a fight, I had no chance of lifting more weight than him.

"Oh, no," Sylvia answered the man. "Not between the two of you. Between me and your manly girlfriend."

Now the girlfriend looked ready to kill Sylvia on the spot, but took her challenge. "Are you joking? You couldn't possibly lift more than me."

That's exactly what I was thinking. What corner had Sylvia painted herself into?

"How much are you willing to bet?" Sylvia challenged.

"Are you crazy or stupid?" the woman asked her. "You actually want to lose your money on this?"

"How much do you want to bet?" Sylvia repeated.

"One hundred dollars," said the man.

Sylvia shook her head.

The woman waved at Sylvia dismissively. "I thought so. All talk."

"A *thousand* dollars," Sylvia said, opening her purse.

She counted out ten hundred-dollar bills. "There's my thousand. Where's yours?"

The man laughed. "We don't need to put any money down because you can't win."

"If you don't lay down a thousand dollars, we don't have a bet." Sylvia folded her arms and stood her ground.

The man quickly found several friends in the gym with the balance of the money, all willing to double their money in the next couple minutes.

"Are you sure this is a good idea?" I whispered in Sylvia's ear.

The other woman's demeanor had changed from outrage to amusement. "Pick any exercise," she challenged. "I'll do more weight and more reps."

Sylvia settled on the leg press. This relieved me since I didn't want Sylvia to injure her back or knees on squats, a more difficult leg exercise.

The other woman set the leg press at 350 pounds and did 12 repetitions. Everyone in the gym gathered around to see what would happen next. Sylvia set the machine at 375 pounds.

"Are you sure about this?" I asked her, wondering how she could possibly win.

"You're going to have to help me," Sylvia said. "With one hand, touch the medallion I gave you and concentrate on me winning. And with your other hand, hold my hand."

"What good will that do?" I asked.

"For starters, it will make me feel better."

Sylvia sat on the machine, carefully keeping her legs together so no one could see up her dress while she did the movement. To everyone's surprise—including mine—she easily moved the platform once, twice, then just kept going, while holding my hand, completely relaxed, for 25 repetitions as everyone counted aloud.

She jumped off the machine and snatched up the

$2,000 sitting on the bench next to us, then turned to the couple and asked, "Would you like to double down and pick another exercise?"

The other gym members now expressed their anger at their friend for losing their money and their amazement at Sylvia.

Before we could get into a fight, I rushed Sylvia out of the gym with Dave at my side as backup. He saw us to my car, then Sylvia and I drove away.

"How did you do that?" I asked.

"I have strong legs. Ice-skating, dancing, bicycling. I'm quite fit, you know."

"Of course, but three hundred and seventy-five pounds for twenty-five repetitions? That's about what *I* would do."

"Yes, Mark, but you really helped me by touching the medallion and holding my hand at the same time. Don't you understand? We're stronger together than we are alone. That's what I've been trying to tell you all along. Now you see the proof with your eyes."

The next day, Dave called and asked if Sylvia and I wanted to go with him and Gail to the jewelry store to pick up their wedding rings. I didn't have to ask Sylvia twice.

"Oh yes! Of course I'd love to go look at jewelry." Pleasure radiated from her eyes and the idea brought a big smile to her face.

Immediately afterwards, I thought, *Oh my God! What have I done?* We'd be in one of San Francisco's most expensive jewelry stores down on Union Square. Sylvia would see Gail's rings and I couldn't afford anything really special for Sylvia.

As Sylvia and I drove downtown in my car, I dreaded going into the store. But I walked in and tried to look happy for Gail as she and Dave greeted us at the counter. Dave had given Gail an engagement ring last year. Now they were picking up the wedding rings just days before the ceremony, but to make things more complicated, Gail now wanted to trade up from the original engagement ring Dave had given her. Gail slipped her half-carat engagement ring off her finger and tried on a larger one-carat ring. She seemed happier with that one and asked about trading the smaller diamond for the bigger one.

"No problem," said the sales clerk, a stylish woman in her forties. "The new diamond is just under ten thousand and you get the full credit for your half-carat diamond of twenty-five hundred. So the balance is just seventy-five hundred." She said it so simply that it really sounded as if there were no problem.

Dave frowned. "Wait. If it's twice the size, why is it four times the price?"

Gail, Sylvia, and the saleswoman looked at him like he was an idiot.

"Larger diamonds are more rare," explained the saleswoman, "so the price goes up exponentially. If you were to get two or three carats, it would drive the price up dramatically."

Dave's eyes expressed alarm at this news. "Let's not even think about those. The wedding itself is costing a fortune."

"Yes," Gail agreed, "but my father's paying half, so we can spend more on a ring. I'll be wearing it for the rest of my life. I don't want a little ring." Then to my surprise, she turned to Sylvia and asked, "Don't you agree?"

"Absolutely," Sylvia said. "Size matters. Ask any woman. Whether it's diamonds or...anything else. The bigger the better."

The saleswoman stifled a giggle at Sylvia's remark, and then regained her composure. She looked at Dave for approval. "So shall we give her the big one that she likes? You do want her to be satisfied?"

Dave nodded his head in defeat. I could see him mentally calculate all the expenses of the wedding in his head.

In the meantime, Sylvia's eyes fixated on something inside the glass case. "Could I see that ring?" She pointed directly at the one with the largest diamond.

"Of course you can," said the saleswoman. "That's one of the nicest engagement rings I've seen. You really have excellent taste."

"Yes, you're right. I do." Sylvia's face glowed with happiness as she slipped the ring on.

Gail addressed the saleswoman: "Sylvia and Mark have only known each other about a week. They're certainly not going to get engaged now."

"You'd be surprised what couples do," answered the saleswoman. "My husband proposed to me after we knew each other for only a month. We've been happily married for over ten years."

"That's wonderful," Sylvia exclaimed. "How romantic!"

The saleswoman started her description: "Your favorite ring here is in a platinum setting. The diamond is over three carats—three point three-three to be exact—heart-shaped, with an ideal cut. The color is D, which is colorless, and the clarity is VVS one. That's why it's one hundred and eighty thousand dollars."

Sylvia held her hand out admiring the fire and sparkle, then turned to me. "Well, Mark, what do you think?"

"About what?" I asked.

"About the *ring*," she said with a sigh.

"I think it's more than I could ever afford. Don't the commercials all say to spend two months salary? This is more than two *years* salary."

"Yes," Sylvia conceded. "But if money were no object, would you buy me this engagement ring?"

As Sylvia asked me this question, Dave and Gail positioned themselves behind her so I could see them, but she couldn't. Both of them shook their heads and silently mouthed the word "No," trying to coach me. I knew they meant well, but what harm could there possibly be in answering Sylvia's hypothetical question?

"Sure," I said. "If money were no object, I'd buy this engagement ring for you right now."

Sylvia stared straight at me with pure joy in her eyes, kissed me on the cheek, and said, "Thank you, Mark. I accept." Then she turned to the saleswoman, smiled, and said, "We'll take it."

I just realized I had accidentally agreed to get engaged by answering Sylvia's hypothetical question. "What I meant is that if I had an extra one hundred and eighty thousand dollars, I'd gladly buy it for you. But I don't have that kind of money."

Sylvia gently placed her hand on my shoulder. "That's alright, Mark. It's not a problem." She reached inside her purse, pulled out a black American Express card and handed it to the saleswoman, who was obviously excited about such a huge sale. Sylvia turned back to me. "If you're really concerned about the cost, you can gradually pay me back. Say, one thousand dollars per year until it's paid off."

"That would take one hundred and eighty years! Long before then, I'll be dead."

"Mark, I'm not unreasonable. I wouldn't expect you to pay anything if you're dead! And as far as getting married, we can wait as long as you want—a month, a year, whatever you like. No pressure there." Sylvia turned to Dave and Gail, who were in shocked amusement at my situation. She held her hand out at them, flashing the large, heart-shaped diamond. "Isn't it wonderful? Mark and I are engaged!"

Chapter Thirteen

When we returned to our apartment building, Sylvia insisted that I come over so she could lend me some books. From her little library, she lent me *The Satanic Bible*, *The Satanic Rituals*, both by Anton LaVey, and an odd assortment of books about demons and possession. She pleaded with me to read them all, promising to explain everything to me fully once I had the necessary background.

"I can't read all of these right now," I protested. "There isn't enough time. If I were to read just one book in the next couple days, where should I start?"

Sylvia thought for a second and then handed me a new trade paperback, *Left and Right of Center—Finding Balance in Your Mundane and Magical Life*, by John Allee and Lillee Allee.

"This sounds like it's about politics, not magic," I said, looking at the title.

"No," Sylvia explained. "It's referring to the left-hand path or the right-hand path—of magic."

"Oh. And what path are you on?"

"*We* are on the left-hand path." Sylvia placed the book in my hand.

Though not a subject I would have studied on my own, I felt now that Sylvia and I had become so seriously involved with each other, I would have to make an attempt to understand her as well as I possibly could. Whether I liked it or not, she and her practice of magic were intermingled, and came together as a package.

For the next couple days, I did extremely well at work, making more sales than I had ever thought possible. I didn't know whether to believe that the medallion was responsible for my recent success, or if it was simply due to the happiness I experienced from being with Sylvia every day.

We continued to see each other Thursday and Friday, and when Saturday rolled around, we were both in cheerful moods. The wedding reception was set for 3 p.m., and we were to meet Dave and Gail at Grace Cathedral at 1:30 to make sure we had everything memorized, since I was to be the best man.

As planned, I knocked on Sylvia's door at noon. Being aware of her sleeping habits, I half expected her to look exhausted from trying to adjust to a different sleeping schedule for this one day, but she looked as lovely as ever. She wore the yellow dress she had just bought a few days before, and the delicately laced pattern around the edges of the material fit the dainty and feminine image that Sylvia always projected. Though the afternoon was to be formal, she chose not to wear her hair up, but wore it as she always did, long and carefree. The glistening black of her hair contrasted sharply with the bright yellow of her dress, and she wore a yellow silk ribbon in her hair, similar to the one she wore the day she came to the gym.

"You look fantastic," I said, as I stepped into her apartment.

"Thank you," she replied with a curtsy. "You look pretty nice yourself. I like you in a tuxedo. Only one thing is missing, though."

"What's that?"

"You need some sort of elegant jewelry, or some gold to add to the look of the clothes."

"If you mean the medallion, it would look awkward around this collar. I'm wearing it, but it's underneath my shirt."

"Yes, I know," she said, nodding.

"Really? How can you tell?"

"I can feel it. But anyway, what you need is something like—like this." With that, she stretched her hand forward to reveal a box that contained a men's watch. She sat me down and started to unfasten my own watch, a Hamilton Ventura, a triangular-shaped, futuristic design.

"Wait a minute," I said. "My watch is perfectly good—and it's a classic. The Hamilton Ventura was the first electric watch when it came out in the fifties. Elvis Presley had one in the movie, *Blue Hawaii*, Rod Serling had one he wore on his show, *The Twilight Zone*, and the two secret agents wore the watch in the movie, *Men in Black*."

"Yes, it's a great design" nodded Sylvia in agreement. "I know all about watches, including yours. That's exactly why I knew you could appreciate this watch from me. It's okay to have two nice watches, you know. It doesn't mean you're cheating on your first watch if you wear a second one occasionally. And mine will be nice to wear at the wedding. But I sure wouldn't wear it to your gym if I were you." Sylvia undid the buckle of my watchband and set it on the table, then handed me the box with the new watch.

Before I even opened it, and saw the watch inside, I recognized the name on the outside—Patek Philippe. Inside the fancy box lay a Patek Philippe Calatrava, in white gold, a very slim classic round wristwatch with hobnail bezel, Roman numerals, and a porcelain dial.

"It's certainly a wonderful gift, but I can't accept it."

"You can't?" she asked with great disappointment. "Why not?"

"Well, it's just too much money."

"Oh, don't worry about that," Sylvia waved my concerns away with her hand. "It's actually one of their least expensive watches."

"Patek Philippe doesn't make any cheap watches just like Rolls Royce doesn't sell any cheap cars. It's beautiful, but it's more than I deserve."

"Didn't you tell me you thought I was beautiful?"

139

"Of course I did."

"So am I more beautiful than you deserve?"

"I ask myself that question every day."

"You should know the answer by now." Sylvia fastened the Patek Philippe around my wrist, then put my Hamilton Ventura inside the box and placed it on the table.

"If I don't wear it, you can still return it and get your money back."

"But I can't return it," Sylvia pleaded. "I bought it from the same store where we went for my diamond ring. Do you want me to look like an idiot?"

"Of course not."

"So you see, you really must keep it. Think of it as a symbol of my love."

"I only wish I had something to give you in return."

"Don't worry. You do." Something in the tone of Sylvia's voice disturbed me, but since I couldn't put my finger on it, I let the remark pass without any reaction from me. "What time is it?" she asked.

I looked at my new watch. "About fifteen minutes after noon."

"We should get going." She hooked her arm around mine and led me out the door.

As we reached the bottom of the stairs, George was checking for his mail. He saw us in our formal clothes and looked a bit surprised since I normally dressed casually. His sweatshirt had several holes in it, and he held a copy of *The Ring* in one hand, showing a picture of a bloody fighter dodging a punch from another boxer. In the other hand, he held a can of beer.

"Well, where are you two kids going so dressed up?"

"We're on our way to a wedding," I answered.

George stared at me incredulously, with his glazed and bloodshot eyes. Apparently, the beer in his hand was not the first of the day. "A wedding!" he repeated, his eyes bulging. "Christ, you kids only known each other a week!" He shook his head.

"Yes," said Sylvia. "We decided that we'd waited long enough. A whole week can be such a very long time, when one's in love, you know. Did you see my new ring?" Sylvia held her hand out to show her diamond engagement ring. I had to keep myself from laughing at George's reaction to Sylvia's remark. He just kept shaking his head, as if he couldn't believe it, but believed it anyway.

"I guess that means that one of your apartments will have to be rented." He held his forehead with his hand, as if he were discovering a headache. "Aw shit. First Harry gets killed, and now this. It seems like I just can't keep these apartments occupied. The Devil must have put a curse on this God damn building, or something." He said this as much to himself as to us, but then turned to us and said, "Well anyway, good luck to the both of you. I hope you have a long and happy marriage." He held his beer can out to toast us.

"Oh, it will be long," answered Sylvia. "I don't believe in divorce."

"You must be Catholic," George remarked, as he nodded in agreement to Sylvia's views on marriage and divorce.

"Not exactly," Sylvia replied, as she cast a smile in my direction.

"I think we better be on our way," I said. "We shouldn't be late." Though I found Sylvia's little game somewhat amusing, it had gone on long enough.

As soon as we stepped outside, Sylvia put on a pair of sunglasses so dark, they looked as if they were made for the blind.

"How do you see out of those things?" I asked.

"The sunlight bothers my eyes."

"What sunlight?" I asked jokingly, for the fog out in

the Richmond District still hadn't burned off. Yet, as I looked towards downtown, I could see that the sun shone stronger there.

Sylvia enjoyed the drive downtown immensely, commenting that it had been so long since she had gone out in the afternoon. I offered to go out with her any afternoon to Golden Gate Park, but she declined, saying that one afternoon outing was sufficient, and that it would be far better if I could quit my job, so that I could stay up all night and sleep all day.

"And what would we do all night?" I asked, testing her.

"Anything we wanted to do. Some new things that you haven't done before."

"Sounds great. When do we start?"

"Very soon," she answered.

"The sooner, the better."

"If you want to," Sylvia answered, "but after you find out what I'm really like, you may wish that you had become involved with someone else. Of course, by that time, it will be too late to change your mind." There was a grave tone in the way she spoke, but I paid no particular attention to it, since I had learned that Sylvia was exceedingly fond of riddles.

I parked the car on Taylor Street, between Pine and California, only half a block from Grace Cathedral. The street amazed Sylvia. All of the cars had to park horizontally because of the steepness of the hill. If that weren't enough, the sidewalk rose at such an extreme angle, that half of the sidewalk consisted of stairs molded into the concrete. This discovery delighted Sylvia, and as we neared the top of the hill at California Street, Grace Cathedral loomed against the sky like a fortress of God reaching up to Heaven, and Sylvia, in her long yellow gown flowing in the San Francisco wind, looked like an angel ascending. When I told her this, she cast me a look of disgust, and crinkled her nose at my analogy.

"And what will I look like," she asked, "when we are walking *down* this hill later on, as it starts to get dark?"

"You'll probably look much better, since you won't be wearing those awful sunglasses and I'll be able to see your beautiful eyes."

She smiled and squeezed my hand as we crossed the street and entered the church through one of the high arched doorways. The interior of the massive cathedral awed Sylvia. She paused to inspect the stained glass windows, which shined high above us. I had heard of the beauty of the cathedral before, but had never realized how amazingly high the ceiling reached. The sheer size of everything made me feel like an ant. Sylvia slowly turned around in a circle, taking in everything with her large and curious eyes. As she examined our surroundings, I watched her, and couldn't help but think how she resembled a mannequin rotating on a stand. So slender and delicate, with glistening black hair that looked almost too perfect, and such a strangely beautiful face, unlike any I had ever seen, she captivated me with an intensity that could only be described as compulsive. A sudden urge to kiss her came upon me as I watched her, and at the exact moment the thought came into my mind, she instantly stopped her examination of our surroundings, and turned towards me instead. Then, without saying a word, she suddenly grabbed my face with both of her dainty hands, and kissed me with a passion that seemed almost inappropriate, considering the solemnity of the gathering and the number of people close to us. Yet, one touch from her soft lips, and I forgot everything and everyone around us.

"Are you two practicing for your own honeymoon?" Dave asked with a laugh, as he walked up to us smiling.

"Yes," answered Sylvia. "After all, we wouldn't want to make any mistakes."

"You do just fine," I told her, with an approving smile.

"I'm glad you're here on time. We're just running over some of the details now. The other guests should be arriving within an hour." Dave then escorted us to the Chapel of Grace, where the wedding ceremony was to be held.

True to Dave's word, the chapel slowly filled with relatives and friends. As close as Dave and I had been, most of these people were unknown to me. Even Dave's parents I had met only twice in ten years, and it had been three years since the last time we saw each other. Dave's father remarked how much larger Dave and I looked compared with the last time he had seen us together, a tribute to our workouts at the gym. Gail's parents walked up at that moment and introduced themselves to me, and I introduced Sylvia to the guests I already knew.

"With a pretty girl like that," said Dave's father as he pointed to Sylvia, "you should be up at the altar yourself, Mark."

"Well, we've only known each other a week," I told him.

"But we've gotten to know each other quite well in such a short time," Sylvia declared to the two sets of parents before us.

She accompanied her statement with a mischievous, sexy smile, and gave me a big hug.

"Indeed?" asked Gail's mother, with apparent contempt in her voice. Evidently, the sexual implication behind Sylvia's remark had upset her. Dave had told me of the religious fervor with which Gail's parents lived their lives, and I was glad to see that only part of it had rubbed off on Gail, and absolutely none of it on Dave.

"Well, at least Gail has saved herself for marriage," her mother declared proudly to Sylvia.

I couldn't see how she could have been so naive to

actually believe what she just said, but I wasn't about to say anything to start an argument with the bride's mother. But then I didn't have to. Sylvia saved me the trouble.

"You can't possibly be serious," Sylvia said to her. "No one is in a relationship for two years without sex — unless they're already married. 'Marriage has many pains, but celibacy has no pleasures,'" retorted Sylvia, with a smile. "I believe it was Samuel Johnson who said that."

Gail's mother stood aghast, while Dave's father rubbed his chin and then nodded. "I believe you're right," he said to Sylvia, "It *was* Samuel Johnson who said that. You're English, aren't you?"

Sylvia nodded.

"I thought I recognized your accent," Dave's father said.

Fortunately, some other relatives and friends wandered into our little circle and interrupted the flow of conversation. I led Sylvia away before she could say anything else to Gail's mother.

"From the way you were talking back there, they all think that we've been in bed with each other from the very second we met."

"What's wrong with that?" Sylvia asked with an air of innocence.

"Nothing would be wrong with it — if it were true. But as things stand, Gail's mother thinks her daughter hasn't been touched by Dave, and the two have been living together, and she thinks we spend all our time in bed, when we've never even had our clothes off together."

"Don't worry about that," Sylvia reassured me. "We'll be going to bed with each other soon enough. I can promise you that."

"That's the nicest thing you've said all day." And it certainly was. Nothing Sylvia could have said would have been more welcome. Though there were perhaps many other people who had known each other for a week or two without the benefit of sex, Sylvia and I had been so close for the short time we had been together that I felt as if I had known her much longer. Additionally, Sylvia seemed to know far more about me than I knew about her. Partly this came about because of the secrecy with which she veiled certain portions of her life. Yet I felt sure that beyond this, there lay another reason, and that this other reason would explain how she had painted a picture of me before we met, and how she happened to move into my apartment after seeing me at the gym just a few days earlier. I didn't press her for these answers too strongly because I felt certain she would be telling me very soon anyway.

Something caught Sylvia's eye and she turned in the other direction and pointed. "Look at that man with the shaved head. He looks like that guy at the gym you almost got into a fight with. Of course it was a good thing he had a shaved head so we could tell him apart from his girlfriend."

I started to laugh until I turned in the other direction and saw the man she was pointing at. Although I hadn't seen him before, I knew who he was from Mary's description months ago, and now he and Mary were headed in our direction. He was the third of the three men Mary had dated during our "relationship." The two others were a dentist and a college professor. But they were passed by—along with me—for this guy, the Harley-riding, tattooed, shaved-head, prison guard. Now Mary had her wedding escort, despite what Gail had told me.

Mary apparently wanted me to see the two of them together, so they approached right away. "Hi Mark. It's nice to see you again. This is Biff."

Biff, I thought. Is she kidding? The name matched his looks. He stood about six-foot-four, a full foot taller than

146

Mary, and quite a bit taller than me, and in size, he matched the muscular guy at the gym. I thought back to months ago, when I fantasized about fighting him, not fully realizing the problem was with Mary, not the men who accepted her invitations.

"Nice to meet you," I said, shaking his hand, wondering if he was going to try to crush my hand, thus forcing me to hit him at Dave's wedding. With his size, a hard punch to the face wouldn't be nearly enough. It would need to be a knife-edge hand to the throat, collapsing his windpipe, or a finger poke to the eyes. As part of my kung-fu training, I had practiced both of these techniques on hard sandbags mounted on the wall.

Mary turned towards Sylvia. "I'm Mary. And I've heard about you from Gail. You must be Sylvia."

"I must be. And of course I've heard about you from Mark." Sylvia looked at me, amused at the awkward situation. She examined Biff and Mary, sizing them up, their noticeable difference in height a contrast with Sylvia and me, since she stood about an inch taller than I.

With Mary's curly blonde hair, blue eyes, and busty figure compared to Sylvia's long black hair, dark exotic eyes, full lips, and slim curvy figure that accentuated her hips and athletic legs, they were a study in contrasts as much as Biff and I looked different from each other.

The priest arrived and began talking with all of the guests, and shortly afterwards the ceremony got under way. I made sure Sylvia and I were seated as far as possible from Gail's parents to avoid potential conflicts. At the end of the ceremony, Gail tossed her bridal bouquet out into the crowd of female guests. It looked like it would go straight to Mary, but Sylvia stood in front of her, and being four or five inches taller, she easily snatched it before it could reach Mary. She stood facing me, sniffed the bouquet, and her eyes met mine as she held the flowers in her hand like an athlete showing off a trophy.

"My, what good luck I'm having today," Sylvia said to me, as she then turned to Mary and handed her the bouquet. "Here. You need this more than I do. Best of luck to you and Biff. I know you'll be perfect for each other." A minute later, Dave and Gail were at our side as I offered them our best wishes.

Dave congratulated Sylvia on catching the bridal bouquet. "They say that whoever catches the bridal bouquet is the next to get married."

Sylvia nodded in agreement happily. Dave's remark had brightened her expression, which had been partly one of boredom while the priest had been reading sections of the Bible during the ceremony.

Everyone gathered to go to the reception, just a block and a half away at the Mark Hopkins Hotel, held in the luxurious Club Lounge. By some cruel seating arrangement—no doubt plotted by Gail—Sylvia and I found ourselves sitting close enough to Mary and Biff so that avoiding conversation with them seemed impossible under the circumstances. Champagne flowed freely, but I knew to sip only a little as it could give me a headache later. This didn't concern Sylvia, who really savored the taste.

"I haven't had champagne in years," she announced.

"Really?" asked Gail. "With your expensive tastes, I would think you drink it all the time." Then turning to her friend, Mary, she asked, "Did you see the nice engagement ring Sylvia bought herself yesterday?"

"Engagement?" Mary asked, bewildered. "Didn't you two just meet?"

Sylvia extended her hand towards Mary's face so she could get the full effect of the three and one-third carat, heart-shaped diamond ring. "We're actually soul mates," Sylvia declared. "We've had dreams about each other for years. Haven't we, Mark?" she added as she turned to me, and I nodded in agreement.

The champagne had added a little color to Sylvia's cheeks and I realized maybe she told the truth when she said she hadn't drank any in years.

"Really?" Mary questioned. "Dreams about each other. Even say, six months ago?" She made sure to include the time we were together.

"Yes, especially then," I admitted. "I think I did a lot of dreaming when I was sleeping alone. You know, when you were out traveling."

"Of course. I had to travel for work," Mary explained, as much to Sylvia as to me. "I have a career." She faced Sylvia. "I sell medical supplies to doctors. And what do *you* do?"

Sylvia took another big sip of champagne, which brought a further flush to her cheeks. "Me? What do I do? I travel. I play the harpsichord and the piano for fun. I have exciting adventures. And now the best romance of my life. That's what I'm doing."

Mary continued to pry, doing Gail's work by proxy. "I meant, what do you do for money?"

"Money?" Sylvia repeated, her voice a little louder now with her third glass of champagne. "If you mean work, I've never worked. I sure would hate to have to. When would I have time for fun?"

"But a ring like that must cost thousands," Mary said.

"I'm sure Gail already told you I paid one hundred and eighty thousand dollars for it." Sylvia took another sip of champagne.

Mary's eyes popped open and she looked to Gail. It surprised me that Gail hadn't told her about the price of the ring. Biff appeared bored with the conversation and had drunk more than anyone else. He excused himself to go to the bathroom and staggered away from the table.

"I didn't know Mark was so impulsive," Mary said. "I guess if we had stayed together, I'd be wearing a ring before now."

"Not with all the men you were dating on your business trips," I countered.

"Those were friends!" Mary protested.

"Yes," I agreed. "Friends like the dentist, the professor, and finally the prison guard you brought here today. All friends. Friends with benefits."

Sylvia put her arm around my shoulder, pulled me close and said, "Well, my *friend*, you're in luck because your benefits start tonight!"

"I can't wait," I said, looking at my watch, wondering when we would start.

Dave, sitting on the other side of me, gasped as he saw my new watch. "Is that a real Patek Philippe?"

"Of course it is," Sylvia replied. "Do you think I'd buy myself this ring and then buy Mark a fake watch?"

"Do you know what that cost?" Dave whispered in my ear.

Somehow, Sylvia heard him, so she responded. "It was about a tenth of the cost of the ring."

Dave nodded. "That's right. About eighteen thousand dollars." Dave knew the price of many expensive things, even those he couldn't afford, because he subscribed to magazines that featured the status symbols he desired.

I turned to Sylvia. "Please tell me you didn't spend that much money on this watch for me."

"Of course I did. I love you, Mark. I couldn't buy that nice ring for myself without getting something nice for you. It would have haunted my conscience." She leaned her cheek against mine and stayed there as if I were holding her up.

"Patek Philippe?" Gail asked. "I think I read some article in the newspaper this week about a Patek Philippe watch."

"And what did the story say?" asked Sylvia, suddenly interested.

"I don't remember," admitted Gail.

Biff stumbled back to the table and slumped into the chair next to Mary. He appeared nauseous and unconcerned with the dinner conversation.

"How can you afford all this if you don't work?" Mary asked Sylvia.

Sylvia took another sip of champagne and leaned forward towards Mary. "If I spent a thousand dollars a day, every day, for the next twenty years, I would still have way more money at the end of those twenty years than I have now."

Gail came to Mary's defense. "Mary may not have the money you have, Sylvia, but she has lots of other good qualities."

Mary nodded, waiting for Gail to elaborate.

Gail thought, then said, "Mary's great at water sports!"

Sylvia's eyes lit up with amusement as she turned back and forth, first at me, then towards Mary, before she raised her voice. "You're great at water sports? Golden showers? How *interesting*. Do you spit or swallow?"

At that remark, Dave lost his composure and his laugh caused him to spray a mouthful of champagne all over Gail's white wedding gown.

Sylvia glanced at Dave, then at me, and pointing her thumb at Dave, told me, "Now Dave, he doesn't swallow. He'd be a spitter. How about you, Mark?"

Gail stared in horror at the yellow champagne stain on her wedding gown and turned to Sylvia. "Now look what you've done!"

Someone told Gail to use club soda to get the stain out and they ordered some right away.

Mary stood up and glared at Sylvia. "When Gail said I was good at water sports, she was referring to me being on the swimming team in college!"

"Oh," said Sylvia softly. "My mistake. I just assumed

that with the *friends* you made on your business travels, you learned some new tricks. When Gail started talking about how great you were at water sports, I thought she meant golden showers. I was just wondering about you and Mark—who was on top and who was on the bottom. *Somebody's* got to swallow!"

"That's disgusting!" remarked Mary.

Suddenly, Biff vomited into his cloth napkin, trying to look discreet as he rushed up from the table and staggered towards the restroom again.

"Now *that's* disgusting," said Sylvia to Mary as she pointed at Biff.

Just in time to break the tension, the waiters arrived with the food and more drinks. I almost stopped the waiter when he asked Sylvia if she wanted more champagne, but to my relief, she changed her mind and suddenly wanted pineapple juice. At least this would give her a chance to sober up. I felt some of her behavior had to be due to the champagne, but then I remembered that she never shied from a conflict.

"I'm glad to see you switched from champagne to pineapple juice," I told her.

"I did it especially for you!" Sylvia replied with a mischievous smile.

The waiters brought more food, and for the first time, I actually got to see Sylvia eat. She ate everything on her plate except for the asparagus. I joked with her that if she didn't eat her vegetables they wouldn't give her any dessert, but we both had plenty of wedding cake.

From that point on, the rest of the reception went smoothly. When Dave and Gail opened the present of the Steuben glass swans from Sylvia and me, the obvious high cost of it so impressed them that Sylvia's earlier comments may have been partly forgiven. After Dave and Gail opened all their wedding gifts, the band began to play. Although several single men asked Sylvia to dance, she would dance only with me. I found it easy to dance with Sylvia, just as it had been when we went to the nightclub before. Mary had to leave early to drive Biff home after he threw up on her new shoes.

Sylvia put her arm around my shoulder. "I hope you don't regret bringing me to the wedding after the trouble I caused."

"Are you kidding? The reactions from Mary were priceless. It was certainly worth any conflict to see her jealousy."

"Do you still feel any love for her?"

"Actually, after my time with you, I wonder if I really loved anyone I was with before you. None of them matter to me anymore."

Then, as Sylvia looked around with her happy expression, her smile turned into a look of horror.

"What's wrong?" I asked her.

"Mark, quick. Get me out of here, and don't leave my side for any reason." She cast a fearful look over at the other end of the church, which was deserted except for one person—a priest standing against the wall, staring at Sylvia, with the same look of horror and recognition in his face as she had shown in hers. An older man, wearing the uniform of a priest, and carrying a black satchel, he hardly had the appearance of one who could strike fear into anyone, and certainly not Sylvia.

"Do you know that priest?" I asked her.

"Yes, I do, Mark, please. You must get me away from here right now. I'll tell you about him later."

The eyes of the priest never left us, and he began to follow us from about a hundred feet away. Sylvia clutched me tightly to her,

"Enough of this nonsense," I said to her, as I stopped walking. "I'm not going to run away from some old man. He's not going to do anything to hurt you while I'm with you. No one is."

"You don't understand. Just do what I ask. No matter what he says or does, don't let go of my hand." She clutched my hand even more tightly than before, then almost dragged me out the door behind her as she hurried down the steep sidewalk to my car. She even insisted on holding my hand as we both got into the Lotus, a most awkward maneuver that appeared unnecessary to me, but Sylvia was so frightened, I accommodated her request.

She begged me to drive as fast as I could to make sure he couldn't possibly follow us. I did as she asked for several blocks, but then it became obvious that we had lost him, so I slowed down. I pulled over at the side of a steep hill, which afforded us a grand view of the San Francisco skyline.

"Safe for the moment," she said, as she caught her breath.

"Would you mind telling me why you're so worried about some old priest?" I asked her.

Sylvia stared at me with her large and melancholy eyes. "His name is Father Callen, and he wants to kill me."

Chapter Fourteen

Unfortunately, Sylvia refused to explain any further regarding Father Callen. We sat inside my Lotus watching the sun's last glimmer of redness on the horizon disappear as the stars came out.

"If I told you the whole truth, you wouldn't believe me," Sylvia said in exasperation. She sat next to me with her hands folded in her lap and stared down at them.

"Please look at me," I said, and immediately she cast her sad eyes at me, as if she were about to cry. "You can tell me anything you want and I promise I'll believe it."

"Oh no!" Sylvia exclaimed. "That would be even worse."

"Now, how do you think I feel, when you tell me that this priest is out to kill you, and you won't tell me why, and I've got to worry that you might be right? If he really is after you, then why don't we just call the police and have him arrested?"

"There's nothing to arrest him for. He hasn't broken any laws here in this country yet, and I don't want to become involved with the police at all. How would you like it if they deported me?"

"I don't know what I'd do then. Maybe I'd have to move to England."

Sylvia's expression brightened at my remark. She gave me a kiss on the cheek, then leaned her body against mine. "I should be safe now. He can't hurt me when I'm with you. If only I had you around all the time."

"That's okay with me," I said quickly. "I'll spend as much time with you as you want."

"But what about during the day, when I sleep?"

I shrugged my shoulders. "I don't know what to do about that. You don't want me to sleep with you, and I work during the day, so that takes care of that, doesn't it?"

"Things will be changing soon enough," Sylvia responded, but didn't bother clarifying just what would be changing.

When we reached the apartment building, I didn't know Sylvia's intentions. At 9 p.m., it was too early to go to sleep, but I didn't know whether to suggest stopping at my apartment. I didn't have to wonder long. With her arm around mine, she led me straight to her apartment. "I hope you didn't think I was teasing when I said your benefits start tonight!" She unlocked the door and we walked in.

"That's great, but I wouldn't want to take advantage of you," I said, noting how much Sylvia had to drink earlier.

Sylvia's mouth dropped open in disbelief. "You take advantage of me? Could a drunk woman do *this*?" She suddenly did a handstand and held it in perfect balance, not wavering in the slightest.

I rushed over to help in case she fell over, but her balance didn't falter. At the same time, I expected her gown to slip down over her head and expose her underwear, but because the gown fit so snugly, it didn't move, so revealed nothing underneath. "It's a good thing you didn't try that at the wedding," I said. "After the conflict tonight, I don't know if they'll ever invite us to anything again."

"Are they planning to have another wedding?" Sylvia asked.

"Of course not."

"Then it doesn't matter. They should be concerned about whether we would invite them to ours." Sylvia gazed at her diamond ring, then smiled at me.

Sylvia motioned for me to follow her into the kitchen, then she opened her refrigerator, which had very little in it. "I need something to drink."

"You don't want more champagne, do you?" I hated

the thought of her getting drunk.

"No. No more champagne," Sylvia assured me. "I want more pineapple juice like I had at the wedding. Why don't you go to the corner store and get a couple bottles?"

It seemed like a reasonable request, so I walked to the store alone to buy the pineapple juice. Just as I left the store, on my way down the sidewalk, a hand tapped me on the shoulder.

I turned around, and there stood Father Callen, right behind me. Up close, he looked like nothing more than an older priest, with grey hair showing underneath his hat, and wire-rimmed spectacles resting on a large nose,

"I'm Father Callen. I wonder if I might have a word with you?"

For a second, I felt frozen to the sidewalk, not knowing what to say or do. Had he seen where Sylvia and I lived? Was he really trying to kill her? How did he find me so quickly? All these questions raced through my mind before I finally asked, "What do you want? And why were you following us?"

"I was not following you, young man. It was the girl. I only learned recently that she had come to America."

"What business is it of yours? And why were you following us?"

"I've been searching for her for many years," he said, with a distant look in his eyes. "You don't know what she is, or what she'll do."

"And what will *you* do if you find her?" I demanded,

"I will bring justice," he said angrily. "Justice for my relatives who died at her hands, justice for the hundreds of people she has murdered in her unholy existence, and perhaps," he added, with a sad nod of his head, "justice for you. For when she has finished with you—for whatever she needs you for—she will surely kill you too."

"You're out of your God damn mind!"

"Am I now? Don't be too sure, until you hear the

157

facts. Do you realize what she is?" he questioned me, his eyes lit up like fire.

"If you're going to warn me about witchcraft, I don't—"

"Witchcraft!" he exclaimed with a laugh. "My, how I wish that was the problem. My son, there are millions of witches all over this world. Quite a few in your own city. People who worship Satan are nothing new, but fortunately, they pose few threats to society or to God. They are just poor misguided souls on their way to Hell. But this girl, by whatever name she goes by now—she is much more than a mere witch."

"So what do you think she is?"

"It is not what I think. It is what I know. What my parents told me since I was a little boy, about how she took a torch to the church in my village in England. How she burned alive half the congregation. One hundred people murdered, among them, one of the earliest known ancestors of my great-grandfather."

"She murdered an *ancestor* of your great-grandfather? Just when did she do this?"

"In 1685!" he declared with a flourish.

"Now you listen to me, you stupid crackpot. If I ever catch you following me or her, I'll—"

"You'll do nothing!" he yelled. "She'll kill you next, you young fool. She's a vampire! And she must be destroyed."

"You're a lunatic!" I shouted. "You're talking about the girl I'll be marrying someday."

"You idiot!" he screamed. "She's not going to marry you. She's going to kill you! You see only her beauty. Do you realize how many men died thinking she was beautiful? You aren't even one out of a hundred. A year after she kills you she won't even remember your name. Do you remember a cockroach you stepped on a year or two ago? You are as important to her as an insect. Her beauty mesmerizes you. You're blind to what she really is."

I grabbed him by the collar and slammed him up against the brick wall of the building, almost cracking his skull.

"Now listen to me, asshole. You don't have to worry about any vampires. All you have to worry about is me. Because if I ever see you following her, or if she ever tells me she's seen you again, I'll kill you myself. Do you understand? If you don't want to have every bone in your body broken, get on a plane today and go back to England." I gave him a shove and bounced him off the building and onto the sidewalk. For a brief second, I wondered how I must have looked, handling a priest in such a manner, until I realized that the man couldn't be a real priest anyway, running around like a madman, ranting about vampires, and threatening to kill my girlfriend.

He slinked away, rubbing his head where it had hit the wall.

"You've been warned," he yelled, as he pointed his finger at me accusingly. "You've chosen Satan instead of God. May your soul burn in Hell."

I watched him climb into his car, which might have been a rental. As he pulled away, I memorized the license plate for future reference. No doubt about it. I would have to call the police now, no matter what Sylvia said to the contrary. I couldn't take the chance that a crazy man like that might get to her alone. But first, I had to tell her what had happened. As much as I would have liked to forget about the whole thing and assure Sylvia that everything was all right, I just had to tell her the truth. At this point, her safety was more important than her peace of mind.

I walked home by going a couple of blocks out of my way to make sure he hadn't tried to follow me back to my apartment. I gave Father Callen's description to George, and told him that if he saw him near the building, or trying to get in, to let me know. In my absence, he was to keep Father Callen out of the building, and if he should try to get in anyway, George was to call the police. George wanted to know the reason for this, so I gave him a twenty-dollar bill. He agreed that was as good a reason as any, and promised me he would keep his eye out for him.

In the wake of Father Callen's raving warning to me, I imagined for a second that perhaps there could be some truth to what he said. I considered the evidence: three people murdered by loss of blood after being wounded in the throat; two of these were connected to me, but that was hardly proof that Sylvia murdered them.

"I've got some bad news for you," I told her as I walked into her apartment and handed Sylvia the two bottles of pineapple juice. "Father Callen came up to me while I was shopping down the street."

"Oh no," cried Sylvia, as she sank into her love seat. "Does he know where we live?"

"I don't think so. I made sure he didn't follow me."

"What happened? What did he say?" she asked, her eyes wide open with curiosity.

I related everything that was said between us, including the details of our physical confrontation, and how I noted down his license plate number.

"So you didn't believe what he said about me?"

"You mean about you being a vampire over three hundred years old who's murdered hundreds of people? Of course not! How could I believe something like that? Everyone knows vampires can't go out during the day, they have long fangs, can't bear the sight of a cross, they certainly wouldn't go to a church wedding — and they cast no reflection, and we've seen ourselves together in a mirror."

"How do you know all these things about vampires?" she asked.

"I've seen lots of movies," I admitted.

"Well, I'm sure thankful for those movies," Sylvia said with a sigh, "and so pleased you're on my side. It will make everything so much easier for me now."

"That's nice to hear, but honestly, I think the police can do more against Father Callen than I can."

"No, the police won't do anything until he breaks the law again."

"Again?" I asked, wondering if that was one of his habits.

"Yes," she answered. "He's already killed two of my closest friends. You wanted to know more about my life and the good and the bad and the people in it. Okay, now you get to satisfy your curiosity and open Pandora's box. Follow me." She grabbed me by the hand, then led me past the Satanic altar in her living room to her bedroom. Sylvia rummaged through her closet and pulled out a folder filled with news clippings and handed one of them to me.

"This is what we're up against," she said. "This article is from London, 1977. Go ahead and read it and find out about Father Callen."

PRIEST SENTENCED TO PRISON

Father William Callen, a self-avowed "vampire hunter," was sentenced to three years in prison today on several counts of grave desecration. Father Callen, who insists he is "only trying to protect humanity from a plague of vampires," was arrested after witnesses saw him and another priest opening up coffins in Highgate Cemetery here in London. At least 12 corpses were mutilated, and relatives of the deceased victims of the attack brought charges against the priest. His accomplice, still unknown to police or Scotland Yard, has not been apprehended.

This case is remarkably similar to that of the mass vampire-hunt that took place on Friday the 13th in 1970 at Highgate Cemetery. Approximately 100 "vampire-hunters" had taken part. While no vampires were found, it is believed that the highly publicized 1970 media event later led to the corpse desecrations over the following months. Although Callen had only one assistant, police believe he is part of a fanatical religious cult, or possibly even the leader.

I handed the article back to Sylvia. "This guy is really crazy," I remarked.

Sylvia nodded. "Yes, I know he is. But he's served his time in prison, and the police can't arrest him, so we'll just have to watch out for him. If we're going to be together all the time, then he'll be after you, too."

"What are you thinking?" I asked, as I noticed Sylvia's far-off gaze in deep thought.

"I don't know," she began, as she shook her head, "It's just that everything was going so well till today with Father Callen. I was so happy when I caught the bridal bouquet today, and now..." Her voice trailed off and she allowed herself to collapse into the loveseat. I sat down next to her and put my arm around her. "Everything was going so well," she repeated, her eyes suddenly welling up. A couple tears ran down her cheeks and so I held her quivering body close to mine. "What am I to do now?" she asked sadly. "I'm in love with you, and we live right next to each other, but now I'll have to move or Father

Callen will find me."

"Move?" I asked, alarmed at losing her. "You can't move *now*!" I told her with disappointment in my voice.

"Why not?"

"Because I'm in love with you, and it would drive me crazy if I couldn't see you," I admitted.

"You do love me?" she asked, as she smiled through her tears.

"Yes. I guess I've just been too much of a jerk to admit the obvious, since we've known each other such a short time, but there's no doubt about it. Short time or not. I love you."

She gave me a big hug, followed by a deep passionate kiss that promised more to come. "Then we'll both move away from here together. I'm not afraid of Father Callen if you're always with me. Will you stay with me?"

"Sure," I said quickly. "I'd love to stay with you."

"Are you absolutely positive?"

"Of course I am. I've always wanted a girlfriend just like you. If I let the opportunity go by for us to live together now, I'd never forgive myself."

"Oh," Sylvia said quietly. "I didn't mean living together as just boyfriend and girlfriend. I was thinking of something on a more permanent basis."

"You mean getting married?"

"Sort of, but not exactly."

"Well then, what? Exactly?"

"I want us to perform a magical ritual. A joining together of our souls and bodies. We could do it right now and then make love right afterwards."

"That sounds like a great idea to me," I agreed. I was about to have sex with the most beautiful woman I had ever seen in my life—a woman I loved, and who loved me back. How could it be anything other than perfect?

"But first, I want to call my friend, Susan and tell her the good news about you and the bad news about Father

Callen. She's one of my oldest and dearest friends and also one of my roommates at the mansion in London." Sylvia dialed the phone and then put it on speakerphone. The ringing tone in London was familiar to me—it came in spurts of two short rings each rather than one long ring, and brought back my own memories of London several years earlier.

After about eight or nine rings, a female British voice answered with a very tired, "Hello?"

"Susan, it's me. Sylvia."

"Do you have any idea what time it is?"

Sylvia looked at my new watch. "Yes, it's ten o'clock."

"It's not ten at night here in London. It's six o'clock in the morning and I was asleep!"

"Sorry. I forgot. Look, I'm here with Mark and he's already saved me from Father Callen."

"Father Callen went to San Francisco to kill you like the others? So you told Mark the truth about…"

"Susan, we're on speakerphone and Mark is right here next to me."

"Oh. I understand. Hello Mark. I've heard so much about you. I hope you're keeping Sylvia safe from that nut case. I've known Sylvia most of my life and I couldn't bear to lose her. You will protect her, won't you?"

"I certainly will. She'll have me by her side all night."

"Then I certainly won't worry about her safety. I'm sure she'll have a wonderful evening. Sylvia, call me back tomorrow and tell me how everything went."

After listening to Sylvia and Susan talk on the phone, Sylvia suddenly became more human to me. Hearing the voice of her friend on the phone took away some of the mystery of Sylvia's life and made me realize she was just like everyone else; she had enemies, but also friends; she hated her enemies, but loved her friends—and most importantly, she loved me.

164

"I'm so glad you had a chance to talk to my friend, Susan. I'm not going to let Father Callen ruin our night together. Our wonderful night together. Not like any other night. What we've both been hoping for and dreaming about for so long. Remember what I said? Be careful what you wish for because you just might get it."

Sylvia took me by the hand and led me to her bedroom, then went straight to her closet and removed two black robes — one for her, and one for me. Amazingly, the robe for me fit exactly, as if it had been custom-made. I asked her where she bought it.

"I didn't buy it. I made it while I was in London."

"Really? You must have had a boyfriend just my size."

"Actually, I made it for you about the same time I painted your portrait."

"How could you, if you didn't know me then?"

She hesitated for a moment, collecting her thoughts, apparently, or at least I hoped that was the reason for her hesitation, rather than to make up some riddle.

"Very well. I'll explain it all to you. But really, you should read the books on magic that I gave you."

I nodded, so she continued, pausing every now and then as she spoke, and then starting again once she felt she had just the right words.

"Demons — or whatever you wish to call them — do not really exist in our physical world. That's why they're invisible. Rather than occupying a different space, they exist in another dimension. They have no physical existence in our dimension, just as we have no physical existence in theirs. As far as I know, there are five dimensions. We live in three dimensions. The fourth dimension is that of time. It is the fifth dimension where the demons or spirits exist."

"Where is this fifth dimension?" I asked. "And what does this have to do with the painting or the robe?"

"I'm getting to that." She placed her arm affectionately on my shoulder. "The fifth dimension is in your mind, or rather, it's in everyone's mind. It is a dimension made of mental activity—the combined mental activity of all thinking beings in the universe. So it's larger than our physical universe. It includes not only everything observed by all intelligent beings, but also everything ever imagined. Notice I said everything ever imagined, and not everything being imagined now. It contains the past and present simultaneously. The difference between our dimension and the fifth dimension is like the difference between being awake and in a dream. The laws of nature do not even exist in the fifth dimension. The impossible happens all the time, because there are no physical laws to prevent it. Inside the fifth dimension, all kinds of strange beings exist: God, Satan, Jesus, demons. A supernatural entity may not have a physical existence in our dimension, but if enough people think about it, then they have created its existence in the fifth dimension. As soon as you think of anything at all, that thought is added to the fifth dimension. To us, they only have a mental existence, but to them, their existence is as real as ours is to us."

"Then does that mean that they can create us too?" I asked.

"Only a very select few have that ability, just as very few can cross into our dimension."

"How could they do that?"

"They must link up with one of us."

"You mean take over our bodies?" I asked, somewhat alarmed.

"No, usually not. Though that happens sometimes. But usually, it just occupies a body without the body even being aware of it, and the two become one unit, but stronger than before, especially if the human can realize the presence of a demon. I recognized such a presence within myself many years ago."

I was stunned and almost couldn't answer what Sylvia had said, so I just asked, "What did you do?"

"I found that it helped with my magic, but I also found out something else."

"Yes?"

"The demon was so powerful, its magical energy was more than I, or any single human could absorb, so half of it remained in the other dimension until it found someone to occupy with the other half. Of course, the demon links me with that other person in such a powerful way, that together, our magical power is incredible. And so, gradually, over a period of several years, a picture began to form in my mind—a picture of that person linked to me. For many years, the picture was so faint, it resembled nothing more than a blurred silhouette, but then, one evening, while performing a magical ritual, I had a vision, and the other person's face came into my mind as sharp as a photograph. So naturally, the first thing I did was to paint a portrait."

"And that's how you painted the portrait of me?" I asked.

"Yes. You are my other half. The other person whom the demon inhabits. We're *twins*, really—born of the same spiritual or demonic seed. With you, I am complete. And with me, you are complete. We form a magical circle so powerful, that—" Sylvia hesitated, and then sighed from her expenditure of effort in explanation. "You remember what happened at the Top of the Mark, to the cocktail waitress?"

I nodded as the grim memory floated through my mind.

"Well that is just a small example of the power that you give me, from your magical essence."

"Then why can't I do these things?" I asked.

"Oh, but you can. You have just as much power as I

167

do—well almost. Only a few minor corrections are necessary."

"What?"

"Don't worry," Sylvia reassured me. "The ritual will take care of everything."

"The ritual?" I wondered what Sylvia had in store for me.

"Yes, our romantic commitment ritual. It's a Satanic ritual, but don't let that worry you. I know exactly what I'm doing. At no point, should you stop the ceremony. Just follow along as best as you can. If I chant something, like 'Hail Satan!' just repeat it. You'll do fine."

"Should we rehearse first?" I asked, feeling nervous. "I'd hate to screw things up."

"It isn't possible to rehearse. This is the kind of thing we can only do once. This is something very different and special—for both of us. We will remember this moment for the rest of our lives, no matter how long that is."

This last remark of Sylvia's I found somewhat puzzling, but then, the last hour with her had been strange enough. Yet, as incredible as it all sounded, I believed her. It all made sense, and I felt curious as to just what would happen during the ritual she had planned. I also had a question regarding the portrait, but it came to mind while she was explaining so many metaphysical points, that by the time we were ready for the actual ritual, I had forgotten what I was going to ask, though I felt that the subject was just on the edge of my memory, just waiting to be remembered.

Suddenly, my cell phone rang, and Sylvia shot me a look of utter exasperation at the interruption. So before answering, I thought I'd return the favor she did when she shared her phone call from Susan in London. I told Sylvia I'd put it on speakerphone. After all, what could be the harm since we trusted each other?

"Mark, it's Dave. Gail has something important she

168

needs to tell you." My cell phone was at its loudest volume, and Sylvia stood next to me, amused that I chose to share my phone call with her, unknown to Dave and Gail.

"Mark, I'm glad I reached you before it was too late," Gail said over my phone.

"Funny you should say that," I remarked, "since it is kind of late." I looked at my new watch. "Did you know it's ten-thirty? I thought by this time, you and Dave might be occupied doing something else."

"Mark, this is serious. It's not a joke. Whatever you do, don't go to Sylvia's apartment!"

Chapter Fifteen

Sylvia perked right up, her eyes wide open after hearing Gail's remark, and she looked at me in anticipation.

"Why shouldn't I go to Sylvia's apartment?" I asked Gail on the phone.

"Remember I said I read something about the watch she gave you? The Patek Philippe Calatrava?"

"Yes. What about it?"

"An article in the paper. An English man from London was murdered in San Francisco a few nights ago—with the exact same watch. And the murder was similar to your last neighbor."

"What are you saying?" I asked. "That Sylvia murdered someone else from London so she could steal his watch and give it to me?"

"That's how it looks to me," Gail explained. "Before you go to Sylvia's apartment, you should read the article."

"That stupid bitch!" Sylvia exclaimed, with a shocked expression on her face.

"Mark, is someone there with you in your apartment?" Gail asked.

"He's not in *his* apartment. He's here in *mine*," Sylvia said, leaning into the phone for Gail to hear. "And speaking of reading the newspaper article, you should have read the whole article before calling."

Sylvia picked up a newspaper that was several days old from the coffee table and searched for the article, then brought it to me stabbing her finger at the paper.

POLICE DISCOVER MURDER PATTERN

With yesterday's discovery of a third blood-drained body in less than two weeks, police believe there may be a pattern in these bizarre murders. The most recent murder was that of English millionaire Clark Graystone, a 45-year-old housing developer from London. Graystone was slain sometime between 2 a.m. and 3 am. on Tuesday morning. His assistant last saw him alive at 11:30 p.m. Monday night, just before retiring.

According to William Frederick, Graystone's assistant, sometime after 2 a.m. he heard breaking glass and a scream from Graystone's bedroom. When he broke down the door, Graystone was already dead. Autopsy has revealed the cause of death to be shock due to extreme loss of blood. A large wound was found on Graystone's throat, right over the jugular vein.

Swenson, the chief investigator on the case, pointed out the similarities between the three murder scenes. All occurred within 10 days. The first murder was that of two young drug dealers in the Mission District, only 10 days ago. However, the two drug dealers were murdered differently. One died of loss of blood, but the other had his neck twisted around and broken. The second murder scene was that of an unemployed rock musician. No links between the three different murders have been found other than the method in which they were killed. All three locations were far from each other.

Robbery has not been considered a motive. It was noted that in Graystone's murder, he was wearing a valuable white gold watch, a Patek Philippe Calatrava, estimated to be worth between $15,000-$20,000. Police were surprised that the murderer did not steal such a valuable watch. Police also cited the large amounts of cash left untouched on the victim's dresser.

At this point, police have no suspects, but are working with the evidence obtained so far.

After I finished reading the article aloud for Gail, I said, "Did you hear the part about how the murder victim still had his watch?"

"I must have missed that detail when I first read it," Gail admitted.

Sylvia opened her purse and pulled out a receipt from the jewelry store and waved it in front of my eyes. There it was, dated the same day she purchased the engagement ring—one Patek Philippe Calatrava watch, white gold case, for $18,900 plus tax.

"Sylvia just showed me her receipt," I told Gail.

"I can forgive you for thinking I'm a murderer," Sylvia said into the phone, "but how could you think I was too cheap to buy Mark a watch?"

"Oh," said Gail, obviously too embarrassed to answer. "Well, what are you going to do now?" Her question seemed aimless and could have been directed at me or Sylvia or perhaps both of us.

"We're going to have sex tonight," Sylvia said to her, "which is exactly what you and Dave should be doing right now since it's your wedding night."

"I'll talk to you both later," I said. "Have a good time."

"Be careful," said Gail.

"What the Hell is that supposed to mean?" asked Sylvia, annoyed again.

"Good night and good luck," I said into the phone, as I hung up.

"Who's next?" Sylvia asked. "Your mother? Your stockbroker? Your ex-girlfriend, Mary? Who's going to call us next tonight?"

"Nobody," I answered, as I turned off my cell phone.

Sylvia led me back into the part of the living room where she had set up the altar. She handed me the black ceremonial robe, which I put on over my white tuxedo shirt and she put hers on over her yellow dress. I stood anxiously in the middle of the room, opposite the large symbol of Baphomet. I felt that the goat inside the pentagram was staring at me, and then I realized it wasn't just a goat, but Satan. Sylvia reached up to the altar and pulled off a silver chalice, which she brought into the kitchen, and then returned immediately with it.

"What are we going to be drinking?" I asked, as I watched her replace the chalice on the black altar.

She turned her exotic eyes in my direction and stared at me for a moment. After a few seconds of silence, she asked, in a somewhat nervous voice, "Drinking?" Her expression resembled that of a little girl caught trying to get into a cookie jar.

"Yes," I answered. "What are we going to be drinking? In the chalice?"

"Oh, in the chalice!" she exclaimed with relief, as she clapped her palm to her breast and sighed. "That pineapple juice you bought at the store. That's all that's in the chalice." She filled it up and drank the entire contents herself, then refilled it for the two of us.

Sylvia stepped to her front door and locked it. I mentioned it to her, and she laughed and replied, "Well, it certainly wouldn't do to have someone walk in on us, now would it?"

Jokingly, I added, "Yes, and I suppose that's one way of keeping me in here if I should change my mind in

173

the middle of the ritual."

Sylvia stared at me sadly, as if about to cry. "Oh please don't tell me you're having second thoughts about this now. I don't know what I would do if you changed your mind."

I put my arm around her and we hugged. Then as we held each other, gazing into each other's eyes, our lips met. Her hands held the back of my head as we kissed. After I caught my breath, I said, "I'm not changing my mind at all. I was only kidding. Though I must admit I'm pretty nervous. I've never taken part in a Satanic ritual before."

"Then you're sure you want to go through with this?"

"Absolutely!" I reassured her. "If I were to let you slip through my fingers now, I'd really feel like a fool. It's going to be great, waking up together every day."

"Then let the ritual begin," she declared, as much to the Baphomet as to me. With that, she lit several black candles on the altar and switched off all the lights in the apartment. We stood in her living room, illuminated solely by the burning candles, which cast strange shadows around the room as they flickered.

She stepped towards the altar and took a bell off of it, then lifted her arm up and down in front of the altar, making it ring, shattering the silence in the room. Then, turning counterclockwise, she repeated the movement, and kept repeating it till she had rung the bell nine times, with the final time in front of the Baphomet.

Sylvia then lit some incense in an ornate silver holder, and the fumes billowed out profusely, casting new shadow and shapes against the walls and us. As the room filled with the pungent aroma of the incense, she raised her hands just slightly above her face, and stretched them out towards the pentagram.

"Hail Satan!" she called out.

"Hail Satan!" I repeated.

"Hail Satan, Lord of Darkness, and friend. We, the children of the night, greet you as a brother and friend. This evening we unite our magical selves with you, as we join our magical and physical selves to each other." Sylvia grasped the chalice in her hand and held it out to me. "With this chalice, we share our magical essence." She drank from it, then handed it back to me. I swallowed the remaining pineapple juice and handed the empty chalice back to her.

By this time, the incense had totally engulfed the apartment, and the thickness of the air changed the atmosphere to such a degree, I felt that at any moment the smoke would clear, and we would be standing at the Gates of Hell.

As this thought came into my consciousness, Sylvia seized the dagger from the altar, and pointed it at the Baphomet, and then called out, "From the South, I call forth Satan," then she turned to her left, pointed the dagger again, and said, "From the East I call forth Lucifer," So the ceremony went; she called for Belial from the North, and Leviathan from the West, until she faced the Baphomet again.

Still facing the Baphomet, she pointed the dagger at it and traced an inverted pentagram in the air. "Thus, with my power, as a Priestess of Satan, do I open the Gates of Hell!"

To my great relief, she replaced the dagger on the altar. It pleased me that it had only a symbolic use, and was not for human sacrifices, especially since I was the only other human in the room with her. Perhaps I was unreasonably cautious, but with all I had heard from sensationalized reports on witchcraft, the ceremony had me nervous, even if Sylvia was the one performing it.

Sylvia took both of my hands in hers, and smiled at me. Her smile emanated as much from those black piercing eyes, as it did from her full and sexy lips. She turned her pretty face towards the altar, then said, "Satan, we have come before you on this night to be joined together as one flesh, one blood. I, Sylvia Martin, pledge myself to Satan, and further, do I pledge myself to Mark Sheridan. Sylvia turned to me, holding both my hands in hers, then asked, "Do you, Mark Sheridan, pledge yourself to me, Sylvia Martin?"

"Yes, I do," I answered.

"Then, by the Powers of Darkness within me, do I join us together as one flesh and one spirit!" So speaking, Sylvia's expression changed from one of formal solemnity to that of delighted glee, and she placed both her arms around my neck and we kissed each other long and passionately.

The ceremony was over, I concluded. How little time it lasted, considering the weight of the event, and its effect upon my life. It seemed to me like a shortened wedding ceremony and now we were heading straight for the honeymoon. I was about to ask Sylvia what we did next, when she answered me first.

"That's the first part," she explained. "We finished the formal ceremony. There are only two more steps needed."

"Oh, I thought that was it," I said. "What is the second step?"

"The second step is lots of fun," she explained, with a sexy smile.

Sylvia led me by the hand out of the incense-filled living room, and back to her bedroom. She lit over a dozen candles in various places close to the bed.

"I want everything to be perfect," she said.

"What could possibly go wrong?"

"Oh, you'd be surprised."

"Okay, surprise me," I said. "I like surprises."

"I'm certainly glad to hear *that*!" Sylvia responded.

She pulled back a black velvet bedspread to reveal

pink satin sheets underneath. She removed my black robe, then started to unbutton my shirt.

After she removed my shirt, her hand reached under my pants. She began to rub me gently, giving me an instant erection. I slowly unzipped her yellow dress. It fell to the floor, revealing Sylvia's matching yellow lace bra and panties. Even in the candlelight, I could make out her nipples pressing against the silk fabric of the bra and the black triangle of her pubic hair under the sheer yellow panties. Slowly, Sylvia lowered herself to her knees, unfastened my belt and pulled down my pants. Then she slid her bra off in a smooth motion, pulled on the elastic and let go, shooting it like a slingshot across the room onto a chair as she laughed.

"Why don't you help me get these panties off?" She pushed down on my shoulders with the palms of her hands to get me on my knees.

She continued standing as I pulled her panties down, and only when I got them to her ankles and my knees were on the floor did she lift each foot to step out of them. Then I stood back a couple feet. My heart skipped and I took a deep breath. I had never seen a woman that perfect—not in person, not in a movie, not in a photo. In her clothes, Sylvia was stunning, but naked, she surpassed anyone. The tiniest waist combined with the curves of her hips focused the eye right to the soft black pubic hair in the center. And she was looking right back at me with such adoration in her eyes. I had never experienced a feeling like that before.

But then, in all my desire for her, I suddenly remembered to say the politically correct and responsible thing. "Oh, I almost forgot. I brought protection."

"Protection?" Sylvia asked. "Protection against what?"

I held up a condom in a foil package.

Sylvia snatched the package from me, opened it,

removed the condom and blew it up like a balloon, then tied a knot at the end. She pulled out a lipstick from her purse and drew a smiley face on the inflated condom. "There you go," she said. "Now you have a new smiling friend to protect you."

"What about safe sex?" I asked.

"Safe sex is an oxymoron," Sylvia replied. "Sex is never safe. You could fall in love with the wrong person."

"What about pregnancy?" I asked.

"I can't get pregnant."

"Well, it's also to protect against diseases. You know — bodily fluids. That sort of thing."

"How unromantic. I want us to exchange as much bodily fluids as possible. Preferably *all* of them."

Sylvia approached and put her arms around my neck and I circled her waist, looking deep into her black, exotic eyes, with their slight upward curve like a perpetual smile. Her long, silky, black hair covered her shoulders, and touched the top of her breasts, but stopped just short of her nipples. We stood and kissed each other, her probing tongue and full lips not just inviting, but aggressive. Sylvia's slight height advantage made our embrace feel more intense, like there were no limits to how strong our passions could be expressed. She was feminine without being delicate. Even the slightest of our movements meshed with each other in perfect harmony. All the feelings I had for Sylvia could be expressed physically now because they were being returned in full measure.

Somehow, we found ourselves on the bed lying down. I noticed the smooth feel of the pink satin sheets, but then something else — a crinkly sound, like a plastic sheet underneath.

"Plastic sheets?" I asked.

"It's a brand new mattress," Sylvia explained.

"Don't you want to take the plastic sheet off?"

"No, it will protect the mattress."

"Protect it from what?" I asked, almost mirroring her words on the condom.

"From getting wet!"

"Wet!" I said with a laugh. "And I thought you were joking with Mary about the golden showers."

Sylvia cocked her head to one side, grinned, and arched an eyebrow.

"You could always put down a towel if you're worried about a wet spot," I said.

"Oh, I'm not worried about a wet spot — I'm planning on one."

Sylvia put her arms around me as we lay together and she grabbed my head and pushed me down the length of her body till my face was in her black pubic hair. She wrapped her thighs around my head and I placed my hands on the sides of her hips. She clutched my hair and pulled my face in between her legs.

"Have you found that wet spot yet?" she asked playfully.

"Yes, it seems to be right here," I said. Sylvia had the most delightful scent and taste. It evoked such an intense feeling, I felt almost as if this were my first sexual experience again.

"Do you like belly dancing?" Her eyes gazed into mine as she held my head.

"I'm sorry," I answered, "but I never learned how."

"No, I mean do you like it if *I* move like that? Like this." And with those words, she started a slow and sensual gyration that had the same mesmerizing effect on both of us. Her movements became faster and stronger and her breathing matched her movements, until finally she grabbed me by the hair firmly as her whole body shuddered and her eyes narrowed to slits that flickered.

We lay there together for a few minutes with her holding my head there, then finally she changed positions, pulling me up so my head rested on the pillow while her head went down. The combination of her skills with her lips and tongue and seeing that beautiful face, with her eyes looking up at me the entire time—worked its magic on me, and she returned the satisfaction I had given her.

"That was great!" I said afterwards. "And you swallowed everything."

"You bet I did!" Sylvia nodded. "I think we're both going to be doing a lot more swallowing before the night is over."

"I don't think we have anything left to swallow," I said, thinking how we were both completely spent.

"We've still got plenty left to swallow," Sylvia replied. "More than you can imagine." Sylvia changed positions. She pulled herself up the length of the bed, so we lay side by side. Then she draped one of her legs over mine and placed her hand on my shoulder so that we faced each other. "Tonight was wonderful. Everything I'd hoped it would be." She shifted position again slightly so that I moved onto my back and she lay partly on top of me. Her hand rested on my shoulder. "I'm wondering if this is a good time for us to be honest with each other."

"It's always a good time to be honest," I answered. "And I have been completely honest with you."

"I know *you've* been honest," Sylvia admitted. "But I was referring to me. Will you still feel the same way about me if I told you everything about me?"

"Of course I would. What could you possibly say that could make me not love you?"

"What if I said that Father Callen was really telling you the truth?"

"Don't be ridiculous!" I answered. "I know he's crazy."

"What if I said that Gail was right, that I killed Graystone and Harry, your last neighbor?"

"I know Gail would say anything to turn me against

180

you. I don't believe her."

"Then what if I said that I killed the two men in the alley right before they were about to kill you? That I saw you put up a great fight, but I knew one of them was going to shoot you, so I grabbed him and ripped his throat open and drank his blood and then snapped the neck of his friend. You remember what you saw — or what you didn't see. You remember the few seconds you thought you blacked out. That was me hypnotizing you not to see, *just as I'm hypnotizing you now so you can't get up or move.*"

With those last words from her, I found my body frozen and utterly paralyzed. But unlike someone paralyzed, I could still feel my entire body. I just couldn't move it. Although her palm and fingers had but the slightest touch on my shoulder and her body weight could not begin to pin me to the bed, some other force kept me lying inert. Was it her voice? Her mind? I didn't know.

But I suddenly realized that her voice had taken on a different quality in that last sentence, like an amplified whisper that echoed inside my head. I recognized where I had heard it before — in the erotic, but frightening dream I had the night my window lock was snapped off. So it hadn't been a dream after all.

"Isn't this hypnotic power wonderful? It has all the sexual advantages of bondage, but without those nasty rope burns. I'd hate to have to put you through *that!*" She nodded happily to show her sincerity. "I really wish I could hypnotize you every night. It has so much potential. It's such a shame I'll only be able to do it tonight. But as long as we're here, let's have fun with it."

I struggled to get away, but without success. My mind and body were now disconnected. I couldn't move even a hand or foot. Sylvia shifted to the side of me again. I could follow her with my eyes, but move my head only slightly. The rest of my body couldn't budge, and I realized then that it didn't matter how much I wanted to escape—whatever happened next would be totally up to her.

"I could do anything I want right now," she explained. She poked me in the shoulder with her sharp fingernail. "Why, I could put a tattoo on your shoulder now. It could say 'Sylvia' inside a heart. I think that would be romantic." Sylvia frowned for a second. "But wait. That would be crazy. A tattoo lasts a lifetime, but yours would only last a night. What would be the point of that?"

I tried to speak, but no words would come out. Sylvia seemed to notice this for the first time.

"Oh, I'm sorry. I didn't mean to stop you from speaking. *You can talk now.*"

"Let me up!" I yelled.

"*No yelling!*" Sylvia insisted as she clapped her hand over my mouth. "Do you want our neighbors to come bursting in here like they did when I killed Harry?"

I tried to nod my head yes.

"Well *I* don't want anyone bursting in on us. I think it's much more romantic with just the two of us alone together. Don't you agree? *Speak quietly, please.*"

I suddenly felt like she had turned down the volume of my voice. I could still speak, but not loudly. "So now you plan to kill me like you did Harry and the guys in the alley."

"Mark, I killed those men in the alley because they were going to kill you. I killed Harry so I could move in next door to you. Can't you see how everything worked out for the best?"

"So Father Callen told me the truth about you murdering hundreds of people?"

"Who counts? Do you count all your sex partners? Who keeps track of such things? I don't even want to think about it right now. I don't want to do anything to spoil the romance of this moment. Let's think happy thoughts!"

"Now I see why you said you've been unlucky in love."

Sylvia smiled. "I'm glad to see you haven't lost your sense of humor. Most men in your position would actually be afraid of dying right now. But not you. You still can see the rainbow through the clouds. I think that's one of the things I like about you."

"Let me leave now and I won't tell anyone what happened tonight."

"Really?" Sylvia asked, cocking her head to one side. "You promise not to tell? I'm so glad to hear you're discreet. But surely, you wouldn't leave me all alone here by myself? Oh, I couldn't bear that, especially after we had such a wonderful night together. No, I have a much better idea. Let's fulfill our sexual fantasies. *Open your mouth wide.*"

Just as before, I found my body unable to resist anything she said. She took her index finger and poked me in the tongue with a sharp fingernail to make sure my mouth was completely open. Then she picked up each of my arms and spread them straight out with my palms up, and I realized that my naked body now lay in the exact same position as a crucifixion. She placed her left knee on the side of my face, then swung her other leg over my head until she was positioned right over my mouth. I still couldn't speak, but I wondered why she felt she had to use her hypnotic power if all she wanted was more oral sex, since I had been happy to give her all she wanted without the hypnosis. But that's not all she wanted.

"Since you can't move, I could pee in your mouth right now. Isn't that wonderful? We can do the golden showers I was talking about at the wedding."

"Wait!" I said, as loudly as I could, which wasn't very loud.

"Wait?" she asked. "Wait for what?"

"Don't do it."

"Why not? I've got the plastic sheet underneath if you can't swallow it all. You're hypnotized so you can't get up or leave. What could be better than that?"

"I can't drink all of your urine."

"That's okay, Mark. Nobody's perfect. Just do the best you can. If you can't swallow it all, the plastic sheet will protect my new mattress."

"I don't want to swallow any of it."

"That's not fair. I swallowed when you came in my mouth. Besides, I've done everything I can to make it enjoyable for the both of us. I skipped the asparagus at dinner because I knew it would ruin the taste and I drank the pineapple juice because I knew it would improve the taste. Surely you can see how considerate I've been."

"If you were considerate, you wouldn't put me through this humiliation while you're trying to kill me."

"Mark, you're not making any sense now. There's nothing humiliating about swallowing. It's probably only about twelve ounces—about as much as a can of soda, only better. I'll be swallowing a lot more than that tonight. I can tell you that."

"I don't want to have a contest with you to see who can drink the most urine," I said.

"Who said anything about *me* drinking urine? I'm going to be drinking your *blood*. You're the one who's going to be drinking my pee. And Mark, this isn't some silly wine tasting where you swish it around in your mouth and then spit it out. That would hurt my feelings. I really want to see and hear you swallow it all. That's what would make me happy. You do want to make me happy, don't you?"

"Not so much right now." I tried to shake my head, but between being frozen by hypnosis and her thighs on each side of my head, I really couldn't move.

184

"Well, Mark, you mustn't be selfish in bed. But then, who am I to judge?"

"Wait!" I said again. "Don't do it."

Sylvia looked down at me and sighed. "I wish you wouldn't speak while I'm trying to pee in your mouth. It's so distracting. You're making me nervous."

"*I'm* making *you* nervous?"

"Yes, of course. I'm as nervous trying to pee in your mouth as you'll be when you're drinking it."

"I don't want to drink your urine."

"Well, okay then, don't think of it as urine. Think of it as recycled pineapple juice. Recycling is good for the environment. It prevents global warming. My God, Mark! Don't you even care about the polar bears?"

She began to hum a musical piece that I didn't recognize by name, but it sounded like Bach. At the same time, she drummed out a sort of rhythm with her fingernails on my forehead as she avoided eye contact. Finally, she spoke again. "Dammit! I hope you're satisfied. With all your protests, you've made me so nervous, I can't pee in your mouth. Oh, I hate it when that happens," she said sadly.

Sylvia dismounted from her position above my head and lay beside me, just inches away. She put her hand on my shoulder. "Do you know what's coming up now?" she asked, her eyes wide with excitement.

"I think so," I answered. "I saw the guys in the alley and Harry." The bloody memory filled my mind with images I didn't want to remember.

"Oh Mark. I love you. I would never do anything like that to you."

"Then you aren't going to drink my blood?" I asked with surprise and relief.

"Of course I'm going to drink your blood. I'm just not going to make a mess like I did with them. But you know what's ironic? I didn't get to drink that much blood from the boys in the alley or from Harry—all because you interrupted me. I'll actually get to drink much more of *your* blood because no one will interrupt us now. Isn't that funny?"

"No, it's not funny."

"I meant funny as in ironic, not humorous. Do you have a headache?"

"If I said I did, would it make a difference in what you're going to do?"

"Yes. It's too bad you don't have a headache because then I could show you how I can take the pain away with my hypnotic power. When I drank blood from Harry and the man in the alley, it hurt them and I didn't care, but I don't want to hurt you. I can bite you and drink all your blood with no pain at all if you like."

"I'd like you to skip the blood drinking altogether."

"I'm sorry, Mark. That's not one of the options. It's either with the pain or without the pain. Take your pick." She held out both hands and emphasized the two choices. When I wouldn't answer her, she went on. "Alright then. *I'll* choose for you. Since I love you, I choose no pain because I wouldn't do anything to hurt you."

She got up from the bed and opened a drawer from the nightstand next to it, then pulled out a pincushion bristling with different size pins. She set it on the bed next to me.

"These pins are much smaller than my teeth, but let me just show you the difference between pain and no pain." She picked the largest pin from the pincushion and jabbed it into my right shoulder.

"Ow!" I protested, but I still couldn't move.

"Now, when I put this pin in your other shoulder, you will feel no pain." True to her word, she jabbed me with a similar pin in my left shoulder. Although I could feel it in there, I felt no pain. "Well, isn't that much better?" she asked.

186

I could see each shoulder had a small trickle of blood from the pins. Sylvia pulled the pins out and licked the blood away with her tongue. As she did that, her eyes half-closed in ecstasy.

When she opened her mouth, I noticed that her canine teeth were now long and sharp. That beautiful face combined with the long, sharp canine teeth had an impact on me that both terrified and titillated me at the same time.

"I don't want you to feel any pain," Sylvia said. She lay on top of me, put her face next to mine and whispered in my ear, "Remember that I love you very, very much." She took both my arms and placed them around her as if I were hugging her. Although I could feel her with my arms, I had neither the power to hug her or push her away. They just stayed in the position she put them in. Then I felt the soft brush of her lips against my neck right before she opened her mouth and her two sharp canine teeth rested against the skin for a second. When she bit down, I felt the piercing of the skin, but under her hypnotic trance, I did not feel the pain. The sensation unnerved me, knowing that blood was coming out of me quickly, some into her mouth, some running down the side of my neck onto the pink satin sheets and then onto the plastic sheet underneath. The odd juxtaposition of her soft lips and embrace with the sharp teeth and the blood loss put me in a state of terror I had never experienced before. This seemed to go on forever. I lost all track of time. I began to feel lightheaded and cold despite Sylvia's warm body on top of mine. The thought suddenly came into my mind that I was going to die in the next few minutes, when an odd revelation came to me. I was 33 — the same age as Bruce Lee and Jesus when they died. Now I was going to die at 33, except that I would be forgotten quickly. It would be as though I had never lived.

I began to feel colder still and about to lose consciousness, though Sylvia's naked body on top of mine felt warm and the skin smoother than the satin sheets below me, now wet with my blood. I struggled to stay awake, certain that if I passed out, I would never wake up again. With Sylvia's cheek against mine, I whispered, "You're killing me." With those words, my life seemed to ebb away, and my hands, which Sylvia had placed around her, fell to my sides.

Sylvia immediately stopped drinking my blood, and sat up, looking down at me. I stared up at her, unable to move. Her mouth was covered with my blood, and small rivulets of the life-giving liquid flowed out of both sides of her lips and down her chin onto her neck. She placed her fingers on my vein, as if she was trying to stop my bleeding, but it did no good. My body felt colder with each passing second.

"Oh no!" she cried, "Don't die on me! Please, you mustn't leave me now!" She hugged me and rocked me back and forth, trying to revive my unresponsive body, repeating, "Don't die!"

Then, holding my head in one hand, her other hand moved to her neck, and in one swift movement, her long sharp nails carved a deep gash over her own jugular vein. She pressed it to my mouth, forcing me to drink her blood. I choked on it, and tried to close my mouth, but she pried it open with her slender fingers.

"*Drink me*," she purred in her hypnotic voice. "*Drink my blood*. You mustn't die!"

Again, my body would not obey me—it would obey only her voice. She forced my mouth open and I swallowed her blood against my will, After several minutes, she let her weight rest upon me, and in a low voice, whispered, "There. It is done. We are of one blood."

I stared at her through glazed eyes. She raised her

head and we looked at each other for a moment, but I could no longer see her clearly.

"I love you so much, Mark," I heard her say. "Please forgive me." I tried to focus my eyes upon her face again, but the image blurred, and I slipped into darkness.

Part Two

Chapter One

Out of the darkness, I awakened. It didn't happen all at once, but rather slowly, like a butterfly emerging from its cocoon. First, I became aware that I couldn't be dead after all, and that perhaps I was only waking from a strange and terrible nightmare. I could feel the side of my naked body against the satin sheets, and pressed against the front of my body, the unmistakably smooth skin of someone else. I opened my eyes slowly and squinted against the harsh glare of the light in the bedroom. Sylvia lay next to me, just inches away, with a smile on her pretty face.

"So," inquired Sylvia, "was it as good for you as it was for me?"

I jerked back in a panic and pushed her away as I looked at her face again. No blood, no mark on her neck where she had cut herself. With one hand, I held her away from me, and with my other, I felt my own neck, then checked my hand. No blood on my hand, either, and the skin on my neck felt smooth and unbroken.

Sylvia frowned at me. "Before we performed the ritual, you said you could wake up to my face forever, and here we are, the first time, and you're pushing me away already. It would have been nice if you had kissed me instead of pushed me away." Sylvia pouted, but refused to budge, and remained right next to me on the bed.

"My neck," I said, as I rubbed it, wondering what had happened to the cuts or bruises I knew should have been there. I felt perhaps I was going mad. Had I dreamt the entire incident?

"What about your neck?" asked Sylvia. "It looks

okay to me."

I took everything in. No blood on Sylvia or me. No cuts or bruises on my neck. No blood on the sheets.

"Was it all a dream?" I asked aloud, as much to myself as to Sylvia.

"Was *what* all a dream? Mark, are you having one of your crazy dreams again? If so, I want to hear all about it. And don't leave out any sexual details."

I held my forehead as if I had a headache. "I dreamt you were trying to kill me."

"Now *that's* a crazy dream for sure. I love you Mark. Why would I want to kill the man I love?"

"It seemed so real," I remembered. "There was blood all over me. All over you. All over the sheets."

I glanced around the room. It was the same room, yet somehow it had *changed*. The lights appeared to be brighter. Even the satin sheets looked different. I stared at them again. They *were* different. They were now purple. I distinctly remembered them being pink when we came into the room.

"Are my eyes playing tricks on me?" I asked Sylvia. "I thought these sheets were pink."

Sylvia burst out laughing. "What a funny thing to say. We wake up together after a wonderful night and you care about the color of the sheets. These are purple. The others were pink."

"What happened to them?" I demanded.

Sylvia rose from the bed, not even aware of her beautiful naked body, and walked to the closet and slid the door open and pulled out the pink sheets. Dried blood covered almost half of the bottom sheet. "So which do you prefer? Pink or purple? I prefer the clean ones myself, but I'm keeping these for a souvenir. I'm sentimental like that."

I could barely speak. "So it wasn't just a dream."

"Yes, it was a dream last night. It was something I

191

had been dreaming of for years—and something you had been dreaming of for years and it finally came true."

"This is a nightmare," I said. "Those sheets."

Sylvia sighed in exasperation. "I don't know why you're so upset about the sheets. We can get more. We'll probably get sheets from Dave and Gail as a wedding present when we're married."

"Married?" I yelled. "You still plan to get married after last night?"

"*Especially* after last night," Sylvia explained. "Why do you think I got this ring?" She held her hand straight out toward me with the large heart-shaped diamond symbolizing our commitment to each other.

"I never agreed to any of this!"

Sylvia's eyes registered shock at my words as she gasped and slumped against the wall. She appeared crushed as her eyes welled up with tears. "So after all I've gone through to be with you, now you don't want me? Oh, why don't you just kill me now and put me out of my misery?"

I suddenly felt sympathy for Sylvia despite the situation. "I never said I didn't want you. But if you're really a vampire, how can we possibly live together? Maybe you'll kill me the next time you drink my blood."

"There isn't going to be a next time," Sylvia assured me. "We never need to drink each other's blood again."

"That's good news. Because I don't want you drinking my blood and I would never want to drink anyone else's blood."

"You misunderstood me," Sylvia explained. "I meant that we only had to drink each other's blood that one time. We still have to drink blood—just from someone else."

"*We?*" I asked. "What do you mean, we? Leave me out of this. I'm never drinking anyone's blood. You're the only vampire here."

A look of amusement crossed Sylvia's beautiful face. "You seemed to notice that the cut on my neck was gone."

I nodded in agreement.

"And the cut on your own neck," Sylvia added.

My hand went to my neck and confirmed what I had felt just minutes ago—no cut on my neck, not even a scab.

Sylvia motioned with her hands for me to get up off the bed. We still had no clothes on. "Pick me up," she said.

"What?" I asked, wondering what she really wanted.

"Pick me up completely, like you're going to carry me across the threshold. You know—like you do right after you get married."

I placed one arm around her neck and one under the back of her legs and lifted her up off the floor. I had never felt anyone so light in my life. I walked around the room, through the doorway, down the hall, into the living room and back to the bedroom. I set her back down on the bed.

"What do you think I weigh?"

I thought of all my weightlifting at the gym. "Less than an empty bar at the gym—and that's only forty-five pounds."

"You're off by almost a hundred pounds."

"Did you hypnotize me again?"

"If I could hypnotize you again, it wouldn't be to make you think I'm lighter than I really am. I'd be a lot more creative than that."

"Why do you feel so light?"

"I'm not lighter. You're stronger now. Do you remember the scar on your leg?"

I knew she was referring to a long scar from a bicycling accident years ago. I looked down and saw the scar had disappeared.

"You're stronger and you heal immediately. That's why I said there would be no point in giving you a tattoo because it would last only one night."

"I thought you meant you were going to kill me. You also said we would remember this night for the rest of our lives, no longer how long that was, and that you thought it was a shame you could hypnotize me for only that night. All that pointed to you killing me right then."

"I'm so sorry to put you through that. You misinterpreted what I said. I meant we would remember that night through the rest of our very *long* lives together. The part about hypnotizing you for one night is the saddest of all. I can never hypnotize you again."

"Why not?"

"Because now you're a vampire, too."

"I'm *not* a vampire!" I yelled.

"No yelling!" Sylvia shouted back at me, clapping her palm over my mouth. "Do you want our neighbors to hear us?" She took her hand off my mouth. "What other evidence do you need to believe? Haven't you noticed your hearing is more acute?"

"Not really." Then I picked up the new Patek Philippe watch Sylvia had given me, which I had laid on the nightstand next to her bed. I tried holding it at arm's length to see if I could hear it ticking. "I can't hear anything." I looked at the watch carefully. "It stopped!"

"Of course," Sylvia replied. "You have to wind it every day. If you don't, it will stop after two days. We came home on Saturday night and you've been out for three days. It's Tuesday night."

"Tuesday night? That means I've lost two days of work. I'll be fired!"

"Fired?" Sylvia stifled a laugh. "That's really the least of your worries."

I read once that losing one's job was one of life's more traumatic incidents, but now Sylvia was right—it didn't compare to this. "You mean I've been here for three days?" I started to sit up, but Sylvia lay on top of me and hugged me.

"Yes, and I've been sitting here watching you for three days, hoping you would wake up. You have no idea how worried I've been. But now, everything's going to be fine. You made it through. You survived. Now you're a vampire too, just like me."

Sylvia slowly slid herself off of me, and then holding my hand, pulled me off of the bed. "Take a look in the mirror if you don't believe me."

I was almost afraid to look, to see that she was right, that I would stare into the mirror and see nothing but an empty room in its reflection.

But when I gazed into the mirror, I saw myself staring back. Not only did I look the same, but I could see Sylvia's reflection too, as she came up behind me and placed her arms around me, giving me a big hug.

"If we're vampires, how come I can see our reflections?" I asked.

"Oh that," Sylvia said, with a wave of her hand, signifying how silly the notion seemed to her. "That's just a superstition. It's interesting how it got started. People used to believe that vampires had lost their souls to Satan, and that since they also believed that a reflection showed a person's soul, then vampires supposedly had no reflection. A most interesting legend, don't you think?"

Sylvia smiled broadly, and looking in the mirror again, I did what needed to be done to clear my mind of this, once and for all. I opened my mouth wide, but saw no fangs as I had half-expected. In the mirror stared my own reflection, the same as it always looked, with but one notable exception—the pupils of my eyes now were the same size as the pupils and iris together—just like Sylvia's eyes—and just as she had painted me in the portrait.

"Oh shit," I muttered, half to myself. "You're telling the truth. I really am a vampire." I sat back down on the bed and felt the world crumbling away.

"Of course I'm telling the truth." Sylvia put her arm

around my neck. "You don't think I'd lie to you, do you?"

"Why not? You never told me that this was part of our relationship. You never said that you were going to turn me into a vampire." I threw my hands up in frustration and began to step away.

"Well, of course not, Mark. How could I have done that? You might have changed your mind if I had explained everything to you first."

"You bet I would have!" I admitted, shaking my fist in the air.

"There now," said Sylvia, pointing her finger at me accusingly. "See, I was right. You would have changed your mind. So I really had no choice but to explain to you afterwards. I couldn't take the chance that you might leave me." Sylvia bowed her head down and sat next to me on the bed, with her hands folded in her lap.

"If I was unconscious for three days, what were you doing all that time?"

Sylvia's eyes widened in alarm. She glanced away briefly before meeting my eyes again. "If I tell you, do you promise not to get angry?"

"At this point, what else could you possibly tell me that would be more upsetting than all of this?"

"So you promise not to get angry?" Sylvia asked again.

"I'll try," I said, as I waited to hear more bad news.

"Very well, then. After we drank each other's blood, we were both quite a mess. I knew you wouldn't wake up for three days, so I thought I'd be nice and clean us off before you woke up. I was thinking of your feelings, you see. I didn't want you to wake up with blood all over both of us. You can see how considerate I was, right?"

"Go on," I said, knowing there was more to come.

"Anyway," Sylvia continued, "you were out cold and covered with blood, so I picked you up and carried you into the bathroom and put you into the bathtub to wash off all the blood. I really had only the best of intentions. But you know, one thing leads to another. Anyway, I was standing over you in the bathtub, about to turn on the water to clean you off and then—well, you remember all the pineapple juice I had to drink at the wedding and also right before we had sex, and how I wanted to do the golden showers and you didn't want to and you made me so nervous I couldn't even pee? Well, by the time I got you into the bathtub, my nervousness had gone away and the urge to go had come back in a big way, and I thought, why waste this 'golden' opportunity?"

"Dammit," I said. "You peed on me in your bathtub? While I was unconscious?"

"*On* you?" Sylvia repeated. "Not exactly. You've been to a carnival before, haven't you? I have, and I love all the games they have. Sometimes when you win a game, you get a prize, like a stuffed teddy bear or some other animal. I like the little polar bears best. I think they're cute. Don't you?"

"What does this have to do with me in the bathtub?" I asked, growing more irritated by the second.

"I was getting to that," Sylvia said. "At these carnivals, they have these clown faces with a balloon on the top of the head. You get a high-powered squirt gun and aim the water into the clown's mouth and if the balloon bursts, you win a stuffed animal."

An image began to form in my mind. "Tell me you didn't pee in my mouth."

"What can I say?" Sylvia asked. "One thing led to another. I agree with what Oscar Wilde once said: 'I can resist anything but temptation.' You were lying there with your mouth open and I had to go right then, so at first the stream just hit your face to wash off the blood, but then I saw I could aim it even though I was standing up, so almost all of it went into your mouth. Unfortunately, you weren't awake, so you couldn't swallow it. If you had, that would have been perfect. But I guess nothing is perfect, right?" Sylvia smiled with her question.

"No, nothing is perfect," I said, controlling my temper. I slipped on my briefs. Now only Sylvia was completely nude.

Sylvia pointed at me. "You promised not to get angry, but I think you *are* angry."

I put on my socks, then stood and buttoned up my shirt.

"Where are you going?" she asked with surprise.

"To my apartment," I said, as I walked to her door.

"Why?" she pleaded.

"To brush my teeth!"

"Now you're being insulting!"

I reached her door before she did.

"Wait!" she called.

"Wait? Wait for what?" I asked, as I slammed the door behind me.

"For your pants!" I heard her yell through the closed door. I looked down and saw that in all the confusion I had forgotten to put my pants on.

Mrs. McCoy, the elderly neighbor, stood in the hallway with a friend of hers and both stared in shock at the sight of me in the hall in my briefs, socks, and shirt, but no pants. I realized then that I couldn't get into my own apartment because the keys were in my pants in Sylvia's apartment. I knocked lightly on Sylvia's door.

She cracked the door open a couple inches with the chain across it. "Oh, what a pleasant surprise to see you again, Mark. Did you bring me my polar bear?"

"Dammit, Sylvia, let me in."

Sylvia nervously peeped through the narrow opening in the door at me. "Are you still angry with me or do you forgive me?"

"We're not alone," I answered.

Sylvia peered down the hall and saw the two

neighbors. They could see only Sylvia's face and didn't know she would be completely nude behind the door.

"I thought that girl would be trouble," Mrs. McCoy said to me.

"You have no idea," I replied.

Sylvia unlatched the chain and grabbed me by my shirt and pulled me in, then slammed the door behind us.

"If you really think brushing your teeth three days after a golden shower is going to accomplish anything, I already bought you a toothbrush and it's in the bathroom."

"Why would you do something like that?" I asked

"I bought you the toothbrush because I thought we'd be sharing this apartment for now."

"No, I mean why did you do the golden showers while I was unconscious?"

"Why?" Sylvia shrugged her shoulders. "Why does anyone do anything? I did it because it was fun."

"Fun?" I repeated. "That's your idea of fun?"

Sylvia gently placed a hand on my shoulder. "Of course, Mark. What could possibly be more fun than peeing in your mouth? *I* can't think of anything. Look, I only did it one time during the three days. You were unconscious. I could have done it over a dozen times in three days, and believe me, it was quite a temptation. At least give me credit for the remarkable restraint I showed."

"It's not even really sexual," I said.

"Oh, it was for me," Sylvia replied. "I masturbated at the same time and had a wonderful orgasm."

"Now I don't believe you. You can't pee and masturbate at the same time."

"Maybe you can't because you're a man, but I can assure you that as a woman I certainly can." Sylvia grabbed my hand. "Here, come with me into the bathroom and lie down in the bathtub and I'll show you."

"I'm not going to do that," I told her as I saw the disappointment register on her face.

"Why not?" Sylvia asked. "Do you have something better planned for tonight?"

"Anything would be better than that."

Sylvia stared at me with sad eyes. "My only regret is that you weren't awake when I was able to do the golden shower."

"Being unconscious is the only thing I don't regret. At least I can't remember it. If I could, it would make it worse."

Sylvia shook her pretty head. "Oh Mark, the only bad thing about a golden shower is it doesn't last long enough. All the fun is over in a minute or two. I wish it could last an hour." Sylvia nodded enthusiastically as she visualized it. A few seconds later, her expression grew more serious. "Well, since we've covered all the major subjects today such as the color of my sheets, how to wind your new watch, and how we both feel about golden showers, now it's time to think about the minor problems—as a vampire you're going to have to drink people's blood and kill them if you're going to survive."

What the Hell would I do now? I wondered. I lay back on the bed and stared at the ceiling, trying to shut out all thoughts about what had happened to me. Sylvia meekly lay next to me and cuddled against my body, unbuttoning my shirt at the same time. Forgetting, or at least trying to forget what she was, and what I now was too, I drew her close to me, and held her tightly. I tried to pretend that everything was completely normal, that we were just like a normal couple waking up on the first day of a honeymoon together, except that I knew Dave and Gail must have had a much different experience waking up together the next morning. I kept trying to tell myself that we were not vampires, that we were just normal people. I repeated the thought to myself again—normal people. Somehow, my mind had numbed itself to the horror, like a person in shock after the death of a loved one. Yet I knew that I would soon have to leave the emotional security of that withdrawal and face the world—and worst of all, myself, and what I had become.

I pulled the sheet up around my body and withdrew from the world as best as I could, but I could not hide from the truth of what Sylvia and I really were.

"Are you going to just stay in bed all night?" Sylvia poked me with her finger.

I shrugged my shoulders and told her that I didn't know what to do about her, myself, or the whole situation. My mind felt numb from shock, and it only gradually dawned on me what our situation was.

Sylvia hugged me tightly. "Well, as long as you don't want to leave the bed now, then let's make love." She smiled at me, with her wicked teeth flashing.

I turned away from her. "I'm too upset right now. I'm really not in the mood."

She grabbed me by the shoulder and shook me. "Come now, Mark. Don't tell me that. I know that vampires don't get headaches. Besides, I thought you liked to make love to me. Surely you can't be tired of me *already!*"

"Love! How dare you speak to me of love!" I yelled. "You lied to me to trick me into becoming a vampire." I jumped out of the bed in frustration.

She sat up and drew her knees to her body, holding them there with her hands. "Sometimes love can be a bit selfish. But we all have our own motives and reasons for loving someone. We all expect to get something. Your love is not any different than mine."

"What do you mean?"

"You agreed to be with me because you wanted to live with me. You wanted to sleep with me and have my company. I wanted the same things from you. So why all

201

the fuss?"

I considered Sylvia's words, and nodded my head in agreement somewhat reluctantly. Perhaps I didn't like what she said, yet it was true. "But if you wanted to live together, why not just do that? Why did you have to make me a vampire, too?"

"Are you kidding?" she laughed. "Can you imagine me going about at night, killing people, and then coming home at all hours to you? Would you have stayed with me if you had known the truth?"

"I suppose not."

"And then there would be the problem of possibly killing you accidentally in bed. It doesn't take much excitement to make me thirsty for blood. Why do you think I wouldn't go to bed with you at first?"

"I really hadn't considered that as a possible reason."

"Of course, that was one of the reasons I made you a vampire, so we could make love together safely. This way, if I should bite you in a fit of excitement, it won't hurt anything."

I rubbed my neck as she said this, as I remembered her two sharp teeth piercing my skin.

"But the main reason I made you a vampire, is that I want you to stay looking the way you are. If we had just gotten married, and you had somehow adjusted to me being a vampire, and if I hadn't killed you accidentally— and you can be sure I would have—even so, the biggest problem would have been watching you grow into an old man, while I stayed young. Now you'll always be the same as you are right now. You'll never grow older. You'll always be thirty-three, just as I will always be around twenty-five."

"I hadn't thought of that," I admitted. In my anger and fear, this fact had slipped my mind, but now, as I considered its full weight, my situation took on a different light. "I'll always stay young?"

"Always." Sylvia smiled and stood next to me, giving me an affectionate hug, happy to see me on her side once more. "Today is the first day of the rest of your life!"

To always be together with her, to see her just as beautiful in thirty or forty years as she looked right that moment, and to see myself stay exactly the same, in the very prime of my life, to have all of this for eternity! My last few years had been spent in rigorous training at the gym, all for the purpose of looking better, and yet, I always knew that though I might slow down my biological timepiece, it would continue to run towards old age, and that in a few years, even all the exercise in the world wouldn't help. Now, nothing could stop me. As an added bonus, I had a beautiful girl who loved me, and who had the same ability to stay young. It was perfect!

There existed just one major obstacle to this perfect life. "But doesn't this mean that we have to kill people every day? And then won't they become vampires, too?"

"Oh no," Sylvia assured me. "No one can become a vampire unless they drink the blood of a vampire. And vampires only give their blood to people they want to be with permanently. That's how vampires are created. If people could become vampires just by being bitten by a vampire, the entire world would be overrun with us in no time at all. And then whom would we have to feed upon?"

"So Harry won't come back as a vampire?"

Sylvia shook her head. "No, He's gone forever. So are the others."

I asked Sylvia how she had killed the guys in the alley and Harry. She explained that upon following me from the gym, with the purpose of finding out where I lived, she had seen the fight on the street, and then watched as it moved into the alley. When she saw the one boy pull out the gun, she grabbed him by the wrist, crushing his hand, and then ripped his throat out with her teeth. It happened so fast, no one could see, and just as I turned around, she blocked my memory with her hypnotic power—thus the reason I felt I had lost several seconds of time in the alley. That part had been blacked out.

Sylvia told me that she had killed Harry in much the same way, climbing up the fire escape and forcing the window open when she discovered it locked. This snapped the lock right off the window. She quickly climbed inside and attacked Harry. He screamed and struggled, which brought the rest of the tenants, including me, to the door. When I tried kicking down the door, she blacked out part of my memory for a second so I wouldn't see her right before she jumped out of the window to exit quickly.

"From four floors up?" I asked.

"Yes, it didn't hurt one bit. There are so many wonderful things we can do together now." Then Sylvia explained how she had come to my window twice before and entered the room, and even slept with me!

"So you did break the lock on my window," I said, "But how did you get into bed with me without waking me up?"

"A form of hypnotism. I didn't want you to wake up and recognize me. I didn't stay long anyway. I just lay in bed with you the first time. On my second visit, I took some blood, but I was careful not to take too much." She gestured with her fingers to show that it was a small amount. "Really, I've been very careful every step of the way. I planned this all quite well. Now everything is perfect."

"Not quite," I objected. "You still haven't answered my question about whether we need to kill people every day."

"Oh no. Not at all." She brushed away my question with a wave of her hand, and then went on to explain just what we needed to survive. "What we need is their life force, which is contained in their blood as long as they are still alive. We can drink small amounts of blood about once a week to maintain our energy. That way, we kill no one at all because their life force is renewed over time. Or, approximately once a month, we can drain someone of his or her blood to the point of death to keep ourselves alive. Take your pick."

I shook my head sadly at this choice Sylvia offered.

She continued, "It's not the amount of blood we drink that's important—it's the amount of life force we take during the blood drinking. It also depends on the size and age of the victim, as well as how much energy we burn up. If we go out during the day, as I did for the wedding, then more blood and life force is needed to make up for the loss of energy that the sun drains out of us. That's why I killed that man the other night—the one who owned the nice watch similar to the one I gave you. I needed the extra energy to be able to stay out in the sun on Saturday. So, actually, if I count the two boys in the alley, your neighbor Harry, and the man last week, I've killed four people in the last two weeks." She considered this for a moment, and then added, "Of course, the past two weeks haven't been typical. Many things have caused quite a strain on me emotionally,"

"Me too," I retorted, somewhat sarcastically.

Sylvia shrugged her shoulders, causing her shiny black hair to glisten under the light in the room. "Don't worry. You'll get accustomed to it. I did. It takes some time, but then time is one thing you won't have to worry about."

Chapter Two

I considered well, Sylvia's statement concerning my time, because for me, time now had little meaning. The way I used to count the days to my paycheck, or the months left till I would be finished with school—these no longer held any importance for me. Before meeting Sylvia, I suppose I had some vague plan for my life, yet now, none of those plans could fit into my new state of being.

"I don't know what I'm going to do about my life now," I explained to her. "Nothing has any meaning anymore. My job, school, my visits to the gym. I'm supposed to live forever and now I can't even do the things I like."

"I give you eternal life and this is the thanks I get? It looks like no good deed goes unpunished." Sylvia sighed.

"Do we have special powers? Can we turn into bats?"

"So, you want me to show you how to turn into a bat? Very well." Sylvia started a little strip tease, taking off her underwear and twirling her bra around in a big circle. She stopped and stared at me. "Come on, now. Take off your clothes."

"What does that have to do with turning into a bat?"

"Have you ever seen a fully-clothed bat?" Sylvia inquired. "We both need to be naked."

Sylvia had a valid point, plus she was now naked herself, so I followed her example. We stood facing each other, about ten feet apart, our clothes scattered on the living room floor between us.

"Now this part will take all your concentration. Put your arms straight out at your sides as if they were wings." Sylvia held her arms out as an example for me to follow, so I mirrored her movements. "Now close your eyes and visualize yourself as a bat. And as you imagine yourself to be a bat, flap your arms up and down as if they were wings, all the while keeping your eyes tightly closed."

I followed Sylvia's instructions and kept my eyes closed, and through my closed eyes, I suddenly saw a flash of light. When I opened my eyes, I was still standing there nude with my arms out and Sylvia was laughing hysterically as she looked at the digital camera she held in her hand.

"What a great photo!" Sylvia exclaimed. "I can't wait to show it to Susan and Yvette in London!"

I made a rush for the camera and Sylvia dashed through the apartment, leading me back to the bedroom, where she jumped on her bed, bouncing up and down while holding the camera high up in the air and laughing uncontrollably. I leaped onto the bed with her and grabbed for the camera, but she tossed it onto the carpet, then flung her arms around my neck as she began to kiss me. "Would you like to make love?" she asked.

"Of course."

"Then let's do it right now." Sylvia pushed me back on the bed and lay on top of me. "I told you I stayed awake for three days and nights watching you, so as long as you're awake and feeling chipper, I'd like to make love again—if you don't mind."

"Fine, we can make love all night if you like. But what I'm wondering is, what are we going to do for the rest of our lives?"

"Who knows, Mark? I'm not a fortuneteller, just a vampire. Why don't we just take life one day at a time? It's easier that way."

I told her I would do the best I could, and she kissed me and rubbed her body against mine, like a cat seeking affection. Her skin felt different to me now. My perceptions were heightened from the transformation, and her smooth skin felt even silkier than it had the first time. I could smell her better than I could before, and it added a new dimension to our sex. It now became obvious to me why dogs behaved the way they did when they discovered a female in heat. Sylvia's velvety skin, her delightful scent, her light and rapid breathing, and even the beating of her heart—these were magnified many times by my heightened senses. Added to this was her appearance, so exquisite as to almost mesmerize me, and a flood of sensory impressions engulfed my consciousness in a new and strange manner. With her, that first evening of my metamorphosis, I discovered the joy and pleasures of the arts of love in a way I had never known, The sensitivity of our bodies allowed us to respond as one, with wave after wave of pleasure and ecstasy. Much later on, we lay in each other's arms and I hugged Sylvia to me tightly. She had taken everything from my life, and I now had nothing left, except for her. Yet, considering how she wanted so very much to be with me, and when I noted the new attributes that she had bestowed upon me with my transformation, I began to see everything in a clearer perspective.

"Maybe this won't be such a bad existence, after all," I remarked.

Sylvia smiled broadly. Ever since she told me the truth about what she really was, her smiles were wide and cheerful; her face appeared far happier than it had the first week I had known her.

"Oh, we shall have such a wonderful time together, you and I. Just wait and see," she exclaimed happily, and she gave me another affectionate hug.

Her body felt so light to me, that she could have stayed in the same position, lying on top of me, forever. I realized that part of the sensation of her lightness was actually my increased strength as a vampire.

"Perhaps I should explain just what we can do as vampires and what we can't do," she said. She then elucidated some of the particular abilities vampires have:

"Heightened senses, increased strength, the ability to see in the dark, the power of controlling someone's will through a sort of hypnotic power—"

"So I'm guessing the legends aren't true about changing into bats?" I interrupted. How about sleeping in coffins? Tell me everything."

Sylvia laughed. "We can't turn into bats, I'm afraid. You see, vampire bats were named after vampires, not the other way around. They're only animals, after all. We're supernatural creatures. Bats have more in common with humans than with us. However, I can teach you how to turn into a polar bear. To do that, of course, you'll have to take off your clothes, get into my bathtub, close your eyes, and open your mouth."

"Not tonight."

"Very well," said Sylvia. "I'll take that as a rain check."

"What about sleeping in coffins?"

"No, we sleep in beds—not coffins."

"Then why have I always heard that vampires slept in coffins?"

"Mainly because you watch too many movies. But part of that belief was due to the plague in the seventeenth century. Many people were buried prematurely, then thought to 'come back to life' when they were never really dead to begin with. Another reason is that in the past, a coffin was one of the few places a vampire could stay undetected. Remember that hundreds of years ago, more people believed in vampires than in our modern enlightened times. They were constantly on the lookout for us. We couldn't blend into society as well as we can now. Cities were far smaller in those days, and people didn't move about from one town to the next as modern people do. When a stranger arrived in town, everyone took notice. No one could ever mind his or her own business. Imagine what would happen if a vampire, with a pale face and nocturnal habits, suddenly moved in among these superstitious townsfolk and tried to fit in! It would only take a few days to see that the vampire didn't eat food often or go out during the day, and the town would be suspicious. And how could one search for victims with such nosy people about? Some vampires tried living among humans, but almost all were discovered and destroyed. Some tried living in barns and deserted houses, but most found that it was easiest to avoid detection by sleeping in coffins. Also, coffins were the first places that vampires emerged from, so both people and vampires believed that that was where vampires lived. After all, if a vampire has lived all of his life as an ignorant peasant in a superstitious village, he usually just becomes an ignorant vampire, full of the same idiotic superstitions as the living. Most vampires did not last long in those days, since so many people were out to get them. Not only did the people get most of the vampires, they killed many more innocent people whom they believed to be vampires. It was much like the witch hunts, only there were fewer victims of vampire-hunters than of witch-hunters, and fortunately, most victims were just corpses anyway, not the living or real vampires. To survive, many vampires tried sleeping in coffins, since graveyards were generally such desolate places, especially at night. Who, in their right mind, would have walked around in a graveyard after dark?

"But as cities and customs changed, vampires changed their habits too. Cities became crowded. People no longer noticed an odd-looking stranger in their midst anymore because there were just too many strangers to account for. That is why there are so many more vampires in cities than out in the country."

"That's strange," I remarked. "I always thought that it was out in the country—the woods in Transylvania, perhaps—that vampires lived."

"Oh no," Sylvia declared. "It's only that the people who lived out in the country always had their eyes open for such things, and if one was found, the whole village would hear of it. But there are far more vampires in cities. It's much easier to find victims and exist undetected, So many crazy murders happen all the time, the police don't know what to do!" Sylvia laughed at her remark, like a little schoolgirl giggling with a group of friends over a joke played on a teacher.

I asked her if she worried about getting caught by the police, as this problem seemed to be our biggest threat.

"I'm careful, but I don't really worry about it too much."

"But what if you were caught?"

"Oh, I have been caught. *Many* times."

"You have?" I asked, somewhat astonished. "How did you get away?"

"How did I get away?" Sylvia appeared amused by my question. "Mark, you must be kidding, I don't have to get away. If anyone catches me, I can I kill them. Or I can hypnotize them to forget that they ever saw me." Her confidence in our ability to defend ourselves reassured me. I needed to feel more secure about what we would be doing. I questioned her some more on the subject, and she told me that the police couldn't shoot us, so the main threat to our existence would be lack of blood if we didn't find a victim when we needed one. She told me not to worry about crucifixes or anything else.

"Then nothing can kill us?"

"Not much. At night, we're too powerful. But by day, we're not as strong. We could be killed in our sleep. We can be wounded like humans in the day, but we recover so quickly that many a vampire-hunter has died trying to drive a stake through the heart of some vampire, only to miss the heart by an inch, and then wake him up. Usually, when vampires had been killed, the deed was done by a group of people during the day. They had several people so they could move swiftly. One man to hold the stake. Another for the hammer. As soon as the hammer pounded in the stake," Sylvia demonstrated by pretending she had driven it into my heart, "then another man would take a hatchet, and cut off the vampire's head." With that, Sylvia drew her finger across my neck, to let me live through the whole experience. "Then they would take the head and body and burn them together. So, if anyone does that to either of us, then that's it. We're finished."

"Then I guess we better find Father Callen before he finds us," I said.

Sylvia readily agreed with a nod of her pretty head. "Yes, we'll have to find him, but right now we have a far more immediate need—one which we will have to fulfill tonight," she explained to me in a serious tone.

I knew she was right. Already I could feel a strange hunger in my stomach and a thirst in my mouth unlike any other. My jaw felt wonderfully powerful, like a beast of prey whose teeth were its primary weapon. I ran my tongue over them with wonder at how strong they now felt in my mouth. Though my canine teeth barely exceeded their former length, I felt especially conscious of them, and realized they would grow when needed, just as Sylvia's did right before she bit me.

Sylvia seemed to know my thoughts. "We'll have to go out tonight, but not right this minute. You've been unconscious for three days. You must be hungry."

Sylvia led me by the hand into her kitchen and asked me what I wanted to eat. I shrugged my shoulders and opened her refrigerator.

"What the Hell?" I asked as I saw bottles of pineapple juice filled one of the racks.

"While you were out cold for three days, I took the liberty of ordering out for more pineapple juice."

"Yeah. That's not the only liberty you took while I

was unconscious. I hope you don't think all that pineapple juice is going to make its way into me second-hand."

"You think I took advantage of you, but now you have the advantage."

"How do you figure that?" I asked.

"I can never hypnotize you again and you'll never be unconscious like you were for three days. I can't repeat what I did the other night. I must rely on just my good looks and charm. I can only do to you what you let me do. My sexual pleasure is all up to you. I'm completely at your mercy."

"I would hardly put it like that."

"Mark, don't you know that *all* women try to change their men? I hope we'll eventually both like the same activities. After all, we're going to be together for eternity anyway, but if we're not both sexually satisfied, eternity will seem so much longer."

"Maybe we'll have to see a marriage counselor later," I said.

"I don't think that will be necessary," Sylvia assured me. "You'll eventually adjust to your new life with me. To be honest with you, I've often peed in a man's mouth after I drank all his blood and I've never had any complaints before. Of course, by then they were already dead, so maybe that's the reason why. Do you think that makes me a bad person?"

"I think some might say you're a bad person," I agreed.

"Okay, so I'm a bad person. No one's perfect—not even me. But I'm a gourmet cook. Would you like eggs Benedict or strawberry waffles?"

"It's nine o'clock at night," I pointed out.

"But it's our first meal of the day, so it's breakfast," Sylvia explained.

After a delicious breakfast of eggs Benedict,

213

strawberry waffles with real maple syrup, and some freshly squeezed orange juice, Sylvia glanced at the old clock ticking away in the living room. It was 10 p.m. "We shall have to go out soon, but first I must show you how to pick victims, and how to deal with them."

Sylvia then demonstrated methods of stalking people on the street. One technique involved approaching from behind the victim, putting a hand to the victim's mouth to cover any screams, then pulling the head back and biting into the neck from behind. Sylvia demonstrated this on me, then went to her next technique, where she walked towards me, then instead of passing by, bumped into me, pulling my head back by covering my mouth with her left hand, and fixed her mouth on the opposite side of my neck from which she had turned my face. Her final standing method involved standing or walking next to me, with her arm around my shoulder. From this position, she clapped her hand over my mouth, jerking my face away from hers, then attacked the side of my neck closest to her. After demonstrating all three techniques, she had me try them on her. As we practiced, we stopped right as our teeth reached their mark.

"Any questions?"

"Yes. How did you drink my blood when you first saw me without waking me up? It seems like these methods you just showed me would be something a victim would remember."

"When I came into your room, I used a form of hypnosis so that you would not awaken. Then I took off all of my clothes and got into bed with you. As a natural reaction, you put your arms around me. I mentally blocked out the pain of the bite to keep you from waking up, but I didn't block out any feelings of pleasure. That's why you only had the vague recollection of an erotic dream. I only extracted a small quantity of blood from your neck, then I licked the small wounds till they closed

214

back up again."

"How could they close back up again after you bit into my neck? Wouldn't the holes be too big?"

"No. You see, if I continue to suck on the vein, the holes stay the same size and the blood keeps flowing out, but if I stop, the blood will clot at the wound, and the bleeding will slow down. But the main reason it stopped is because something in a vampire's saliva has a healing effect."

"You must be joking," I said with a laugh.

"No, I'm not. If you had cut your hand, and I had licked it, the cut would close up and heal. But I can't show you such a demonstration anymore."

When I asked Sylvia why, she brought me into the living room and then took down her ceremonial dagger from the altar. She held the blade to her wrist, and before I could stop her, she drew it across in one sweeping motion. Nothing happened, Her wrist looked the same as before. "You see?" she asked, and then as further proof held the blade to my wrist. I pulled it away and Sylvia started at my unwillingness to participate in her little demonstration. "Don't be silly, Mark. It can't hurt you." She grabbed my hand and slashed across my wrist with the blade of the dagger. It felt as dull as a butter knife. My wrist couldn't be cut. I stared at it in amazement.

"We can't be hurt." I felt my wrist and marveled at the thought.

"Unless we want to," Sylvia explained.

"Why would we want to?"

"Who knows? For whatever reasons we should so choose. Here, look at this." She drew the blade across her wrist once more, but this time it sliced right through her skin and the blood ran into her hand as she cupped her palm. "Here, try some," she said, offering her bloody hand to me, as she smiled at her little demonstration.

"Are you crazy?" I yelled, as I glanced around the

room in a panic for something to stop the bleeding.

Sylvia grabbed me by the shoulder and pointed at her wrist. The bleeding had stopped by itself. She licked the spot where the blade had passed, cleaning off the blood from her hand with her tongue. I looked at her wrist again. The cut had disappeared.

"Thanks for your concern, Mark. But you see, you needn't worry. I can bleed when I want to, like when I cut my throat to let you drink my blood."

"So we can't bleed unless we want to."

"With one exception."

"What's that?"

"We can make each other bleed if we bite each other. But that shouldn't be a problem." Sylvia paused for a moment in reflection, and then in a solemn tone, added, "At least I hope not."

"Why would that be a problem?" I felt somewhat suspicious about the manner in which she spoke.

"Oh, don't worry." She turned her head away from me, something I had never seen her do while talking to me. "Everything will work out. I just know it will."

Somehow, her tone didn't sound reassuring, and I hoped that the time for any secrets between us had passed. Perhaps there was no secret. Perhaps it was only an overreaction on my part to her tone of voice, yet she conveyed a sense of melancholy that unsettled me and aroused my curiosity.

"Is there anything else I need to know about this?"

"No, not really. I'll explain things as they come up. It's really not that complicated. But we should probably get dressed and go out. This is a good time to find someone. Then we'll have the whole night afterwards to do as we please."

We dressed quickly, and before we left, I looked at my new watch. It was only 10:30. I looked out the window. The stars twinkled from a clear black sky, just

216

like the lights of downtown off in the distance. I turned around and Sylvia stood staring at me, waiting for us to go out together.

"This whole thing has me kind of nervous. I don't want to kill anyone."

Sylvia buttoned up her black velvet jacket. "Yes, I know. I understand. I really do. So how's this? Tonight we won't kill anyone. We'll just drink enough blood to get by for a while. Maybe that will make this first time easier for you." She stared at me with a certain amount of sympathy, then motioned that we had to leave. She withdrew a key from her pocket and locked it as we left.

"Do I get a key to this place too?" I asked her.

"Here, take this one." Sylvia handed it to me. "It's the only one I have, but we'll be together all of the time anyway, so it doesn't matter who carries the keys."

Though Sylvia had absolutely no qualms about what we were about to do, and I felt apprehensive, we strode out into the crisp night air arm in arm, with the same irresistible and growing thirst.

Chapter Three

As we drove downtown, Sylvia entertained me by singing along with the radio. She draped an arm around my neck and leaned against my shoulder. I steered with my left hand and held her with my right, which was awkward when I had to shift gears. I don't know whether she held me tighter out of affection or if I held her tighter for the same reason, or if it stemmed from my nervousness.

I told Sylvia not to expect many people out on a Tuesday night, especially since she had asked me to drive to a poorer section of the city. We settled on the Tenderloin, known for its prostitutes, junkies, alcoholics, and muggers, as well as its senior citizens in sleazy hotels, and a Vietnamese community. The Tenderloin was, for some, a temporary place to stay when new to the city, until luck or hard work brought them out. But for others, it remained a bleak and dangerous neighborhood. By day, it looked far more cheerful, as it was one of the sunniest areas in San Francisco. Indeed, many times my own apartment out in the Richmond District had been shrouded in fog, while the Tenderloin and all of the Downtown area basked in the sun. But now it was night, and the darkness covered the entire city without regard to the wealth or social status of its inhabitants.

Sylvia had specifically requested that we find an area that had the most violence so we would raise less suspicion in case there were any "complications."

We circled the neighborhood several times, and then Sylvia asked me to park on Geary and Mason Street. From there we walked down Mason towards Market Street and on the way a veritable sideshow of humanity opened to Sylvia's curious eyes. Transvestites, fully dressed in garish outfits, stood outside the entrances to nightclubs and winked at passersby. Pimps dressed in bright-colored suits stood leaning against their equally bright-colored Cadillacs. Junkies made deals with each other, eyes furtively glancing in every direction before making their transactions with eager hands.

"When I first met you, I never thought I'd be taking you for a walk in this neighborhood," I said, shaking my head.

"Life is just full of surprises, isn't it?" Sylvia flashed her wicked smile.

She stopped for a moment and looked around, taking stock of our location, then suggested we move to somewhere less crowded. I led her down to Turk Street, where we turned right. Only a few people could be seen on the dreary street.

"And now for the moment of truth!" Sylvia announced to me with a flourish. "Take your pick from any of these fine specimens here on this street." She glanced at a prostitute walking towards us. "She's quite pretty. You might enjoy her."

"But she's so young. I would feel guilty in case something went wrong and I drank enough blood to kill her."

Sylvia pointed across the street to a black man, dressed in stylish, but well-worn clothes. "He's probably a drug dealer. You could kill him. You'd be doing the police and the community a public service." Sylvia nodded her head.

"To tell you the truth, I don't feel like killing anybody. And you said we didn't have to. That we could just take a little blood."

Sylvia pointed at an elderly woman hobbling by with a shopping bag filled with old clothes, apparently a hobo who lived out of the bag she carried, and slept on the sidewalks. "Take *her*," cried Sylvia. "She has nothing to live for. Any joy or happiness allotted for her lifetime by fate has been spent many years ago. Her future is only a succession of sleepless nights on hard pavements. *Take* her!" Sylvia nodded and pushed me in the woman's direction.

I wanted to tell Sylvia that I wouldn't do it, but I knew she was right. I could feel the thirst building up inside my mouth. It started with dryness on my tongue. I moved it against the roof of my mouth and then across my teeth. My fangs were longer and sharper than they were just seconds ago, and they felt as if they were the very center of my entire body. My heartbeat quickened in anticipation. Perhaps Sylvia was right. The woman had little time left to her, after all. Even if I ignored her, she probably wouldn't live that much longer anyway. I needed her blood right away. The choice became clear—her or me. Yet I still felt I could do what Sylvia suggested earlier—take just enough blood to survive and no more.

Sylvia gestured to me again and gave me a gentle nudge. I took a few steps and she instantly joined me, linking her arm in mine, and we started for the old woman. She had no idea that Sylvia and I were following her until we were almost upon her. At the last moment, she turned to face us, and when we stopped just right behind her, she gave us a curious look, as if surprised, but not frightened.

"Can you spare some change?" she asked us.

I opened my mouth wide and bent forward to bite her neck. She let out a scream as my teeth clamped down on her collar, then swung her shopping bag in my face. While the blow gave me no pain, it distracted me for an instant, and she ran down the street as fast as her legs could carry her, screeching all the way.

I turned to Sylvia with a questioning look in my eyes. She was laughing so hard, I thought she would fall down on the sidewalk. She grabbed me by the arm and led me in the direction we originally came from, walking as quickly as she could without arousing suspicion.

She stared at me out of the corners of her eyes with a

mixture of amusement and fondness. As we walked, she shook her head and smiled broadly, revealing her sharp canine teeth, which, in anticipation of a kill, had grown considerably in length. "You cover the victim's mouth first. *Then* you bite them."

"Maybe we better go home," I suggested. "She might be getting the police after us."

Sylvia shrugged her shoulders, and her black hair glistened under the neon lights of Mason Street. "Don't worry about it. Let's just find someone else. This time, let's try it my way."

We walked to Ellis Street and turned into an alleyway. Though darkened and a dead end, I could see perfectly well, and Sylvia focused her large eyes up at one of the buildings, which hemmed us in. I knew what had caught her attention—a window on the fifth floor, slightly ajar.

"I guess that must be their way of saying that vampires are welcome," Sylvia whispered with a smile. "Follow me."

With that, she leaped up into the air and grabbed the bottom of the fire escape that hung above us. It lowered down to us and Sylvia motioned for me to follow her up the stairs. I realized then how she had gotten inside my apartment.

"You're holding me up," she whispered. "Come on. I'm waiting for you." She took one of her hands off of the fire escape and motioned for me to follow her.

"Where are you going?" I asked.

"Shh," she said, putting her finger to her lips. She motioned for me to climb up to her level and peek inside the window.

Looking inside, I could see a young woman asleep in a large bed. I could hear the hum of her electric alarm clock and her deep, heavy breathing.

"Follow me inside," Sylvia whispered in my ear.

"Don't say or do anything. Just watch."

Sylvia climbed in the window and I followed. Though all the lights in the room were out, I could see as clearly as if it were brightly lit. Sylvia stepped quietly across the carpeted floor and sat on the edge of the bed. The face of the woman now came into my view. She must have been in her late twenties, so she looked just a couple of years older than Sylvia. She had long blonde hair that lay scattered across the pillow in disarray. Sylvia bent over the woman, so close to her face that it looked as if she were about to kiss her, then stared at the closed eyes of our unsuspecting prey.

"*Listen,*" commanded Sylvia to her sleeping victim.

The woman woke with a start. She appeared about to scream, but froze in that position with her mouth open. Sylvia's dark eyes stared into hers with a burning intensity, as if some demonic energy radiated out of them.

"*You no longer have any will of your own,*" Sylvia directed, in a voice both gentle and compelling, "*My will is your will, and you must obey. You shall not scream, nor struggle, nor feel any pain. And when you wake, you shall not remember this night.*"

The young woman's eyes appeared empty, and devoid of any feeling or knowledge regarding her predicament.

Sylvia turned to me. "Do you want to go first, or shall I?"

I motioned nervously for Sylvia to go. She smiled at me. "So, your chivalry allows a lady to go first? Very well then." She curtsied to me, then turned to the girl lying on the bed, who appeared somewhat dead already, as she stared blankly at the ceiling.

Sylvia turned the victim's head to one side, then bit into her jugular vein. I could hear the sucking noises as her lips worked on the girl's neck, and the sound of Sylvia swallowing the blood in small, but frequent gulps. The woman remained impassive, in a trance, and showed no hint of perceiving what Sylvia was doing to her. It seemed to me a long time that Sylvia spent on her, yet it must have been less than a minute. It only felt longer, because I, too, now experienced the same thirst that Sylvia had, and my anticipation of satisfying that thirst stretched out each waiting second.

Sylvia placed a finger on the woman's vein to slow the bleeding, then turned her face to me. She had blood smeared all over her lips, and a thin line trickled down each side of her mouth to her chin. She licked the blood from her lips with a circular motion from her long red tongue, like a little girl who just finished off her first ice cream cone. "It's your turn, Mark," she whispered.

My heartbeat quickened in anticipation, as I could smell the blood from the tiny punctures that Sylvia had bestowed upon the victim. With a smooth motion, Sylvia slid her finger off just as my mouth covered the two little holes over the young woman's jugular in. I began to suck slowly, with a certain hesitation at first, then bit down harder, opening the holes just slightly larger than before. The blood flowed into my mouth easily now, with only the slightest amount of sucking needed on my part. It tasted somehow different than I had remembered it as a human; the flavor now consumed and intoxicated me in a way I never would have dreamed possible, and after my first few gulps, a strange sensation came over my body.

It started as a slight tingling, as one feels when a hand or foot has fallen asleep, yet this strange feeling was not one of numbness, but of increased sensitivity in all parts of my body. This feeling started in my tongue, then I felt it in my mouth, my head, my heart, and then it quickly spread to all my extremities. Soothing warmth accompanied this tingling sensation, and this heat spread throughout my body at the same time. I could hear a sound like the breaking of a wave, which started at an almost inaudible level at first, and then, as the seconds went by, became almost deafening.

Through this sound, there came another—that of Sylvia's soft voice behind me, yet in the frenzied state in which I found myself, I could not hear her words through the rapid heartbeat of the woman on the bed. Her pulse quickened its tempo, then gradually faded, and I could, at last, hear Sylvia's words as she shook me by the shoulder.

"Stop. You've drunk too much. You'll drain her completely."

Sylvia pulled me off the young woman, then placed her finger over the wound, which had grown in size. I felt both dazed and invigorated simultaneously, and I regarded Sylvia with some curiosity as she held her finger to the girl's throat for a moment, then frowned.

"I'm afraid you've killed her," she said, then shrugged her shoulders and sighed. "That's why I was trying to get you to stop. I thought we might leave her alive, and then there would be nothing more to arouse the police. Oh, well. Don't worry about it. It's only a minor inconvenience, since the police have no clues linking us to her."

Then a fit of remorse struck me and I felt like crying.

"I didn't mean to kill her," I explained to Sylvia. "I just couldn't hear you. I heard her heart beating. I thought she would live and we would go after we were through."

"Yes, I know. But things don't always go as planned. Especially when you have two vampires on just one human. The strain was too much for her." Sylvia gently closed the victim's eyelids, which made her appear as if she were only sleeping.

"Then it was I who killed her, since she was still alive after you finished with her."

"Not necessarily," Sylvia pointed out. "After all, if I hadn't gone first, the amount of blood you took wouldn't have killed her. And anyway, like I said before, it's not really the amount of blood that's important—it's the life force."

I sat on the bed and stared at the lifeless woman who appeared to be sleeping, then turned back toward Sylvia. "Then we're both guilty."

Sylvia shook her head. "No. We're both innocent."

"What?" I asked, as I looked at Sylvia questioningly.

"I'll explain it to you in a few minutes. But first, let's leave this place. I find death depressing at times."

We climbed down the fire escape and walked back towards Mason Street, then towards my car. Though I felt guilty for what we had done, I could not hide the wonderful sensation the blood had given. It renewed and energized me, causing a feeling of euphoria so great, that even the poor young woman's death could not blot it out.

In the car, Sylvia leaned up against me. Her body was warmer than usual, due to the increased blood, and she kissed me on the cheek, spreading her warmth across my face with her soft lips.

"I understand how you feel, Mark, but neither of us is guilty of murder. We're innocent."

"How can that be?" I asked. "We just killed someone."

"But we must drink the blood of humans to survive," Sylvia protested. "So it's not murder at all. It's just like a hunter killing for food."

"That's different. A hunter kills *animals* for food— and we're killing other *people*."

"So? What difference does it make?" Sylvia shrugged her shoulders and threw her hands up in mock exasperation.

"The difference is when a hunter kills an animal, he's killing a lower form of life, not other humans."

"Just as we are killing humans, which are a lower form of life. We don't kill other vampires. We only kill

225

humans. And humans are definitely a lower form of life compared to us."

"But what gives us the right to take another human life?"

"*Another* human life?" laughed Sylvia. "Mark, we're not humans. We're vampires. I suppose you still think of yourself as human, but you're certainly not, anymore than I am."

I considered this thought for a moment as I drove through downtown on the way back to the apartment. Not human. Of course I was human. I still felt human. I was about to respond to this, but Sylvia moved on to her next point, punctuating it by first holding a finger up in the air for emphasis.

"And as far as our right to take a human life, we have the right to survive, just like any other form of life. When the right to life of two living beings can only be enjoyed by one of the two, the stronger one survives. We are stronger, so we survive and they die. It's really very simple."

"It may be simple, but it's still not right to me,"

"Then let me put it this way. I needed blood tonight to survive. So did you. And so did the girl we killed. Who would you have preferred to die in her place—me—or you?"

I told her I had no answer to this, and conceded that she was right, though I also explained that being right didn't make me feel any better about what we had done.

"I understand just how you feel," she responded. Her voice conveyed true sympathy, and she moved even closer to me. She sighed. "I felt the same way when I first became a vampire. It was so long ago, yet I can remember it all as if it just happened. At times, I wish my memory were not so vivid. I hate living in the past, and yet it's so easy when one has such a powerful capacity to remember every single incident. How terrible it is to be haunted by my past. To be trapped in such a lonely existence, and never have anyone to tell it all to—" Sylvia's voice cracked, as if she were about to cry, and she hugged me so hard, I almost lost control of the car. Fortunately, we had almost reached the apartment.

"I'd like to hear all about your life, if you'd tell me," I told her.

Sylvia's expression brightened and a cheerful smile adorned her beautiful face. I parked the car and we walked upstairs arm in arm. As we reached our floor, I asked, "My place or yours?"

"Oh that's right," she remarked with a laugh. "We have two apartments now. We better stay in mine. I have special window shades to keep out the light while we sleep during the day, and I have better locks on my doors and windows to keep out unwanted guests."

As soon as we reached the bedroom, we took off our clothes and slid into bed. Sylvia lit a candle on the nightstand, and to our eyes, it illuminated the room quite well.

"So you want to hear my life story?" Sylvia asked. "Oh, how I longed to tell you the truth when I first met you, but couldn't. It isn't fair for one to have so many memories with no one to tell them to. I'm so glad I have you."

"So am I," I answered, and gave her a hug.

"It will take a long time to tell you everything," Sylvia said, as she looked at the clock, which showed the time to be just a little before 1 a.m.

"That's okay. I'm not going anywhere."

"There is so much to tell," cried Sylvia in a perplexed tone. "Oh, I don't know where to begin!"

"Begin at the beginning," I suggested, and so she did.

Chapter Four

"You know what Charles Dickens wrote in *A Tale of Two Cities*. 'It was the best of times, it was the worst of times.' He obviously wasn't talking about London when I was born—1666—because it clearly was the worst of times. The year before, the bubonic plague killed almost a hundred thousand people in London. And that was out of a population of less than half a million. Then in 1666, just three months after I was born, the Great Fire of London burned down most of the city.

"I came from a relatively small family, considering the times. I only had one brother and one sister, both several years older than I. Another brother and sister had died in infancy, which was quite common then. We were a small, but close-knit family, my father being a farmer who owned a large parcel of land about a two-day ride north of London. We earned more than enough to survive. Because my family owned more land than we could work ourselves, others in the village came to work for my father. They got employment and money and our family prospered. We had a nice house and my parents bought me a harpsichord—an English bentside spinet— when I was just thirteen years old. They taught me how to read and write—something most of the other girls didn't learn. Our neighbors depended upon my family for survival, yet jealousy was always just under the surface.

"People in our village went to church regularly each week, but my family sometimes missed services. This aroused the suspicions of our neighbors, and not totally without cause. You see, my parents both knew about herbs and potions, and this knowledge could be incriminating back then. They secretly practiced magic, even while going to church—not with any intentions of doing anything evil, but just common everyday sorts of uses, like improving the crops, or banishing sickness.

228

They asked for nothing more in their practice of magic than Christians commonly pray for, yet this was strictly forbidden. I wasn't even aware that we were different until I played with some of the other children, and their parents felt that something must be wrong with my family since we didn't attend church as often as everyone else. When I was a little girl, one of the neighbors accused my family of witchcraft. The charges didn't stick. My family was found not guilty, but the suspicions remained for years.

"It wasn't until the death of one of the church officials, that our most serious troubles began. This man had wanted my father to sell our land for a paltry sum. My father refused, and there were threats on both sides. Not long afterwards, the man died in his sleep. It was believed that he was killed by a vampire."

"Were you already a vampire at that time?" I asked Sylvia.

"Oh no! Certainly not! Why, I didn't even practice witchcraft. I had no idea what the magical incantations meant, or how my parents used them, only that they never used magic to harm others. They did nothing to hurt the man. I learned later that he was indeed killed by a vampire.

"But the people in the village, a superstitious bunch of fools, believed that vampires and witches were all together, and that if my father and mother didn't always attend church with everyone else, then they were possibly vampires as well as witches. Eventually, some of my father's enemies felt the only way to rid the village of their 'curse' would be to kill the vampire-witch family. Little did they realize, that not only were they after innocent people, but they were about to create a self-fulfilling prophecy that would bring about their own destruction.

"Late one afternoon near sunset, my family had gone back inside the house to take a rest from our work. I had stayed in the field, picking flowers, when I saw a mob of angry people from the village approach. Though I had lived a sheltered life for all of my nineteen years, I certainly wasn't stupid. I knew why they had come—to take us all away from our farm and execute us for being witches. And as I watched in horror, crouching in the fields out of fear that they would kill me too, the one thought which ran through my mind at the time was that I couldn't do a thing to prevent it. I, a mere girl, against dozens of maddened people armed with various weapons—what could I do?"

Sylvia began to sob, and I held her gently in my arms. Her tears rolled off of her face and onto my neck. "You don't have to go on with this if it hurts too much," I said.

Sylvia shook her head. "No. I must tell you. I've been holding this in for so long."

I held her tightly to me till she could go on with her story, then loosened my embrace just enough for her to talk when I could see that she was ready to continue.

"I had to cower out in the field, shaking from fright like a little mouse. They were less than a hundred feet from where I hid, so I could see everything clearly. The mob dragged my parents and my brother and sister out in front of the house and before my eyes, they hung everyone from the big tree in front. I could not stop them. All I could do was scream. Of course they heard the scream and knew it was I. 'Sylvia! That must be Sylvia! We must get her too!' About a dozen of them started to chase me. The rest stayed behind to ransack my family's house and steal whatever they could find of value.

"I don't know how I kept from going completely insane. One minute I was picking flowers, and the next minute I witnessed the murder of my family. A moment later I was running for my life. Any rest or pause would result in capture and my death. Because I knew the woods around our land better than they did and because I was younger than the men who chased me, I kept ahead of them. And as it started to get dark, I felt that if I could just stay ahead of them for a while, maybe I could lose them in the darkness of the forest. But they wouldn't stop. Breathing became difficult. I gasped for air. When I thought I had put some distance between my pursuers and myself, I suddenly slipped on a rock and twisted my foot with a loud and painful snap. I had broken my ankle and lay on the ground, unable to run or even walk. In my desperation, I said the only kind of prayer I could imagine: 'Satan! They called my family witches and said we are aligned with you. Alas, it wasn't true. If it had been, perhaps you would have saved us from them. I ask you now for your help and if you give it to me, I will pledge myself to you.'

"Right after I pronounced those words, one of the villagers appeared with a pitchfork in his hand and a smile on his face. 'I found her!' he yelled out. 'I found Sylvia the witch, praying to the Devil.' His voice would bring the others, perhaps three or four who had kept up and not turned back from exhaustion. I couldn't run, so I just hoped he wouldn't stab me with his pitchfork.

"We both listened for the others, but heard nothing. He yelled out for them again, but with no answer. Finally, there came a crackling of branches as another man strode through the trees and approached. 'She's trapped,' the villager with the pitchfork proudly announced to the approaching man.

"'Actually, you're the one who's trapped,' said the stranger. In one swift movement, he snatched the pitchfork from the villager's hand and drove the points through his foot pinning him to the ground.

"The villager screamed hysterically, then yelled, 'My friends will be here in seconds and they will kill you—you witch.'

"'I'm not a witch,' replied the stranger. 'And your friends aren't coming. I've already killed them.' With that, he grabbed the villager's head with both hands and turned it completely around, snapping his neck. He turned in my direction and began to walk towards me.

"'You came just at the right time,' I told him.

"'So did you,' he answered, and as he came closer, I saw his long, sharp, canine teeth, and I suddenly realized why he had saved me. He bit into my neck, spurting blood all over as he drank. Then he ripped off my dress and raped me, which is how I lost my virginity. Finally, when I thought he would leave me for dead, he opened one of his veins and forced me to drink his blood. As you can guess, I woke up three days later as a vampire.

"Of course, I hated him for what he had done to me, but now, not knowing anything about how to survive as a vampire, I had to stay with him for a few days to learn what my new existence was all about. It turned out his name was Alex and he had decided to make me a vampire because he wanted a female companion. The feeling was not mutual. I hated him, and resolved to escape as soon as possible.

"I perceived that the only advantage in my new condition lay in my greater ability to seek vengeance for the death of my family. I questioned Alex about our strengths and weaknesses, so I could carry out my plans, one of which was to leave him after he told me what I wanted to know. He must have realized that I was considering this, for he threatened to kill me, should I try to leave him, and what's more, declared he would kill anyone else I decided to stay with instead of him.

"Perhaps he made these threats out of loneliness, but he had raped me and turned me into a vampire. I cared nothing for his problems. I had enough of my own. If he had been truly capable of love, he wouldn't have taken me the way he did. But then, Alex was a brute, and had no idea how to love. I wouldn't let him touch me, and each time I would shun his amorous advances, he would threaten to kill me.

"Several days later, we prepared to go to our sleep at dawn. I waited until I knew he was asleep in his coffin in the mausoleum where we hid, and then I left, walking towards the village in broad daylight, but making sure to stay off any well-worn trails, so I could remain unseen. The sunlight bothered my newly sensitive eyes, so I made it a point to walk under as many trees as possible, and thus take advantage of the shade. As I'm sure you've guessed by now, when I woke as a vampire, my broken ankle had already healed and my strength had increased many times.

"By nightfall, I reached the edge of the village, and my craving for blood consumed me so powerfully, I knew I had to slake my growing thirst, and do it quickly, for the trip from the mausoleum in daylight had sapped every bit of my energy. As I walked, I tried to decide whom I should go after first, but the decision seemed fated for me. A young woman, whom I had seen with her husband as two of the people who murdered my family, was walking towards me, when she suddenly screamed as she recognized me, Naturally, she was the first to die.

"I felt absolutely no remorse after my first kill, the way that you did with yours tonight. At other times, I certainly did, but not with anyone in my village, for they had all conspired to murder my family.

"I was only about a hundred feet or so from the church that everyone in the village attended. I decided it to be appropriate that I drag her to the church and leave her on the steps for everyone to find. Then, later that night, I stole a wig from a shop, which made me a blonde. I wore this the next day while walking around the town, together with a dress which I stole from another shop, so I could walk among the humans the next day, without them realizing who I was. The disguise worked well enough, and I found out bits of gossip as I eavesdropped on the villagers throughout the day. Of course, being out in the sun for two days in a row with no sleep taxed my body in the most incredible way. It drained my energy totally, yet I knew it wouldn't be a serious problem, because I didn't have to worry about keeping a low profile by killing people at a slow rate. I knew I would drink my fill again that night, and the night after. Instead of maybe draining one victim every two weeks, and sleeping in a coffin by night, I opted for walking around in the daylight and forgoing all sleep. The fact that I would have to kill someone new every single night to make up for such a drain on my energy didn't bother me in the least, because I knew that each victim would be one of the villagers who had murdered my family. I wanted to see the villagers squirm as they saw each other dying off from a vampire, and watch them scurry around in a panic trying to decide how to escape the fate I had in store for them.

"The next day everyone in the village heard that two people had been murdered by a vampire and then placed on the church steps. They were expecting a third victim on the third night, and that is precisely what I gave them. The next evening, in the wee hours while everyone slept, I wrote a large note and then I tacked it up on the church door so everyone would read it.

"The note stated that something had to be done about the murders of the good people of our town and that there would be a special meeting that night at the church to discuss methods of exterminating the vampire. It promised the appearance of a renowned vampire-hunter, just returned from a successful mission in Transylvania, where he successfully killed a vampire who had plagued people for many years. In the text, I asked for all the people who had helped to kill the Martin family, the family of vampires, to be the only people to attend the first meeting, as their experience in dealing with these matters would be needed. I promised that the vampire-hunter would come to talk with these people alone, and that they were to meet the very next night inside the church at eight o'clock.

"The evening before the meeting, I prepared some rags in oil in the basement of the church, and just as the meeting began, I lit them. The old wooden church went up quickly. Just as they discovered the smoke from downstairs, I boarded up the doors with some heavy beams and long spikes. They were trapped like the pack of rats that they were, and as far as I knew at the time, I had killed every single person who had a hand in my family's death,

"Once that was accomplished, I had no reason to remain, so I stole two horses, a carriage, and some other supplies from victims of the fire. I also reclaimed money and jewels stolen from my family by the villagers and I took anything they had of value that could be carried — gold, diamonds, anything. Before I left the village, I buried my family and loaded my harpsichord onto the carriage. And then I spent the next couple days riding to London. I stayed in the city from 1685 to 1766, and then decided to return to my old village for a visit just out of curiosity.

"By that time, I had already accumulated a large bank account. I had a new identity and my own house in London, which was magnificently furnished in the best French Provincial. I had read many books on a wide variety of subjects, and had become quite accomplished at playing the harpsichord. In 1764, I got to see a piano concert of a wonderfully gifted eight-year-old boy named Mozart. Quite inspiring. But to me, hearing him on the piano, all I could think about was that the piano meant the death of the harpsichord. It actually put it into hibernation for over a century. Little did I realize it at the time, but just two years later, the same thing would happen to me.

"In eighty-one years after becoming a vampire in 1685, I hadn't changed much physically. I had only aged about five or six years, so I looked about twenty-five. I also grew about an inch taller. "One of the men who died in the church blaze was named William Callen. It especially pleased me that he died, since he was the man who killed my mother. What I had forgotten was that the man had a young son when I had set the church fire. This son later had a son, and then eventually a grandson, now in his sixties in 1766. Indeed, I was the only person who hadn't changed much. What a fool I was to return! Of course they recognized me from the descriptions they had heard from their ancestors. Now they were smarter, however, and they planned their revenge upon me with more cleverness than I had thought them capable of.

"Just on a whim—a very stupid whim—I thought it would be interesting if I were to spend one day's rest inside the first coffin I slept in, back at the deserted mausoleum. How quaint I thought it would be to wake up at the same place where just eighty-one years earlier I had become a vampire.

"I awoke to a sharp pain in my chest as a stake pierced my flesh. I screamed as my eyes flew open, and above me, I saw William Callen's great-grandson, his arm raised, and then traveling down again as he hit the stake once more with his hammer. The pain lasted only a few seconds, followed by a sensation of numbness over my whole body. I couldn't move or speak, but I could still feel the stake in my chest, hear the voices of all the villagers surrounding the coffin, and see those who stood above me, peering into my coffin.

"A more horrifying scene one couldn't possibly imagine; here I was with all my enemies surrounding me, as I lay on the verge of death. I could hear their shouts of joy at 'having killed the vampire at last,' and above me, they stood grinning like ogres. My muscles refused to work at all. I couldn't even move my eyes; I could only see what happened to cross my field of vision. Yet in my panic, I realized I was still alive, and that they somehow believed me to be dead, due to the cataleptic state I now found myself in. I hoped that perhaps they would leave now, believing me to be dead, and that *somehow*, I would awaken to remove the stake, though I couldn't foresee much hope for this possibility.

"They lifted my hand and let it drop. They felt for my pulse. And when some were satisfied that I was really dead, several suggested that they depart. At this point, Callen objected violently, declaring that the only way to make sure I couldn't rise again would be to chop off my head!

"How I longed to jump up and run out of the mausoleum and not stop running until I was far away. Yet I couldn't even move my eyes to follow the movements of my tormentors as they walked around the coffin in which I lay imprisoned.

"They all argued back and forth, and at last, some old man declared that the desecration of a corpse would be against the law of God, and that he had a better solution. With that, he opened my mouth and stuffed a piece of garlic inside, then lifted my head up slightly, and placed a crucifix about my neck. Then he asked the other villagers who among them believed that the Devil could defeat the power of Jesus Christ? Other than Callen, all the others agreed with him, and congratulated the old man, as if he had personally fought Satan in a battle of wits. I could hear that Callen was not satisfied, and still wished to cut off my head, but by this time, the crowd had swayed in opinion toward the side of the old man, and they screamed that if Callen persisted in cutting off my head, they would nail him up in the coffin with me. He swore at them; then I could hear his voice fade as he left. The last sight I saw was the sad face of the old man, who sprinkled some holy water on my inert body, and crossed himself, muttering a prayer in Latin.

"He closed the coffin; then I heard the sound of several people hammering the lid shut. Darkness overcame me, and I wasn't aware of ever closing my eyes, just the blackness inside the casket, and then the silence as I lay in the tomb.

"And gradually, after sight, sound, and feeling fled my senses, my thoughts grew vague, as one's do right at the onset of sleep, and my last glimmer of consciousness faded into limbo."

Chapter Five

"After a length of time passed, how much time I had no way to judge, consciousness returned. The first minute or so, it was simply the knowledge that I was still alive, and that I could think. Attempts to move, speak, or in any way validate my physical existence proved impossible, yet I could feel myself lying inside the coffin, just as I knew my eyes were now closed. I opened them in anticipation, but found I could see only absolute darkness.

"Then came the unmistakable sound of footsteps outside the mausoleum. So my hearing hadn't been affected! I hoped that perhaps my sight would also return once the coffin lid was opened. But then, as I heard the old door open, not with a creak as it did before, but smashed down with great force, terror gripped me once again.

"That someone had broken into the mausoleum to get to me, I felt sure of. But the violence with which the heavy door crashed down frightened me just as much as what their possible motives might be. I wondered if William Callen's great-grandson had returned to cut off my head, and I tried in vain to at least move my body, to prove to myself that I wasn't helpless, but it was a futile attempt.

"Voices now surrounded my coffin—*unfamiliar* voices.

"I could recognize no one as being part of the group that had tried to kill me. I heard a hand slide along the outside surface of my coffin, then grip the edge of it, ripping the top right off, as if it were merely cardboard, instead of a coffin that had been nailed shut.

"A bright light shone into my eyes—at least it seemed very bright after absolute darkness inside the coffin. I squinted against its glare. The light was close to me and I feared that perhaps I would get burned if it were to come any closer to my face. My eyes must have become accustomed to the darkness of the coffin, I reasoned, for the light from a single candle so overwhelmed me that the faces around me looked like mere silhouettes, I later realized that the change in my vision was not due to the darkness, but to a change in my *eyes*.

"They all gathered around the coffin to look at me, and then I heard one of them say, 'Yes, I believe she is Sylvia Martin.'

"They knew my name! I wondered if they had seen it before they opened the coffin, or if they had recognized me. They stood around me, then one of the men gently picked up my hand, felt for a pulse, then let go as he watched my hand fall limply, 'What shall we do with her?' he asked the group.

"I had no idea what they wanted from me. They didn't seem to be in any hurry to drive another stake through me, but now another fear came to mind. Perhaps they were grave robbers, and meant to sell me to some school of medicine, where I would be dissected.

"Another hand reached for me, this time that of a girl, who touched my face, then stroked it gently. 'How pretty she is,' she remarked to the others, 'and see how well she has kept.'

"The others nodded in agreement, then a murmur went through the group. They passed the candle around in front of their faces so I could make out the features of all of them quite distinctly, They numbered eight—four men and four women, all appearing to be in their twenties and thirties. I could tell by the way they dressed, that they couldn't have been from the village. They certainly weren't simple country people. All were clothed in garments that marked them as being wealthy city people, perhaps from London. They couldn't have been more out of place, in a deserted mausoleum at the edge of a small village. Nevertheless, what startled me was how strangely they were dressed. The men wore hats I had never seen before. The young ladies had unfamiliar hairstyles and wore dresses that seemed just as out of place as the men's strange garb.

"'Can you hear us?' one of the girls asked me. I couldn't answer her, and so she turned to the others and asked them what they should do about me. In answer to her question, one of the men produced a large bowl made of silver, and placed it upon my stomach, just below the wound that the stake had made. The others in the group nodded, and one of the other girls reached inside her purse and brought forth a sharp dagger.

"She stepped towards me, and in my horror, I felt certain she would plunge it into me, and that my poor body would suffer even more. But to my great surprise, she took the dagger and slashed her wrist, holding it so the blood would run into the bowl. After about half a minute, she put a finger over the vein she had cut, then passed the dagger to the others, and each repeated the same procedure till they had filled the bowl with their blood.

"Then the girl who had initiated this strange ceremony put the palm of one her hands on my chest and with her other hand jerked the stake out of my chest. I gasped! All sensations of my body started to flow back into me. The girl put her fingers to my lips and parted my mouth as one of the men slowly poured part of the blood into my mouth. At first, it just ran down into my throat, but then I swallowed it and took an active part in drinking it. I raised my hands to the bowl and held it to my lips, and at the same time, several members of the group placed their hands behind my head and helped me to sit up. In this position, I finished off the contents of the bowl, then laid it in my lap. Looking down, I saw the bloodstained hole made from the stake had now disappeared entirely, and only the bloodstained dress I wore, with its large rip in the middle, gave evidence that I had even been impaled with a stake. I sat in a stupor for a few seconds, and then my curiosity overcame me, since I perceived I could now speak.

"'Who are you?' I asked. 'And why have you helped me? Don't you realize I'm a vampire?'

"They all laughed uproariously at my question, as if they didn't believe me. 'Excuse us for laughing,' said one of the girls, 'but we *know* that you're a vampire, Sylvia.'

"'And yet you're not afraid?' I asked.

"'Why should we be? After all, we're vampires, too.' She smiled as she said this, and I could see her sharp canine teeth gleam from the candlelight.

"I felt like an idiot for not discerning this when they had been able to cut themselves on the wrist the way they did without harming themselves. They helped me out of the coffin, and I stood among them, feeling very odd, my clothes looking as if they were so old that the material would crumble into dust at any time. I asked them what had happened to make my dress age like that, as I remarked almost to myself that it must have been the lack of air in the coffin. I then asked why they were dressed so strangely.

"They responded that it was I who was dressed so strangely, not them, but I looked around at all of them and could see that they were wrong. Their clothes may have been new, while mine appeared old for some reason, but they were the strange-looking ones. The men wore trousers instead of stockings and britches. They had formal jackets with tails in the back. Their hats, I learned, were called Derbies and stovepipes, and the ladies wore long dresses with bustles in the rear and high lace collars. " 'Such modest dress is appropriate for a religious order,' I remarked to the ladies. 'Yet you're *vampires*?'

"Everyone laughed at my question, then one of the other girls turned to the one who had just spoken to me

242

and said to her, 'Of course, Sylvia has been used to seeing different fashions than ours. She was buried in 1766.'

"I looked at the girl who had just finished saying this, and suddenly felt very apprehensive. 'What do you mean?' I asked. 'How long have I been in here?'

"A dreadful silence filled the mausoleum. I glanced around, gazing at one face, then another, for an answer to my question.

"'Are you saying it's not 1766 anymore? That I've been trapped in this coffin for over an entire year? Is that what you mean?'

"They all looked at each other, then one of the men answered, 'You've been here for a very long time.' He paused for a moment, then added, 'It's now 1866.'

"I gasped at his answer and held my head in my hands as I slumped to the floor and cried uncontrollably. I had lost an entire century of my life, and would now have to live in a world I couldn't understand, where people dressed funny and where I certainly wouldn't fit in. And yet, perhaps I cried partly through the joy that somehow, a group of people had actually tried to help me even though they knew what I was. Of course, they weren't really people, but rather, other vampires, similar to me, but the last thing I had expected was to be rescued intentionally. If I ever held any hope of being released from my cataleptic state, I felt certain it would happen of its own accord or that someone would unwittingly revive me through some accidental means.

"'Why did you help me to live again?' I asked them.

"'You can help us,' replied one of the girls,

"I was aghast at her answer. What could I possibly do for them? After all, they had revived me. I couldn't do anything like that for them. After my unexplained disappearance from London a hundred years earlier, I was presumed to be dead. Most money or property I owned in 1766 would have been claimed by someone else

243

years ago—except, of course, some jewelry and gold I had buried just in case of emergencies. What could they ever want from me?

"Then the girl explained that they needed help against a group of people who still hunted vampires—a group that had originated in my village, but now had chapters in London, as well as other cities. This group, led by a descendant of the same Callen who drove the stake through me, now dug up graves in their search for vampires. It seems these religious fanatics had already murdered two of the vampires on the outskirts of London. The eight who had saved me knew these two vampires, and now they wanted revenge.

"'But how can I help?' I inquired of them.

"The girl explained. 'We know that your family practiced magic. We do, too, and are more powerful than any humans, for we alone on this earth exist as supernatural creatures. Humans have many limitations, but vampires are a higher form of life. Our magic is far stronger. With your help, we can defeat our enemies. We need your magical powers allied with ours.'

"I laughed at her suggestion. 'But I don't have any magical powers. My family practiced a little magic, but I learned almost nothing. I'm grateful for your help, but I can't do very much in return, I'm afraid.'

"They all glanced around at each other uneasily, then stared at me. I became afraid that perhaps I shouldn't have told them I was of no use to them, and worried that maybe they would kill me.

"The girl I had spoken to saw the fear in my eyes. 'You don't have to worry about us. We're your friends. Your only friends. We know that your family was murdered by the villagers for witchcraft, so we all have a common bond here.'

"I tried to explain to them that my family only practiced a very simple form of witchcraft, which only revolved around farming a better crop or banishing sickness, and that I hadn't learned any of it anyway. Apparently, they must have thought I was only being modest, for they persisted in believing I had some sort of magical power that would help them, even if I didn't know about it. They explained that their combined magical powers had enabled them to find me, in the same way a divining rod in the right person's hands might lead to water.

"'Now that you've found me,' I said to them, 'what do you intend to do with me?'

"'You are free to do whatever you wish,' answered one of the girls, 'but you may stay with us if you like.'

"'Oh yes, please do,' said one of the other girls.

"'We have a beautiful mansion in London,' one of the men said, 'and we'd like to have you as our guest for as long as you want.'

"I looked around the mausoleum at the dust covering the stone floor, at the coffin where I had lain for all those wasted years, at the walls and ceilings strung with cobwebs, and at a rat scurrying across the floor. Then I glanced down at my once elegant dress, now tattered and stained with blood that had dried a century ago. My future—what was it anyway? My past consisted mostly of lying inside a coffin in that mausoleum. The eighty-one years I had spent in London would not be of much help in learning to adapt to a new time. I knew things had changed, though to what extent still remained a mystery.

"'Yes. I'll come with you,' I told them. 'I'll be happy to join you.'

"'Good!' exclaimed several of them, as they nodded their approval of my decision.

"Their smiles turned to expressions of contempt as they all suddenly stared at the same place—my neck. I swallowed nervously, as I put my hand to my throat, the place where all their eyes had focused with almost obsessive attention. The crucifix, which the old man had hung around my neck, still lay there. Its presence clearly upset my new acquaintances, and I certainly had no need for it I explained to them how it got there.

"One of the men stepped forward and removed it from my neck.

"'Let us be rid of this wretched symbol,' he said, as he held it at arms-length between his fingers, like something that reeked of an unpleasant odor. He turned from me and dropped it back into my coffin and shut the lid.

"'This will be your new ornament,' said one of the girls, as she stepped towards me, and placed a silver chain with the symbol of Baphomet around my neck. 'Now you're one of us.'

"I looked around the room. Every single one of them wore the same medallion. I fingered the fine silver and saw it gleam under the dim light. 'You're all Satanists,' I remarked to them as I inspected the fine detail in my new medallion—the very same medallion, incidentally, which you now have around your neck."

I looked down at the medallion around my neck. "I had no idea it had such a long history behind it. But what happened to you then? Did you go live with them like they asked you to?"

Sylvia nodded. "Of course. What else could I have done? I needed the security of the group for a while, at least until I became financially secure once more. I was so afraid of being discovered by anyone again.

"After I agreed to go with them, one of the girls produced a beautiful satin dress, which I changed into before we left, after I first asked the men to turn around while I slipped out of my old one.

"'What will we do if any of the villagers try to stop us from leaving the area?' I asked, fearful of a confrontation with more vampire-hunters.

"'Don't worry,' explained one of the men. 'We're

generous here. If we run into any of the villagers on the way, we'll share them.'

"At that, they all burst into laughter, and I followed, too. It made me realize just how silly my fears were. After all, who *could* stop nine vampires—not just ordinary vampires—but vampires magically united, and possessed of Satan's power?

"'Besides, we're not walking out of here,' answered one of the girls. 'We're taking two coaches from here to the train station.'

"'Train station?' I asked. 'What is a "train station"?'

"'That's where we catch a train to London,' the girl answered.

"'Let me make sure I understand you. We must capture some kind of wild animal, which you call a 'train,' before we may return to London. Is that not correct?' I looked around the mausoleum at the group, and perceived they were stifling laughter again.

"They led me out into the night and explained some of the changes in England over the past century. We rode down the narrow country road, in two luxurious carriages, leaving behind the crumbling mausoleum with its nightmarish memories. As we sped away past the village on our way to London, I felt my life had taken a turn for the best. I liked my new friends so much. And the ride on the train to London just amazed me. I could never have imagined such a thing.

"The mansion we stayed in was quite roomy, having thirteen large bedrooms. In addition to the luxury of the furnishings, we had several trustworthy servants, for the vampires had so much money among all of them that they had no trouble finding people they could trust. Only on rare occasions would they have a problem of loyalty, and of course any threats of blackmail on the part of a servant would result in death immediately. Fortunately, this happened rarely, and we had little trouble finding competent help.

"I had to catch up on what I had missed during my century-long sleep. I learned that the colonies had revolted against King George III only a decade after the beginning of my long sleep. Of course, the war had long been over by the time I woke. Although there were only two bridges in London in 1766, by 1866 almost all of London's bridges had already been constructed, including a *new* London Bridge to replace the old one. The railways had been built, too. People could travel great distances easily. An industrial revolution was on, and the disparity between the rich and the poor became even more extreme, though people in general seemed to have improved their lot materially. With the Twentieth Century came war with Germany, and the Americans who fought against us in the American Revolution were now our allies. How times changed from one year to the next. It seemed to me that it was never clear whom the real enemies or allies were, for they changed from one war to the next. I came to the conclusion that the real enemy was war itself, for after each war finished, little had been accomplished, except for slight changes in the countries' governments and boundaries, and these were surely not worth the price paid in suffering—especially since these changes were temporary. For, at the conclusion of the following war, everything might be changed once again. So they killed each other for nothing. At least as vampires, we have a reason to kill, because it is essential if we are to survive. But humans kill for the most trivial reasons.

"Times were happier after the war, and we had such freedom. If someone had professed to be a witch or a Satanist back in the time of my childhood, it would have meant certain death. But times had changed, and in the 1920s, witchcraft was even practiced openly by some people, like Aleister Crowley. While it wasn't accepted, we were nonetheless free from government persecution. The nine of us had a powerful coven. I soon realized after going with them that night in the mausoleum, that what they said was true—I did have powers I had been unaware of. When I prayed to Satan on the day my family was murdered—when I asked for Satan's help for revenge—he decided to send the vampire to save me and to transform me. Even when the villagers trapped me in the coffin for an entire century—lying in that coffin somehow transformed me—turned me into a different type of vampire. And just as Christians believe that faith gives salvation, a similar point works in Satanism and magic. One who considers herself a Satanist and aligns herself with Satan does not necessarily have to perform arcane rites and rituals. Indeed, many of the rituals performed by magicians in the past included steps to 'protect' the magician from the Satanic forces she should have been aligned with, instead of trying unsuccessfully to control.

"And so we used our magical powers to accumulate wealth. As the years went on, I amassed a fortune, but felt no reason to leave the others and strike out on my own. I liked our mansion, and besides, I would have been dreadfully lonely by myself. As it was, my loneliness hurt me more than anything else. For although I did have the company of eight other vampires, all of whom I came to love like brothers and sisters, I was the only odd one. Yes, it was no accident that there were four men and four women in the group. Everyone had already paired off years before they had rescued me from the mausoleum. To them, I was like a younger sister, and I always felt a little strange at being the only one to be alone. Yet, what could I do?"

"I don't know. What *did* you do?" I asked. "You're not telling me that you've been alone all this time, are you? Since 1866?"

Sylvia frowned for a moment, as if she didn't want to answer, but since I kept looking at her for a continuation of her tale, she had to either explain or look away. She didn't look away.

"Yes, on occasion I did become involved with some men romantically, but it never worked out."

"Why not?"

Sylvia bit her lip, then looked away for a moment before returning her gaze back to me. "I usually killed them before much happened between us." Sylvia paused and swallowed nervously as she tried to read my reaction in my eyes. "You see, if I have sex, my heartbeat quickens and many times it will cause a need for blood. I bite them without wanting to, and before I know it, I've killed them. That's why I didn't make love with you right away. I wanted to be sure you would feel all right about staying with me and becoming a vampire. I gambled that you would want to stay with me. If you hadn't drunk my blood, you would have just died. I'm glad everything worked out."

I asked Sylvia about some of the other men she had become romantically involved with, and she explained that they either left her when she wouldn't have sex with them, or made love to them, which sometimes ended with her accidentally killing them. I thought this over for a few seconds.

"But didn't you ever try turning them into vampires like you did with me?"

"Yes, a few times. But there were certain complications."

"Complications?" I didn't like the sound of that.

"Most of them didn't want to become vampires, so they just died after I drank their blood."

"And the others?" I asked, fascinated by Sylvia's strange past.

Sylvia fidgeted with her hair, twining a strand

around her finger, as she stared down at the sheets, then at me. "It doesn't always work, you know. It's not that easy to make someone a vampire."

"I don't know what you mean. It seemed easy enough to me. You drank my blood and then made me drink yours. It seems you could make all the vampires you want that way."

"Yes, but you see, it usually doesn't work for *me*. The human body usually rejects *my* blood. My other vampire friends can turn anyone into a vampire, but not me. My blood has killed more people than it has transformed. My blood is different. I'm different from other vampires—and now, so are you. Sylvia avoided my eyes, and added, "I had no guarantee that it would work with you either. True, I had had a vision about you while I was still in London, and we performed a Satanic ceremony together, but I didn't know for sure that it would work. Your body could have rejected my blood, in which case you would have died immediately."

"You gambled with my life," I said, with some annoyance.

Sylvia nodded. "Yes, I did. Please forgive me. But, I just had to have you for myself. I had to take the risk."

"It seems like the risk fell on me, not you."

"Not really. If I had killed you, you would have died instantly with no suffering, but I would have had to live with what I had done. I may have killed many people in my lifetime, but most of them I didn't love. You are the first man I've ever really loved like this. If I had killed you, I don't know what I would have done." Sylvia's eyes welled up with tears.

I put my arm around her. "Well, you don't have to worry about it anymore. Now that I'm a vampire, too, everything's okay. You can't kill me now that we're both vampires, right?"

Sylvia continued to cry softly as she hugged me

tightly.

"Please don't cry," I said to her. "There's nothing to worry about. Everything worked out, so what are you crying about? There's no sense in getting depressed over what could have happened."

"I'm not worried anymore over what already happened," Sylvia said through her tears.

"Well then, what are you crying about?"

"What *could* happen later." Sylvia dried her tears, and regained her composure, but would explain no further.

Chapter Six

What a joy it was to wake in Sylvia's embrace. Her arms held me to her tightly, as if she were afraid I would leave while she was asleep, and one of her legs wrapped itself around my body like a snake coiling around its victim. Her eyes were closed, and her long lashes made her look so peaceful and innocent. After staring at her sleeping for a few seconds, she woke, as if my stare had pierced her slumber.

"Good morning," I said, as I kissed her.

She returned the kiss with even more passion, and then whispered softly, "It's not morning anymore."

I glanced over at the clock. It was almost 6 p.m., and I suddenly realized it would always be like this. We would always wake around dark and now mornings were a thing of the past. They would be passed by in the beginning of our sleep. But then, I thought, *So what?* I never did like getting up in the morning anyway. Now I had a perfectly valid excuse to wake up as late as I wanted.

"Should we be doing anything special?" I asked. "I mean, what do vampires do when they wake up?"

Sylvia rubbed her smooth body against mine in a slow rhythmical motion that emphasized her sensuality. "Sex is always good when you wake up. Or, actually anytime."

Fortunately for us, it wasn't until after we finished making love that the doorbell rang. I groaned when I heard it, and hated the thought of getting out of bed at all. Sylvia slipped on a dress, and I put on my pants as we walked to the door.

"I'll bet you ten dollars it's Dave and Gail," Sylvia challenged me as we made our way through the living room.

I pressed the buzzer to let whoever it was into the building, and a minute later we opened the door to Dave and Gail.

"I've been trying to call you since yesterday," said Dave, as he and Gail walked into our apartment. "They said you hadn't shown up for work this week. Are you feeling okay?"

"I never felt better." It was true. I never felt stronger, yet I wondered if they could sense or see anything different.

Dave pointed an accusing finger at Gail. "See! I told you she didn't kill him."

Sylvia and I glanced at each other, then at them. Gail avoided Sylvia's eyes as we all remembered her phone call to me warning me not to go to Sylvia's apartment.

Dave went on to describe their three-day cruise to Mexico, which they had left for late Saturday night. They had only returned late this afternoon, and Dave had tried to call me without luck, and when he called my job, they said they hadn't seen me all week, and as far as they were concerned at the paper, I was fired. In addition, no one at the gym had seen me since Friday. He wanted to know if anything was wrong.

"I guess I may as well tell you the truth," I began, and Sylvia stared at me in horror, not knowing what to expect. "Sylvia and I made a special commitment to each other while you and Gail were on your honeymoon."

Sylvia almost swooned with relief, as if she had been afraid I would have told Dave the whole story. Dave blinked as if he just saw an unbelievable hallucination.

"You did what?"

Sylvia nodded. "Yes, it's true, it really is. I guess you and Gail are responsible. If it wasn't for attending your wedding, we might never have thought of it."

Dave contemplated Sylvia's words as he dragged himself inside the living room and slumped into a French Provincial sofa. Gail glared at Sylvia, as if she didn't believe what she had said and angry with Sylvia for joking about marriage.

"So you got married?" asked Dave.

"No," answered Sylvia, with a frown. "We haven't gotten married yet. But we did perform a special ceremony."

"What kind of ceremony?" Gail asked. Her words were more like a challenge than a question.

I didn't know how to answer her. Certainly I couldn't tell her the truth. I glanced at Sylvia to see what she wanted to tell them.

"You could call it a romantic commitment ceremony. We performed it here." Sylvia waved her hand across the living room. "I wish you could have been here."

Dave and Gail stared at us suspiciously. "No church or minister?" Gail asked in an accusing tone.

"None were necessary," answered Sylvia, as she threw her hands up. "It was a Satanic ceremony, and we were the only people in it."

Gail fumed at this revelation, and asked Dave to leave with her. Dave sat on the sofa, not moving a muscle. "Don't get so excited," he told her. "They're only kidding. Besides, a private ceremony isn't legal anyway."

His words caused such an uproar, that now both Gail and Sylvia united against him, though for different reasons. Gail berated him for condoning Satanism, while Sylvia responded to his accusations concerning the legitimacy of our relationship. He sat on the sofa like a dog stretched out before the hearth, oblivious to the words of both women.

"Who cares about legitimacy?" said Sylvia, the volume of her soft voice now rising. "We're not lawyers. A piece of paper means nothing. It's the quality of love and how long it lasts that matters."

"That's right," I said to Dave, in support of Sylvia. "Believe me, Sylvia and I will be together longer than any other couple you've ever known. As a matter of fact, we may set a new world record."

Sylvia smiled at me, as only she understood that I had spoken so literally; Dave and Gail couldn't have possibly comprehended the full meaning of my statement.

Dave turned to Gail. "See. They're just like us. The four of us were probably doing the exact same thing late last Saturday night."

"I really doubt that," I said.

Sylvia's eyes widened in shock as if anticipating a complete retelling of our first night together, with details on the sex, the blood-drinking—and what she did afterwards while I was unconscious.

"I don't imagine our nights were similar at all," I said to Dave.

Sylvia's eyebrows went up and the slightest smile played on the edge of her lips. "Well, maybe not exactly the same. I think Mark and I had a unique experience."

"That's for sure," I agreed. "Definitely unique."

Dave shifted uncomfortably. "Naturally. We're all unique. So we're all the same." Dave shrugged his shoulders. "I guess you two are really serious then. Great! The best of luck to both of you! But if you ever have a real wedding, you should invite us yours since you went to ours."

Sylvia stretched out her left hand towards Dave and Gail. "Do you really think I would have spent one hundred and eighty thousand dollars on this ring if I had no intention of marrying Mark? Of course we'll have a wedding later and naturally, you'll be invited!"

Dave and Gail looked at each other, then at us, and seemed to approve.

Sylvia asked if they would like to hear Bach's *Partita 6 in E minor* on her harpsichord. Dave and I endorsed the idea, while Gail ignored the question completely.

Sylvia sat on the little bench and her slender fingers gracefully floated across the keyboard as she played incredibly. I loved to watch her as she played, with her long, glistening, black hair spilling over her shoulders and down her back to her tiny waist. Her wonderfully large eyes sometimes looked down at the keys, and sometimes not, for she knew each melody so well, she could divert her attention elsewhere, which she often did by casting her gaze around the room, and then holding it on me while she continued to play without missing a note.

Gail resigned herself to sitting down beside Dave and listening. The fact that she enjoyed Sylvia's music seemed to annoy Gail even more, because it kept her from disliking everything about her, and forced her to confront the fact that Sylvia perhaps was not as bad as she made her out to be. Of course, if Gail had any inkling as to what Sylvia, or for that matter, now I, were really like, she would have probably rushed out of the apartment in search of the nearest priest. With my luck, it would have been Father Callen.

At the end of the piece, Sylvia rose from the bench in front of the harpsichord, and curtsied, as if at the end of a performance. Dave and I clapped, and Sylvia smiled.

"All this entertainment has made me hungry," Dave announced. "Why don't we all go out for some pizza to celebrate?"

Sylvia stopped smiling, and looked at me pleadingly as if to say we shouldn't. She hadn't explained anything about how often we would eat, so I thought I would wait to see her reaction, especially since I didn't feel the slightest bit hungry. I thought perhaps I had better take a hint from the wary look she cast me.

"Gee, thanks Dave," I said, "but we're not really hungry right now."

"Why don't you let Sylvia answer for herself?" Gail challenged. "Do you make decisions for the both of you? Or can you each make up your own mind?"

"We stick by each other's decisions," Sylvia declared.

"We're both intuitive enough to know what each other wants."

Gail, resentful at her inevitable failure at trying to pit Sylvia against me, stood up, thus signaling to Dave her intention to leave. He watched her stand, but remained seated, to her great frustration. "We're not in any hurry," he told her.

She sulked and sat down next to him again. I could feel a wave of resentment passing between the two of them, like a cloud covering the sun. I tried to suggest an alternate activity, such as watching a movie, in the hope that the situation could somehow be mended, but I was too late. Gail fidgeted and made faces while Dave started talking about food again.

Nothing I could have suggested would have changed that. Dave placed his hands on his knees and then stood up. "Well, I guess we'll have to eat without you then," he said to me. Gail rose quickly, and started for the door.

"See you at the gym tomorrow then?" Dave asked me.

Sylvia glanced at me, and I caught what she was thinking. "No, I don't think I'll be coming into the gym tomorrow," I told Dave.

He shifted his stare from me to Sylvia, and then back to me again.

He knew something strange was going on, but best friend or not, I certainly couldn't tell him.

"You're going to miss a workout? Why? You've sure got plenty of time, now that you're not working." Since I didn't answer right away, Dave used the pause in the conversation to avoid any awkward silences that threatened to take over. "Why *did* you miss work all week?" Dave's voice sounded suspicious.

"Why did you?" I countered.

"Because Gail and I just got married, and we were on our honeymoon." Dave hesitated, then laughed. "I guess

258

you have as good a reason as I do. But you should have at least called your boss. What are you going to do now?"

I didn't know how to answer him because I really had no idea what Sylvia and I would do. Obviously, I couldn't hold a daytime job, but from the way Sylvia had acted, I felt that any job might be unnecessary. She hadn't mentioned anything about money in the few hours of my new existence, and I was just as curious as Dave concerning my future.

"We haven't made any definite plans yet," Sylvia answered, "but everything will work out just fine." She smiled and nodded, without giving Dave any further explanation.

Gail stood by the door, waiting silently, as Sylvia and I crossed the room with Dave, They were just about to turn and leave, when the bright hall light glared down at us, illuminating our features more clearly than the more subdued light in Sylvia's apartment, Dave stared at my face with an expression of alarm, then quickly regained his composure and said goodbye to us,

As he and Gail walked slowly down the hall towards the stairs, I heard Gail ask him what was wrong. He bent toward her, then whispered, "His eyes! Did you see his eyes?"

"What about them?" Gail asked, annoyed, in a voice much louder than Dave's whisper.

"They're just like Sylvia's!"

I closed the door quietly. So Dave had been able to perceive a slight difference in me, after all. I sighed and sat down on the love seat. Sylvia sat down beside me and tenderly placed her hand upon my shoulder.

"It could have been worse," she pointed out. "If you had smiled the wrong way while you had a strong thirst, he would have seen your teeth."

"Now I wish he hadn't come over. I didn't want him to notice the change."

"Better now than later. The changes aren't so apparent, Not all of them, anyway."

I started from the sofa. "What other changes?"

"Just look at your skin, for one thing."

I looked at it, then told Sylvia it looked the same as before. "Yes, but not for long," she laughed. "After you've been out of the sun for weeks and then months, it will become lighter—like mine."

"Sunbathing is a bore anyway. I never liked it. I don't care what color my skin is. Are there any other changes which will happen to my body?"

Sylvia thought for a moment. "The only other one which may annoy you is—" and then she hesitated as she stared at my body. "Well, I'm sure you realize that if you drink blood and eat less, then you're bound to lose a little weight."

"Shit!" I yelled, as I stood up. "You mean to tell me that every pound of muscle I had to work so hard for in the last three years all of it is going to go away?"

Sylvia flinched from my loud words as if she were expecting me to hit her. "Please don't raise your voice at me. You'll hurt my feelings if you do."

I sank into the love seat again. "All those years at the gym. All that exercise. And all for nothing. Now I'll look just like I did before weightlifting—skinny—except with pale skin."

"Oh, come now, Mark. Cheer up. It's not so bad. You'll still look quite fit. You'll just be—lighter. Maybe ten or fifteen pounds less. As a matter of fact, you'll probably look even better. You won't have an ounce of fat, and you'll be much stronger than you ever were before. Don't you realize how strong you are *now*?"

"I don't know. I haven't been to the gym for a week." I tried to recall how much I had lifted the last time there, but Sylvia interrupted me.

"Even I could lift way more than that!" she

exclaimed. "Now that you're a vampire, you're even stronger than I am. Either one of us could lift more weight than anyone in your gym."

I smiled. Things weren't so bad after all. I could still retain some of the things that I enjoyed as a human. Certain activities and abilities would improve, while others, such as bodybuilding would not. But it could have been worse.

Sylvia put her arm around me again and gave me a hug. "Besides, with the gifts you now have, it would be such a waste to spend any of your time in the gym."

Sylvia then explained how we could read many thousands of words per minute with total comprehension, how we could perform mathematical calculations which a human could only accomplish with a computer, how we could learn to paint like the best artists of all time, play music on all instruments, and move with the ability of an Olympic gymnast.

"With all the things we can do, we'll be busy just trying to live up to our almost unlimited potential. Don't you see? This is the reason that vampires are here on earth. To fulfill Satan's role here. We are his children — the children of the night. It is we, alone, of all creatures on this planet, who have this ability. We mustn't let ourselves go to waste. We must grow magically, increase our power, so that one day, we will no longer have to fear any attacks upon us by humans. We must constantly strengthen ourselves, for we are alone."

"Not anymore," I said, as I placed my arm around Sylvia and drew her towards me.

"No. Not anymore. Now you and I are as one, and our strength together is such that no one can stand against it. You can't imagine what sorts of things lie ahead for you as you become more involved in magic!" Sylvia spoke with excitement. She suddenly stood up and pulled me by the hand to her bookshelf, where many books, mostly about magic, witchcraft, and various aspects of the supernatural sat, just waiting for a special kind of reader to browse through their esoteric contents. Sylvia enthusiastically gave a brief summary of some of her favorite books, and explained how many of them were extremely rare.

"It's great that we'll be able to work magic," I said. "But with all that power, I still can't go out much during the day. I can't do any more bodybuilding, and I can't even confide in my best friend. Dave and I have been best friends for years, but tonight when he left, I felt like we were both strangers."

"Mark, you must accept that Dave isn't your best friend anymore. I am."

"You!" I answered with a laugh, "But you're my girlfriend or my fianceé now, not my best friend."

"No. I'm both. A friend is someone you share your innermost secrets with. Someone you share your favorite activities with. Someone you can trust to help you when you're in trouble. Not only is Dave no longer your best friend, he's not even your friend now. He was the best friend of the old Mark—the human Mark. Go tell him we're vampires—how we drank the blood of that girl last night till she died. Tell him how much you enjoyed the taste of her blood, the feel of your sharp teeth against her soft neck, and how you're going to do this again. Not to just one or two more victims, but to thousands of people over the coming centuries, Tell him all of this. Tell him the truth about yourself, just like you would tell the truth to a 'best friend.' What do you think he'll do then?"

I shook my head sadly. "I don't know."

"I'll *tell* you what he'll do. He'll call the police, that's what. And as crazy as the story may sound to the police, you can be sure they'll come after us anyway."

I nodded my head, then admitted that Sylvia was right. As much as I liked Dave, I could never share the

262

truth with him now.

"So that's why I said I'm your best friend—in fact, your only friend. I'm the only one you can trust with the truth. I love you for what you are, not for anything you have to pretend to be."

"Yes, I suppose that's true."

"Love is caring for another and accepting them as they are, not as something they may pretend to be. True love can only exist when both people know each other completely. Without that honesty and trust, what exists is merely a silly romantic charade. And by the way, in case you're interested, that's one of the reasons I picked you. I felt you had the ability to love me despite who and what I am."

I had to agree with Sylvia on these points, though I certainly felt sad at realizing that my life as I had known it would no longer exist. Yet, for all I gave up, it seemed worth the price, since I got Sylvia for myself forever. This alone made it all worthwhile. True, she had cost me not only my life, but also my soul. However, being now "undead" seemed to be as good as eternal life, and I really had no use for my soul anyway. Satan could have it as long as I could have Sylvia.

We spent the rest of the night going through the many volumes on her bookshelf, and didn't get back to bed until almost 5 a.m. I happily curled up with her, eager to wake up to her beautiful face the next evening.

And so I was not prepared for what awaited me.

Chapter Seven

When I opened my eyes, strangely enough, it took a few seconds to properly focus them. Yet after I blinked for a second, the sight did not change or go away. Sylvia faced towards me, just as she had the previous night when I had awoken. But tonight her lips and cheek were smeared with dried blood. My first reaction was terror—that perhaps she had died in her sleep.

I shook her by the shoulder, calling her name. To my great relief, she woke immediately, so I smiled, happy that she was all right. She did not return my smile. The second her eyes opened and saw me, she screamed so loud, I clapped my hand over her mouth so she wouldn't be heard by a neighbor. I didn't want them calling the police. We needed our privacy.

"What's wrong?" I asked, as I removed my hand from her mouth.

She pointed at me in horror, and I looked at my chest. A dried river of blood ran from my neck down my chest to my stomach. I felt my neck with my hand and could feel the dried blood caked there, but no holes.

Sylvia began to cry. "I was afraid this might happen. Oh, what am I to do now?"

I lay there like a stone, bewildered and stunned. Sylvia had drunk my blood while I was sleeping, and the wounds healed before I even woke. But why had she done it?

"I'm sorry, Mark," she blurted through her tears. "I didn't mean to do it. It must have happened in my sleep."

"It's okay. I'm all right. So don't worry about it." I tried to sound as reassuring as I could, but even I didn't believe what I told her.

"It's *not* okay!" she sobbed. "I might have killed you!"

I felt my neck again, and this time swallowed nervously. Perhaps I did feel a little weaker than normal.

Sylvia pulled me towards her and hugged me as she rocked back and forth, until her tears stopped. "I don't know what I'd do if I lost you."

"Have you done this in your sleep before?"

I felt Sylvia nod her head against my shoulder. "Yes," she said, almost at a whisper. "It's happened before."

"Would you like to tell me about it?"

"I told you before that I had tried to make other men vampires, but without much success. They usually died from loss of blood, or their bodies rejected my blood, and that killed them. But once, about thirty years ago, I was successful in creating another vampire. It turned out badly from the start. He hated me just as I had hated Alex for turning me into a vampire. Yet he stayed with me, possibly because he didn't want to be alone quite yet. One evening I awoke to see his blood on my mouth and his neck. He was quite dead, and I couldn't revive him even with my own blood. I had killed him while we slept, just as I almost did to you last night."

I sat up in bed, watching Sylvia's bloodstained mouth as she told her story. "What can we do?" I asked.

She shrugged her shoulders. "I don't know. I'm afraid it might happen again, but maybe it won't. I hope you won't leave me."

"No, of course not. This is *our* problem, and we'll defeat it together. Somehow." I realized I was only talking nonsense. "But what I don't understand is how did both of us sleep through this? Are you sure you didn't hypnotize me in my sleep like you did before you moved into the apartment?"

Sylvia's eyes narrowed at my suggestion. "Mark! Do you really think I would hypnotize you in your sleep and drink your blood now? Don't you know that I would never want to hurt you or risk losing you? I already told you that I could no longer hypnotize you because you're a vampire, too." Sylvia's eyes suddenly changed to a

265

happier expression as another thought came into her head. "Besides, if I *could* still hypnotize you, it wouldn't be to drink your blood—it would be to make you drink my pee. Not all the time, mind you. Just twice."

"Twice?" I asked. "You mean like on Christmas and your birthday?"

Sylvia frowned at this suggestion. "Twice a year? Certainly not!" Then her face brightened into a mischievous smile as she visualized something. "Twice means we do it as soon as I wake up right before sex and then late at night right before having sex again before we go to sleep. Just twice a day. That would be perfect for me. Yes, *that's* what I would do if I could still hypnotize you."

"Now I understand why you said you've been unlucky in love," I replied.

"I'd feel a lot luckier if I could still hypnotize you. Then you'd do exactly what I want. Oh, why do relationships have to be so difficult?" Sylvia stared at me and sighed.

"I guess it's not safe for me to sleep again. When I'm asleep you either drink my blood or piss in my mouth."

"Wait a minute," Sylvia said. "The blood drinking was a mistake. I did it in my sleep. As far as peeing in your mouth—you were unconscious for three days. What did you expect me to do to pass the time?"

"Watch TV or read a book."

"I can do that alone."

"You can pee alone, too," I pointed out.

"It's not as much fun alone. A golden shower needs two people. Without another person, it's just going to the toilet."

"With another person, it's still going to the toilet, but you're using *me* as your toilet."

Sylvia's eyes half-closed in ecstasy. "Oh, I just love it when you talk dirty to me about sex. I know everything

266

will work out between us. I have great expectations."

"And I don't know what to expect." I rose from the bed, and washed off the blood from my neck in the bathroom. Sylvia joined me and cleaned off the crimson trail around her lips. I made sure to tell her that I felt just fine, other than a slight weakness. Yet, aside from the languor that had stolen over my body, I perceived something else—a growing thirst—and the need to replace my lost blood.

We showered and dressed with an awkward interval of silence, during which, Sylvia avoided my gaze as if deeply ashamed of what had happened. Finally, she cast her melancholy eyes upon mine and said, "We must go out again tonight."

I nodded. Her meaning was clear. Even though we had just found a victim, we would have to find another one right away. Sylvia could quench her own voracious thirst, and I could renew my strength, which she had consumed from me during our sleep.

"Let's go back to where we went the other night," she suggested. "No one will be missed from there too much."

I glanced at the slim white gold watch Sylvia had given me. It was now 7 p.m., and I asked Sylvia if it were perhaps a little early to search for a victim. After all, the streets were still crowded and most people would still be awake.

"We can't wait till after midnight. You're going to feel ill unless you get some more blood in you soon, and I don't want to repeat what I did to you last night. As long as I get some more blood now, I can be sure that won't happen."

"I suppose you're right," I agreed.

"Besides," Sylvia explained, "if we can get this out of the way early in the evening, we'll still have time to go to a movie or do something afterward."

Her plans sounded logical enough, so we left

immediately, and as I drove, she read the entertainment section of the *San Francisco Chronicle*, searching for a good movie that started later on. She mentioned that *Spirits of the Dead* was playing at nine. I had seen the movie before, and enjoyed it, since it portrayed three separate stories by Edgar Allan Poe, as interpreted by three different directors. I told Sylvia she reminded me of one of the characters in the movie.

"I'll bet I can guess which one," she said, since she had seen the movie before, too.

"She was in the third story—the one Fellini directed, based on Poe's short story, 'Never Bet the Devil Your Head'."

Sylvia smiled in recognition. "The girl with the ball?"

"Yes," I answered. So Sylvia remembered her, too. Terence Stamp kept seeing this strangely beautiful young girl, in a white dress, bouncing a large ball. Since no one else could see her, he believed her to be the Devil. At the end of the movie, he pursues her in his Ferrari when he sees her on the other side of a demolished bridge. As the car leaps the gap from one side to the other, a thin wire on the other side decapitates him. The movie ends with the girl setting her ball aside, and picking up Terence Stamp's severed head. As she smiles into the camera, the audience realizes Terence Stamp wasn't crazy after all—she really was the Devil.

"Thank you," said Sylvia. "I consider that a compliment."

"Well, that's how I meant it, of course. She was very pretty, and you both look somewhat alike, except for the color of your eyes and hair."

Sylvia nodded. "But there's another difference."

"What's that?"

"I love you. The girl in the movie didn't love him. And that makes all the difference in the world."

"True, it does."

"But I'd still like to go see the movie again, so let's see if we can make it there by nine o'clock."

We drove to the same area where we had found our victim just two nights before, and parked on Taylor Street this time. As we had expected, because it was still early, the streets were fairly crowded. Sylvia did not appear happy at the prospect of finding a new victim with so many potential witnesses walking around. She suggested that we keep searching for more deserted streets and alleys.

When we walked along the streets, we couldn't find anyone because there were too many possible witnesses, but when we searched the alleys, we couldn't find any victims. We were in a predicament. Sylvia wanted new blood soon, but I needed it immediately. Her somnambulistic feast on me had left me in a state of thirst like I had never known before.

"What are we to do?" She paced nervously.

I placed my arm around her and held her to me tightly as we made our way through one of the alleys, past garbage cans in relative darkness compared to the brightly lit streets.

"Maybe we need to go to another area of town," I suggested.

Without really thinking, we had wandered into an alley that did not go through to another street. It came to a dead end under a building that had no lights on. Just as we were about to turn around, I heard footsteps coming up behind us,

We turned around, and behind us were two men, apparently in their twenties, approaching slowly and quietly, as if trying to take us by surprise. They had crude, vacant faces, with glazed eyes that leered at us in the darkness. Both men kept their hands in their pockets.

One of them glanced back at the entrance to the alley—an entrance that they now blocked—as if he were

269

checking to see if anyone had seen them walk in. The two of them peered around the alley, then up the sides of the buildings that hemmed us in, then they looked at each other with knowing smiles. They ran their eyes up and down Sylvia's body, then fixed their attention upon my gold watch, which seemed to have caught what little illumination existed.

"Hey, man, like what time is it?" the one closest to me asked. He stood only four or five feet away, and his accomplice moved to his side to give any assistance deemed necessary.

"I don't know," I answered, but didn't bother to look at my watch.

I was aware of how muggers often asked this question, then hit their victim as he would try to tell the time.

"You don't know!" the other one answered, "Ain't that a watch you got? You can't tell time? Or what?"

"I'm afraid my eyesight is very poor. I can hardly see in this light. And the solid gold of my watch makes it difficult to see in the dark."

Sylvia looked at me and smiled, then she covered her mouth and stifled a laugh.

"Lemme see that watch!" commanded one of them. He pulled his hands out of his pockets, and his switchblade opened in the middle of his movement. "Gimme the watch or I cut you and your girlfriend."

"I paid eighteen-thousand dollars for that watch," Sylvia declared, "and one hundred and eighty-thousand dollars for my ring. Just try to take them."

The man with the knife stepped forward.

An expression of recognition rose in Sylvia's face and she poked me in the side with her finger in excitement. "Oh, don't you remember him? He's the one you knocked out in the alley."

The guy with the knife suddenly had his own

moment of recognition as he heard Sylvia's words. He pointed the knife at me. "You're the one who killed my homeboys a few weeks ago."

"No," Sylvia corrected him. "He's the one who knocked you out," pointing at me. "*I'm* the one who killed your two friends."

His face scrunched up in confusion. "My friends were big. How could a bitch like you kill my two friends?"

"Like *this*!" Sylvia covered the distance in a split second. A blur of form and her hand clapped over his mouth and twisted his head to the side exposing his throat. The boy's knife clattered to the pavement.

His partner turned to me with his own knife. I threw a punch at his head. Right before it connected, I saw Sylvia turn to me and yell, "No!" as if she were trying to stop me from hitting him.

But it was too late. My fist cracked his skull as if it had been made of papier-mâché. He died before the knife had even dropped from his lifeless hand, and his body collapsed on the ground in a heap, like a broken marionette. He fell in such a way that his dead eyes seemed to fix upon his friend.

I stared in surprise at my fist, covered with blood.

Sylvia shook her head at me, then wagged her finger in my direction. "I told you not to hit him. Now that you've killed him, you can't drink his blood anymore. It has no life in it. We've only got this one left for the two of us."

Her words reached the other man, and in a panic he struggled to free himself, yet his movements seemed so slow, perhaps due to his fear. With one hand, Sylvia jerked his head back, while she covered his mouth with the other hand. Her fangs tore his throat open in an instant. She drank his blood swiftly, swallowing in large gulps, then handed his almost lifeless body over to me. I drained him completely in less than a minute, then let him drop to the pavement. I felt a rush of energy as my heart pounded. The new blood jolted me with a strange feeling of physical pleasure that started in the middle of my chest and spread throughout my extremities.

Sylvia glanced around the alley, then turned to me, her lips and cheeks smeared with blood, which she occasionally licked with a large sweep of her tongue.

"My goodness, what a mess!" she exclaimed. "We can't leave them like this." She pointed at a dumpster and suggested we place the bodies inside, so they might go undetected a little while longer.

Sylvia reached into her purse and pulled out a plastic bag with two washcloths, already moistened, handed one to me and used the other to wipe the blood from her face. I followed her example and then she put the washcloths back into the plastic bag in her purse. We hid the bodies in the dumpster.

"What time is it?" she asked, as we walked towards Geary Street, hand in hand.

"It's a quarter after eight," I answered, now filled with energy.

"Oh that's wonderful," Sylvia said cheerfully. "We can still see the movie."

I nodded and sighed, "I hope it's not going to be like this every night."

"Me too," Sylvia agreed. "But don't worry. Soon you'll be able to take just enough blood without killing them each time. You'll do it by the power of your will, so they won't even know it's happened or be able to recognize you afterwards. When you can do that, you'll never have to go thirsty or worry about the police."

We were only one block from the car when I heard a voice behind me screech, "That's them! He's the one who tried to kill me!"

Sylvia and I turned around. Twenty feet behind us

272

stood the old woman, who, just two nights before, had almost become my first victim. Her eyes nearly bulged out of their sockets in recognition as she pointed at the two of us, with her withered finger shaking in the air. A policeman stood next to her.

"Just a minute, you two," he said. "I'd like to have a word with you."

We stopped and waited while the old woman kept stabbing a finger in our direction and yelled, "They're the ones! Arrest them!"

"What's the meaning of this?" asked Sylvia indignantly. She directed her question at the woman, then stared at the policeman, waiting for him to explain himself.

"This woman claims you two attacked her two nights ago." He scrutinized our faces as if trying to determine our guilt. "I'd like to see your I.D."

I handed him my driver's license and Sylvia showed her passport. He inspected them carefully, then wrote something onto a small notepad.

"Now then," he resumed. "This lady just came up to me and said you two attacked her a couple of nights ago. Tuesday night. What do you have to say to that?"

"This is ridiculous. Why would anyone attack her?" I pointed at her ragged dirty clothes. "Money?"

The officer looked at the way the old woman was dressed. It appeared as if she hadn't changed her clothes in months. She carried a blanket inside her shopping bag, used to sleep on the sidewalk, no doubt. I had on a brown turtleneck and tan pants. Sylvia wore an orange velvet dress under a snakeskin coat. He looked us over and then turned to the woman. "Why did you say they attacked you?"

She pointed at me and shook her finger as her whole body trembled. "He tried to bite me!"

"Bite you?" the officer asked, with a puzzled

273

expression on his face.

"Yes, bite me!" she screamed angrily. "They're both vampires!"

An expression of embarrassment came across the cop's face. He glared at the old woman for a second, then turned to us and handed back our identification. "Sorry to have taken up your time."

"Wait!" screamed the old woman, as she grabbed him by the sleeve. "Look at their teeth! That will prove it! I saw his teeth. They're this long!" She motioned with her hands to show that my teeth were several inches long,

The policeman shook his head, then told her that he was only walking a regular beat, and that he wasn't in charge of vampire investigations. "Make him show you his teeth," the woman insisted as she grabbed his sleeve again.

He pulled his arm away, then looked at us and pointed with his thumb at the woman. "Would you smile for the lady so she can see you're not vampires?" Sylvia and I smiled. The cop nodded his head as he turned to the woman and said, "See? No vampires. Just regular teeth." He grinned at us and shrugged his shoulders. "Sorry folks."

We turned to walk away.

"Oh, and miss?" he called.

"Yes?" Sylvia answered, as she turned around.

"Not everyone in San Francisco is crazy. It just seems that way when you come downtown." He winked at us.

We smiled and waved good-bye to him.

Sylvia held her hand to her forehead, as if experiencing a headache.

"A close call. Too close. From now on, if you don't put your victims in a trance to make them forget you, then you'll just have to kill them."

I nodded, but with some regret. "Well, no witnesses

from tonight's episode."

"Yes, but my, what a mess. *Never* hit anyone as hard as you can. Just a light tap is sufficient. Remember, you're stronger now. Next time, I'm going to show you how to put humans into a trance. That way, you can drink their blood without killing them and still not have to worry about them identifying you later."

I told her that sounded like a very practical ability, and that if she didn't teach it to me soon, every cop in the city would be on our trail before long.

We reached the theater just in time to see *Spirits of the Dead* begin at 9 p.m. Sylvia squirmed in her seat out of boredom during the first two segments, but when the third segment started, she poked me in the arm with her finger excitedly, and said, "Here it comes!" We both watched intently during the short scenes where the young girl appeared. Her white face and bright red lips reminded me so much of Sylvia. When the movie ended with the girl picking up Terence Stamp's severed head and smiling demonically into the camera, Sylvia turned to me and sighed. "And I so wanted the two of them to have a meaningful relationship."

"I guess they're just like us."

Sylvia's large eyes met mine with a hurt expression on her face, "What do you mean?" she asked sadly.

"I've lost my head over you, too."

She repressed a laugh, but a large smile came through. "Let's get out of here before you get any cornier."

When we arrived back at the apartment, we noticed the door stood open to George's apartment on the first floor. He sat watching a movie on television, and looked up when we came into the hall. "Hi kids. Have a good time tonight?"

"Oh yes," answered Sylvia. "We always do. By the way, did you know that Mark and I are together now?"

275

"Sure do. Remember? I saw you both on the way to church last Saturday afternoon." George smiled and took a long swig of his beer.

Sylvia frowned, "Oh yes, of course. Last Saturday." Her voice trailed off, as if she were about to correct George and explain that we were only on our way to Dave and Gail's wedding last weekend, but she evidently decided not to give him the full details on our Satanic ceremony. I felt it was a wise decision.

"So what are you going to do now?" he asked. "Keep both apartments, or one, or move?"

I shrugged my shoulders and told him we weren't sure yet.

"By the way, before I forget, this guy came by here tonight looking for the two of you."

Sylvia's eyes widened. "What did he look like?"

"Nothing special. Just a priest."

Chapter Eight

George assured us he sent Father Callen away, and that he would be unlikely to return.

Sylvia glanced at me nervously, and George noticed her anxiety. "Don't worry. I told him that neither of you lived here. But tell me. Why the Hell are you afraid of some damn priest anyway?"

Sylvia appeared too distraught to answer George, so I spoke for her. "He's crazy and very dangerous."

"If he comes by again, do you want me to call the police?"

"No," I answered. "Just call us."

George promised to warn us if Father Callen came by again, so Sylvia and I made our way upstairs. "We're either going to have to move, or kill him," Sylvia whispered in my ear. "Before he finds us and kills us first."

A couple hours later, around 2 a.m., her phone rang. I looked at Sylvia questioningly. She knitted her eyebrows together, as if puzzled, "Now, who could that be?" she asked.

She picked up the receiver and said, "Hello?" then smiled with delight a second later. "Oh Yvette, I'm so happy to hear from you. But surprised. Isn't it only ten o'clock in the morning in London? Yes, I did! Of course I am. Yes, he's right here. Want to hear him say, 'Hello'?" Sylvia turned to me. "Say hello." She handed the receiver to me.

"Hello," I said, and a female voice with a British accent on the other end of the line said, "Hello," back. With a name like Yvette, I was expecting maybe a French accent instead.

Sylvia snatched the phone from me and spoke to the mysterious caller. "I met him just a few weeks ago. Mark. Last Saturday was when I did it. No, just fine. He woke up Tuesday, and we've been out twice since then. We'll have to move, though. Father Callen's around and looking for us. Okay. Good. We need all the help we can get. Great. Talk to you soon."

Sylvia hung up and smiled, then gave me a big hug.

I asked her what was going on.

"That was Yvette. She's one of the vampires I live with in London. She's been a friend for a long time, ever since she and her friends opened my coffin and brought me back to life in 1866."

"So she's one of the vampires."

"Yes," said Sylvia with a smile. "They're all in London, and they want us to come to see them. In the meantime, though, she told me that she'd have all of them perform a ritual to protect us from Father Callen. That won't stop him necessarily, but it could help."

"It sounded like she knew you were going to meet me here in San Francisco," I noted.

"She did. We performed a Satanic ritual together when I had a vision. That's when I saw your face and knew I'd find you in San Francisco. So the others knew why I came here. She's very happy for us, and all the other vampires want to meet you."

"How odd it is to hear that a group of vampires want to meet me."

"Yes, and we mustn't disappoint them. It's time for lessons again." With those words, Sylvia stepped over to the bookshelf and with a sweeping motion of her hand, pointed out approximately a dozen volumes. "You must read these so that you'll be able to talk about magic with them."

"How soon do I have to read them?"

Sylvia stroked her delicate chin with her fingers as she immersed herself in thought for a second. "Let's see," she began. "It's two o'clock now. We must go to sleep by about five. We need an hour or two to make love properly. So you have one hour of study time."

"To read a dozen books! Are you out of your mind? I'd be lucky to finish one."

"All right, then. One book in one hour." Sylvia proceeded to demonstrate how to speed read. I had once taken a course in the subject in school, but had fallen out of practice, and my speed had returned to normal. What Sylvia showed me didn't really differ that much from what I had already known, but what was different was the ease with which I could now do it. It seemed that no matter how quickly I turned the pages, as long as I kept my eyes on the words and concentrated on the subject, I could understand everything.

"Time's up!" announced Sylvia.

I looked up from a copy of *Inner Traditions of Magic*. Sylvia stood before me in naked innocence, with her hands folded in front of her. She smiled for a second, then bent forward and began to undress me. We left a trail of clothes all the way to the bedroom.

Apparently, she was in no mood to discuss the book I just read, but that didn't bother me. Just seeing her naked in front of me had a way of diverting my mind from anything else I was doing at the time. I felt that perhaps when we awoke, we would find it more convenient to go over all the new material I had learned in so short a time.

Instead of waking after a good day's sleep, the buzzer rousted us from our daytime rest. I cursed the unknown disturber of our sleep, then Sylvia rolled onto her side and looked at the clock. It was 5 p.m., so the sun was about to set anyway.

"I guess we would have gotten up soon, regardless," Sylvia said with a frown. "But I wish people would quit dropping by when we're in bed."

We slipped on some clothes swiftly as we prepared to open the door. Sylvia mentioned that next time, we'd move to an apartment with an intercom. I nodded wearily, and with Sylvia by my side, opened the door. Out in the hall stood Lieutenant Swenson, a cigarette dangling from his mouth.

"You're a hard man to get a hold of," he said. "Mind if I come in?" He stepped forward, but Sylvia stood in his way, blocking the door.

"Put that cigarette out before you come in," she told him.

He looked around, then asked, "Have an ashtray?"

"No" she replied icily.

He stared at the growing ash then around the carpeted hallway. Reluctantly, he crushed it out on the sole of his shiny black shoes, then placed the cigarette butt inside his coat pocket.

"I need to ask you a few questions."

Sylvia motioned for him to step inside. The Baphomet on the wall caught his eye immediately. He arched his eyebrows, then turned to Sylvia. "Are you a Satanist?"

She nodded, and I could see the irritation slowly rising to her face.

"I'm a Christian myself. My family goes to church every Sunday," he said in a condescending tone.

Sylvia rolled her eyes, then sighed in exasperation. "I suppose everyone has their cross to bear."

Lieutenant Swenson shot her an angry stare, then addressed us both. "I need to know where you two were on several different nights, starting with last night."

"We went to the movies," I told him.

"Which one?"

"*Spirits of the Dead*," Sylvia answered.

"What time?"

"From nine to eleven," I replied.

"Where were you from seven-thirty to nine?"

"Oh, just walking around." Sylvia left it vague

enough to irritate him.

"Where? *Precisely*?"

"Oh, just around," said Sylvia, as she watched his irritation grow. "Why do you want to know? Are we in some kind of trouble?"

The inspector pulled a small notepad from his inside coat pocket and began to read from it. "You were stopped by a policeman last night at eight-thirty when a woman identified you as assailants from Tuesday night." He looked up from his notepad and stared intently at us. "There was a murder on Tuesday night. A young woman."

"What a shame," Sylvia answered him. "But what has that to do with us? Or with the crazy old woman?"

Lieutenant Swenson flipped another page of the notepad. "There were two murders last night, right before the policeman stopped you. There were certain *similarities*."

"And what were those similarities?" I asked.

"The way they were killed." He pointed at his notepad. "The murder of the man in Pacific Heights in his home late last Monday night and two drug dealers in the Mission killed in an alley a couple weeks ago. Do you know what they all have in common?"

"I could never guess," taunted Sylvia.

"They were all killed like your next-door neighbor. Throats cut or ripped open, and missing a lot of blood. A murder happened right here in this apartment just two weeks ago, but I guess you wouldn't be curious about that, would you?"

We didn't bother to answer him. I wondered just how much he really knew, or if he had simply hatched this theory out of the circumstances. As long as he had no witnesses, there would be little he could do.

"So far, all you've told me is you have some kind of suspicion regarding me," I said.

"It's more than just a suspicion, and I think it's more than just you. I think you're *both* in on this." He cast a hostile glance towards Sylvia, then back at me. "I think you knew each other before any of these murders."

"Well, you're wrong," interrupted Sylvia. "We just met when I moved here two weeks ago. And that was after the murder in this apartment." She stood defiantly, with her arms akimbo. "And another thing. If you're so clever in your police work, tell me what our motive would have been."

The inspector averted his eyes from Sylvia's fiery and piercing stare. He looked at the floor for a moment, then lifted his gaze back to us. "There may not be a rational motive," he said. "Murderers don't always think in a logical manner."

"Apparently detectives don't either," Sylvia countered.

An arrogant sneer crossed Swenson's lips as he turned to me. "Gold's Gym closed just minutes before the murder. The manager said you were the last to leave."

"This is ridiculous," I said. "Dozens of members leave Gold's Gym at closing time. Why pick me?"

"You match the description given a couple weeks ago by the surviving witness—brown hair and a muscular build."

"That describes most of the members of my gym."

"Who's this witness?" Sylvia asked.

Lieutenant Swenson nodded and pointed at both of us. "That's the other thing. The witness to the murders two weeks ago was just killed last night with a friend—in the same area where you were stopped by the police."

"You mean your witness is dead?" Sylvia asked. "I have a Ouija board if you want to try to contact him."

The detective glared at her.

"Wait a minute," I said to him. "You told me the night of Harry's murder that I wasn't a suspect because I was out in the hall with all my neighbors during the murder. From what you're saying, all these murders are related, so you're looking for someone other than us."

"Unless you think *I'm* the one who single-handedly overpowered all of these male victims," Sylvia pointed out to him.

"Are you arresting us?" I asked.

I noticed that as he talked, he folded his arm, so that his right hand came to rest on his left side—just inches away from his shoulder holster. He seemed to be contemplating our words and his next move. "No, I'm not arresting you."

"Very well," replied Sylvia. "But first, look into my eyes and tell me what you see."

"What?" asked Inspector Swenson. His eyes involuntarily met hers, then he froze, unable to break her hypnotic gaze.

"*I now control your will,*" Sylvia commanded. "*Do you understand?*" Her voice took on the same eerie quality I remembered both from my dream about her and also the night she hypnotized me in her own bed.

The detective stared straight ahead without exhibiting any sign of thought or emotion. "Yes. I understand." He stood completely frozen in the same pose, with his hand near his holster. Only his mouth moved, as if the rest of his body were a cartoon, and the artist too lazy to draw any movement on the figure except for the mouth.

Sylvia motioned to me. "Mark, I need your help. Please hold my hand."

I stared at her with some curiosity over her odd request. "Sure, I'll hold your hand, but how does that help?"

"Just concentrate with me on controlling his mind. Lend me your magical essence."

The detective still stood immobilized in front of us.

His eyes appeared glassy and his gaze detached, as if he had just gone through a frontal lobotomy.

"*Does anyone else know you're here?*" she asked him.

"No."

"*Do you have any recording or listening devices on your person?*"

"No."

"*Have you mentioned us to any other police?*"

"No."

Sylvia smiled. "Well, that's nice isn't it?" she remarked as she nodded to me.

"*You want to catch the killer, don't you?*" she asked Inspector Swenson.

"Yes."

"*Good. The killer is a gang member you've arrested before. You have to figure out which one it is. You'll just keep pursuing a gang member for the murder. That's your duty. It would be wrong to let him escape, wouldn't it?*"

"Yes."

"*Then there's only one thing for you to do, isn't there? You must kill him yourself. You're going to do that right now, aren't you?*"

"Yes."

"*Wonderful!*" exclaimed Sylvia. "*And before you leave, just one more thing. You will not remember our conversation. You will forget you ever considered Mark and me as suspects. And if someone should ever hypnotize you, they will not be able to override my commands and make you remember. Do you understand?*"

"Yes,"

"*Fine. When I snap my fingers, you will awaken with no knowledge of this conversation. You will be friendly to us and then leave quickly to kill the gang member you think is the murderer. How many bullets are in your gun?*"

"Ten."

"*How nice. Be sure to use them all.*" Sylvia snapped her fingers.

284

He blinked several times, and then looked at his watch. "God, it's late, Please excuse me. I must be going. It's been a pleasure talking to you," He reached out and shook my hand heartily. "I hate to leave, but you know, police business." He grinned sheepishly,

"Yes." Sylvia smiled. "We understand." She waved good-bye to him as he left.

I told Sylvia I felt unsure about whether she did the right thing or not.

"Of course it was the right thing. Do you think we should have killed him right here?"

"No."

"Should we have gone to the police station and answered a million questions?" she asked with a laugh.

"Of course not."

"Then we really had no choice. This way, we remove any suspicion about us and solve all the murders."

"How do we solve all the murders? If Swenson kills some gang member, he could get sent to prison for life."

"Oh, come now, Mark. You know that won't happen. Just look at what happened when your own mayor was murdered."

Sylvia was right. Dan White, a city supervisor and ex-cop, gunned down Mayor Moscone and Supervisor Harvey Milk in 1978, using six bullets for each of them, yet the jury only convicted White for manslaughter—not murder. I related this information to Sylvia.

She nodded. "Yes, I know. And when Detective Swenson kills another gang member, a man with a record of drugs and assault and maybe an arrest record for murder—well, he'll be a hero for ridding San Francisco of a dangerous killer."

"Until the murders start again."

"There aren't going to be any more murders by us."

I looked at Sylvia questioningly. "What do you mean?"

"We're leaving. We must. Father Callen's after us. The police will renew their search for us if we continue to kill people. Let the detective kill the 'murderer' and the whole case is closed."

"Do you want to go to London, then?" I asked.

"Yes. But first we're going to take a little vacation for fun and earn some money at the same time. We'll take a trip to the gambling casinos and play some card games. Then, after we win, we'll come back here for our things and be off to London." Sylvia smiled, then suddenly became solemn as she stared sadly into my eyes. She ran her slender fingers through my hair, then held my head with her hands. "Oh, Mark. Are you sure you don't mind all this moving about? The gambling trip? The move to London?"

I kissed her gently, then held her close to me. "Of course I don't mind. I love you. And nothing will ever drive us apart. Remember, we're together for eternity."

Chapter Nine

Sylvia immediately began to pack a small suitcase in preparation for our trip. I asked her where we were going, and she told me Reno would be the best place.

"But what about Las Vegas? Aren't there more casinos there than Reno?"

"Yes, but no one knows me in Reno. There might be some dealers or pit bosses who would recognize me in Las Vegas. Remember, I was there only three weeks ago, and I won quite a bit of money."

"How much?" I asked.

In answer to my question, she lifted an attaché case out of her closet and set it on the bed. "Take a look inside." She smiled at me

I opened it. Inside were stacks of $100 bills held together with rubber bands. I picked some of them up and held them in my hand. I had never seen so much cash stacked up in front of me before. "It looks like you just robbed a bank," I said with a chuckle.

"Yes, only this is legal. I broke no laws to make the money." Sylvia thought for a moment, then added, "Except for tax evasion, I suppose." She shrugged her shoulders. "Anyway, I came by it all legally. The casinos aren't too happy about it, but then they make plenty of money anyway."

"How much is here?" I stared in awe at the attaché case.

"About fifty-thousand. But in the next couple days, we'll have two or three times that amount at least. We need money to make money. We'll stay in the best hotels, wear our finest clothes, and do everything possible to create an impression of great wealth. In that way, it will look less suspicious when we win so much. But even so, there will be risks. As you know, casinos don't like card counters."

"I've heard. We better be careful. But it sounds like fun. I guess you could say this is like our honeymoon in a way."

Sylvia frowned. "Not really. We'll be concerned about money and the chance of getting caught every minute that we're there. Our real honeymoon starts when we leave for London. That's when most of our problems will be over and Father Callen will be left behind."

With those hopes in mind, Sylvia made a plane reservation and then late the next afternoon, we made our way to San Francisco International Airport. The flight to Reno lasted only forty-five minutes, and while the night covered the beauty of the mountains, the city itself looked incredible from the sky as we made our descent. Reno, a twenty-four-hour city, sparkled like a jewel as all the lights glittered in the night.

We took a taxi to the Atlantis, one of Reno's larger casinos. It had been years since I had been to Reno, and this was the first time I had been to this casino. In keeping with its name, the design theme featured aquariums, waterfalls, and parts that resembled a rain forest. At 7 p.m. on a Saturday, every square inch of the casino bustled with frenzied activity. Bells rang constantly as jackpots were won, and people swore as money was lost.

Two bellhops carried our luggage, but I carried the attaché case. Both Sylvia and I would have been in quite a predicament had they dropped it and opened the case accidentally. I held it in one hand, and held Sylvia with my other hand.

"Just look at this!" she cried, as she pointed happily to all the flashing lights, the plush carpets, the ocean designs on the walls, and the well-dressed gamblers. "Oh, what fun we shall have here!"

After tipping the bellhops, we stood alone in the room and hugged each other for a moment. A king-size bed dominated the room. A glance through the twenty-seventh floor window revealed a view of all the downtown lights two miles away. Sylvia looked out the window with me.

"I like Nevada," she said to me. "Everything's going twenty-four hours a day. Plenty of people out at night, so many places to go, it's okay to sleep during the day, and we can dispose of bodies in the desert. It's really a perfect place for us."

"I think I'd prefer London, myself. There must be a lot to do there."

"Yes, there is." Sylvia turned away from the window and faced me. "But this is a wonderful place to make money quickly." She winked and smiled. "Come. Let us go out into the night." She took me by the hand and a moment later we were descending towards the main floor in a plushly carpeted elevator.

Busy gaming tables beckoned the eye. I looked around, wondering where we should start. We walked hand in hand, and Sylvia zipped through the casino floor with such speed, I thought at first that she must have seen a table she wanted to bet on. To my surprise, she passed them all and pulled me by the hand right out the front door.

"Where are we going?" I asked-

"I don't want to gamble here," she explained. "We're guests. If we're to win thousands of dollars at a casino, it simply won't do to have our names registered at their front desk. I'd rather win at a different casino."

We immediately took a taxi to the downtown area, then wandered around on Virginia Street, where most of the casinos were. Sylvia glanced around at the three short blocks of neon and a sign that hung over the street in an arc. It proclaimed Reno to be "The Biggest Little City in the World"—an apt title.

"It's not big *enough*," Sylvia said with a frown. "This

place is much smaller than I expected it to be. Much smaller than Las Vegas. We must make our money and then leave quickly."

We entered Harrah's, one of the more established casinos downtown, and headed for the twenty-one tables. Sylvia had explained the card counting procedure to me on the plane, so I knew exactly what she was going to do. We started by changing some of our cash into hundred dollar chips.

Sylvia seated herself at the far left of the card table, to avail herself of a good view of the cards which had already been played, I sat directly to her right, and watched the couple on my right look at each other as Sylvia opened her bet with one hundred dollars. They appeared to be in their sixties and were wearing polyester leisure suits. Each was betting one dollar at a time.

The table limit was five hundred dollars, so the dealer hardly noticed the size of Sylvia's bet. She just dealt out the cards with machine-like efficiency. Her bright red hair stood above her emotionless face with equal stiffness. Sylvia handled the cards with a dexterity which far surpassed the dealer's own movements. Sylvia received a ten and a seven, and decided to stay. I watched her expression as the dealer showed a ten and an eight, then cleared Sylvia's hundred dollars off the table in a sweeping movement with her cards. Only the slightest frown crossed Sylvia's face, then she quickly set up another hundred-dollar chip. The couple in polyester stared at her.

The cards were dealt again, and again Sylvia lost, this time for going over twenty-one. She placed another hundred-dollar chip on the table without hesitation, and I noted, with some satisfaction, that her eyes glanced around at the cards of the dealer and the couple playing with us. It was a swift glance, but with her quick eyes, long enough so she would remember each card that had been played. The next few hands varied in the outcome. Sometimes the dealer won, sometimes Sylvia. But as the game progressed, Sylvia gradually began to win more hands than the dealer, and with each bet, she increased the amount of the wager.

Within half an hour, Sylvia was betting five hundred dollars on each hand, and winning the majority of the time. A pit boss in an expensive suit and a large diamond ring signaled to one of the cocktail waitresses. In seconds, she hovered at our side to offer us complimentary drinks. Sylvia dismissed her with a shake of her head and went back to concentrating on the game. I stifled a laugh as I watched the frustration in the face of the pit boss as he learned we wouldn't drink. In a few more minutes, we had over twenty thousand dollars in chips stacked up on our side of the table. Just as the pit boss motioned for one of his assistants to watch us, Sylvia gathered up the chips, and we strode to the cashier's booth to exchange them for currency.

"Are you sure you want the whole thing in cash?" the woman asked. "I can issue you a cashier's check or give you credit. It's risky to carry so much money on you."

"We'll take the cash, thank you," answered Sylvia curtly.

Sylvia had to produce her passport and they took a fingerprint of her index finger in order to get paid. I asked her how she planned to remain anonymous.

"This passport is fake and I put something on my index finger that has a different fingerprint. It can't be matched to me."

Across the gaming area, some thirty or forty feet away, the pit boss stood, pointing us out to a couple of other men. I couldn't tell whether they held the same position that he did, or whether they were security guards in plain clothes. I mentioned it to Sylvia.

She shot a quick glance in their direction, then

turned to me. "I think it's time for us to go." She hooked her arm in mine, as she sauntered towards the door with me.

"Back to the hotel?" I questioned her.

"Not a chance," Sylvia answered with a grin. She passed the attaché case to me and walked briskly to the Silver Legacy, another casino on the other side of Virginia Street. We repeated the process again, this time winning almost thirty thousand dollars before leaving. A large group of gamblers and employees had noticed our winning streak, and watched attentively, apparently hoping to learn our secrets of success.

Finally, Sylvia stopped concentrating on the game as she looked around at the people staring at us. Pressing her lips against my ear, she whispered that we should leave. I couldn't have agreed with her more.

Back on the sidewalk once again, we walked slowly away from the Silver Legacy, glancing over our shoulders frequently to see if we were being followed. Several people were looking in our direction, but we decided that if we wandered around some more, we could determine whether they were following us or not.

"Let's go this way," said Sylvia, She pointed away from the bright lights and glitter of Virginia Street.

We strolled along Commercial Row until we reached Lake Street, then stopped and looked around. Only a few winos leaning against buildings were present. The tourists were several blocks away. The street stood nearly deserted, and as we made our way along the sidewalk, pieces of broken glass cracked under our shoes.

"Perhaps we should go back to the hotel now," I suggested. "This is kind of a sleazy area, and now we have about a hundred-thousand dollars with us."

Sylvia surveyed the street and nodded in agreement. Arm in arm, we reversed direction, and headed back towards the casinos to catch a taxi. We had only taken a few steps, when a shiny black Cadillac Escalade pulled up alongside of us. Two young men sat in the front, and one in the back. He opened the rear door and motioned to us. He and the two others looked like gang members in their twenties.

"Get in!" he commanded, his voice like gravel.

"Get *lost*!" snapped Sylvia, as she turned her nose up at them.

We continued walking along the sidewalk, but the car jerked forward twenty feet, then screeched to a halt. Two of the men jumped out of the car at us, leaving the doors open. They glanced around swiftly, then noticing we were alone, they both pulled their guns.

"I said to get in," repeated the man angrily. He and his partner were dressed in the standard baggy clothes and wearing gold chains and big gold watches.

"Where to?" I asked.

"We're just going for a little ride, that's all," answered the other. He grinned at his partner, who then nodded and smirked.

"What do you think?" I asked Sylvia.

She shrugged her shoulders. "It's okay with me. It couldn't hurt. I can never drink too much, you know. I'm always ready for more."

The men puzzled over Sylvia's remark to me, then quickly forgot about it as we entered the rear door of the SUV. One of the men sat in the back seat with us and pointed his gun in our direction. The other sat in the front seat, but turned to face us. With two guns trained on us, they must have felt quite confident about carrying out their plans. The car accelerated quickly and headed north on Virginia Street until we were on a dark highway. They pulled over onto a dirt road and drove for about a quarter of a mile.

"Hand over the money," the man demanded of me. He held his hand out.

Sylvia nodded to me. I passed it to him, and he opened up the attaché case and began counting the money. "Shit!" he yelled. "There must be over thirty thousand dollars in here!"

"Actually, it's about one-hundred-thousand," Sylvia corrected.

The men stared at her in amazement, puzzled by her lack of concern.

"What now?" I asked.

"We're almost at our destination." The driver pulled the car up to a spot he had apparently been to before.

"Well, let's see," said Sylvia to me, as she began to count on her fingers. "There were five the first two weeks, and now three tonight. I haven't felt so alive in a long time!" she announced cheerfully.

"Enjoy it while you can," growled the man in the back seat.

Sylvia turned to me. "Even though this big car is comfortable, I would feel guilty driving one all the time. It must get terrible gas mileage. Think what it's doing to the environment. Think about the polar bears."

"If I think about the polar bears again, you know what it's going to remind me of," I said.

Sylvia nodded and smiled. "Yes, I know."

The man next to her with the gun sneered at her. "I wouldn't be worried about no polar bears if I was you."

"You're *not* me," Sylvia replied.

The car stopped, and could no longer be seen by any cars on the highway. The men opened the doors and got out first.

"End of the ride," announced the man from the back seat as he motioned for us to get out, too.

We stood, and Sylvia took a deep breath and sighed. "What nice clean mountain air they have here. On the ride back, I think I'll keep the window rolled down."

The man next to us shook his head. "You're crazy as

shit, lady. There ain't gonna be any ride back." He pointed the gun at her.

"Not for you," taunted Sylvia, as she glared at him. "Mark, would you please remove the driver from our new car? I don't want to get any blood on the nice clean seats."

The two men stared at Sylvia in disbelief, and then at me as I opened the car door. The driver pulled his gun, but before he could aim it, I grabbed him by the collar and jerked him out of the car. With one hand, I lifted him off his feet. In his surprise, he dropped the gun. His legs dangled several inches above the ground, and he squirmed in my grip, which by now had almost choked him entirely.

"Let him down," threatened one of the men behind me, "or I'll pull this trigger." He stuck the barrel of his gun against the back of my head.

"All right," I answered, and threw the driver on top of him, knocking both of them onto a large sagebrush.

The other man pointed his gun at my face and fired. I flinched as a normal reaction from the noise of the blast just a few feet away, but I felt absolutely nothing. It was as if the gun had been loaded with blanks. The man stared for a moment in shock, then fired again with the same result. His eyes stared disbelievingly, first at my face, then at his gun.

Sylvia slapped the gun out of his hand and snapped his neck back in one smooth motion, Her mouth lunged forward like a wolf, and her teeth ripped into his neck, tearing off a piece of flesh the size of a golf ball. Her movement knocked him to the ground, and she crouched over him, sucking his blood.

Before I could move, one of the other men fired his weapon at Sylvia. She turned towards him, her eyes ablaze in fury, like an animal jealously guarding its kill from predators. Blood stained her mouth and ran down her chin. Her fangs had reached full length in her blood lust, the sharp points extending beyond her bottom lip.

By now, I could smell the blood from the man's wound, and feel my own canine teeth longer than just seconds before. I ran my tongue across their surface, and felt all of my energy focus there. The two other men leapt to their feet, and one of them fired his gun at me as I approached them for the kill. The bullets blasted through the front of my jacket, yet I couldn't feel them on my body even though they ripped my jacket to shreds. Still, I felt no anger over my ruined suit, no fear of the gun. Only one emotion remained—the thirst—the all-consuming thirst.

His eyes acknowledged the true situation that he now found himself in, a condemned man with no chance of a reprieve. The gun dropped from his hands as I snapped his head back and bit into his throat. The coppery taste of his blood filled my mouth, and I felt my pulse rise and my face flush with warmth as I drained the life from his veins.

The last surviving victim, the driver, stumbled into the car, his eyes bulging and wild with terror.

Sylvia glanced up. "Stop him, Mark!"

I grabbed the bumper of the car. The man started the engine, but when he stepped on the gas, the wheels spun fruitlessly as I held on as tightly as I could. Sylvia dropped her victim's head to the ground and slowly rose. Her hand tried the door, but found it locked. The man inside panicked, his nervous eyes darting around the car's interior, as if searching for some way to keep us out, when Sylvia arrested his attention by pointing at the door lock. She then pointed at her eyes and his stare focused there. His eyes went blank as Sylvia's hypnotic power did its magic. Sylvia pointed at the lock, just on the other side of the car window. She gestured with her finger, flicking it upwards and the man obeyed, flicking up the door lock like a marionette having its strings pulled by an unseen hand. My grip loosened on the bumper, and a few seconds later, Sylvia raised her blood-covered face and motioned for me to finish him off.

After I drained his last drop of life, I stood for a few seconds, overwhelmed by the sensations that came to me. The warmth, which had been slight when Sylvia and I shared the girl in San Francisco, now fully intoxicated me with its intensity. The stars seemed to shine more brightly as they winked at us from above.

"It's different, isn't it?" Sylvia asked.

I nodded in agreement, feeling the new blood flow through my veins giving me new strength and energy.

"It's like that," she explained, "when you drink more than you need."

Her words stuck in my mind. We didn't need so much blood, even if the murders were justified. I could not feel any guilt over their deaths, yet I wondered whether I could resist the temptation to do whatever necessary to experience the same sensation again.

Sylvia stared at me, as if reading my thoughts, then said, "Yes, sometimes I do."

"Do what?" I asked.

"Kill just because it feels good. Because more blood than I need makes me feel stronger. Because it gives me energy. Because it increases my magical power." She lowered her eyes, "That's just the way we are," she said softly. "We have to take blood to survive, but how much we take is up to us."

"What should we do about them?" I pointed at the bodies of the men.

"Do? We don't have to do anything. Just leave them for the natural predators and take their car. After all, what's left will still make a good meal for some poor animal."

I nodded, and was about to enter the car, when

Sylvia's bloodstained face caught my attention. "We've got blood all over our faces," I said. "We can't go back to the hotel like this." I rubbed my face with my hands, but the blood had already dried and would not come off.

Sylvia laughed at my frustration, then walked over to me and placed her arms around my neck. "This is how you get rid of it," she explained. She pressed her smooth face against mine, then began to lick the dried blood. Her tongue lapped against my cheeks and lips like a cat giving her kitten a bath. When she finished, I did the same for her, then we kissed long and passionately.

The drive back to downtown Reno afforded us a magnificent view of the city, and Sylvia kept the window open, letting the wind blow her hair as she sang to the radio. "Oh, I like this car," she remarked in her usual cheerful voice. "But not as much as my Aston Martin. Maybe when we get to London, we'll buy a new Lotus Evora. I think you'd like it more than your Lotus Esprit."

"Can we afford it?"

"Sure we can. We have over one hundred-thousand dollars with us, and I've got millions more back in London. We can buy anything we want."

We parked the SUV a block from the Atlantis Casino and Hotel and glanced around to see if anyone had noticed us, but there were so many other cars, we just blended in. Sylvia and I wiped off the door handles and steering wheel to remove any possible fingerprints, then deserted the car and entered the casino.

From our hotel room, I admired the great view of downtown Reno and the surrounding mountains. I stared at it and pondered the events of the past two weeks. It all seemed like a dream. Yet it also felt more real and alive and intense than any other period of my life. I gazed out at the stars, which stretched out for infinity, and tried to think of what time without end would be like, and it struck me as being just like the stars. Some could be seen already. Others were far away and would have to be traveled to later on. But there would be plenty of time.

"Mark, it's three-thirty. Please come to bed."

I turned to see Sylvia stretched out on the bed, her smooth bare skin luring me. She held her arms out to me. Without hesitation, I slipped off my clothes.

The extra blood we had consumed served as an aphrodisiac, magnifying our already strong passion for each other. After making love, we lay in each other's arms and held each other tightly.

"Are you glad I made you a vampire?" Sylvia's eyes probed mine.

I paused and thought a moment. "I don't know. I'm glad we're together, but I'd be just as happy if we were together as two humans. And I definitely wouldn't be happy being a vampire by myself. Too lonely."

Sylvia nodded. "Yes, I know. That's why I made you a vampire."

"I'm just glad to be with you. If you were to leave me, I wouldn't enjoy being a vampire."

"I'm not leaving—ever. You don't have to worry about that," she said with a smile. "I'm yours 'till death do us part,' and I'm certainly not ready to die."

Chapter Ten

The tranquility of my sleep was shattered by Sylvia's scream. I sprang up to see Father Callen's arm ready for another swing of his hammer. The wooden stake had already pierced the center of Sylvia's chest, and a widening circle of crimson spread across her delicate frame.

I leaped out of bed and slammed him against the wall. He bounced once onto the floor, then lay inert, his hammer next to him on the carpet.

Sylvia stared up at the ceiling, motionless. I knelt beside her and whispered her name, but received no reply. I picked up her hand and held it to my face, but it was limp, and I slowly laid it against her body. My eyes welled up with tears, then without holding back, I cried and screamed as I collapsed on the bed, my face resting on one of her breasts. My tears rolled down her breast and found its way to the wooden stake, which still impaled her.

"No!" I screamed. "You can't die!"

Sylvia's body remained frozen in place. Her large eyes appeared blank and lifeless. In a rage, I turned to Father Callen to exact revenge, but he too, lay on the floor as deathly still as Sylvia. I could not murder someone twice, so I was cheated of the satisfaction I would have received by killing him deliberately.

I turned my tear-filled eyes back to her. By then, my voice had almost failed me. "Please don't die," I whispered. "I love you Sylvia. I won't live without you."

She didn't answer. No words came from her sweet lips. Her soft melodious voice said nothing. Her melancholy eyes conveyed only death.

I held her to me tightly, and kissed her on the lips, as my tears ran down my face and onto hers.

How could I live without her? What would I do?

What would have been the purpose in going on as a vampire by myself, once I had tasted her love and companionship?

Then the inspiration came to me. I remembered what she told me about how she had been staked before, how she had slept for a hundred years before the other vampires revived her with their blood. If they did it, why couldn't I?

In her brief struggle for life, her canine teeth had grown to their full length. They stood out against the bright red of her lips, the points sharp as two ice picks. I scraped the inside of my wrist across her two fangs, slicing my veins. It felt good to have her sharp teeth press against my skin, and I let my blood flow from the gash in my wrist. It trickled down my hand and a small stream spilled onto her lips.

"In a few minutes, we shall be together again," I told her, as I watched the blood flow down my hand and fingers and then into her mouth. How fitting, I thought, that Sylvia had given me eternal life and now I would give it back to her. These thoughts played over and over in my mind. My thinking became cloudy, and I felt a growing chill in the room as well as a thirst—the same thirst that had preceded my immediate need for blood. As I watched my life drain from my wrist and spill into Sylvia's mouth, I waited and hoped to see some sign of life in her eyes, but instead, just felt weak and lightheaded as my blood flowed from my wrist to her mouth. I promised Sylvia that we would be together again, and through the fog which now clouded my brain, the chill which overtook my body, and the thirst which consumed my entire being, I intended to keep my vow to her.

My eyes fought a war with me. They tried to close, but I refused to let them. In a compromise, they began to flicker, my body began to tremble from the chills, and my fangs had grown to their full length, as if readying for a kill. But there would be no kill. I would just let the blood flow till there was none left, until she came back to life — if it was the last thing I did. My vision blurred slightly and numbness overtook my entire body. I could feel almost nothing except for the sharp pain across my wrist.

But gradually through this mental fog, there came another sensation. Intermingled with the sharp pain in my wrist, there was softness. Fighting to keep my eyes open, I slowly glanced down,

Sylvia's lips were moving!

Her tongue slowly lapped at the blood on my hand, and her eyes flickered slightly. I pressed my wrist to her lips, and she started sucking the blood, gradually at first, then increasing till her mouth worked as energetically as before.

I wanted to scream for joy! To hug and kiss her! But I didn't dare move an inch, fearing that any sudden change in position could prevent her recovery. It wasn't until she spoke that I dared to stir.

"Mark," she whispered softly. "The stake. Pull out the stake."

Slowly, and as gently as I could, I removed the stake from her chest. She winced as it came out, and a small quantity of blood oozed from the wound. In a matter of seconds, the horrible gash in her chest closed itself up, and the skin once again was perfectly smooth.

I hugged her to me and cried from joy that I had not lost her. She smothered my face with kisses, then gazed affectionately into my eyes. "I would have died without you," she said.

"And I would have died *with* you, " I replied. "I would do anything to keep you with me."

"*Anything*?" Sylvia asked with her mischievous smile.

She stared at my slashed wrist, still wet from my own blood.

"Oh, Mark," she cried, as her eyes welled up with

tears. "You saved me. Father Callen would have killed me if it wasn't for you."

She hugged me tightly to her, then gradually loosened her grip as she noticed his body on the floor.

"You killed him?"

"I guess so," I answered.

Her expression was one of disappointment. "I'm glad he's finally dead, only — "

"What?"

"I wish I had killed him," she replied as she stared at him angrily. Not receiving any response from him, Sylvia began to get dressed. "Goodness, won't you be popular with the other vampires in London when they find out what you've done!"

I asked Sylvia what she thought we should do with the body. She considered it as I dressed and started to pack our bags. As if in answer to my question, Father Callen slowly stirred back to consciousness.

At the sound of his movement, Sylvia's eyes darted to her side. Never had I seen such intensity, such glaring hatred in those huge-pupiled eyes. He had started to prop himself back up on one arm as her eyes met his. The second her eyes clicked into place, he fell back onto the floor, as if the power of her stare knocked him down. She stood, and her magical power filled the room, negative energy flowing from her to the priest on the floor.

In desperation, he reached inside his jacket and pulled out a white plastic crucifix. He held it in front of him, as if to ward off Sylvia's attack

Sylvia gripped his hand, which held the crucifix, then she laughed. It was the high, musical laugh I had heard so many times before, but this time it was uttered more in derision than amusement. Father Callen grimaced in pain as Sylvia squeezed his hand tighter around the crucifix, then jerked it from his feeble grip.

"This!" she yelled, holding the crucifix in the air.

"You use this silly little piece of plastic as a weapon against me? You fool! Don't you know what I am?"

He cowered against the wall, unable to speak.

"I'm a vampire. And a Satanist, A real Satanist. If you were a real Christian, you wouldn't be here right now, trying to kill vampires. You'd be out trying to feed the poor or heal the sick."

Sylvia held the cross in her slender fingers, then snapped it in half. "Your crucifix is as good as your faith." Father Callen stared at her in horror.

"You don't need this," she said, holding out the broken pieces of the cross in her hands. *You're* not a Christian. Christians don't go about trying to kill people. Jesus never killed anyone. He had the power. He used it to help those who suffered, not to kill those he felt were wrong."

Father Callen backed away from her as much as he could. The expression of terror which now had spread over his face showed he was more concerned with what Sylvia would do rather than with what she was saying.

"Since you don't follow Christ, perhaps you want the moral freedom of a Satanist. After all, you don't mind killing your enemies. Beware! A Christian who plays the game of life by Satan's rules has neither God's mercy nor Satan's power, and must die at one of their hands. *And you know who I am.*"

Sylvia turned to me. "Mark, would you please open the window? Father Callen is leaving."

I stepped over to the window and discovered it didn't open. The bright sun of the new day made me squint against the harsh glare. Not a cloud in the sky, and the cars in the parking lot sparkled in the light twenty-seven floors below.

Sylvia realized we couldn't throw him out the window and obviously didn't want to leave any evidence at the hotel linking us all together. She then addressed

Father Callen with that eerie voice she used when she hypnotized someone.

"You will go to the roof and look down at the people below. You will see me looking up at you. At that time, you will become an angel and spread your wings. When you see me pointing at you, you can then fly off the building to Heaven."

Father Callen left the hotel room in a trance, and we checked out at the lobby, then walked to the parking lot. By the time we got there, we could see him on the roof. Several other people were in the parking lot with us. Sylvia announced in a loud voice to everyone, "Look. Someone's on the roof. I think he's going to jump."

She pointed to Father Callen, and as she did, he lifted his arms like wings and took off headfirst from the roof. The others in the parking lot gasped or screamed in shock as they saw his fall and then watched his body splatter all over the parking lot.

Sylvia turned from the scene and sighed. "Father Callen finally left his mark on the world. That's what he gets for killing my friends and trying to kill me."

She picked up her suitcase, then turned to me. "I think we better be off now."

Several security guards ran out of the front entrance to keep any bystanders away while they waited for the police to arrive.

We carried our suitcases and the attaché case past the crowd of people. Just as our taxi left the parking lot for the airport, a police car, with lights flashing and siren wailing, passed us on its way to the casino.

Once back at the apartment in San Francisco, we packed the rest of the things we needed and called a moving company to handle Sylvia's harpsichord and French Provincial furniture. A few days later, the moving company loaded all our belongings in cardboard boxes for shipment to London by air, an expensive proposition, but far faster than by sea.

As the jet screamed off the runway, I watched the San Francisco Bay Area skyline slowly shrink below us. How beautiful it looked during the sunny afternoon, a sight Sylvia and I would see only rarely.

Sylvia held my hand and smiled fondly. "This is it. The beginning of our future. And we'll have a home in London." Her eyes beamed with pleasure. "And friends, too." She nodded her head happily.

"What about Father Callen's friends?" I asked.

She frowned. "Yes, they'll still be after us. But we'll have friends of our own to help us."

The flight attendant came by and asked what we would like to drink, and Sylvia ordered two Perriers. I glanced out the window. The view of the sunny scene below began to recede, and both of us squinted against the harsh light until I pulled down the shade.

The flight attendant returned with two bottles of Perrier, which Sylvia poured. She handed one of the glasses to me.

"I propose a toast," Sylvia declared, raising her glass.

I raised my glass to meet hers. "What shall we toast to?"

Sylvia smiled broadly, revealing all her teeth. "To an eternity together."

We clinked our glasses together and drank.

The End